The White Ladies of Worcester
A Romance of the Twelfth Century

Florence L. Barclay

The White Ladies of Worcester: A Romance of the Twelfth Century

ISBN: 978-1-64799-971-1

TO
FAITHFUL HEARTS
ALL THE WORLD OVER

CONTENTS

CHAPTER I

THE SUBTERRANEAN WAY

The slanting rays of afternoon sunshine, pouring through stone arches, lay in broad, golden bands, upon the flags of the Convent cloister.

The old lay-sister, Mary Antony, stepped from the cool shade of the cell passage and, blinking at the sunshine, shuffled slowly to her appointed post at the top of the crypt steps, up which would shortly pass the silent procession of nuns returning from Vespers.

Daily they went, and daily they returned, by the underground way, a passage over a mile in length, leading from the Nunnery of the White Ladies at Whytstone in Claines, to the Church of St. Mary and St. Peter, the noble Cathedral within the walls of the city of Worcester.

Entering this passage from the crypt in their own cloisters, they walked in darkness below the sunny meadows, passed beneath the Fore-gate, moving in silent procession under the busy streets, until they reached the crypt of the Cathedral.

From the crypt, a winding stairway in the wall led up to a chamber above the choir, whence, unseeing and unseen, the White Ladies of Worcester daily heard the holy monks below chant Vespers.

To Sister Mary Antony fell the task of counting the five-and-twenty veiled figures, as they passed down the steps and disappeared beneath the ground, and of again counting them as they reappeared, and moved in stately silence along the cloister, each entering her own cell, to spend, in prayer and adoration, the hours until the Refectory bell should call them to the evening meal.

This counting of the White Ladies dated from the day, now more than half a century ago, when Sister Agatha, weakened by prolonged fasting, and chancing to walk last in the procession, fainted and, falling silently, remained behind, unnoticed, in the solitude and darkness.

It was the habit of this saintly lady to abide in her own cell after Vespers, dispensing with the evening meal; thus her absence was not discovered until the following morning when Mary Antony, finding the cell empty, hastened to report that Sister Agatha having long, like Enoch, walked with God, had, even, as Enoch, been translated!

The nuns who flocked to the cell, inclining to Mary Antony's view of the strange happening, kneeled upon the floor before the empty couch, and worshipped.

The Prioress of that time, however, being of a practical turn of mind, ordered the immediate lighting of the lanterns, and herself descended to search the underground way.

She did not need to go far.

1

The saintly spirit of Sister Agatha had indeed been translated.

They found her frail body lying prone against the door, the hands broken and torn by much wild beating upon its studded panels.

She had run to and fro in the dank darkness, beating first upon the door beneath the Convent cloisters, then upon the door, a mile away, leading into the Cathedral crypt.

But the nuns were shut into their cells, beyond the cloister; the good people of Worcester city slept peacefully, not dreaming of the despairing figure running to and fro beneath them—tottering, stumbling, falling, arising to fall again, yet hurrying blindly onwards; and the Cathedral Sacristan, when questioned, confessed that, hearing cries and rappings coming from the crypt at a late hour, he speedily locked the outer gate, said an "Ave," and went home to supper; well knowing that, at such a time, none save spirits of evil would be wandering below, in so great torment.

Thus, through much tribulation, poor Sister Agatha entered into rest; being held in deepest reverence ever after.

More than fifty years had gone by. The Prioress of that day, and most of those who walked in that procession, had long lain beside Sister Agatha in the Convent burying-ground. But Mary Antony, now oldest of the lay-sisters, never failed to make careful count, as each veiled figure passed, nor to impart the mournful reason for this necessity to all new-comers. So that the nun whose turn it was to walk last in the procession, prayed that she might not hear behind her the running feet of Sister Agatha; while none went alone into the cloisters after dark, lest they should hear the poor thin hands of Sister Agatha beating upon the panels of the door.

Thus does the anguish of a tortured brain leave its imperishable impress upon the surroundings in which the mind once suffered, though the freed spirit may have long forgotten, in the peace of Paradise, that slight affliction, which was but for a moment, through which it passed to the eternal weight of glory.

Of late, the old lay-sister, Mary Antony, had grown fearful lest she should make mistake in this solemn office of the counting. Therefore, in the secret of her own heart, she devised a plan, which she carried out under cover of her scapulary. Twenty-five dried peas she held ready in her wallet; then, as each veiled figure, having mounted the steps leading from the crypt doorway, moved slowly past her, she dropped a pea with her right hand into her left. When all the holy Ladies had passed, if all had returned, five-and-twenty peas lay in her left hand, none remained in the wallet.

This secret dropping of peas became a kind of game to Mary Antony. She kept the peas in a small linen bag, and often took them out and played with them when alone in her cell, placing them all in a row, and settling, to her own satisfaction, which peas should represent the various holy Ladies.

2

A large white pea, of finer aspect than the rest, stood for the noble Prioress herself; a somewhat shrivelled pea, hard, brown, and wizened, did duty as Mother Sub-Prioress, an elderly nun, not loved by Mary Antony because of her sharp tongue and strict fault-finding ways; while a pale and speckled pea became Sister Mary Rebecca, held in high scorn by the old lay-sister, as a traitress, sneak, and liar, for if ever tale of wrong or shame was whispered in the Convent, it could be traced for place of origin to the slanderous tongue and crooked mind of Sister Mary Rebecca.

When all the peas in line upon the floor of her cell were named, old Mary Antony marked out a distant flagstone, on which the sunlight fell, as heaven; another, partially in shadow, purgatory; a third, in a far corner of exceeding darkness, hell. She then proceeded, with well-directed fillip of thumb and middle finger, to send the holy Ladies there where, in her judgment, they belonged.

If the game went well, the noble Prioress landed safely in heaven, without even the most transitory visit to purgatory; Mother Sub-Prioress, rolling into purgatory, remained there; while the pale and speckled pea went straight to hell!

When these were safely landed, Mary Antony rubbed her hands and, chuckling gleefully, finished the game at gay hap-hazard, it being of less importance where the rest of the holy Ladies chanced to go.

CHAPTER II

SISTER MARY ANTONY DISCOURSES

As Mary Antony shuffled slowly from the shadow into the sunshine, a gay little flutter of wings preceded her, and a robin perched upon the parapet behind the stone seat upon which it was the lay-sister's custom to await the sound of the turning of the key in the lock of the heavy door beneath the cloisters.

"Thou good-for-nothing imp!" exclaimed Mary Antony, her old face crinkling with delight. "Thou little vain man, in thy red jerkin! Beshrew thine impudence, intruding into a place where women alone do dwell, and no male thing may enter. I would have thee take warning by the fate of the baker's boy, who dared to climb into a tree, so that he might peep over the wall and spy upon the holy Ladies in their garden. Boasting afterward of that which he had done, and making merry over that which he pretended to have seen, our great Lord Bishop heard of

3

it, and sent and took that baker's boy, and though he cried for mercy, swearing the whole tale was an empty boast, they put out his bold eyes with heated tongs, and hanged him from the very branches he had climbed. They'd do the like to thee, thou little vain man, if Mary Antony reported on thy ways. Wouldst like to hang, in thy red doublet?"

The robin had heard this warning tale many times already, told by old Mary Antony with infinite variety.

Sometimes the tongue of the baker's boy was cut out at the roots; sometimes he lost his ears, or again, he was tied to a cart-tail, and flogged through the Tything. Often he became a pieman, and once he was a turnspit in the household of the Lord Bishop himself. But, whatever the preliminaries, and whether baker, pieman, or turnspit, his final catastrophe was always the same: he was hanged from a bough of the very tree into which, impious and greatly daring, he had climbed.

This was an ancient tale. All who might vouch for it, saving the old lay-sister, had passed away; and, of late, Mary Antony had been strictly forbidden by the Reverend Mother, to tell it to new-comers, or to speak of it to any of the nuns.

So, daily, she told it to the robin; and he, being neither baker's lad, pieman, nor turnspit, and having a conscience void of offence, would listen, wholly unafraid; then, hopping nearer to Mary Antony, would look up at her, eager inquiry in his bright eyes.

On this particular afternoon he flew up into the very tree climbed by the prying and ill-fated baker's lad, settled on a bough which branched out over the Convent wall, and poured forth a gay trill of song.

"Ha, thou little vain man, in thy brown and red suit!" chuckled Mary Antony, leaning her gnarled hands on the stone parapet, as she stood framed in one of the cloister arches overlooking the garden. "Is that thy little 'grace before meat'? But, I pray thee, Sir Robin, who said there was cheese in my wallet? Nay, is there like to be cheese in a wallet already containing five-and-twenty holy Ladies on their way back from Vespers? Out upon thee for a most irreverent little glutton! I fear me thou hast not only a high look, thou hast also a proud stomach; just the reverse of the great French Cardinal who came, with much pomp, to visit us at Easter time. He had a proud look and a— Come down again, thou little naughty man, and I will tell thee what the Lord Cardinal had under his crimson sash. 'Tis not a thing to shout to the tree-tops. I might have to recite ten Paternosters, if I let thee tempt me so to do. For whispering it in thine ear, I should but say one; for having remarked it, none at all. Facts are facts; and, even in the case of so weighty a fact, the responsibility rests not upon the beholder."

Mary Antony leaned over the parapet, looking upward. The afternoon sunlight fell full upon the russet parchment of her kind old face, shewing the web of wrinkles spun by ninety years of the gently turning wheel of time.

4

But the robin, perched upon the bough, trilled and sang, unmoved. He was weary of tales of bakers and piemen. He was not at all curious as to what had been beneath the French Cardinal's crimson sash. He wanted the tasty morsels which he knew lay concealed in Sister Mary Antony's leathern wallet. So he stayed on the bough and sang.

The old face, peering up from between the pillars, softened into tenderness at the robin's song.

"I cannot let thy little grace return unto thee void," she said, and fumbled at the fastenings of her wallet.

A flick of wings, a flash of red. The robin had dropped from the bough, and perched beside her.

She doled out crumbs, and fragments of cheese, pushing them toward him along the parapet; leaving her fingers near, to see how close he would adventure to her hand.

She watched him peck a morsel of cheese into five tiny pieces, then fly, with full beak, on eager wing, to the hidden nest, from which five gaping mouths shrieked a shrill and hungry welcome. Then, back again—swift as an arrow from the archer's bow—noting, with bright eye, and head turned sidewise, that the hand resting on the coping had moved nearer; yet brave to take all risks for the sake of those yellow beaks, which would gape wide, in expectation, at sound of the beat of his wings.

"Feed thyself, thou little worldling!" chuckled old Antony, and covered the remaining bits of cheese with her hand. "Who art thou to come here presuming to teach thy betters lessons of self-sacrifice? First feed thyself; then give to the hungry, the fragments that remain. Had I five squealing children here—which Heaven forbid—I should eat mine own mess, and count myself charitable if I let them lick the dish. The holy Ladies give to the poor at the Convent gate, that for which they have no further use. Does thy jaunty fatherhood presume to shame our saintly celibacy? Mother Sub-Prioress did chide me sharply because, to a poor soul with many hungry mouths to feed, I gave a good piece of venison, and not the piece which was tainted. Truth to tell, I had already made away with the tainted piece; but Mother Sub-Prioress was pleased to think it was in the pot, seething for the holy Ladies' evening meal; and wherefore should Mother Sub-Prioress not think as she pleased?

"'Woman!' she cried; 'Woman!'—and when Mother Sub-Prioress says 'Woman!' the woman she addresses feels her estate would be higher had God Almighty been pleased to have let her be the Man, or even the Serpent, so much contempt does Mother Sub-Prioress infuse into the name—'Woman!' said Mother Sub-Prioress, 'wouldst thou make all the Ladies of the Convent ill?'

"'Nay,' said I, 'that would I not. Yet, if any needs must be ill,

5

'twere easier to tend the holy Ladies in their cells, than the Poor, in humble homes, outside the Convent walls, tossing on beds of rushes.'

"'Tush, fool!' snarled Mother Sub-Prioress. "'The Poor are not easily made ill.'

"Tush indeed! I tell thee, little bright-eyed man, old Antony, can 'tush' to better purpose! That night there were strong purging herbs in the broth of Mother Sub-Prioress. Yet she did but keep her bed for one day. Like the Poor, she is not easily made ill! . . . Well, have thy way; only peck not my fingers, Master Robin, or I will have thee flogged through the Tything at the cart-tail, as was done to a certain pieman, whose history I will now relate.

"Once upon a time, when Sister Mary Antony was young, and fair to look upon—Nay, wink not thy naughty eye—"

At that moment came the sound of a key turning slowly in the lock of the door at the bottom of the steps leading from the crypt to the cloister.

CHAPTER III

THE PRIORESS PASSES

A key turned slowly in the lock of the oaken door at the entrance to the underground way.

The old lay-sister seized her wallet and pulled out the bag of peas.

Below, the heavy door swung back upon its hinges.

Mary Antony dropped upon her knees to the right of the steps, her hands hidden beneath her scapulary, her eyes bent in lowly reverence upon the sunlit flagstones, her lips mumbling chance sentences from the Psalter.

The measured sound of softly moving feet drew near, slightly shuffling as they reached the steps and began to mount, up from the mile-long darkness, into the sunset light.

First to appear was a young lay-sister, carrying a lantern. Hastening up the steps, she extinguished the flame, grown sickly in the sunshine, placed the lantern in a niche, and, dropping upon her knees, opposite old Mary Antony, sought to join in the latter's pious recitations.

"Adhaesit pavimento anima mea," chanted Mary Antony. "Wherefore are the holy Ladies late to-day?"

6

"One fell to weeping in the darkness," intoned the young lay-sister, "whereupon Mother Sub-Prioress caused all to stand still while she strove, by the light of my lantern held high, to discover who had burst forth with a sob. None shewing traces of tears, she gave me back the lantern, herself walking last in the line, as all moved on."

"Convertentur ad vesperam, and the devil catch the hindmost," chanted Mary Antony, with fervour.

"Amen," intoned Sister Abigail, eyes bent upon the ground; for the tall figure of the Prioress, mounting the steps, now came into view.

The Prioress passed up the cloister with a stately grace of motion which, even beneath the heavy cloth of her white robe, revealed the noble length of supple limbs. Her arms hung by her sides, swaying gently as she walked. There was a look of strength and of restfulness about the long fingers and beautifully moulded hands. Her face, calm and purposeful, was lifted to the sunlight. Suffering and sorrow had left thereon indelible marks; but the clear grey eyes, beneath level brows, were luminous with a light betokening the victory of a pure and noble spirit over passionate and most human flesh.

No sinner, in her presence, ever felt crushed by hopeless weight of sin; no saint, before the gaze of her calm eyes, felt sure of being altogether faultless.

So truly was she woman, that all humanity seemed lifted to her level; so completely was she saint, that sin did slink away abashed before her coming.

They who feared her most, were most conscious of her kindness. They who loved her best, were least able to venture near.

In the first bloom of her womanhood she had left the world, resigning high rank, fair lands, and the wealth which makes for power. Her faith in human love having been rudely shattered, she had sought security in Divine compassion, and consolation in the daily contemplation of the Man of Sorrows. In her cell, on a rough wooden cross, hung a life-size figure of the dying Saviour.

She had not reached her twenty-fifth year when, fleeing from the world, she joined the Order of the White Ladies of Worcester, and passed into the seclusion and outward calm of the Nunnery at Whytstone.

Five years later, on the death of the aged Prioress, she was elected, by a large majority, to fill the vacant place.

She had now, during two years, ruled the Nunnery wisely and well.

She had ruled her own spirit, even better. She had won the victory over the World and the Flesh; there remained but the Devil. The Devil, alas, always remains.

As she moved, with uplifted brow and mien of calm detachment, along the sunlit cloister to the lofty, stone passage, within, the Convent, she was feared by many, loved by most, and obeyed by all.

And, as she passed, old Mary Antony, bowing almost to the ground, dropped a large white pea, from between her right thumb and finger, into the horny palm of her left hand.

Behind the Prioress there followed a nun, tall also, but ungainly. Her short-sighted eyes peered shiftily to right and left; her long nose went on before, scenting possible scandal and wrong-doing; her weak lips let loose a ready smile, insinuating, crafty, apologetic. She walked with hands crossed upon her breast, in attitude of adoration and humility. As she moved by, old Mary Antony let drop the pale and speckled pea.

Keeping their distances, mostly with shrouded faces, bent heads, and folded hands, all the White Ladies passed.

Each went in silence to her cell, there kneeling in prayer and contemplation until the Refectory bell should call to the evening meal.

As the last, save one, went by, the keen eyes of the old lay-sister noted that her hands were clenched against her breast, that she stumbled at the topmost step, and caught her breath with a half sob.

Behind her, moving quickly, came the spare form of the Sub-Prioress, ferret-faced, alert, vigilant; fearful lest sin should go unpunished; wishful to be the punisher.

She must have heard the half-strangled sob burst from the slight figure stumbling up the steps before her, had not old Mary Antony been suddenly moved at that moment to uplift her voice in a cracked and raucous "Amen."

Startled, and vexed at being startled, the Sub-Prioress turned upon Mary Antony.

"Peace, woman!" she said. "The Convent cloister is not a hen-yard. Such ill-timed devotion well-nigh merits penance. Rise from thy knees, and go at once about thy business."

The Sub-Prioress hastened on.

Scowling darkly, old Antony bent forward, looking, past Mother Sub-Prioress, up the cloister to the distant passage.

Sister Mary Seraphine had reached her cell. The door was shut.

Old Antony's knees creaked as she arose, but her wizened face was once more cheerful.

"Beans in her broth to-night," she said. "One for 'woman'; another for the hen-yard; a third for threatening penance when I did but chant a melodious 'Amen.' I'll give her beans—castor beans!"

Down the steps she went, pushed the heavy door to, locked it, and drew forth the key; then turned her steps toward the cell of the Reverend Mother.

On her way thither, she paused at a certain door and listened, her ear against the oaken panel. Then she hurried onward, knocked upon the door of the Reverend Mother's cell and, being bidden to enter, passed within, closed the door behind her, and dropped upon her knees.

The Prioress stood beside the casement, gazing at the golden glory of the sunset. She was, for the moment, unconscious of her surroundings. Her mind was away behind those crimson battlements.

Presently she turned and saw the old woman, kneeling at the door.

"How now, dear Antony?" she said, kindly. "Get up! Hang the key in its appointed place, and make me thy report. Have all returned? As always, is all well?"

The old lay-sister rose, hung the massive key upon a nail; then came to the feet of the Prioress, and knelt again.

"Reverend Mother," she said, "all who went forth have returned. But all is not well. Sister Mary Seraphine is uttering wild cries in her cell; and much I fear me, Mother Sub-Prioress may pass by, and hear her."

The face of the Prioress grew stern and sad; yet, withal, tender. She raised the lay-sister, and gently patted the old hands which trembled.

"Go thy ways, dear Antony," she said. "I myself will visit the little Sister in her cell. None will attempt to enter while I am there."

CHAPTER IV

"GIVE ME TENDERNESS," SHE SAID

The Prioress knelt before a marble group of the Virgin and Child, placed where the rays of evening sunshine, entering through the western casement, played over its white beauty, shedding a radiance on the pure face of the Madonna, and a halo of golden glory around the Infant Christ.

"Mother of God," prayed the Prioress, with folded hands, "give me patience in dealing with wilfulness; grant me wisdom to cope with unreason; may it be given me to share the pain of this heart in torment, even as—when thou didst witness the sufferings of thy dear Son, our Lord, on Calvary—a sword pierced through thine own soul also.

"Give me this gift of sympathy with suffering, though the cross be not mine own, but another's.

"But give me firmness and authority: even as when thou didst say to the servants at Cana: 'Whatsoever He saith unto you, do it.'"

The Prioress waited, with bowed head.

9

Then, of a sudden she put forth her hand, and touched the marble foot of the Babe.

"Give me tenderness," she said.

CHAPTER V

THE WAYWARD NUN

Sister Mary Seraphine lay prone upon the floor of her cell.

Tightly clenched in her hands were fragments of her torn veil.

She beat her knuckles upon the stones with rhythmic regularity; then, when her arms would lift no longer, took up the measure with her toes, in wild imitation of a galloping horse.

As she lay, she repeated with monotonous reiteration: "Trappings of crimson, and silver bells: mane and tail, like foam of the waves; a palfrey as white as snow!"

The Prioress entered, closed the door behind her, and looked searchingly at the prostrate figure; then, lifting the master-key which hung from her girdle, locked the door on the inside.

Sister Mary Seraphine had been silent long enough to hear the closing and locking of the door.

Now she started afresh.

"Trappings of crimson, and silver bells—"

The Prioress walked over to the narrow casement, and stood looking out at the rosy clouds wreathing a pale green sky.

"Oh! . . . Oh! . . . Oh! . . ." wailed Sister Mary Seraphine, writhing upon the floor; "mane and tail, like foam of the waves; a palfrey as white as snow!"

The Prioress watched the swallows on swift wing, chasing flies in the evening light.

So complete was the silence, that Sister Mary Seraphine—notwithstanding that turning of the key in the lock—fancied she must be alone.

"Trappings of crimson, and silver bells!" she declaimed with vehemence; then lifted her face to peep, and saw the tall figure of the Prioress standing at the casement.

Instantly, Sister Mary Seraphine dropped her head.

"Mane and tail," she began—then her courage failed; the "foam of the waves" quavered into indecision; and indecision, in such a case, is fatal.

10

For a while she lay quite still, moaning plaintively, then, of a sudden, quivered from head to foot, starting up alert, as if to listen.

"Wilfred!" she shrieked; "Wilfred! Are you coming to save me?"

Then she opened her eyes, and peeped again.

The Prioress, wholly unmoved by the impending advent of "Wilfred," stood at the casement, calmly watching the swallows.

Sister Mary Seraphine began to weep.

At last the passionate sobbing ceased.

Unbroken silence reigned in the cell.

From without, the latch of the door was lifted; but the lock held.

Presently Sister Mary Seraphine dragged herself to the feet of the Prioress, seized the hem of her robe, and kissed it.

Then the Prioress turned. She firmly withdrew her robe from those clinging hands; yet looked, with eyes of tender compassion, upon the kneeling figure at her feet.

"Sister Seraphine," she said, "—for you must shew true penitence e'er I can permit you to be called by our Lady's name—you will now come to my cell, where I will presently speak with you."

Sister Seraphine instantly fell prone.

"I cannot walk," she said.

"You will not walk," replied the Prioress, sternly. "You will travel upon your hands and knees."

She crossed to the door, unlocked and set it wide.

"Moreover," she added, from the doorway, "if you do not appear in my presence in reasonable time, I shall be constrained to send for Mother Sub-Prioress."

The cell of the Prioress was situated at the opposite end of the long, stone passage; but in less than reasonable time, Sister Seraphine crawled in.

The unwonted exercise had had a most salutary effect upon her frame of mind.

Her straight habit, of heavy cloth, had rendered progress upon her knees awkward and difficult. Her hands had become entangled in her torn veil. Each moment she had feared lest cell doors, on either side, should open; old Antony might appear from the cloisters, or— greatest disaster of all—Mother Sub-Prioress might advance toward her from the Refectory stairs! In order to attain a greater rate of speed, she had tried lifting her knees, as elephants lift their feet. This mode of progress, though ungainly, had proved efficacious; but would have been distinctly mirth-provoking to beholders. The stones had hurt her hands and knees far more than she hurt them when she beat upon the floor of her own cell.

She arrived at the Reverend Mother's footstool, heated in mind and body, ashamed of herself, vexed with her garments, in fact in an altogether saner frame of mind than when she had called upon

11

"Wilfred," and made reiterated mention of trappings of crimson and silver bells.

Perhaps the Prioress had foreseen this result, when she imposed the penance. Leniency or sympathy, at that moment, would have been fatal and foolish; and had not the Prioress made special petition for wisdom?

She was seated at her table, when Sister Seraphine bumped and shuffled into view. She did not raise her eyes from the illuminated missal she was studying. One hand lay on the massive clasp, the other rested in readiness to turn the page. Her noble form seemed stately calm personified.

When she heard Sister Seraphine panting close to her foot, she spoke; still without lifting her eyes.

"You may rise to your feet," she said, "and shut to the door."

Then the waiting hand turned the page, and silence fell.

"You may arrange the disorder of your dress," said the Prioress, and turned another page.

When at length she looked up, Sister Seraphine, clothed and apparently in her right mind, stood humbly near the door.

The Prioress closed the book, and shut the heavy clasps.

Then she pointed to an oaken stool, signing to the nun to draw it forward.

"Be seated, my child," she said, in tones of infinite tenderness. "There is much which must now be said, and your mind will pay better heed, if your body be at rest."

With her steadfast eyes the Prioress searched the pretty, flushed face, swollen with weeping, and now gathering a look of petulant defiance, thinly veiled beneath surface humility.

"What was the cause of this outburst, my child?" asked the Prioress, very gently.

"While in the Cathedral, Reverend Mother, up in our gallery, I, being placed not far from a window, heard, in a moment of silence, the neighing of a horse in the street without. It was like to the neighing of mine own lovely palfrey, waiting in the castle court at home, until I should come down and mount him. Each time that steed neighed, I could see Snowflake more clearly, in trappings of gay crimson, with silver bells, amid many others prancing impatiently, champing their bits as they waited; for it pleased me to come out last, when all were mounted. Then the riders lifted their plumed caps when I appeared, while Wilfred, pushing my page aside, did swing me into the saddle. Thus, with shouting and laughter and winding of horn, we would all ride out to the hunt or the tourney; I first, on Snowflake; Wilfred, close behind."

Very quietly the Prioress sat listening. She did not take her eyes from the flushed face. A slight colour tinged her own cheeks.

"Who was Wilfred?" she asked, when Sister Seraphine paused for breath.

12

"My cousin, whom I should have wed if—"

"If?"

"If I had not left the world."

The Prioress considered this.

"If your heart was set upon wedding your cousin, my child, why did you profess a vocation and, renouncing all worldly and carnal desires, gain admission to our sacred Order?"

"My heart was not set on marrying my cousin!" cried Sister Seraphine, with petulance. "I was weary of Wilfred. I was weary of everything! I wanted to profess. I wished to become a nun. There were people I could punish, and people I could surprise, better so, than in any other way. But Wilfred said that, when the time came, he would be there to carry me off."

"And—when the time came?"

"He was not there. I never saw him again."

The Prioress turned, and looked out through the oriel window. She seemed to be weighing, carefully, what she should say.

When at length she spoke, she kept her eyes fixed upon the waving tree-tops beyond the Convent wall.

"Sister Seraphine," she said, "many who embrace the religious life, know what it is to pass through the experience you have now had; but, as a rule, they fight the temptation and conquer it in the secret of their own hearts, in the silence of their own cells.

"Memories of the life that was, before, choosing the better part, we left the world, come back to haunt us, with a wanton sweetness. Such memories cannot change the state, fixed forever by our vows; but they may awaken in us vain regrets or worldly longings. Therein lies their sinfulness.

"To help you against this danger, I will now give you two prayers, which you must commit to memory, and repeat whenever need arises. The first is from the Breviary."

The Prioress drew toward her a black book with silver clasps, opened it, and read therefrom a short prayer in Latin. But seeing no light of response or of intelligence upon the face of Sister Seraphine, she slowly repeated a translation.

Almighty and Everlasting God, grant that our wills be ever meekly subject to Thy will, and our hearts be ever honestly ready to serve Thee. Amen.

Her eyes rested, with a wistful smile, upon the book.

"This prayer might suffice," she said, "if our hearts were truly honest, if our wills were ever yielded. But, alas, our hearts are deceitful above all things, and our wills are apt to turn traitor to our good intentions.

"Therefore I have found for you, in the Gregorian Sacramentary, another prayer—less well-known, yet much more ancient, written over six hundred years ago. It deals effectually with the deceitful heart, the

13

insidious, tempting thoughts, and the unstable will. Here is a translation which I have myself inscribed upon the margin."

The Prioress laid her folded hands upon the missal and as she repeated the ancient sixth-century prayer, in all its depth of inspired simplicity, her voice thrilled with deep emotion, for she was giving to another that which had meant infinitely much to her own inner life.

Almighty God, unto Whom all hearts be open, all desires known, and from Whom no secrets are hid: Cleanse the thoughts of our hearts by the inspiration of Thy Holy Spirit, that we may perfectly love Thee, and worthily magnify Thy Holy Name, through Christ our Lord. Amen.

The Prioress turned her face from Sister Seraphine's unresponsive countenance and fixed her eyes once more upon the tree-tops. She was thinking of the long years of secret conflict, known only to Him from Whom no secrets are hid; of the constant cleansing of her thoughts, for which she had so earnestly pleaded; of the fear lest she should never worthily magnify that Holy Name.

Presently—her heart filled with humble tenderness—she turned to Sister Seraphine.

"These prayers, my child, which you will commit to memory before you sleep this night, will protect you from a too insistent recollection of the world you have resigned; and will assist you, with real inward thoroughness, to die daily to self, in order that the Holy Name of our dear Lord may be more worthily magnified in you."

But, alas! this gentle treatment, these long silences, this quiet recitation of holy prayers, had but stirred the naughty spirit in Sister Seraphine.

Her shallow nature failed to understand the deeps of the noble heart, dealing thus tenderly with her. She measured its ocean-wide greatness, by the little artificial runnels of her own morbid emotions. She mistook gentleness for weakness; calm self-control, for lack of strength of will. Her wholesome awe of the Prioress was forgotten.

"But I do not want to die!" she exclaimed. "I want to live—to live—to live!"

The Prioress looked up, astonished.

The surface humility had departed from the swollen countenance of Sister Seraphine. The petulant defiance was plainly visible.

"Kneel!" commanded the Prioress, with authority.

The wayward nun jerked down upon her knees, upsetting the stool behind her.

The Prioress made a quick movement, then restrained herself. She had prayed for patience in dealing with wilfulness.

"We die that we may live," she said, solemnly. "Sister Seraphine, this is the lesson your wayward heart must learn. Dying to self, we live unto God. Dying to sin, we live unto righteousness. Dying to the world, we find the Life Eternal."

On her knees upon the floor, Sister Seraphine felt her position to be such as lent itself to pathos.

14

"But I want to live to the world!" she cried, and burst into tears.

Now Convent life does not tend to further individual grief. Constant devout contemplation of the Supreme Sorrow which wrought the world's salvation lessens the inclination to shed tears of self-pity.

The Prioress was startled and alarmed by the pathetic sobs of Sister Seraphine.

This young nun had but lately been sent on to the Nunnery at Whytstone from a convent at Tewkesbury in which she had served her novitiate, and taken her final vows. The Prioress now realised how little she knew of the inner working of the mind of Sister Seraphine, and blamed herself for having looked upon the outward appearance rather than upon the heart, taken too much for granted, and relied too entirely upon the reports of others. Her sense of failure, toward the Community in general, and toward Seraphine in particular, lent her a fresh stock of patience.

She raised the weeping nun from the floor, put her arm around her, with protective gesture, and led her before the Shrine of the Madonna.

"My child," she said, "there are things we are called upon to suffer which we can best tell to our blessèd Lady, herself. Try to unburden your heart and find comfort . . . Does your mind hark back to the thought of the earthly love you resigned in order to give yourself solely to the heavenly? . . . Are you troubled by fears lest you wronged the man you loved, when, leaving him, you became the bride of Heaven?"

Sister Seraphine smiled—a scornful little smile. "Nay," she said, "I was weary of Wilfred. But—there were others."

The voice of the Prioress grew even graver, and more sad.

"Is it then the Fact of marriage which you desired and regret?"

Sister Seraphine laughed—a hard, self-conscious, little laugh.

"Nay, I could not have brooked to be bound to any man. But I liked to be loved, and I liked to be First in the thought and heart of another."

The Prioress looked at the pretty, tear-stained face, at the softly moulded form. Then an idea came to her. To voice it, lifted the veil from the very Holy of Holies of her own heart's sufferings; but she would not shrink from aught which could help this soul she was striving to uplift.

With her eyes resting upon the Babe in the arms of the Virgin Mother, she asked, gravely and low:

"Is it the ceaseless longing to have had a little child of your own to hold in your arms, to gather to your breast, to put to sleep upon your knees, which keeps your heart turning restlessly back to the world?"

Sister Seraphine gazed at the Prioress, in utter amazement.

"Nay, then, indeed!" she replied, impatiently. "Always have I

15

hated children. To escape from the vexations of motherhood were reason enough for leaving the world."

Then the Prioress withdrew her protective arm, and looked sternly upon Sister Seraphine.

"You are playing false to your vows," she said; "you are slighting your vocation; yet no worthy or noble feeling draws your heart back to the world. You do but desire vain pomp and show; all those things which minister to the enthronement of self. Return to your cell and spend three hours in prayer and penitence before the crucifix."

The Prioress lifted her hand and pointed to the figure of the Christ, hanging upon the great rugged cross against the wall, facing the door. The sublimity of a supreme adoration was in her voice, as she made her last appeal.

"Surely," she said, "surely no love of self can live, in view of the death and sacrifice of our blessèd Lord! Kneel then before the crucifix and learn—"

But the over-wrought mind of Sister Seraphine, suddenly convinced of the futility of its hopeless rebellion, passed, in that moment, altogether beyond control.

With a shout of wild laughter, she flung back her head, pointing with outstretched finger at the crucifix.

"Death! Death! Death!" she shrieked, "helpless, hopeless, terrible! I ask for life, I want to live; I am young, I am gay, I am beautiful. And they bid—bid—bid me kneel—long hours—watching death." Her voice rose to a piercing scream. "Ah, HA! That will I NOT! A dead God cannot help me! I want life, not death!"

Shrieking she leapt to her feet, flew across the room, beat upon the sacred Form with her fists; tore at It with her fingers.

One instant of petrifying horror. Then the Prioress was upon her.

Seizing her by both wrists she flung her to the floor, then pulled a rope passing over a pulley in the wall, which started the great alarm-bell, in the passage, clanging wildly.

At once there came a rush of flying feet; calls for the Sub-Prioress; but she was already there.

When they flung wide the door, lo, the Prioress stood—with white face and blazing eyes, her arms outstretched—between them and the crucifix.

Upon the floor, a crumpled heap, lay Sister Mary Seraphine.

The nuns, in a frightened crowd, filled the doorway, none daring to speak, or to enter; till old Mary Antony, pushing past the Sub-Prioress, kneeled down beside the Reverend Mother, and, lifting the hem of her robe, kissed it and pressed it to her breast.

Slowly the Prioress let fall her arms.

"Enter," she said; and they flocked in.

"Sister Seraphine," said the Prioress, in awful tones, "has profaned the crucifix, reviling our blessèd Lord, Who hangs thereon."

16

All the nuns, falling upon their knees, hid their faces in their hands.

There was a terrifying quality in the silence of the next moments.

Slowly the Prioress turned, prostrated herself at the foot of the cross, and laid her forehead against the floor at its base. Then the nuns heard one deep, shuddering sob.

Not a head was lifted. The only nun who peeped was Sister Mary Seraphine, prone upon the floor.

After a while, the Prioress arose, pale but calm.

"Carry her to her cell," she said.

Two tall nuns to whom she made sign lifted Sister Seraphine, and bore her out.

When the shuffling of their feet died away in the distance, the Prioress gave further commands.

"All will now go to their cells and kneel in adoration before the crucifix. Doors are to be left standing wide. The Miserere is to be chanted, until the ringing of the Refectory bell. Mother Sub-Prioress will remain behind."

The nuns dispersed, as quickly as they had gathered; seeking their cells, like frightened birds fleeing before a gathering storm.

The tall nuns who had carried Sister Seraphine returned and waited outside the Reverend Mother's door.

The Prioress stood alone; a tragic figure in her grief.

Mother Sub-Prioress drew near. Her narrow face, peering from out her veil, more than ever resembled a ferret. Her small eyes gleamed with a merciless light.

"Is mine the task, Reverend Mother?" she whispered.

The Prioress inclined her head.

Mother Sub-Prioress murmured a second question.

The Prioress turned and looked at the crucifix.

"Yes," she said, firmly.

Mother Sub-Prioress sidled nearer; then whispered her third question.

The Prioress did not answer. She was looking at the carved, oaken stool, overthrown. She was wondering whether she could have acted with better judgment, spoken more wisely. Her heart was sore. Such noble natures ever blame themselves for the wrong-doing of the worthless.

Receiving no reply, Mother Sub-Prioress whispered a suggestion.

"No," said the Prioress.

Mother Sub-Prioress modified her suggestion.

The Prioress turned and looked at the tender figure of the Madonna, brooding over the blessèd Babe.

"No," said the Prioress.

Mother Sub-Prioress frowned, and made a further modification; but in tones which suggested finality.

17

The Prioress inclined her head.

The Sub-Prioress, bowing low, lifted the hem of the Reverend Mother's veil, and kissed it; then passed from the room.

The Prioress moved to the window.

The sunset was over. The evening star shone, like a newly-lighted lamp, in a pale purple sky. The fleet-winged swallows had gone to rest.

Bats flitted past the casement, like homeless souls who know not where to go.

Low chanting began in the cells; the nuns, with open doors, singing Miserere.

But, as she looked at the evening star, the Prioress heard again, with startling distinctness, the final profanity of poor Sister Seraphine: "I want life—not death!"

Along the corridor passed a short procession, on its way to the cell of Mary Seraphine.

First went a nun, carrying a lighted taper.

Next, the two tall nuns who had borne Mary Seraphine to her cell.

Behind them, Mother Sub-Prioress, holding something beneath her scapulary which gave to her more of a presence than she usually possessed.

Solemn and official,—nay, almost sacrificial—was their measured shuffle, as they moved along the passage, and entered the cell of Mary Seraphine.

The Prioress closed her door, and, kneeling before the crucifix, implored forgiveness for the sacrilege which, all unwittingly, she had provoked.

The nuns, in their separate cells, chanted the Miserere. But—suddenly—with one accord, their voices fell silent; then hastened on, in uncertain, agitated rhythm.

Old Mary Antony below, playing her favourite game, also paused, and pricked up her ears: then filliped the wizen pea, which stood for Mother Sub-Prioress, into the darkest corner, and hurried off to brew a soothing balsam.

So, when the Refectory bell had summoned all to the evening meal, the old lay-sister crept to the cell of Mary Seraphine, carrying broth and comfort.

But Sister Seraphine was better content than she had been for many weeks.

At last she had become the centre of attention; and, although, during the visit of Mother Sub-Prioress to her cell, this had been a peculiarly painful position to occupy, yet to the morbid mind of Mary Seraphine, the position seemed worth the discomfort.

Therefore, her mind now purged of its discontent, she cheerfully supped old Antony's broth, and applied the soothing balsam; yet planning the while, to gain favour with the Prioress, by repeating to

18

her, at the first convenient opportunity, the naughty remarks concerning Mother Sub-Prioress, now being made for her diversion, by the kind old woman who had risked reproof, in order to bring to her, in her disgrace, both food and consolation.

CHAPTER VI

THE KNIGHT OF THE BLOODY VEST

"Nay, I have naught for thee this morning," said Mary Antony to the robin; "naught, that is, save spritely conversation. I can tell thee a tale or two; I can give thee sage advice; but, in my wallet, little Master Mendicant, I have but my bag of peas."

The old lay-sister sat resting in the garden. She had had a busy hour, yet complicated in its busy-ness, for, starting out to do weeding, she had presently fancied herself intent upon making a posy, and now, sat upon the stone seat beneath the beech tree, holding a large nosegay made up of many kinds of flowering weeds, arranged with much care, and bound round with convolvulus tendrils.

Keen and uncommon shrewd though old Antony certainly was in many ways, her great age occasionally betrayed itself by childish vagaries. Her mind would start off along the lines of a false premise, landing her eventually in a dream-like conclusion. As now, when waking from a moment's nodding in the welcome shade, she wondered why her old back seemed well-nigh broken, and marvelled to find herself holding a big posy of dandelions, groundsel, plantain, and bindweed.

On the other end of the seat, stood the robin. The beech was just near enough to the cloisters, the pieman's tree, and his own particular yew hedge, to come within his little kingdom.

Having mentioned her bag of peas, Mary Antony experienced an irresistible desire to view them and, moreover, to display them before the bright eyes of the robin.

She laid the queer nosegay down upon the grass at her feet, turned sidewise on the stone slab, and drew the bag from her wallet.

"Now, Master Pieman!" she said. "At thine own risk thou doest it; but with thine own bright eyes thou shalt see the holy Ladies; the Unnamed, all like peas in a pod, as the Lord knows they do look, when they walk to and fro; but first, if so be that I can find them, the Few which I distinguish from among the rest."

19

Presently, after much peering into the bag, the fine white pea, the wizened pea, and the pale and speckled pea, lay in line upon the stone.

"This," explained Mary Antony, pointing, with knobby forefinger, to the first, "is the Reverend Mother, Herself—large, and pure, and noble. . . . Nay, hop not too close, Sir Redbreast! When we enter her chamber we kneel at the threshold, till she bids us draw nearer. True, we are merely soberly-clad, holy women, whereas thou art a gay, gaudy man; bold-eyed, and, doubtless, steeped in sin. But even thou must keep thy distance, in presence of this most Reverend Pea of great price.

"This," indicating the shrivelled pea, "is Mother Sub-Prioress, who would love to have the whipping of thee, thou naughty little rascal!

"This is Sister Mary Rebecca who daily grows more crooked, both in mind and body; yet who ever sweetly smileth.

"Now will I show thee, if so be that I can find her, Sister Teresa, a kindly soul and gracious, but with a sniff which may be heard in the kitchens when that holy Lady taketh her turn at the Refectory reading. And when, the reading over, having sniffed every other minute, she at length, feels free to blow, beshrew me, Master Redbreast, one might think our old dun cow had just been parted from a newly-born calf. Yea, a kind, gracious soul; but noisy about the nose, and forgetful of the ears of other people, her own necessity seeming excuse enough for veritable trumpet blasts."

Mary Antony, half turning as she talked, peered into the open bag in search of Sister Teresa.

Then, quick as thought, the unexpected happened.

Three rapid hops, a jerky bend of the red breast, a flash of wings—

The robin had flown off with the white pea! The shrivelled and the speckled alone remained upon the seat.

Uttering a cry of horror and dismay, the old lay-sister fell upon her knees, lifting despairing hands to trees and sky.

Down by the lower wall, in earnest meditation, the Prioress moved back and forth, on the Cypress Walk.

Mary Antony's shriek of dismay, faint but unmistakable, reached her ears. Turning, she passed noiselessly up the green sward, on the further side of the yew hedge; but paused, in surprise, as she drew level with the beech; for the old lay-sister's voice penetrated the hedge, and the first words she overheard seemed to the Prioress wholly incomprehensible.

"Ah, thou Knight of the Bloody Vest!" moaned Mary Antony. "Heaven send thy wicked perfidy may fall on thine own pate! Intruding thyself into our most private places; begging food, which could not be refused; wheedling old Mary Antony into letting thee have a peep at the holy Ladies—thou bold, bad man!—and then carrying off the Reverend Mother, Herself! Ha! Hadst thou but caught away Mother Sub-Prioress, she would have reformed thy home, whipped thy children,

20

and mended thine own vile manners, thou graceless churl! Or hadst thou taken Sister Mary Rebecca, she would have brought the place about thine ears, telling thy wife fine tales of thine unfaithfulness; whispering that Mary Antony is younger and fairer than she. But, nay, forsooth! Neither of these will do! Thou must needs snatch away the Reverend Mother, Herself! Oh, sacrilegious fiend! Stand not there mocking me! Where is the Reverend Mother?"

"Why, here am I, dear Antony," said the Prioress, in soothing tones, coming quickly from behind the hedge.

One glance revealed, to her relief, that the lay-sister was alone. Tears ran down the furrows of her worn old face. She knelt upon the grass; beside her a large nosegay of flowering weeds; upon the seat, peas strewn from out a much-used, linen bag. Above her on a bough, a robin perched, bending to look, with roguish eye, at the scattered peas.

To the Prioress it seemed that indeed the old lay-sister must have taken leave of her senses.

Stooping, she tried to raise her; but Mary Antony, flinging herself forward, clasped and kissed the Reverend Mother's feet, in an abandonment of penitence and grief.

"Nay, rise, dear Antony," said the Prioress, firmly. "Rise! I command it. The day is warm. Thou hast been dreaming. No bold, bad man has forced his way within these walls. No 'Knight of the Bloody Vest' is here. Rise up and look. We are alone."

But Mary Antony, still on her knees, half raised herself, and, pointing to the bough above, quavered, amid her sobs: "The bold, bad man is there!"

Looking up, the Prioress met the bright eye of the robin, peeping down.

Why, surely? Yes! There was the "Bloody Vest."

The Prioress smiled. She began to understand.

The robin burst into a stream of triumphant song. At which, old Mary Antony, still kneeling, shook her uplifted fist.

The Prioress raised and drew her to the seat.

"Now sit thee here beside me," she said, "and make full confession. Ease thine old heart by telling me the entire tale. Then I will pass sentence on the robin if, true to his name, he turns out to be a thief."

So there, in the Convent garden, while the robin sang overhead, the Prioress listened to the quaint recital; the dread of making mistake in the daily counting; the elaborate plan of dropping peas; the manner in which the peas became identified with the personalities of the White Ladies; the games in the cell; the taming of the robin; the habit of sharing with the little bird, interests which might not be shared with others, which had resulted that morning in the display of the peas, and this undreamed of disaster—the abduction of the Reverend Mother.

The Prioress listened with outward gravity, striving to conceal all

21

signs of the inward mirth which seized and shook her. But more than once she had to turn her face from the peering eyes of Mary Antony, striving anxiously to gather whether her chronicle of sins was placing her outside the pale of possible forgiveness.

The Prioress did not hasten the recital. She knew the importance, to the mind with which she dealt, of even the most trivial detail. To be checked or hurried, would leave Mary Antony with the sense of an incomplete confession.

Therefore, with infinite patience the Prioress listened, seated in the sunlit garden, undisturbed, save for the silent passing, once or twice, of a veiled figure through the cloisters, who, seeing the Reverend Mother seated beneath the beech, did reverence and hastened on, looking not again.

When the garrulous old voice at last fell silent, the Prioress, with kind hand, covered the restless fingers—clasping and unclasping in anxious contortions—and firmly held them in folded stillness.

Her first words were of a thing as yet unmentioned.

"Dear Antony," she said, "is that thy posy lying at our feet?"

"Ah, Reverend Mother," sighed the old lay-sister, "in this did I again do wrong meaning to do right. Sister Mary Augustine, coming into the kitchens with leave, from Mother Sub-Prioress, to make the pasties, and desiring to be free to make them heavy—unhampered by my advice which, of a surety, would have helped them to lightness—bade me go out and weed the garden.

"Weeding, I bethought me how much liefer I would be gathering a posy of choicest flowers for our sweet Lady's shrine; and, thus thinking, I began to do, not according to Sister Mary Augustine's hard task, but according to mine own heart's promptings. Yet, when the posy was finished, alack-a-day! it was a posy of weeds!"

Tears filled the eyes of the Prioress; at first she could not trust her voice to make reply.

Then, stooping she picked up the nosegay.

"Our Lady shall have it," she said. "I will place it before her shrine, in mine own cell. She will understand—knowing how often, though the hands perforce do weeding, yet, all the time, the heart is gathering choicest flowers.

"Aye, and sometimes when we bring to God offerings of fairest flowers, He sees but worthless weeds. And, when we mourn, because we have but weeds to offer, He sees them fragrant blossoms. Whatever, to the eye of man, the hand may hold, God sees therein the bouquet of the heart's intention."

The Prioress paused, a look of great gladness on her face; then, as she saw the old lay-sister still eyeing her posy with dissatisfaction: "And, after all, dear Antony," she said, "who shall decide which flowers shall be dubbed 'weeds'? No plant of His creation, however humble, was called a 'weed' by the Creator. When, for man's sin, He cursed the

22

ground, He said: 'Thorns also and thistles shall it cause to bud.' Well? Sharpest thorns are found around the rose; the thistle is the royal bloom of Scotland; and, if our old white ass could speak her mind, doubtless she would call it King of Flowers.

"Nowhere in Holy Books, is any plant named a 'weed.' It is left to man to proclaim that the flowers he wants not, are weeds.

"Look at each one of these. Could you or I, labouring for years, with all our skill, make anything so perfect as the meanest of these weeds?

"Nay; they are weeds, because they grow, there where they should not be. The gorgeous scarlet poppy is a weed amid the corn. If roses overgrew the wheat, we should dub them weeds, and root them out.

"And some of us have had, perforce, so to deal with the roses in our lives; those sweet and fragrant things which overgrew our offering of the wheat of service, our sacrifice of praise and prayer.

"Perhaps, when our weeds are all torn out, and cast in a tangled heap before His Feet, our Lord beholds in them a garland of choice blossoms. The crown of thorns on earth, may prove, in Paradise, a diadem of flowers."

The Prioress laid the posy on the seat beside her.

"Now, Antony, about thy games with peas. There is no wrong in keeping count with peas of those who daily walk to and from Vespers; though, I admit, it seems to me, it were easier to count one, two, three, with folded hands, than to let fall the peas from one hand to the other, beneath thy scapulary. Howbeit, a method which would be but a pitfall to one, may prove a prop to another. So I give thee leave to continue to count with thy peas. Also the games in thy cell are harmless, and lead me to think, as already I have sometimes thought, that games with balls or rings, something in which eye guides the hand, and mind the eye, might be helpful for all, on summer evenings.

"But I cannot have thee take upon thyself to decide the future state of the White Ladies. Who art thou, to send me to Paradise with a fillip of thine old finger-nail, yet to keep our excellent Sub-Prioress in Purgatory? Shame upon thee, Mary Antony!" But the sternness of the Reverend Mother's tone was belied by the merriment in her grey eyes.

"So no more of that, my Antony; though, truth to tell, thy story gives me relief, answering a question I was meaning to put to thee. I heard, not an hour ago, that Sister Antony had boasted that with a turn of her thumb and finger she could, any night, send Mother Sub-Prioress to Purgatory."

"Who said that of me?" stuttered Mary Antony. "Who said it, Reverend Mother?"

"A little bird," murmured the Prioress. "A little bird, dear Antony; but not thy pretty robin. Also, the boast was taken to mean

23

poison in the broth of Mother Sub-Prioress. Hast thou ever put harmful things in the broth of Mother Sub-Prioress?"

Mary Antony slipped to her knees.

"Only beans, Reverend Mother, castor beans; and, when her temper was vilest, purging herbs. Nothing more, I swear it! Old Antony knows naught of poisons; only of mixing balsams—ah, ha!—and soothing ointments! Our blessèd Lady knows the tale is false."

Hastily the Prioress lifted the nosegay and buried her face in bindweed and dandelions.

"I believe thee," she said, in a voice not over steady. "Rise from thy knees. But, remember, I forbid thee to put aught into Mother Sub-Prioress's broth, save things that soothe and comfort. Give me thy word for this, Antony."

The old woman humbly lifted the hem of the Prioress's robe, and pressed it to her lips.

"I promise, Reverend Mother," she said, "and I do repent me of my sin."

"Sit beside me," commanded the Prioress. "I have more to say to thee. . . . Think not hard thoughts of the Sub-Prioress. She is stern, and extreme to mark what is done amiss, but this she conceives to be her duty. She is a most pious Lady. Her zeal is but a sign of her piety."

Mary Antony's keen eyes, meeting those of the Prioress, twinkled.

Once again the Prioress took refuge in the posy. She was beginning to have had enough of the scent of dandelions.

"Mother Sub-Prioress is sick," she said. "The cold struck her last evening, after sunset, in the orchard. I have bidden her to keep her bed awhile. We must tend her kindly, Antony, and help her back to health again.

"Sister Mary Rebecca is also sick, with pains in her bones and slight fever. She too keeps her bed to-day. Strive to feel kindly toward her, Antony. I know she oft thinks evil where none was meant, telling tales of wrong which are mostly of her own imagining. But, in so doing, she harms herself more than she can harm others.

"By stirring up the mud in a dark pool, you dim the reflection of the star which, before, shone bright within it. But you do not dim the star, shining on high.

"So is it with the slanderous thoughts of evil minds. They stir up their own murkiness; but they fail to dim the stars.

"We must bear with Sister Mary Rebecca."

"Go not nigh them, Reverend Mother," begged old Antony. "I will tend them with due care and patience. These pains in bones, and general shiverings, are given quickly from one to another. I pray you, go not near. Remember—you were taken—alas! alas!—and they were left!"

At this the Prioress laughed, gaily.

"But I was not taken decently, with pains in my bones and a-bed, dear Antony. I was carried off by a bold, bad man—thy Knight of the Bloody Vest."

"Oh, pray!" cried the old lay-sister. "I fear me it is an omen. The angel Gabriel, Reverend Mother, sent to bear you from earth to heaven. 'The one shall be taken, and the other left.' Ah, if he had but flown off with Mother Sub-Prioress!"

The Prioress laughed again. "Dear Antony, thy little bird took the first pea he saw. Had there but been a crumb, or a morsel of cheese, he would have left thee thy white pea. . . Hark how he sings his little song of praise! . . . Is it not wonderful to call to mind how, centuries ago, when white-robed Druids cut mistletoe from British oaks, the robin redbreast hopped around, and sang; when, earlier still, men were wild and savage, dwelling in holes and caves and huts of mud, when churches and cloisters were unknown in this land and the one true God undreamed of, robins mated and made their nests, the speckled thrushes sang, 'Do it now—Do it now,' as they sought food for their young, the blackbirds whistled, and the swallows flashed by on joyous wing. Aye, and when Eve and Adam walked in Eden, amid strange beasts and gaily plumaged birds, here—in these Isles—the robin redbreast sang, and all our British birds busily built their nests and reared their young; living their little joyous lives, as He Who made them taught them how to do.

"And, in the centuries to come, when all things may be changed in this our land, when we shall long have gone to dust, when our loved cloisters may have crumbled into ruin; still the hills of Malvern will stand, and the silvery Severn flow along the valley; while here, in this very garden—if it be a garden still—the robin will build his nest, and carol his happy song.

"Mark you this, dear Mary Antony: all things made by man hold within them the elements of change and of decay. But nature is at one with God, and therefore immutable. Earthly kingdoms may rise and wane; mighty cities may spring up, then fall into ruin. Nations may conquer and, in their turn, be conquered. Man may slay man and, in his turn, be slain. But, through it all, the mountains stand, the rivers flow, the forests wave, and the redbreast builds his nest in the hawthorn, and warbles a love-song to his mate."

The Prioress rose and stretched wide her arms to the sunlit garden, to the bough where the robin sang.

"Oh, to be one with God and with Nature!" she cried. "Oh, to know the essential mysteries of Life and Light and Love! This is Life Eternal!"

She had forgotten the old lay-sister; aye, for the moment she had forgotten the Convent and the cloister, the mile-long walk in darkness, the chant of the unseen monks. She trod again the springy heather of her youth; she heard the rush of the mountain stream; the sigh of the

25

great forest; the rustle of the sunlit glades, alive with, life. These all were in the robin's song. Then—

Within the Convent, the Refectory bell clanged loudly.

The Prioress let fall her arms.

She picked up the nosegay of weeds.

"Come, Antony," she said, "let us go and discover whether Sister Mary Augustine hath contrived to make the pasties light and savoury, even without the aid of the advice she might have had from thee."

Old Mary Antony, gleeful and marvelling, followed the stately figure of the Prioress. Never was shriven soul more blissfully at peace. She had kept back nothing; yet the Reverend Mother had imposed no punishment, had merely asked a promise which, in the fulness of her gratitude, Mary Antony had found it easy to give.

Truly the broth of Mother Sub-Prioress should, for the future, contain naught but what was grateful and soothing.

But, as she entered the Refectory behind the Reverend Mother and saw all the waiting nuns arise, old Mary Antony laid her finger to her nose.

"That 'little bird' shall have the castor beans," she said, "That 'little bird' shall have them. Not my pretty robin, but the other!"

And, sad to say, poor Sister Seraphine was sorely griped that night, and suffered many pangs.

CHAPTER VII

THE MADONNA IN THE CLOISTER

The Prioress knelt, in prayer and meditation, before the figure of the Virgin Mother holding upon her knees the holy Babe.

Moonlight flooded the cell with a pure radiance.

Mary Antony's posy of weeds, offered, according to promise, at the Virgin's shrine, took on, in that silver splendour, the semblance of lilies and roses.

The Prioress knelt long, with clasped hands and bowed head, as white and as motionless as the marble before her. But at length she lifted her face, and broke into low pleading.

"Mother of God," she said, "help this poor aching heart; still the wild hunger at my breast. Make me content to be at one with the Divine, and to let Nature go. . . . Thou knowest it is not the man I want. In all the long years since he played traitor to his troth to me, I have not

26

wanted the man. The woman he wed may have him, unbegrudged by me. I do not envy her the encircling of his arms, though time was when I felt them strong and tender. I do not want the man, but—O, sweet Mother of God—I want the man's little child! I envy her the motherhood which, but for her, would have been mine. . . . I want the soft dark head against my breast. . . . I want sweet baby lips drawing fresh life from mine. . . . I want the little feet, resting together in my hand. . . . All Nature sings of life, and the power to bestow life. Yet mine arms are empty, and my strength does but carry mine own self to and fro. . . . Oh, give me grace to turn my thoughts from Life to Sacrifice."

The Prioress rose, crossed the floor, and knelt long in prayer and contemplation before the crucifix.

The moonlight fell upon the dying face of the suffering Saviour, upon the crown of thorns, the helpless arms out-stretched, the bleeding feet.

O, Infinite Redeemer! O, mighty Sacrifice! O, Love of God, made manifest!

The Prioress knelt long in adoring contemplation. At intervals she prostrated herself, pressing her forehead against the base of the cross.

At length she rose and moved toward the inner room, where stood her couch.

But even as she reached the threshold she turned quickly back, and kneeling before the Virgin and Child clasped the little marble foot of the Babe, covered it with kisses, and pressed it to her breast.

Then, lifting despairing eyes to the tender face of the Madonna: "O, Mother of God," she cried, "grant unto me to love the piercèd feet of thy dear Son crucified, more than I love the little, baby feet of the Infant Jesus on thy knees."

A great calm fell upon her after this final prayer. It seemed, of a sudden, more efficacious than all the long hours of vigil. She felt persuaded that it would be granted.

She rose to her feet, almost too much dazed and too weary to cross to the inner cell.

A breath of exquisite fragrance filled the air.

At the feet of the Madonna stood a wondrous bouquet of lilies of the valley and white roses.

Pale but radiant, the Prioress passed into her sleeping-chamber. The loving heart of old Mary Antony had been full of lilies and roses. It was not her fault that her old hands had been filled with weeds. Divine Love, understanding, had wrought this gracious miracle.

As the Prioress stretched herself upon her couch, she murmured softly: "The Lord seeth not as man seeth: for man looketh on the outward appearance, but the Lord looketh on the heart.

"And, after all, this miracle of the Divine perception doth take place daily.

27

"Alas, when our vaunted roses and lilies appear, in His sight, as mere worthless weeds.

"The Lord looketh on the heart."

* * * * * *

When the Prioress awoke, the sunlight filled her chamber.

She hastened to the archway between the cells, and looked.

The dandelions seemed more gaily golden, in the morning light. The bindweed had faded.

The Prioress was disappointed. She had counted upon sending early for old Mary Antony. She had pictured her bewildered joy. Yet now the nosegay was as before.

Morning light is ever a test for transformations. Things are apt to look again as they were.

But a fragrance of roses and lilies still lingered in the chamber.

The blessèd Virgin smiled upon the Babe.

And there was peace in the heart of the Prioress. Her long vigil, her hours of prayer, had won for her the sense of a calm certainty of coming victory.

Strong in that certainty, she bent, and gently kissed the little feet of the holy Babe.

Then, as was her wont, she sounded the bell which called the entire community to arise, and to begin a new day.

CHAPTER VIII

ON THE WINGS OF THE STORM

In the afternoon of that day, Mary Antony awaited, in the cloisters, the return of the White Ladies from Vespers. Twenty only, had gone; and, fearful lest she should make mistake with the unusual number, the old lay-sister spent the time of waiting in counting the twenty peas afresh, passing them back and forth from one hand to the other.

Mother Sub-Prioress was still unable to leave her bed.

Sister Mary Augustine stayed to tend her.

Sister Teresa was in less pain, but fevered still, and strangely weak.

28

The Reverend Mother forbade her to rise.

Shortly before the bell rang calling the nuns to form procession in the cloisters, Sister Seraphine declared herself unable for the walk, and begged to be allowed to remain behind. The Prioress found herself misdoubting this sudden indisposition of Sister Seraphine who, though flushed and excited, shewed none of the usual signs of sickness.

Not wishing, however, to risk having a third patient upon her hands, the Reverend Mother gave leave for her to stay, but also elected to remain behind, herself; letting Sister Mary Rebecca, who had recovered from her indisposition, lead the procession.

Thus the Reverend Mother contrived to keep Sister Seraphine with her during the absence of the other nuns, giving her translations from the Sacramentaries to copy upon strips of vellum, until shortly before the hour when the White Ladies would return from Vespers, when she sent her to her cell for the time of prayer and meditation.

Left alone, the Prioress examined the copies, fairly legible, but sadly unlike her own beautiful work. She sighed and, putting them away, rose and paced the room, questioning how best to deal with the pretty but wayward young nun.

Two definite causes led the Prioress to mistrust Sister Seraphine: one, that she had called upon "Wilfred" to come and save her, and had admitted having expected him to appear and carry her off before she made her final profession; the other, that she had tried to start an evil report concerning the old lay-sister, Mary Antony. The Prioress pondered what means to take in order to bring Sister Seraphine to a better mind.

As the Prioress walked to and fro, unconsciously missing the daily exercise of the passage to the Cathedral, she noted a sudden darkening of her chamber. Going to the window, she saw the sky grown black with thunder clouds. So quickly the storm gathered, that the bright summer world without seemed suddenly hung over with a deep purple pall.

Birds screamed and darted by, on hurried wing; then, reaching home, fell silent. All nature seemed to hold its breath, awaiting the first flash, and the first roll of thunder.

Still standing at her window, the Prioress questioned whether the nuns were returned, and safely in their cells. While underground they would know nothing of it; but they loved not passing along the cloisters in a storm.

The Prioress wondered why she had not heard the bell announcing their return, and calling to the hour of prayer and silence. Also why Mary Antony had not brought in the key and her report.

Thinking to inquire into this, she turned from the window, just as a darting snake of fire cleft the sky. A crash of thunder followed; and, at that moment, the door of the chamber bursting open, old Mary Antony, breathless, stumbled in, forgetting to knock, omitting to kneel,

29

not waiting leave to speak, both hands outstretched, one tightly clenched, the other holding the great key: "Oh, Reverend Mother!" she gasped. Then the stern displeasure on that loved face silenced her. She dropped upon her knees, ashen and trembling.

Now the Prioress held personal fear in high scorn; and if, after ninety years' experience of lightning and thunder, Mary Antony was not better proof against their terrors, the Prioress felt scant patience with her. She spoke sternly.

"How now, Mary Antony! Why this unseemly haste? Why this rush into my presence; no knock; no pause until I bid thee enter? Is the storm-fiend at thy heels? Now shame upon thee!"

For only answer, Mary Antony opened her clenched hand: whereupon twenty peas fell pattering to the floor, chasing one another across the Reverend Mother's cell.

The Prioress frowned, growing suddenly weary of these games with peas.

"Have the Ladies returned?" she asked.

Mary Antony grovelled nearer, let fall the key, and seized the robe of the Prioress with both hands, not to carry it to her lips, but to cling to it as if for protection.

With the clang of the key on the flags, a twisted blade of fire rent the sky.

As the roar which followed rolled away, echoed and re-echoed by distant hills, the old lay-sister lifted her face.

Her lips moved, her gums rattled; the terror in her eyes pleaded for help.

This was the moment when it dawned on the Prioress that there was more here than fear of a storm.

Stooping she laid her hands firmly, yet with kindness in their strength, on the shaking shoulders.

"What is it, dear Antony?" she said.

"Twenty White Ladies went," whispered the old lay-sister. "I counted them. Twenty White Ladies went; but—"

"Well?"

"Twenty-one returned," chattered Mary Antony, and hid her face in the Reverend Mother's robe.

Two flashes, with their accompanying peals of thunder passed, before the Prioress moved or spoke. Then raising Mary Antony she placed her in a chair, disengaged her robe from the shaking hands, passed out into the cell passage, and herself sounded the call to silence and prayer.

Returning to her cell she shut the door, poured out a cordial and put it to the trembling lips of Mary Antony. Then taking a seat just opposite, she looked with calm eyes at the lay-sister.

"What means this story?" said the Prioress.

"Reverend Mother, twenty holy Ladies went—"

30

"I know. And twenty returned."

"Aye," said the old woman more firmly, nettled out of her speechlessness; "twenty returned; and twenty peas I dropped from hand to hand. Then—when no pea remained—yet another White Lady glided by; and with her went an icy wind, and around her came the blackness of the storm.

"Down the steps I fled, locked the door, and took the key. How I mounted again, I know not. As I drew level with the cloisters, I saw that twenty-first White Lady, for whom—Saint Peter knows—I held no pea, passing from the cloisters into the cell passage. As I hastened on, fain to see whither she went, a blinding flash, like an evil twisting snake, shot betwixt her and me. When I could see again, she was gone. I fled to the Reverend Mother, and ran in on the roar of the thunder."

"Saw you her face, Mary Antony?"

"Nay, Reverend Mother. But, of late, the holy Ladies mostly walk by with their faces shrouded."

"I know. Now, see here, dear Antony. Two peas dropped together, the while you counted one."

"Nay, Reverend Mother. Twenty peas dropped one by one; also I counted twenty White Ladies. And, after I had counted twenty, yet another passed."

"But how could that be?" objected the Prioress. "If twenty went, but twenty could return. Who should be the twenty-first?"

Then old Mary Antony leaned forward, crossing herself.

"Sister Agatha," she whispered, tremulously. "Poor Sister Agatha returned to us again."

But, even as she said it, swift came a name to the mind of the Prioress, answering her own question, and filling her with consternation and a great anger. "Wilfred! Wilfred, are you come to save me?" foolish little Seraphine had said. Was such sacrilege possible? Could one from the outside world have dared to intrude into their holy Sanctuary?

Yet old Antony's tale carried conviction. Her abject fear was now explained.

That the Dead should come again, and walk and move among the haunts of men, seeking out the surroundings they have loved and left, seems always to hold terror for the untutored mind, which knows not that the Dead are more alive than the living; and that there is no death, saving the death of sin.

But to the Reverend Mother, guarding her flock from sin or shame, a visitor from the Unseen World held less of horror than a possible intruder from the Seen.

A rapid glance as she sounded the bell, had shown her that the passage was empty.

Which cell now sheltered two, where there should be but one?

The Prioress walked across to a recess near the south window,

31

touched a spring, and slid back a portion of the oak panelling. Passing her hand into a secret hiding place in the wall, she drew forth a beautifully fashioned dagger, with carved ivory handle, crossed metal thumb-guard, blade of bevelled steel, polished and narrowing to a sharp needle point. She tested the point, then slipped the weapon into her belt, beneath her scapulary. As she closed the panel, and turned back into the chamber, a light of high resolve was in her eyes. Her whole bearing betokened so fine a fearlessness, such noble fixity of purpose that, looking on her, Mary Antony felt her own fears vanishing.

"Now listen, dear Antony," said the Prioress, holding the old woman with her look. "I must make sure that this twenty-first White Lady of thine is but a trick played on thee by thy peas. Should she be anywhere in the Convent I shall most certainly have speech with her.

"Meanwhile, go thou to thy kitchens, and give thy mind to the preparing of the evening meal. But ring not the Refectory bell until I bid thee. Nay, I myself will sound it this evening. It may suit me to keep the nuns somewhat longer at their devotions.

"Should I sound the alarm bell, let all thy helpers run up here; but go thou to the cell of Mother Sub-Prioress and persuade her not to rise. If needful say that it is my command that she keep her bed. . . . Great heavens! What a crash! May our Lady defend us! The lightning inclines to strike. I shall pass to each cell and make sure that none are too greatly alarmed."

"Now, haste thee, Antony; and not a word concerning thy fears must pass thy lips to any; no mention of a twenty-first White Lady nor"—the Prioress crossed herself—"of Sister Agatha, to whom may our Lord grant everlasting rest."

Mary Antony, kneeling, kissed the hem of the Prioress's robe. Then, rising, she said—with unwonted solemnity and restraint: "The Lord defend you, Reverend Mother, from foes, seen and unseen," and, followed by another blinding flash of lightning, she left the cell.

CHAPTER IX

THE PRIORESS SHUTS THE DOOR

The Prioress waited until the old lay-sister's shuffling footsteps died away.

Then she passed out into the long, stone passage, leaving her own door open wide.

Into each cell the Prioress went.

In each she found a kneeling nun, absorbed in her devotions. In no cell were there two white figures. So simple were the fittings of these cells, that no place of concealment was possible. One look, from the doorway, sufficed.

Outside the cell of Sister Seraphine the Prioress paused, hearing words within; then entered swiftly. But Sister Seraphine was alone, reciting aloud, for love of hearing her own voice.

The Prioress now moved toward the heavy door in the archway leading into the cloisters. It opened inwards, and had been left standing wide, by Mary Antony. Indeed, in summer it stood open day and night, for coolness.

As the Prioress walked along the dimly lighted passage, she could see, through the open door, sheets of rain driving through the cloisters. The storm-clouds had burst, at last, and were descending in floods.

The Prioress stood in the shelter of the doorway, looking out into the cloisters. The only places she could not view, were the entrance to the subterranean way, and the flight of steps leading thereto. She would have wished to examine these; but it seemed scarcely worth passing into the driving rain, now sweeping through the cloister arches. After all, whatever possible danger lurked down those steps, the safety of the Convent would be assured if she closed this door, between the passage and the cloisters, and locked it.

Stepping back into the passage, she seized the heavy door and swung it to, noting as she did so, how far too heavy it was for the feeble arms of old Mary Antony, and deciding for the future to allot the task of closing it to a young lay-sister, leaving to Mary Antony merely the responsibility of turning the key in the lock.

This the Prioress was herself proceeding to do, when something impelled her to turn her eyes to the angle of wall laid bare by the closing of the door.

In that dark corner, motionless, with shrouded face, stood a tall figure, garbed in the dress of the nuns of the Order of the White Ladies of Worcester.

Perhaps the habit of silence is never of greater value than in moments of sudden shock and horror.

One cry from the Prioress would have meant the instant opening of many doors, and the arrival, on flying feet, of a score of frightened nuns.

Instead of screaming, the Prioress stood silent and perfectly still; while every pulse in her body ceased beating, during one moment of uncontrollable, cold horror. Then, with a leap, her heart went on; pounding so loudly, that she could hear it in the silence. Yet she kept command of every impulse which drove to sound or motion.

Before long her pulses quieted; her heart, beating steadily, was

33

once again the well-managed steed upon which her high courage could ride to victory.

And, all the while, her eyes never left the white figure; knowing it knew itself discovered and observed.

Her hand was still upon the key.

She turned it, and withdrew it from the lock.

A deafening crash of thunder shook the walls. A swirl of wind and rain beat on the door.

When the last echo of the thunder had died away, the Prioress spoke; and that calm voice, sounding amid the storm, fell on the only ears that heard it, like the Voice of Power on Galilee, which bid the tempest cease, and the wild waves be still.

"Who art thou, and what doest thou here?"

The figure answered not.

"Art thou a ghostly visitor come back amongst us, from the Realm of the Unseen?"

The figure made no sign. "Art thou then flesh and blood, and mortal as ourselves?"

Slowly the figure bowed its head.

"Now I adjure thee by our blessèd Lady to tell me truly. Art thou, in very deed a holy nun, a member of our sacred Order? Answer me, yea or nay?"

The figure shook its head.

The Prioress advanced a step, passed the key into her left hand and, slipping her right beneath her scapulary, took firm grip of the dagger at her girdle.

"Then, masquerader in our sacred dress," she said, "to me you have to answer for double sacrilege: the wearing of these robes, and your presence here, unbidden. I warn you that your life has never hung by frailer thread than now it hangs. Your only hope of safety lies in doing as I bid you. Pass before me along this passage until you reach a chamber on the right, of which the door stands open. Enter, and place yourself against the wall on the side farthest from the door. There I will speak with you."

With the shuffling steps of a woman, and the bent shoulders of the very old, the figure moved slowly forward, stepped upon the front of the white robe, stumbled, but recovered.

The Prioress watching, laughed—a short scornful laugh, holding more of anger than of merriment.

With an abrupt movement the figure straightened, stood at its full height, and strode forward. The Prioress marked the squaring of the broad shoulders; the height, greater than her own, though she was more than common tall; the stride, beneath the folds of the long robe; and she knit her level brows, for well she knew with whom she had to deal. She was called to face a desperate danger. Single-handed, she had to meet a subtle foe. She asked no help from others, but she took no needless risks.

34

As she passed the cell of Mary Seraphine, using her master-key, she locked that lady in!

CHAPTER X

"I KNOW YOU FOR A MAN"

Entering her cell, the Prioress saw at once that her orders had been obeyed.

. The hooded figure stood on the far side of the chamber, leaning broad shoulders against the wall. Under the cape, the arms were folded; she could see that the feet were crossed beneath the robe. The dress was indeed the dress of a White Lady, but the form within it was so obviously that of a man—a big man, at bay, and inclined to be defiant—that, despite the strange situation, despite her anger, and her fears, the contrast between the holy habit and its hidden wearer, forced from the Prioress an unwilling smile.

Closing the door, she drew forward a chair of dark Spanish wood, the gift of the Lord Bishop; a chair which well betokened the dignity of her high office.

Seating herself, she laid her left hand lightly upon the mane of one of the carved lions which formed, on either side, the arms of the chair; but her right hand still gripped unseen the ivory hilt; while leaning slightly forward, with feet firmly planted, she was ready at any moment to spring erect.

"I know you for a man," she said.

The thunder rumbled far away in the distance.

The rain still splashed against the casement, but the storm had spent itself; the sky was brightening. A pale slant of sunshine broke through the parting clouds and, entering the casement, gleamed on the jewelled cross at the breast of the Prioress, and kindled into peculiar radiance the searching light of her clear eyes.

"I know you for a man," she said again. "You stand there, revealed; and surely you stand there, shamed. By plotting and planning, by assuming our dress, you have succeeded in forcing your undesired presence into this sacred cloister, where dwells a little company of women who have left the world, never to return to it again; who have given up much in order to devote themselves to a life of continual worship and adoration, gaining thereby a power in

35

intercession which brings down blessing upon those who still fight life's battles in the world without.

"But it has meant the breaking of many a tender tie. There are fathers and brothers dear to them, whom the nuns would love to see again; but they cannot do so, save, on rare occasions, in the guest-room at the gate; and then, with the grille between.

"Saving Bishop or Priest, no foot of man may tread our cloisters; no voice of man may be heard in these cells.

"Yet—by trick and subterfuge—you have intruded. Methinks I scarce should let you leave this place alive, to boast what you have done."

The Prioress paused.

The figure stood, with folded arms, immovable, leaning against the wall. There was a quality in this motionless silence such as the Prioress had not connected with her idea of Mary Seraphine's "Cousin Wilfred."

This was not a man to threaten. Her threat came back to her, as if she had flung it against a stone wall. She tried another line of reasoning.

"I know you, Sir Wilfred," she said. "And I know why you are here. You have come to tempt away, or mayhap, if possible, to force away one of our number who but lately took her final vows. There was a time, not long ago, when you might have thwarted her desire to seek and find the best and highest. But now you come too late. No bride of Heaven turns from her high estate. Her choice is made. She will abide by it; and so, Sir Knight, must you."

The rain had ceased. The storm was over. Sunshine flooded the cell.

Once more the Prioress spoke, and her voice was gentle.

"I know the disappointment to you must be grievous. You took great risks; you adventured much. How long you have plotted this intrusion, I know not. You have been thwarted in your evil purpose by the faithfulness of one old woman, our aged lay-sister, Mary Antony, who never fails to count the White Ladies as they go and as they return, and who reported at once to me that one more had returned than went.

"Do you not see in this the Hand of God? Will you not bow in penitence before Him, confessing the sinfulness of the thing you had in mind to do?"

The shrouded head was lifted higher, as if with a proud gesture of disavowal. At the same time, the hood slightly parting, the hand of a man, lean and brown, gripped it close.

The Prioress looked long at that lean, brown hand.

Then she rose slowly to her feet.

"Shew me—thy—face," she said; and the tension of each word was like a naked blade passing in and out of quivering flesh.

At sound of it the figure stood erect, took one step forward, flung

36

back the hood, tore open the robe and scapulary, loosing his arms from the wide sleeves.

And—as the hood fell back—the Prioress found herself looking into a face she had not thought to see again in life—the face of him who once had been her lover.

CHAPTER XI

THE YEARS ROLL BACK

"Hugh!" exclaimed the Prioress.

And again, in utter bewilderment: "Hugh?"

And yet a third time, in a low whisper of horror, passing her left hand across her eyes, as if to clear from her outer vision some nightmare of the inner mind: "Hugh!"

The silent Knight still made no answer; but he flung aside the clinging robes, stepped from out them, and strode forward, both arms outstretched.

"Back!" cried the Prioress. But her hand had left the hilt of the dagger. "Come no nearer," she commanded.

Then she sank into her chair, spreading her trembling hands upon the carven manes of the lions.

The Knight, still silent, folded his arms across his breast.

Thus for a space they gazed on one another—these two, who had parted, eight years before, with clinging lips and straining arms, a deep, pure passion of love surging within them; a union of heart, made closer by the wrench of outward separation.

The Knight looked at the lips of the noble woman before him; and as he looked those firm lips quivered, trembled, parted—

Then—the years rolled back—

* * * * *

It was moonlight on the battlements. The horses champed in the courtyard below. They two had climbed to the topmost turret, that they might part as near the stars as possible, and that, unseen by others, she might watch him ride away.

How radiant she looked, in her robe of sapphire velvet, jewels at her breast and girdle, a mantle of ermine hanging from her shoulders.

37

But brighter than any jewels were the eyes full of love and tears; and softer than softest velvet, the beautiful hair which, covered her, as with a golden veil. Standing with his arms around her, it flowed over his hands. Silent he stood, looking deep into her eyes.

Below they could hear Martin Goodfellow calling to the men-at-arms.

Her lips being free, she spoke.

"Thou wilt come back to me, Hugh," she said. "The Saracens will not slay thee, will not wound thee, will not touch thee. My love will ever be around thee, as a silver shield."

She flung her strong young arms about him, long and supple, enfolding him closely, even as his enfolded her.

He filled his hands with her soft hair, straining her closer.

"I would I left thee wife, not maid. Could I have wed thee first, I would go with a lighter heart."

"Wife or maid," she answered, her face lifted to his, "I am all thine own. Go with a light heart, dear man of mine, for it makes no difference. Maid or wife, I am thine, and none other's, forever."

"Let those be the last words I hear thee say," he murmured, as his lips sought hers.

So, a little later, standing above him on the turret steps, she bent and clasped her hands about his head, pushing her fingers into the thickness of his hair. Then: "Maid or wife," she said, and her voice now steady, was deep and tender; "Maid or wife, God knows, I am all thine own." Then she caught his face to her breast. "Thine and none other's, forever," she said; and he felt her bosom heave with one deep sob.

Then turning quickly he ran down the winding stair, reached the courtyard, mounted, and rode out through the gates of Castle Norelle, and into the fir wood; and so down south to follow the King, who already had started on the great Crusade.

And, as he rode, in moonlight or in shadow, always he saw the sweet lips that trembled, always he felt the soft heave of that sob, and the low voice so tender, said: "Thine and none other's, forever."

* * * * * *

And now—

The Prioress sat in her chair of state.

Each moment her face grew calmer and more stern.

The Knight let his eyes dwell on the fingers which once crept so tenderly into his hair.

She hid them beneath her scapulary, as if his gaze scorched them.

He looked at the bosom against which his head had been pressed.

A jewelled cross gleamed, there where his face had laid hidden.

Then the Knight lifted his eyes again to that stern, cold face. Yet still he kept silence.

At length the Prioress spoke.

"So it is you," she said.

"Yes," said the Knight, "it is I."

Wroth with her own poor heart because it thrilled at his voice, the Prioress spoke with anger.

"How did you dare to force your way into this sacred cloister?"

The Knight smiled. "I have yet to find the thing I dare not do."

"Why are you not with your wife?" demanded the Prioress; and her tone was terrible.

"I am with my wife," replied the Knight. "The only wife I have ever wanted, the only woman I shall ever wed, is here."

"Coward!" cried the Prioress, white with anger. "Traitor!" She leaned forward, clenching her hands upon the lions' heads. "Liar! You wedded your cousin, Alfrida, less than one year after you went from me."

"Cease to be angry," said the Knight. "Thine anger affrights me not, yet it hurts thyself. Listen, mine own belovèd, and I will tell thee the cruel, and yet blessèd, truth.

"Seven months after I left thee, a messenger reached our camp, bearing letters from England; no word for me from thee; but a long missive from thy half-sister Eleanor, breaking to me the news that, being weary of my absence, and somewhat over-persuaded, thou hadst wedded Humphry; Earl of Carnforth.

"It was no news to me, that Humphry sought to win thee; but, that thou hadst let thyself be won away from thy vow to me, was hell's own tidings.

"In my first rage of grief I would have speech with none. But, by-and-by, I sought the messenger, and asked him casually of things at home. He told me he had seen thy splendid nuptials with the lord of Carnforth, had been present at the marriage, and joined in the after revels and festivities. He said thou didst make a lovely bride, but somewhat sad, as if thy mind strayed elsewhere. The fellow was a kind of lawyer's clerk, but lean, and out at elbow.

"Then I sought 'Frida, my cousin. She too had had a letter, giving the news. She told me she long had feared this thing for me, knowing the heart of Humphry to be set on winning thee, and that Eleanor approved his suit, and having already heard that of late thou hadst inclined to smile on him. She begged me to do nothing rash or hasty.

"'What good were it,' she said, 'to beg the King for leave to hasten home? If you kill Humphry, Hugh, you do but make a widow of the woman you have loved; nor could you wed the widow of a man yourself had slain. If Humphry kills you—well, a valiant arm is lost to the Holy

Cause, and other hearts, more faithful than hers, may come nigh to breaking. Stay here, and play the man.'

"So, by the messenger, I sent thee back a letter, asking thee to write me word how it was that thou, being my betrothed, hadst come to do this thing; and whether Humphry was good to thee, and making thy life pleasant. To Humphry I sent a letter saying that, thy love being round him as a silver shield, I would not slay him, wound him, or touch him! But—if he used thee ill, or gave thee any grief or sorrow, then would I come, forthwith, and send him straight to hell.

"These letters, with others from the camp, went back to England by that clerkly messenger. No answers were returned to mine.

"Meanwhile I went, with my despair, out to the battlefield.

"No tender shield was round me any more. I fought, like a mad wild beast. So often was I wounded, that they dubbed me 'The Knight of the Bloody Vest.'

"At last they brought me back to camp, delirious and dying. My cousin 'Frida, there biding her time, nursed me back to life, and sought to win for herself (I shame to say it) the love which thou hadst flouted. I need not tell thee, my cousin 'Frida failed. The Queen herself as good as bid me wed her favourite Lady. The Queen herself had to discover that she could command an English soldier's life, but not his love.

"Back in the field again, I found myself one day, cut off, surrounded, hewn down, taken prisoner; but by a generous foe.

"Thereafter followed years of much adventure; escapes, far distant wanderings, strange company. Many months I spent in a mountain fastness with a wise Hebrew Rabbi, who taught me his sacred Scriptures; going back to the beginning of all things, before the world was; yet shrewd in judgment of the present, and throwing a weird light forward upon the future. A strange man; wise, as are all of that Chosen Race; and a faithful friend. He did much to heal my hurt and woo me back to sanity.

"Later, more than a year with a band of holy monks in a desert monastery, high among the rocks; good Fathers who believed in Greek and Latin as surest of all balsams for a wounded spirit, and who made me to become deeply learned in Apostolic writings, and in the teachings of the Church. But, for all their best endeavours, I could not feel called to the perpetual calm of the Cloister. We are a line of fighters and hunters, men to whom pride of race and love of hearth and home, are primal instincts.

"Thus, after many further wanderings and much varying adventure, having by a strange chance heard news of the death of my father, and that my mother mourned. In solitude, the opening of this year found me landed in England—I who, by most, had long been given up for dead; though Martin Goodfellow, failing to find trace of me in Palestine, had gone back to Cumberland, and staunchly maintained his belief that I lived, a captive, and should some day make my escape, and return.

"I passed with all speed to our Castle on the moors, knowing a mother's heart waited here, for mothers never cease to watch and hope. And, sure enough, as I rode up, the great doors flew wide; the house waited its master; the mother was on the threshold to greet her son. Aye! It was good to be at home once more—even in the land where my woman was bearing children to another man.

"We spent a few happy days, I and my mother, together. Then— the joy of hope fulfilled being sometimes a swifter harbinger to another world than the heaviest load of sorrow—she passed, without pain or sickness, smiling, in her sleep; she passed—leaving my home desolate indeed.

"Not having known of my betrothal to thee, because of the old feud between our families, and my reluctance to cross her wish that I should wed Alfrida, thy name was not spoken between us; but I learned from her that my cousin 'Frida lay dying at her manor, nigh to Chester, of some lingering disease contracted in eastern lands."

"With the first stirrings of Spring in forest and pasture, I felt moved to ride south to the Court, and report my return to the King; yet waited, strangely loath to go abroad where any turn of the road might bring me face to face with Humphry. I doubted, should we meet, if I could pass, without slaying him, the man who had stolen my betrothed from me. So I stayed in my own domain, bringing things into order, working in the armoury, and striving by hard exercise to throttle the grim demon of despair.

"April brought a burst of early summer; and, on the first day of May, I set off for Windsor.

"Passing through Carnforth on my way, I found the town keeping high holiday. I asked the reason, and was told of a Tourney now in progress in the neighbourhood, to which the Earl had that morning ridden in state, accompanied by his Countess, who indeed was chosen Queen of Beauty, and was to sit enthroned, attended by her little daughter, two tiny sons acting as pages.

"A sudden mad desire came on me, to look upon thy face again; to see thee with the man who stole thee from me; with the children, who should have been mine own.

"Ten minutes later, I rode on to the field. Pushing in amid the gay crowd, I seemed almost at once to find myself right in front of the throne.

"I saw the Queen of Beauty, in cloth of gold. I saw the little maiden and the pages in attendance. I saw Humphry, proud husband and father, beside them. All this I saw, which I had come to see. But— the face of Humphry's Countess was not thy face! In that moment I knew that, for seven long years, I had been fooled!

"I started on a frenzied quest after the truth, and news of thee.

41

"Thy sister Eleanor had died the year before. To thy beautiful castle and lands, so near mine own, Eleanor's son had succeeded, and ruled there in thy stead. He being at Court just then, I saw him not, nor could I hear direct news of thee, though rumour said a convent.

"Then I remembered my cousin, Alfrida, lying sick at her manor in Chester. To her I went; and, walking in unannounced—I, whom she had long thought dead—I forced the truth from her. The whole plot stood revealed. She and Eleanor had hatched it between them. Eleanor desiring thy lands for herself and her boy, and knowing children of thine would put hers out of succession; Alfrida—it shames me to say it—desiring for herself, thy lover.

"The messenger who brought the letters was bribed to give details of thy supposed marriage. On his return to England, my letters to thee and to Humphry he handed to Eleanor; also a lying letter from 'Frida, telling of her marriage with me, with the Queen's consent and approval, and asking Eleanor to break the news to thee. The messenger then mingled with thy household, describing my nuptials in detail, as, when abroad, he had done thine. Hearing of this, my poor Love did even as I had done, sent for him, questioned him, heard the full tale he had to tell, and saw, alas! no reason to misdoubt him.

"By the way, my cousin 'Frida knew where to lay her hand upon that clerkly fellow. Therefore we sent for him. He came in haste to see the Lady Alfrida, from whom, during all the years, he had extorted endless hush-money.

"I and my men awaited him.

"He had fattened on his hush-money! He was no longer lean and out at elbow.

"He screeched at sight of me, thinking me risen from the dead.

"He screeched still louder when he saw the noose, flung over a strong bough.

"We left him hanging, when we rode away. That Judas kind will do the darkest deeds for greed of gain. The first of the tribe himself shewed the way by which it was most fitting to speed them from a world into which it had been good for them never to have been born.

"From Alfrida I learned that, as Eleanor had foreseen, thy grief at my perfidy drove thee to the Cloister. Also that thy Convent was near Worcester.

"To Worcester I came, and made myself known to the Lord Bishop, with whom I supped; and finding him most pleasant to talk with, and ready to understand, deemed it best, in perfect frankness, to tell him the whole matter; being careful not to mention thy name, nor to give any clue to thy person.

"Through chance remarks let fall by the Bishop while giving me the history of the Order, I learned that already thou wert Prioress of the White Ladies. 'The youngest Prioress in the kingdom,' said the Bishop, 'yet none could be wiser or better fitted to hold high authority.' Little did he dream that any mention of thee was as water to the parched desert; yet he talked on, for love of speaking of thee, while I sat praying he might tell me more; yet barely answering yea or nay, seeming to be absorbed in mine own melancholy thoughts.

"From the Bishop I learned that the Order was a strictly close one, and that no man could, on any pretext whatsoever, gain speech alone with one of the White Ladies.

"But I also heard of the underground way leading from the Cathedral to the Convent, and of the daily walk to and from Vespers.

"I went to the crypt, and saw the doorway through which the White Ladies pass. Standing unseen amid the many pillars, I daily watched the long line of silent figures, noted that they all walked veiled, with faces hidden, keeping a measured distance apart. Also that several were above usual height. Then I conceived the plan of wearing the outer dress, and of stepping in amongst those veiled figures just at the foot of the winding stair in the wall, leading down from the clerestory to the crypt. I marked that the nun descending, could not keep in view the nun in front who had just stepped forth into the crypt; while she, moving forward, would not perceive it if, slipping from behind a pillar, another white figure silently joined the procession behind her. Once within the Convent, I trusted to our Lady to help me to speech alone with thee; and our blessèd Lady hath not failed me.

"Now I have told thee all."

With that the Knight left speaking; and, after the long steady recitation, the ceasing of his voice caused a silence which, seemed, to hold the very air suspended.

Not once had the Prioress made interruption. She had sat immovable, her eyes upon his face, her hands gripping the arms of her chair. Long before the tale was finished her sad eyes had overflowed, the tears raining down her cheeks, and falling upon the cross at her breast.

When he had told all, when the deep, manly voice—now resolute, now eager, now vibrant with fierce indignation, yet tender always when speaking of her—at last fell silent, the Prioress fought with her emotion, and mastered it; then, so soon as she could safely trust her voice, she spoke.

CHAPTER XII

ALAS, THE PITY OF IT!

At length the Prioress spoke.

"Alas," she said, "the pity of it! Ah, the cruel, cruel pity of it!"

Her voice, so sweet and tender, yet so hopeless in the unquestioning finality of its regret, struck cold upon the heart of the Knight.

"But, my belovèd, I have found thee," he said, and dropping upon one knee at her feet, he put out his hands to cover both hers. But the Prioress was too quick for him. She hid her hands beneath her scapulary. The Knight's brown fingers closed on the lions' heads.

"Touch me not," said the Prioress.

The Knight flushed, darkly.

"You are mine," he said. "Mine to have and to keep. During these wretched years we have schooled ourselves each to think of the other as wedded. Now we know that neither has been faithless. I have found thee, my belovèd, and I will not let thee go."

"Hugh," said the Prioress, "I am wedded. You come too late. Saw you not the sacred ring upon my hand? Know you not that every nun is the bride of Christ?"

"You are mine!" said the Knight, fiercely; and he laid his great hand upon her knee.

From beneath her scapulary, the Prioress drew the dagger.

"Before I went to the cloister door," she said, "I took this from its hiding-place, and put it in my girdle. I guessed I had a man to deal with; though, Heaven knows, I dreamed not it was thou! But I tell thee, Hugh, if thou, or any man, attempt to lay defiling touch upon any nun in this Priory—myself, or another—I strike, and I strike home. This blade will be driven up to the hilt in the offender's heart."

The Knight rose to his feet, stepped to the window and leaned, with folded arms, against the wall.

"Put back thy weapon," he said, sternly, "into its hiding-place. No other man is here; yet, should another come, my sword would well suffice to guard thine honour, and the honour of thy nuns."

She looked at his dark face, scornful in its pain; then went at once, obedient, to the secret panel.

"Yes, Hugh," she said. "That much of trust indeed I owe thy love."

As she placed the dagger in the wall and closed the panel, something fell from her, intangible, yet real.

For so long, she had had to command. Bowing, kneeling,

44

hurrying women flew to do her behests. Each vied with the others to magnify her Office. Often, she felt lonely by reason of her dignity.

And now—a man's dark face frowned on her in scornful anger; a man's stern voice flung back her elaborate threat with a short command, which disarmed her, yet which she obeyed. Moreover, she found it strangely sweet to obey. Behind the sternness, behind the scornful anger, there throbbed a great love. In that love she trusted; but with that love she had to deal, putting it from her with a finality which should be beyond question.

Yet the "Prioress" fell from her, as she closed the panel. It was the Woman and the Saint who moved over to the window and stood beside the Knight, in the radiance of a golden sunset after storm.

There was about her, as she spoke, a wistful humbleness; and a patient sadness, infinitely touching.

"Sir Hugh," she said, "my dear Knight, whom I ever found brave and tender, and whom I now know to have been always loyal and true— there is no need that I should add a word to your recital. The facts you wrung from Alfrida—God grant forgiveness to that tormented heart— are all true. Believing the messenger, not dreaming of doubting Eleanor, my one thought was to hide from the world my broken heart, my shattered pride. I hastened to offer to God the love and the life which had been slighted by man. I confess this has since seemed to me but a poor second-best to have brought to Him, Who indeed should have our very best. But, daily kneeling at His Feet, I said: 'A broken and a contrite heart, Lord, Thou wilt not despise.' My heart was 'broken,' when I brought it here. It has been 'contrite' since. And well I know, although so far from worthy, it has not been despised."

She lifted her eyes to the golden glory behind the battlements of purple cloud.

"Our blessèd Lady interceded," she said, simply; "she, who understands a woman's heart."

The Knight was breathing hard. The folded arms rose and fell, with the heaving of his chest. But he kept his lips firm shut; though praying, all the while, that our Lady might have, also, some understanding of the heart of a man!

"I think it right that you should know, dear Hugh," went on the sad voice, gently; "that, at first, I suffered greatly. I spent long agonizing nights, kneeling before our Lady's shrine, imploring strength to conquer the love and the longing which had become sin."

A stifled groan broke from the Knight.

The golden light shone in her steadfast eyes, and played about her noble brow.

"And strength was given," she said, very low.

"Mora!" cried the Knight—She started. It was so long since she had heard her own name—"You prayed for strength to conquer, when you thought it sin; just as I rode out to meet the foe, to fight and slay,

45

and afterward wrestled with unknown tongues, doing all those things which were hardest, while striving to quench my love for you. But when I knew that no other man had right to you or ever had had right, why then I found that nothing had slain my love, nor ever could. And Mora, now you know that I am free, is your love dead?"

She clasped her hands over the cross at her breast. His voice held a deep passion of appeal; yet he strove, loyally, to keep it calm.

"Listen, Hugh," she said. "If, thinking me faithless, you had turned for consolation to another; if, though you brought her but your second best, you yet had won and wed her; now, finding after all that I had not wedded Humphry, would you leave your bride, and try to wake again your love for me?"

"You seek to place me," he said, "in straits in which, by mine own act, I shall never be. Loving you as I love you, I could wed no other while you live."

She paled, but persisted.

"But, if, Hugh? If?"

"Then, no," he said. "I should not leave one I had wed. But—"

"Hugh," she said, "thinking you faithless, I took the holy vows which wedded me to Heaven. How can I leave my heavenly Bridegroom, for love of any man upon this earth?"

"Not 'any man,'" he answered; "but your betrothed, returned to claim you; the man to whom you said as parting words: 'Maid or wife, I am all thine own; thine and none other's forever.' Ah, that brings the warm blood to thy cheek! Oh, my Heart's Life, if it was true then, it is true still! God is not a man that he should lie, or rob another of his bride. If I had wed another woman, I should have done that thing, honestly believing thee the wife of another man. But, all these years, while thou and I were both deceived, He, Who knoweth all, has known the truth. He knew thee betrothed to me. He heard thee say, upon the battlements, when last we stood together: 'God knows, I am all thine own.' He knew how, when I thought I had lost thee, I yet lived faithful to the pure memory of our love. The day thy vows were made, He knew that I was free, and thou, therefore, still pledged to me. Shall a man rob God? Ay, he may. But shall God rob a man? Nay, then, never!"

She trembled, wavered; then fled to the shrine of the Virgin, kneeling with hands outstretched.

"Holy Mother of God," she sobbed, "teach him that I dare not do this thing! Shew him that I cannot break my vows. Help him to understand that I would not, if I could."

He followed, and kneeled beside her; his proud head bent; his voice breaking with emotion.

"Blessèd Virgin," he said. "Thou who didst dwell in the earthly home at Nazareth, help this woman of mine to understand, that if she break her troth to me, holding herself from me, now when I am come to

46

claim her, she sends me forth to an empty life, to a hearth beside which no woman will sit, to a home forever desolate."

Together they knelt, before the tender image of Mother and Child; together, yet apart; he, loyally mindful not so much as to brush against a fold of her veil.

The dark face, and the fair, were lifted, side by side, as they knelt before the Madonna. For a while so motionless they kneeled, they might have been finely-modelled figures; he, bronze; she, marble.

Then, with a sudden movement, she put out her right hand, and caught his left.

Firmly his fingers closed over hers; but he drew no nearer.

Yet as they knelt thus with clasped hands, his pulsing life seemed to flow through her, undoing, in one wild, sweet moment, the work of years of fast and vigil.

"Ah, Hugh," she cried, suddenly, "spare me! Spare me! Tempt me not!"

Loosing her hand from his, she clasped both upon her breast.

The Knight rose, and stood beside her.

"Mora," he said, and his voice held a new tone, a tone of sadness and solemnity; "far be it from me to tempt you. I will plead with you but once again, in presence of our Lady and of the Holy Child; and, having so done, I will say no more.

"I ask you to leave this place, which you would never have entered had you known your lover was yours, and needing you. I ask you to keep your plighted word to me, and to become my wife. If you refuse, I go, returning not again. I leave you here, to kneel in peace, by night or day, before the shrine of the Madonna. But—I bid you to remember, day and night, that because of this which you have done, there can be no Madonna in my home. No woman will ever sit beside my hearth, holding a little child upon her knees.

"You leave to me the crucifix—heart broken, love betrayed; feet and hands nailed to the wood of cruel circumstance; side pierced by spear of treachery—lonely, forsaken. But you take from me all the best, both in life and in religion; all that tells of love, of joy, of hope for the years to come.

"Oh, my belovèd, weigh it well! There are so many, with a true vocation, serving Heaven in Convent and in Cloister. There is but one woman in the whole world for me. In the sight of Heaven, nothing divides us. Convent walls now stand between—but they were built by man, not God. Vows of celibacy were not meant to sunder loving hearts. Mora? . . . Come!"

The Prioress rose and faced him.

"I cannot come," she said. "That which I have taught to others, I must myself perform. Hugh, I am dead to the world; and if I be dead to the world, how can I live to you? Had I, in very deed, died and been entombed, you would not have gone down into the vaults and forced

47

my resting-place, that you might look upon my face, clasp my cold hand, and pour into deaf ears a tale of love. Yet that is what, by trick and artifice, you now have done. You come to a dead woman, saying; 'Love me, and be my wife.' She must, perforce, make answer: 'How shall I, who am dead to the world, live any longer therein?' Take a wife from among the Living, Hugh. Come not to seek a bride among the Dead."

"Mother of God!" exclaimed the Knight, "is this religion?"

He turned to the window, then to the door. "How can I go from here?"

The stifled horror in his voice chilled the very soul of the woman to whom he spoke. She had, indeed at last made him to understand.

"I must get you hence unseen," she said. "I dare not pass you out by the Convent gate. I fear me, you must go back the way you came; nor can you go alone. We hold the key to unlock the door leading from our passage into the Cathedral crypt. I will now send all the nuns to the Refectory. Then I myself must take you to the crypt."

"Can I not walk alone," asked the Knight, brusquely; "returning you the key by messenger?"

"Nay," said the Prioress, "I dare run no risks. So quickly rumours are afloat. To-morrow, this strange hour must be a dream; and you and I alone, the dreamers. Now, while I go and make safe the way, put you on again the robe and hood. When I return and beckon, follow silently."

The Prioress passed out, closing the door behind her.

CHAPTER XIII

"SEND HER TO ME!"

The Prioress stood for a moment outside the closed door. The peaceful silence of the passage helped her to the outward calm which must be hers before she could bring herself to face her nuns.

Moving slowly to the farther end, she unlocked the cell of Sister Mary Seraphine, feeling a shamed humility that she should have made so sure she had to deal with "Wilfred," and have thought such scorn of him and Seraphine. Alas! The wrong deeds of those they love, oft humble the purest, noblest spirits into the soiling dust.

Next, the Prioress herself rang the Refectory bell.

The hour for the evening meal was long passed; the nuns hastened out, readily.

As they trooped toward the stairs leading down to the Refectory, they saw their Prioress, very pale, very erect, standing with her back to the door of her chamber.

Each nun made a genuflexion as she passed; and to each, the Prioress slightly inclined her head.

To Sister Mary Rebecca, who kneeled at once, she spoke: "I come not to the meal this evening. In the absence of Mother Sub-Prioress, you will take my place."

"Yes, Reverend Mother," said Sister Mary Rebecca, meekly, and kissed the hem of the robe of the Prioress; then rising, hastened on, charmed to have a position of authority, however temporary.

When all had passed, the Prioress went into the cloisters, walked round them; looked over into the garden, observing every possible place from which prying eyes might have sight of the way from the passage to the crypt entrance. But the garden, already full of purple shadows, was left to the circling swifts. The robin sang an evening song from the bough, of the pieman's tree.

The Prioress returned along the passage, looking into every cell. Each door stood open wide; each cell was empty. The sick nuns were on a further passage, round the corner, beyond the Refectory stairs. Yet she passed along this also, making sure that the door of each occupied cell was shut.

Standing motionless at the top of the Refectory steps, she could hear the distant clatter of platters, the shuffling feet of the lay-sisters as they carried the dishes to and from the kitchens; and, above it all, the monotonous voice of Sister Mary Rebecca reading aloud to the nuns while they supped.

Then the Prioress took down one of the crypt lanterns and lighted it.

* * * * * *

Meanwhile the Knight, left alone, stood for a few moments, as if stunned.

He had played for a big stake and lost; yet he felt more unnerved by the unexpected finality of his own acquiescence in defeat, than by the firm refusal which had brought that defeat about.

It seemed to him, as he now stood alone, that suddenly he had realised the extraordinary detachment wrought by years of cloistered life. Aflame with love and longing he had come, seeking the Living among the Dead. It would have been less bitter to have knelt beside her tomb, knowing the heart forever still had, to the last, beat true with love for him; knowing the dead arms, lying cold and stiff, had he come sooner, would have been flung around him; knowing the lips, now silent in death, living, would have called to him in tenderest greeting.

49

But this cold travesty of the radiant woman he had left, said: "Touch me not," and bade him seek a wife elsewhere; he, who had remained faithful to her, even when he had thought her faithless.

And yet, cold though she was, in her saintly aloofness, she was still the woman he loved. Moreover she still had the noble carriage, the rich womanly beauty, the look of vital, physical vigour, which marked her out as meant by Nature to be the mother of brave sons and fair daughters. Yet he must leave her—to this!

He looked round the room, noted the low archway leading to the sleeping chamber, took a step toward it, then fell back as from a sanctuary; marked the great table, covered with missals, parchments, and vellum. It might well have been the cell of a learned monk, rather than the chamber of the woman he loved. His eye, travelling round, fell upon the Madonna and Child.

In the pure evening light there was a strangely arresting quality about the marble group; something infinitely human in the brooding tenderness of the Mother, as she bent over the smiling Babe. It spoke of home, rather than of the cloister. It struck a chord in the heart of the Knight, a chord which rang clear and true, above the jangle of disputation and bitterness.

He put out his hand and touched the little foot of the Holy Babe.

"Mother of God," he said aloud, "send her to me! Take pity on a hungry heart, a lonely home, a desolate hearth. Send her to me!"

Then he lifted from the floor the white robe and hood, and drew them on.

CHAPTER XIV

FAREWELL—HERE, AND NOW

When the Prioress, a lighted lantern in her hand, opened the door of her chamber, a tall figure in the dress of the White Ladies of Worcester stood motionless against the wall, facing the door.

"Come!" she whispered, beckoning; and, noiselessly, it stood beside her. Then she closed the door and, using her master-key, locked it behind her.

Silently the two white figures passed along the passage, through the cloister, and down the flight of steps into the Convent crypt. The Prioress unlocked the door and stooping they passed under the arch, and entered the subterranean way.

Placing the lantern on the ground, the Prioress drew out the key, closed the door, and locked it on the inside.

She turned, and lifting the lantern, saw that the Knight had rid himself of his disguise, and now stood before her, very straight and tall, just within the circle of light cast by her lantern.

With the closing and locking of the door a strange sense came over them, as of standing together in a third world—neither his nor hers—tomblike in its complete isolation and darkness; heavy with a smell of earth and damp stones; the slightest sound reverberating in hollow exaggeration; yet, in itself, silent as the grave.

This tomblike quality in their surroundings seemed to make their own vitality stronger and more palpitating.

The seconds of silence, after the grating of the key in the lock ceased, seemed hours.

Then the Knight spoke.

"Give me the lantern," he said.

She met his eyes. Again the dignity of her Office slipped from her. Again it was sweet to obey.

He held the lantern so that its light illumined her face and his.

"Mora," he said, "it is long since thou and I last walked together over the sunny fields, amid buttercups and cowslips, and the sweet-smelling clover. To-night we walk beneath the fields instead of through them. We are under the grass, my sweet. I seem to stand beside thee in the grave. And truly my hopes lie slain; the promise of our love is dead, and shall soon be buried. Yet thou and I still live, and now must walk together side by side, the sad ghosts of our former selves.

"So now I ask thee, Mora, for the sake of those past walks among the flowers, to lay thy hand within my arm and walk with me in gentle fellowship, here in this place of gloom and darkness, as, long ago, we walked among the flowers."

His dark eyes searched her face. An almost youthful eagerness vibrated in his voice.

She hesitated, lifting her eyes to his. Then slowly moved toward him and laid her hand within his arm.

Then, side by side, they paced on through the darkness; he, in his right hand, holding the lantern, swinging low, to light their feet; she, leaning on his left arm, keeping slow pace with him.

Over their heads, in the meadows, walked lovers, arm in arm; young men and maidens out in the gathering twilight. All nature, refreshed, poured forth a fragrant sweetness. But the rose, with its dewy petals, seemed to the youth less sweet than the lips of the maid. This, he shyly ventured to tell her; whereupon, as she bent to its fragrance, her cheeks reflected the crimson of those delicate folds.

So walked and talked young lovers in the Worcester meadows; little dreaming that, beneath their happy feet, the Knight and the Prioress paced slowly, side by side, through the darkness.

51

No word passed between them. With, her hand upon his arm, her face so near his shoulder, his arm pressing her hand closer and closer against his heart, silence said more than speech. And in silence they walked.

They passed beneath the city wall, under the Foregate.

The Sheriff rode home to supper, well pleased with a stroke of business accomplished in a house in which he had chanced to shelter during the storm.

The good people of Worcester bought and sold in the market. Men whose day's work was over, hastened to reach the rest and comfort of wife and home. Crowds jostled gaily through the streets, little dreaming that beneath their hurrying, busy feet, the Knight and the Prioress paced slowly, side by side, through the darkness.

Had the Knight spoken, her mind would have been up in arms to resist him. But, because he walked in silence, her heart had leisure to remember; and, remembering, it grew sorely tender.

At length they reached the doorway leading into the Cathedral crypt.

The Prioress carried the key in her left hand. Freeing her right from the grip of his arm, she slipped the key noiselessly into the lock; but, leaving it there unturned, she paused, and faced the Knight.

"Hugh," she said, "I beg you, for my sake and for the sake of all whose fair fame is under my care, to pass through quickly into the crypt, and to go from thence, if possible, unseen, or in such manner as shall prevent any suspicion that you come from out this hidden way. Tales of wrong are told so readily, and so quickly grow."

"I will observe the utmost caution," said the Knight.

"Hugh," she said, "I grieve to have had, perforce, to disappoint you." The brave voice shook. "This is our final farewell. Do you forgive me, Hugh? Will you think kindly, if you ever think on me?"

The Knight held the lantern so that its rays illumined both her face and his.

"Mora," he said, "I cannot as yet take thine answer as final. I will return no more, nor try to speak with thee again. But five days longer, I shall wait. I shall have plans made with the utmost care, to bear thee, in safety and unseen, from the Cathedral. I know the doors are watched, and that all who pass in and out are noted and observed. But, if thou wilt but come to me, belovèd, trust me to know how to guard mine own. . . . Nay, speak not! Hear me out.

"Daily, after Vespers, I shall stand hidden among the pillars, close to the winding stair. One step aside—only one step—and my arm will be around thee. A new life of love and home will lie before us. I shall take thee, safely concealed, to the hostel where I and my men now lodge. There, horses will stand ready, and we shall ride at once to Warwick. At Warwick we shall find a priest—one in high favour, both in

52

Church and State—who knows all, and is prepared to wed us without delay. After which, by easy stages, my wife, I shall take thee home."

He swung the lantern high. She saw the lovelight and the triumph, in his eyes. "I shall take thee home!" he said.

She stepped back a pace, lifting both hands toward him, palms outward, and stood thus gazing, with eyes full of sorrow.

"My poor Hugh," she whispered; "it is useless to wait. I shall not come."

"Yet five days," said the Knight, "I shall tarry in Worcester. Each day, after Vespers, I shall be here."

"Go to-day, dear Hugh. Ride to Warwick and tell thy priest, that which indeed he should know without the telling: that a nun does not break her vows. This is our final farewell, Hugh. Thou hadst best believe it, and go."

"Our last farewell?" he said.

"Our last."

"Here and now?"

"Here and now, dear Hugh."

Looking into that calm face, so lovely in its sadness, he saw that she meant it.

Of a sudden he knew he had lost her; he knew life's way stretched lonely before him, evermore.

"Yes," he said, "yes. It is indeed farewell—here and now—forever."

The dull despair in the voice which, but a few moments before, had vibrated with love and hope, wrung her heart.

She still held her hands before her, as if to ward him off.

"Ah, Hugh," she cried, sharply, "be merciful, and go! Spare me, and go quickly."

The Knight heard in her voice a tone it had not hitherto held. But he loved her loyally; therefore he kept his own anguish under strong control.

Placing the lantern on the ground, he knelt on one knee before her.

"Farewell, my Love," he said. "Our Lady comfort thee; and may Heaven forgive me, for that I have disturbed thy peace."

With which he lifted the hem of her robe, and pressed his lips upon it.

Thus he knelt, for a space, his dark head bent.

Slowly, slowly, the Prioress let drop her hands until, lightly as the fall of autumn leaves,—sad autumn leaves—they rested upon his head, in blessing and farewell.

But feeling his hair beneath her hands, she could not keep from softly smoothing it, nor from passing her fingers gently in and out of its crisp thickness.

Then her heart stood still, for of a sudden, in the silence, she heard a shuddering sob.

With a cry, she bent and gathered him to her, holding his head first against her knees, then stooping lower to clasp it to her breast; then as his strong arms were flung around her, she loosed his head, and, as he rose to his feet, slipped her arms about his neck, and surrendered to his embrace.

His lips sought hers, and at once she yielded them. His strong hands held her, and she, feeling the force of their constraint, did but clasp him closer.

Long they stood thus. In that embrace a life-time of pain passed from them, a life-time of bliss was born, and came with a rush to maturity, bringing with it a sense of utter completeness. A world of sweetest trust and certainty filled them; a joy so perfect, that the lonely vista of future years seemed, in that moment, to matter not at all.

All about them was darkness, silence as of the tomb; the heavy smell of earth; the dank chill of the grave.

Yet theirs was life more abundant; theirs, joy undreamed of; theirs, love beyond all imagining, while those moments lasted.

Then—

The hands about his neck loosened, unclasped, fell gently away.

He set free her lips, and they took their liberty.

He unlocked his arms, and stepping back she stood erect, like a fair white lily, needing no prop nor stay.

So they stood for a space, looking upon one another in silence. This thing which had happened, was too wonderful for speech.

Then the Prioress turned the key in the lock.

The heavy door swung open.

A dim, grey light, like a pearly dawn at sea, came downwards from the crypt.

Without a word the Knight, bending his head, passed under the archway, mounted the steps, and was lost to view among the many pillars.

She closed the door, locked it, and withdrawing the key, stood alone where they had stood together.

Then, sinking to the ground, she laid her face in the dust, there where his feet had been.

It was farewell, here and now; farewell forever.

* * * * * *

After a while the Prioress rose, took up the lantern, and started upon her lonely journey, back to the cloister door.

54

CHAPTER XV

"SHARPEN THE WITS OF MARY ANTONY"

When the Prioress started upon her pilgrimage to the Cathedral with the Knight, she locked the door of her chamber, knowing that thus her absence would remain undiscovered; for if any, knocking on the door, received no answer, or trying it, found it fast, they would hasten away without question; concluding that some special hour of devotion or time of study demanded that the Reverend Mother should be free from intrusion.

The atmosphere of the empty cell, charged during the past hour with such unaccustomed forces of conflict and of passion, settled into the quietude of an unbroken stillness.

The Madonna smiled serenely upon the Holy Babe. The dead Christ, with bowed head, hung forlorn upon the wooden cross. The ponderous volumes in black and silver bindings, lay undisturbed upon the table; and the Bishop's chair stood empty, with that obtrusive emptiness which, in an empty seat, seems to suggest an unseen presence filling it. The silence was complete.

But presently a queer shuffling sound began in the inner cell, as of something stiff and torpid compelling itself to action.

Then a weird figure, the wizen face distorted by grief and terror, appeared in the doorway—old Mary Antony, holding a meat chopper in her shaking hands, and staring, with chattering gums, into the empty cell.

That faithful soul, although dismissed, had resolved that the adored Reverend Mother should not go forth to meet dangers—ghostly or corporeal—alone and unprotected.

Hastening to the kitchens, she had given instructions that the evening meal was not to be served until the Reverend Mother herself should sound the bell.

Then, catching up a meat chopper, as being the most murderous-looking weapon at hand, and the most likely to strike terror into the ghostly heart of Sister Agatha, old Antony had hastened back to the passage.

Creeping up the stairs, hugging the wall, she had reached the top just in time to see, in the dim distance, the two tall white figures confronting one another.

Clinging to her chopper, motionless with horror, she had watched them, until they began, to come toward her, moving in the direction of the Reverend Mother's cell. They were still thirty yards away, at the cloister end of the passage. Old Antony was close to the open door.

Through it she had scurried, unheard, unseen, a terrified black shadow; yet brave withal; for with her went the meat chopper. Also she might have turned and fled back down the stairs, rather than into the very place whither she knew the Reverend Mother was conducting this tall spectre of the long dead Sister Agatha, grown to most alarming proportions during her fifty years' entombment! But being brave and faithful old Antony had sped into the inner cell, and crouched there in a corner; ready to call for help or strike with her chopper, should need arise.

Thus it came to pass that this old weaver of romances had perforce become a listener to a true romance so thrilling, so soul-stirring, that she had had to thrust the end of the wooden handle of the chopper into her mouth, lest she should applaud the noble Knight, cry counsel in his extremities, or invoke blessings on his enterprise. At each mention of the Ladies Eleanor and Alfrida, she shook her fist, and made signs with her old fingers, as of throttling, in the air. And when the clerkly messenger, arriving to speak with the Lady Alfrida—who, Saint Luke be praised, was by that time dying—found the Knight awaiting him with a noose flung over a strong bough, old Antony had laid down the chopper that she might the better hug herself with silent glee; and when the Knight rode away and left him hanging, she had whispered "Pieman! Pieman!" then clapped her hands over her mouth, rocking to and fro with merriment. When the Knight made mention that they called him "Knight of the Bloody Vest," old Antony had started; then had shaken her finger toward the entrance, as she was used to shake it at the robin, and had opened her wallet to search for crumbs of cheese. But soon again the story held her and, oblivious of the present, she had been back in the realms of romance.

Not until the Knight ceased speaking and the Reverend Mother's sad voice fell upon her ear, had old Antony realised the true bearing of the tale. Thereafter her heart had been torn by grief and terror. When they kneeled together, before the Madonna, with uplifted faces, Mary Antony had crawled forward and peeped. She had seen them kneeling—a noble pair—had seen the Prioress catch at his hand and clasp it; then, crawling back had fallen prostrate, overwhelmed, a huddled heap upon the floor.

The ringing of the Refectory bell had roused her from her stupor in time to hear the impassioned appeal of the Knight, as he kneeled alone before the Virgin's shrine.

Then, the Knight and the Prioress both being gone, Mary Antony had arisen, lifted her chopper with hands that trembled, and now stood with distraught mien, surveying the empty cell.

At length it dawned upon her that she and her weapon were locked into the Reverend Mother's cell; she, who had been most explicitly bidden to go to the kitchens and to remain there. It had been a sense of the enormity of her offence in having disobeyed the

Reverend Mother's orders which, unconsciously, had caused her to stifle all ejaculations and move without noise, lest she should be discovered.

Yet now her first care was not for her own predicament, but for the two noble hearts, of whose tragic grief she had secretly been a witness.

Her eye fell on the Madonna, calmly smiling.

She tottered forward, kneeling where the Prioress had knelt.

"Holy Mother of God," she whispered, "teach him that she cannot do this thing!"

Then, moving along on her knees to where the Knight had kneeled: "Blessèd Virgin!" she cried, "shew her that she cannot leave him desolate!"

Then shuffling back to the centre, and kneeling between the two places: "Sweetest Lady," she said, "be pleased to sharpen the old wits of Mary Antony."

Looking furtively at the Madonna, she saw that our Lady smiled. The blessèd Infant, also, looked merry. Mary Antony chuckled, and took heart. When the Reverend Mother smiled, she always knew herself forgiven.

Moreover, without delay, her request was granted; for scarcely had she arisen from her knees, when she remembered the place where the Reverend Mother kept the key of her cell; and she, having locked the door, on leaving, with her own master-key, the other was quickly in old Antony's hand, and she out once more in the passage, locking the door behind her; sure of being able to restore the key to its place, before it should be missed by the Reverend Mother.

Sister Mary Antony slipped unseen past the Refectory and into the kitchens. Once there, she fussed and scolded and made her presence felt, implying that she had been waiting, a good hour gone, for the thing for which she had but that moment asked.

The younger lay-sisters might make no retort; but Sister Mary Martha presently asked: "What have you been doing since Vespers, Sister Antony?"

By aid of the wits our Lady had sharpened, old Antony, at that moment, realised that sometimes, when you needs must deceive, there is nothing so deceptive as the actual truth.

"Listening to a wondrous romantic tale," she made answer, "told by the

Knight of the Bloody Vest."

"You verily are foolish about that robin, Sister Antony," remarked Mary Martha; "and you will take your death of cold, sitting out in the garden in the damp, after sunset."

"Well—so long as I take only that which is mine own, others have no cause to grumble," snapped Mary Antony, and turned her mind upon the making of a savoury broth, favoured by the Reverend Mother.

And all the while the Devil was whispering in the old woman's ear: "She will not return. . . . Make thy broth, fool; but she will not be here to drink it. . . . The World and the Flesh have called; the Reverend Mother will not come back. . . . Stir the broth well, but flavour it to thine own taste. Thou wilt sup on it thyself this night. When the World and the Flesh call loudly enough, the best of women go to the Devil."

"Liar!" said Mary Antony, brandishing her wooden spoon. "Get thee behind me—nay, rather, get thee in front of me! I have had thee skulking behind me long enough. Also in front of me, just now, being into the fire, thou wilt feel at home, Master Devil! Only, put not thy tail into the Reverend Mother's broth."

When the White Ladies passed up from the Refectory, Mary Antony chanced to be polishing the panelling around the picture of Saint Mary Magdalen, beside the door of the Reverend Mother's cell.

Presently Sister Mary Rebecca, arriving, lifted her hand to knock.

"Stay!" whispered Mary Antony. "The Reverend Mother may not be disturbed."

Sister Mary Rebecca veiled her scowl with a smile.

"And wherefore not, good Sister Antony?"

"'Wherefore not' is not my business," retorted old Antony, as rudely as she knew how. "It may be for special study; it may be for an hour of extra devotion; it may be only the very natural desire for a little respite from the sight of two such ugly faces as yours and mine. But, be the reason what it may, Reverend Mother has locked her door, and sees nobody this even." After which old Antony proceeded to polish the outside of the Reverend Mother's door panels.

Sister Mary Rebecca lifted her knuckles to rap; but old Antony's not over clean clout was pushed each time between Sister Mary Rebecca's tap, and the woodwork.

Muttering concerning the report she would make to the Prioress in the morning, Sister Mary Rebecca went to her cell.

When all was quiet, when every door was closed, the old lay-sister crept into the cloisters and, crouching in an archway just beyond the flight of steps leading to the underground way, watched and waited.

Storm clouds were gathering again, black on a purple sky. The after-glow in the west had faded. It was dark in the cloisters. Thunder growled in the distance; an owl hooted in the Pieman's tree.

Mary Antony's old bones ached sorely, and her heart failed her. She had sat so long in cramped positions, and she had not tasted food since the mid-day meal.

The Devil drew near, as he is wont to do, when those who have fasted long, seek to keep vigil.

"The Reverend Mother will not return," he whispered. "What wait you for?"

"Be off!" said Mary Antony. "I am too old to be keeping company, even with thee. Also Sister Mary Rebecca awaits thee in her cell."

58

"The Reverend Mother ever walked with her head among the stars," sneered the Devil. "Why do the highest fall the lowest, when temptation comes?"

"Ask that of Mother Sub-Prioress," said Mary Antony, "next time she bids thee to supper."

Then she clasped her old hands upon her breast; for, very softly, in the lock below, a key turned.

Steps, felt rather than heard, passed up into the cloister.

Then, in the dim light, the tall figure of the Prioress moved noiselessly over the flagstones, passed through the open door and up the deserted passage.

Peering eagerly forward, the old lay-sister saw the Prioress pause outside the door of her chamber, lift her master-key, unlock the door, and pass within.

As the faint sound of the closing of the door reached her straining ears, old Mary Antony began to sob, helplessly.

CHAPTER XVI

THE ECHO OF WILD VOICES

When the Prioress entered her cell, she stood for a moment bewildered by the rapid walk in the darkness. She could hardly realise that the long strain was over; that she had safely regained her chamber.

All was as she had left it. Apparently she had not been missed, and had returned unobserved. Hugh was by now safely in the hostel at Worcester. None need ever know that he had been here.

None need ever know—Yet, alas, it was that knowledge which held the Prioress rooted to the spot on which she stood, gazing round her cell.

Hugh had been here; and when he was here, her one desire had been to get him speedily away.

But now?

Dumb with the pain of a great yearning, she looked about her.

Yes; just there he had stood; here he had knelt, and there he had stood again.

This calm monastic air had vibrated to the fervour of his voice.

It had grown calm again.

Would her poor heart in time also grow calm? Would her lips stop trembling, and cease to feel the fire of his?

Yet for one moment, only, her mind dwelt upon herself. Then all thought of self was merged in the realisation of his loneliness, his suffering, his bitter disillusion. To have found her dead, would have been hard; to have lost her living, was almost past bearing. Would it cost him his faith in God, in truth, in purity, in honour?

The Prioress felt the insistent need of prayer. But passing the gracious image of the Virgin and Child, she cast herself down at the foot of the crucifix.

She had seen a strong man in agony, nailed, by the cruel iron of circumstance, to the cross-beams of sacrifice and surrender. To the suffering Saviour she turned, instinctively, for help and consolation.

Thus speedily had her prayer of the previous night been granted. The piercèd feet of our dear Lord, crucified, had become more to her than the baby feet of the Infant Jesus, on His Mother's knee.

Yet, even as she knelt—supplicating, interceding, adoring—there echoed in her memory the wicked shriek of Mary Seraphine: "A dead God cannot help me! I want life, not death!" followed almost instantly by Hugh's stern question: "Is this religion?"

Truly, of late, wild voices had taken liberty of speech in the cell of the Prioress, and had left their impious utterances echoing behind them.

CHAPTER XVII

THE DIMNESS OF MARY ANTONY

The Prioress had been back in her cell for nearly an hour, when a gentle tap came on the door.

"Enter," commanded the Prioress, and Mary Antony appeared, bearing broth and bread, fruit and a cup of wine.

The Prioress sat at her table, parchment and an open missal before her. Her face was very white; also there were dark shadows beneath her eyes. She did not smile at sight of old Antony, thus laden.

"How now, Antony?" she said, almost sternly. "I did not bid thee to bring me food."

"Reverend Mother," said the old lay-sister, in a voice which strove to be steady, yet quavered; "for long hours you have studied, not heeding that the evening meal was over. Chide not old Antony for bringing you some of that broth, which you like the best. You will not sleep unless you eat."

The Prioress looked at her uncomprehendingly; as if, for the moment, words conveyed no meaning to her mind. Then she saw those old hands trembling, and a sudden flood of colour flushed the pallor of her face.

This sweet stirring of fresh life within her own heart gave her to see, in the old woman's untiring devotion, a human element hitherto unperceived. It brought a rush of comfort, in her sadness.

She closed the volume, and pushed aside the parchment. "How kind of thee, dear Antony, to take so much thought for me. Place the bowls on the table. . . . Now draw up that stool, and stay near me while I sup. I am weary this night, and shall like thy company."

Had the golden gates of heaven opened before her, and Saint Peter himself invited her to enter, Sister Mary Antony would not have been more astonished and certainly could hardly have been more gratified. It was a thing undreamed of, that she should be bidden to sit with the Reverend Mother in her cell.

Drawing the carven stool two feet from the wall, Mary Antony took her seat upon it.

"Nearer, Antony, nearer," said the Prioress. "Place the stool here, close beside the corner of my table. I have much to say to thee, and would wish to speak low."

Truly Sister Antony found herself in the seventh heaven!

Yet, quietly observing, the Prioress could not fail to note the drawn weariness on the old face, the yellow pallor of the wizen skin, which usually wore the bright tint of a russet apple.

The Prioress took a portion of the broth; then pushed the bowl from her, and turned to the fruit.

"There, Antony," she said. "The broth is excellent; but I have enough. Finish it thyself. It will pleasure me to see thee enjoy it."

Faint and thankful, old Antony seized the bowl. And as she drank the broth, her shrewd eyes twinkled. For had not the Devil said she would sup on it herself; knowing that much, yet not knowing that she would receive it from the hand of the Reverend Mother?

It has been ever so, from Eden onwards, when the Devil tries his hand at prophecy.

For a while the Prioress talked lightly, of flowers and birds; of the garden and the orchard; of the gift of three fine salmon, sent to them by the good monks of the Priory at Worcester.

But, presently, when the broth was finished and a faint colour tinted the old cheeks, she passed on to the storm and the sunset, the rolling thunder and the torrents of rain. Then of a sudden she said:

"By the way, Antony, hast thou made mention, to any, of thy fearsome tale of the walking through the cloisters, in line with the White Ladies, of the Spectre of the saintly Sister Agatha?"

"Nay, Reverend Mother," said Mary Antony. "Did not you forbid me to speak of it?"

"True," said the Prioress. "Well, Antony, I went in the storm, to look for her; but—I found not Sister Agatha."

"That I already knew," said Mary Antony, nodding her head sagaciously.

The Prioress cast upon her a quick, anxious look.

"What mean you, Antony?"

Then old Mary Antony fell upon her knees, and kissed the hem of the Prioress's robe. "Oh, Reverend Mother," she stammered, "I have a confession to make!"

"Make it," said the Prioress, with white lips.

"Reverend Mother, when you sent me from you, after making my report, I went first, as commanded, to the kitchens. But afterward, in my cell, I found these."

Mary Antony opened her wallet and drew out the linen bag in which she kept her peas. Shaking its contents into the palm of her hand, she held out six peas to view.

"Reverend Mother," she said, "there were twenty-five in the bag. I thought I had counted twenty out into my hand; so when all the peas had dropped and yet another holy Lady passed, I thought that made twenty-one. But when I found six peas in my bag, I became aware of my folly. I had but counted nineteen, and had no pea to let fall for the twentieth holy Lady. Yet I ran in haste with my false report, when, had I but thought to look in my wallet, all would have been made clear. Will the Reverend Mother forgive old Mary Antony?"

She shot a quick glance at the Prioress; and, at sight of the immense relief on that loved face, felt ready for any punishment with which it might please Heaven to visit her deceit.

"Dear Antony," began the Reverend Mother, smiling.

"Dear Antony—" she said, and laughed aloud.

Then she placed her hand beneath the old woman's arm, and gently raised her. "Mistakes arise so easily," she said. "With the best of intentions, we all sometimes make mistakes. There is nothing to forgive, my Antony."

"I am old, and dim, and stupid," said the lay-sister, humbly; "but I have begged of our sweet Lady to sharpen the old wits of Mary Antony."

After which statement, made in a voice of humble penitence, Mary Antony, unseen by the thankful Prioress, did give a knowing wink with the eye next to the Madonna. Our blessèd Lady smiled. The sweet Babe looked merry. The Prioress rose, a great light of relief illumining her weary face.

"Let us to bed, dear Antony; then, with the dawn of a new day we shall all arise with hearts refreshed and wits more keen. So now—God rest thee."

Left alone, the Prioress knelt long in prayer before the shrine of the Madonna. Once, she reached out her right hand to the empty space where Hugh had knelt, striving to feel remembrance of his strong clasp.

At length she sought her couch. But sleep refused to come, and presently she crept back in the white moonlight, and kneeling pressed her lips to the stone on which Hugh had kneeled; then fled, in shame that our Lady should see such weakness; and dared not glance toward the shadowy form of the dead Christ, crucified. For with the coming of Love to seek her, Life had come; and where Life enters, Death is put to flight; even as before the triumphant march of the rising sun, darkness and shadows flee away.

Yet, even then, our Lady gently smiled, and the Babe on her knees looked merry.

CHAPTER XVIII

IN THE CATHEDRAL CRYPT

On the day following, in the afternoon, shortly before the hour of Vespers, a stretcher was carried through the streets of Worcester, by four men-at-arms wearing the livery of Sir Hugh d'Argent.

Beside it walked the Knight, with bent head, his eyes upon the ground.

The body of the man upon the stretcher was covered by a fine linen sheet, over which lay a blue cloak, richly embroidered with silver. His head was swathed in a bandage of many folds, partially concealing the face.

The little procession passed through the Precincts; then entered the Cathedral by the great door leading into the nave.

Here a monk stood, taking careful note of all who passed in or out of the building. As the stretcher approached, he stepped forward with hand upraised.

There was a pause in the measured tramp of the bearers' feet.

The Knight lifted his eyes, and seeing the monk barring the way, he drew forth a parchment and tendered it.

"I have the leave of the Lord Bishop, good father," he said, "to carry this man upon the stretcher daily into the crypt, and there to let him lie before the shrine of Saint Oswald, during the hour of Vespers; from which daily pilgrimage and prayer, we hope a great recovery and restoration."

At sight of the Lord Bishop's signature and seal, the monk made deep obeisance, and hastened to call the Sacristan, bidding him attend the Knight on his passage to the crypt and give him every facility in placing the sick man there where he might most conveniently lie before the holy altar of the blessèd Saint Oswald.

So presently, the stretcher being safely deposited, the men-at-arms stood each against a pillar, and the Knight folded back the coverings, in order that the man who lay beneath, might have sight of the altar and the shrine.

As the Knight stood gazing through the vista of many columns, he found the old Sacristan standing at his elbow.

"Most worshipful Knight," said the old man, with deference, "our Lord Bishop's mandate supersedes all rules. Were it not so, it would be my duty to clear the crypt before Vespers. See you that stairway yonder, beneath the arch? Not many minutes hence, up those steps will pass the holy nuns from the Convent of the White Ladies at Whytstone— noble ladies all, and of great repute for saintliness. Daily they come to Vespers by a secret way; entering the crypt, they pass across to a winding stair in the wall, and so arrive at a gallery above the choir, from which they can, unseen, hear the chanting of the monks. I must to my duties above. Will you undertake, Sir Knight, that your men go not nigh where the White Ladies pass, nor in any way molest them?"

"None shall stir hand or foot, as they pass, nor in any way molest them," said the Knight.

Hugh d'Argent was kneeling before the altar, his folded hands resting upon the cross on the hilt of his sword, when the faint sound of a key turning in a distant lock, caught his ear.

Then up the steps and across the crypt passed, in silent procession, the White Ladies of Worcester.

There was something ghostly and awe-inspiring about those veiled figures, moving noiselessly among the pillars in the dimly-lighted crypt; then vanishing, one by one, up the winding stairway in the wall.

The Knight did not stir. He stayed upon his knees, his hands clasped upon his sword-hilt; but he followed each silent figure with his eyes.

The last had barely disappeared from view when, from above, came the solemn chanting of monks and choristers.

This harmony, descending from above, seemed to uplift the soul all the more readily, because the sacred words and noble sounds reached the listener, unhampered by association with the personalities, either youthful or ponderous, of the singers. All that was of the earth remained unseen; while that which was so near akin to heaven, entered the listening ear.

Kneeling in lowly reverence with bowed head, the Knight found himself wondering whether the ascending sounds reached that distant gallery in the clerestory where the White Ladies knelt, as greatly softened, sweetened, and enriched, as they now came stealing down into the crypt. Were the hearts of those veiled worshippers also lifted heavenward; or—being already above the music—did the ascending voices rather tend to draw them down to earth?

Upon which the Knight fell to meditating as to whether that which is higher always uplifts; whereas that which is lower tends to debase. Certainly the upward look betokens hope and joy; while the downward casting of the eye, is sign of sorrow and despondency.

"Levavi oculos meos in montes"—chanted the monks, in the choir above.

He certainly looked high when he lifted the eyes of his insistent desire to the Prioress of the White Ladies. So high did he lift them, and so unattainable was she, that most men would say he might as well ask the silvery moon, sailing across the firmament, to come down and be his bride!

He had held her high, in her maiden loveliness and purity. But now that he had found her, a noble woman, matured, ripened by sorrow rather than hardened, yet firm in her determination to die to the world, to deny self, crucify the flesh, and resist the Devil—he felt indeed that she walked among the stars.

Yet he could not bring himself to regard her as unattainable. It had ever been his firm belief that a man could win any woman upon whom he wholly set his heart—always supposing that no other man had already won her. And this woman had been his own betrothed, when treachery intervened and sundered them. Yet that did not now count for much.

He had left a girl; he had come back to find a woman. That woman had infinitely more to give; but it would be infinitely more difficult to persuade her to give it.

At the close of their interview in her cell, the day before, all hope had left him. But later, as they paced together in the darkness, hope had revived.

The strange isolation in which they then found themselves—between locked doors a mile apart, earth above, earth beneath, earth all around them, they two alone, entombed yet vividly conscious of glowing life—had brought her nearer to him; and when at last the moment of parting arrived and again he faced it as final, there had come—all unheralded—the sudden wonder of her surrender.

True, she had afterwards withdrawn herself; true, she had sent him from her; true, he had gone, without a word. But that was because no promise could have been so binding, as that silent embrace.

He had gone from her on the impulse of the sweetness of obeying instantly her slightest wish; buoyed up by the certainty that no Convent walls could long divide lips which had met and clung with such a passion of mutual need.

That evening when, after much adventure, he at length gained the streets of the city, he had trodden them with the mien of a victor.

65

That night he had slept as he had not slept since the hour when his whole life had been embittered by a lying letter and a traitorous tongue.

But morning, alas, had brought its doubts; noon, its dark uncertainties; and as the hour of Vespers drew near, he had realised, with the helpless misery of despair, that it was madness to expect the Prioress of the White Ladies to break her vows, leave her Nunnery, and fly with him to Warwick.

Yet he carried out his plan, and kept to his undertaking, though here, in the calm atmosphere of the crypt, holy chanting descending from above, the remembrance still with him of the aloofness of those stately white figures gliding between the pillars in the distance, he faced the madness of his hopes, and the mournful prospect of a life of loneliness.

Presently he arose, crossed the crypt, and took up his position behind a pillar to the right of the exit from the winding stair.

The chanting ceased. Vespers were over.

He heard the sound of soft footsteps drawing nearer.

The White Ladies were coming.

They came.

The Knight was not kept long in suspense. The Prioress walked first. Her face was hidden, but her height and carriage revealed her to her lover. She looked neither to right nor left but, turning away from the pillar behind which the Knight stood concealed, crossed to the steps leading down to the subterranean way, and so passed swiftly out of sight.

The Knight stood motionless until all had appeared, and had vanished once more from view.

One, tall but ungainly, crooked of body, and doubtless short of vision, missed her way among the columns and passed perilously near to the Knight. With his long arm, he could have clasped her. How old Antony would have chuckled, could she but have known! "Sister Mary Rebecca embraced by the Knight of the Bloody Vest? Nay then; the Saints forbid!"

The stretcher, borne by four men-at-arms, passed out from the Cathedral.

The Knight walked beside it, with bent head, and eyes upon the ground.

As it passed through the Precincts, the Lord Bishop himself rode out on his white palfrey, on his way to the Nunnery at Whytstone.

The Knight, being downhearted, did not lift his eyes.

The Bishop looked, kindly, upon the stretcher and upon the Knight's dark face.

The Bishop had known Hugh d'Argent as a boy.

He grieved to see him thus in sorrow.

Yet the Bishop smiled as he rode on.

Perhaps he did not put much faith in the efficacy of relics, for so heavily bandaged a broken head as that upon the stretcher.

For there was a whimsical tenderness about the Bishop's smile.

CHAPTER XIX

THE BISHOP PUTS ON HIS BIRETTA

Symon, Lord Bishop of Worcester, having received a letter from the Prioress of the White Ladies, praying him for an interview at his leisure, sent back at once a most courtly and gracious answer, that he would that same day give himself the pleasure of visiting the Reverend Mother, at the Nunnery, an hour after Vespers.

The great gates were thrown open, and the Bishop rode his palfrey into the courtyard.

The Prioress herself met him at the door and, kneeling, kissed his ring; then led him through the lower hall, where the nuns knelt to receive his blessing, and up the wide staircase, to the privacy of her own cell.

There she presently unfolded to him the history of her difficulties with that wayward little nun, Sister Mary Seraphine.

"But the point which I chiefly desire to lay before you, Reverend Father," concluded the Prioress, "is this: If the neighing of a palfrey calls more loudly to her than the voice of God; if her mind is still set upon the things of the world; if she professed without a true vocation, merely because she wished to be the central figure of a great ceremony, yet was all the while expecting a man to intervene and carry her off; if all this bespeaks her true state of heart, then to my mind there comes the question: Is she doing good, either to herself or to others, by belonging to our Order? Would she not be better away?

"My lord, I fear I greatly shock you by naming such a possibility. But truly I am pursued by the remembrance of that young thing, beating the floor with her hands, and singing a mournful dirge about the crimson trappings of her palfrey. And, alas! when I reasoned with her and exhorted, she broke out, as I have told you, Reverend Father, into grievous blasphemy—for which she was severely dealt with by Mother Sub-Prioress, and has since been outwardly amenable to rules and discipline.

"But, though she may outwardly conform, how about her inward state? Well I know that our vows are lifelong vows; all who belong to our Order are wedded to Heaven; we are thankful to know that the calm of the Cloister shall be exchanged only for the greater peace of Paradise. But, supposing a young heart has mistaken its vocation; supposing the voice of an earthly lover calls when it is too late; would it seem right or possible to you, Reverend Father, to grant any sort of absolution from the vows; tacitly to allow the opening of the cage door, that the little foolish bird might, if it wished, escape into the liberty for which it chafes and sighs?"

The Bishop sat in the Spanish chair, drawn up near the oriel window, so that he could either gaze at the glories of the distant sunset, or, by slightly turning his head, look on the beautiful but grave face of the Prioress, seated before him.

While she was speaking he watched her keenly, with those bright searching eyes, so much more youthful than aught else about him. But now that he must make reply, he looked away to the sunset.

The light shone on the plain gold cross at his breast, and on the violet silk of his cassock. His face, against the background of the black Spanish wood, looked strangely white and thin; strong in contour, with a virile strength; in expression, sensitive as a woman's. He had removed his biretta, and placed it upon the table. His silvery hair rolled back from his forehead in silky waves. His was the look of the saint and the scholar, almost of the mystic—save for the tender humour in those keen blue eyes, gleaming like beacon lights from beneath the level eyebrows; eyes which had won the confidence of many a man who else had not dared unfold his very human story, to one of such saintly aspect as Symon, Bishop of Worcester. They were turned toward the sunset, as he made answer to the Prioress.

"The little foolish bird," said the Bishop—and he spoke in that gently musing tone, which conveys to the mind of the hearer a sense of infinite leisure in which to weigh and consider the subject in hand— "The little foolish bird might soon wish herself back in the safety of the cage. On such as she, the cruel hawks of life do love to prey. Absorbed in the contemplation of her own charms, she sees not, until too late, the dangers which surround her. Such little foolish birds, my daughter, are best in the safe shelter of the cloister. Moreover, of what value are they in the world? None. If Popinjays wed them, they do but hatch out broods of foolish little Popinjays. If true men, caught by mere surface beauty, wed them, it can mean naught save heartbreak and sorrow, and deterioration of the race. Women of finer mould"—for an instant the Bishop's eyes strayed from the sunset—"are needed, to be the mothers of the men who, in the years to come, are to make England great. Nay, rather than let one escape, I would shut up all the little foolish birds in a Nunnery, with our excellent Sub-Prioress to administer necessary discipline."

With his elbows resting upon the arms of the chair, the Bishop put his fingers together, so that the tips met most precisely; then bent his lips to them, and looked at the Prioress.

She, troubled and sick at heart, lifting deep pools of silent misery, met the merry twinkle in the Bishop's eyes, and sat astonished. What was it like? Why it was like the song of a robin, perched on a frosty bough, on Christmas morning! It was so young and gay; so jocund, and so hopeful.

Meeting it, the Prioress realised fully, what she had many times half-divined, that the revered and reverend Prelate sitting opposite, for all his robes and dignity, his panoply of Church and State, had the heart of a merry schoolboy out on a holiday.

For the moment she felt much older than the Bishop, infinitely sadder; more travel-worn and worldly-wise.

Then she looked at the silver hair; the firm mouth, with a shrewd curve at either corner; the thoughtful brow.

And then she looked at the Bishop's ring.

The Bishop wore a remarkable ring; not a signet, but a large gem of great value, beautifully cut in many facets, and clear set in massive gold. This precious stone, said to be a chrysoprasus, had been given to the Bishop by a Russian prince, in acknowledgment of a great service rendered him when he came on pilgrimage to Rome. The rarity of these gems arose partly from the fact that the sovereigns of Russia had decreed that they should be held exclusively for royal ornament, forbidding their use or purchase by people of lesser degree.

But its beauty and its rarity were not the only qualities of the precious stone in the Bishop's ring. The strangest thing about it was that its colour varied, according to the Bishop's mood and surroundings.

When the Prioress looked up and met the gay twinkle, the stone in the Bishop's ring was a heavenly blue, the colour of forget-me-nots beside a meadow brook, or the clear azure of the sky above a rosy sunset. But presently he passed his hand over his eyes, as if to shut out some bright vision, and to turn his mind to more sober thought; and, at that moment, the stone in his ring gleamed a pale opal, threaded with flashes of green.

The Prioress returned to the subject, with studied seriousness.

"I did not suppose, Reverend Father, that it was to be of any advantage to the world, that Sister Seraphine should return to it. The advantage was to be to her, and also to this whole Community, well rid of the presence of one who finds our sacred exercises irksome; our beautiful Nunnery, a prison; her cell, a living tomb. She cries out for life. 'I want to live,' she said, 'I am young, I am gay, I am beautiful! I want life.'"

"To such as Sister Seraphine," remarked the Bishop, gravely, "life is but a mirror which reflects themselves. Other forms and faces may flit by, in the background; dimly seen, scarcely noticed. There is but one face and form occupying the entire foreground. Life is, to such, the mirror which ministers to vanity. Should a husband appear in the picture, he is soon relegated to the background, receiving only occasional glances over the shoulder. If children dance into the field of vision, they are petulantly driven elsewhere. Tell me? Did Sister Seraphine's desire for life include any expression of the desire to give life?"

Involuntarily the Prioress glanced at the sweet Babe upon the Virgin's knees.

"No," she said, very low.

"I thought not," said the Bishop. "Self-centred, shallow natures are not capable of the sublime passion for motherhood; partly, no doubt, because they themselves possess no life worth passing on."

The Prioress rose quickly and, moving to the window, flung open a second casement. It was imperative, at that moment, to hide her face; for the uncontrollable flood of emotion at her heart, could scarce fail to send a tell-tale wave to disturb the calm of her countenance.

Whereupon the Bishop turned, to see at what the Prioress had glanced before answering his question.

"No," he mused, as she resumed her seat, his eyes upon the tree-tops beyond the casement, "the Seraphines have not the instinct of motherhood. And the future greatness of our race depends upon those noble women who are able to pass on to their sons and daughters a life which is true, and brave, and worthy; a life whose foundation is self-sacrifice, whose cornerstone is loyalty, and from whose summit waves the banner of unsullied love of hearth and home.

"A woman with the true instinct of motherhood cannot see a little child without yearning to clasp it to her bosom. When she finds her mate, she thinks more of being the mother of his children than the object of his devotion, because the Self in her is subservient to the maternal instinct for self-sacrifice. These women are pure as snow, and they hold their men to the highest and the best. Such women are needed in the world. Our Lady knoweth, I speak not lightly, unadvisedly nor wantonly; but were Seraphine such an one as this, I should say; 'Leave the door on the latch. Without permission, yet without reproach—let her go.'"

"Were Seraphine such an one as that, my lord," said the Prioress, firmly, "then would there be no question of her going. If the cornerstone of character be loyalty, the very essential of loyalty is the keeping of vows."

"Quite so," murmured the Bishop; "undoubtedly, my daughter. Unless, by some strange fatality, those vows were made under a total misapprehension. You tell me Sister Seraphine expected a man to intervene?"

The Bishop sat up, of a sudden keenly alert. His eyes, no longer humorous and tender, became searching and bright—young still, but with the fire of youth, rather than its merriment. As he leaned forward in his chair, his hands gripped his knees. Looking at his ring the Prioress saw the stone the colour of red wine.

"What if, after all, I can help you in this," he said. "What if I can throw light upon the whole situation, and find a cause for the little foolish bird's restless condition, proving to you that she may have heard something more than the mere neighing of a palfrey! Listen!

"A Knight arrived in this city, rather more than a month ago; a very noble Knight, splendid to look upon; one of our bravest Crusaders. He arrived here in sore anguish of heart. His betrothed had been taken from him during his absence from England, waging war against the Turks in Palestine—taken from him by a most dastardly and heartless plot. He made many inquiries concerning this Nunnery and Order, rode north again on urgent business, but returned, with a large retinue, five days since."

The Prioress did not stir. She maintained her quiet posture as an attentive listener. But her face grew as white as her wimple, and she folded her hands to steady their trembling.

But the Bishop, now eagerly launched, had no interest in pallor, or possible palsy. His vigorous words cut the calm atmosphere. The gem on his finger sparkled like red wine in a goblet.

"I knew him of old," he said; "knew him as a high-spirited lad, yet loving, and much belovèd. He came to me, in his grief, distraught with anguish of heart, and told me this tale of treachery and wrong. Never did I hear of such a network of evil device, such a tragedy of loving hearts sundered. And when at last he returned to this land, he found that the girl whom he had thought false, thinking him so, had entered a Nunnery. Also he seemed convinced that she was to be found among our White Ladies of Worcester. Now tell me, dear Prioress, think you she could be Seraphine?"

The Prioress smiled; and truly it was a very creditable smile for a face which might have been carved in marble.

"From my knowledge of Sister Mary Seraphine," she said, "it seems unlikely that for loss of her, so noble a Knight as you describe would be distraught with anguish of heart."

"Nay, there I do not agree," said the Bishop. "It is ever opposites which attract. The tall wed the short; the stout, the lean; the dark, the fair; the grave, the gay. Wherefore my stern Crusader may be breaking his heart for your foolish little bird."

"I do not think so," said the Prioress, shortly; then hastened to add: "Not that I would presume to differ from you, Reverend Father. Doubtless you are better versed in such matters than I. But—if it be as you suppose—what measures do you suggest? How am I to deal with Sister Mary Seraphine?"

The Bishop leaned forward and whispered, though not another soul was within hearing; but at this juncture in the conversation, a whisper was both dramatic and effective. Also, when he leaned forward, he could almost hear the angry beating of the heart of the Prioress.

The Bishop held the Prioress in high regard, and loved not to distress her. But he did not think it right that a woman should have such complete mastery over herself, and therefore over others. A fine quality in a man, may be a blemish in a woman. For which reason the Bishop leaned forward and whispered.

"Let her fly, my daughter; let her fly. If his arms await her, she will not have far to go, nor many dangers to face. Her lover will know how to guard his own."

"My lord," said the Prioress, now flushed with anger, "you amaze me! Am I to understand that you would have me open the Convent door, so that a renegade nun may escape to her lover? Or perhaps, my lord, it would better meet your ideas if I bid the porteress stand wide the great gates, so that this high-spirited Knight may ride in and carry off the nun he desires, in sight of all! My Lord Bishop! You rule in Worcester and in the cities of the diocese. But I rule in this Nunnery; and while I rule here, such a thing as this shall never be."

The Prioress flashed and quivered; rose to her feet and towered; flung her arms wide, and paced the floor.

"The Knight has bewitched you, my lord," she said. "You forget the rules of our holy Church. You fail in your trust toward the women who look to you as their spiritual Father and guide."

The Prioress walked up and down the cell, and each time she passed her chair she wheeled, and gripping the back with her strong fingers, shook it. Not being able to shake the Bishop, she needs must shake something.

"You amaze me!" she said. "Truly, my lord, you amaze me!"

The Bishop put on his biretta.

Only once before, in his eventful life, had he made a woman as angry as this. Very young he was, then; and the angry woman had seized him by his hair.

The Bishop did not really think the Prioress would do this; but it amused him to fancy he was afraid, and to put on his biretta.

Then, as he leaned back in his chair, and his finger tips met, the stone in his ring was blue again, and his eyes were more than ever the eyes of a merry schoolboy out on a holiday.

Yet, presently, he sought to calm the tempest he had raised.

"My daughter," he said, "I did but agree to that which you yourself suggested. Did you not ask whether it would seem to me right or possible to grant absolution from her vows, tacitly to allow the opening of the cage door, that the little foolish bird might, if she wished it, escape? Why this exceeding indignation, when I do but yield to your arguments and fall in with your suggestions?"

"I did not suggest that a lover's arms were awaiting one of my nuns," said the angry Prioress.

"You did not mention arms," replied the Bishop, gently; "but you most explicitly mentioned a voice. 'Supposing the voice of an earthly lover calls,' you said. And—having admitted that I am better versed in such matters than you—you must forgive me, dear Prioress, if I amaze you further by acquainting you with the undoubted fact, recognised, in the outer world, as beyond dispute, that when a lover's voice calls, a lover's arms are likely to be waiting. Earthly lovers, my daughter, by no means resemble those charming cherubs which you may have observed on the carved woodwork in our Cathedral. Otherwise you might have just a voice, flanked by seraphic wings. Some such fanciful creation must have been in your mind for Sister Mary Seraphine; for, until I made mention of the noble Knight who had arrived in Worcester distraught with anguish of heart by reason of his loss, you had decided leanings toward tacitly allowing flight. Therefore it was not the fact of the broken vows, but the idea of Seraphine wedded to the brave Crusader, which so greatly roused your ire."

The Prioress stood silent. Her hot anger cooled, enveloped in the chill mantle of self-revelation and self-scorn.

It seemed to her that the gentle words of the Bishop indeed expressed the truth far more correctly than he knew.

The thought of Hugh, consoling himself with some foolish, vain, unworthy, little Seraphine, had stung with intolerable pain.

Yet, how should she, the cause of his despair, begrudge him any comfort he might find in the love of another?

Then, suddenly, the Prioress knelt at the feet of the Bishop.

"Forgive me, most Reverend Father," she said. "I did wrong to be angry."

Symon of Worcester extended his hand, and the Prioress kissed the ring. As she withdrew her lips from the precious stone, she saw it blood-red and sparkling, as the juice of purple grapes in a goblet.

The Bishop laid his biretta once more upon the table, and smiled very tenderly on the Prioress, as he motioned her to rise from her knees and to resume her seat.

"You did right to be angry, my daughter," he said. "You were not angry with me, nor with the brave Crusader, nor with the foolish Seraphine. Your anger, all unconsciously, was aroused by a system, a method of life which is contrary to Nature, and therefore surely at variance with the will of God. I have long had my doubts concerning these vows of perpetual celibacy for women. For men, it is different. The creative powers in a man, if denied their natural functions, stir him to great enterprise, move him to beget fine phantasies, creations of his brain, children of his intellect. If he stamp not his image on brave sons and fair daughters, he leaves his mark on life in many other ways, both brave and fair. But it is not so with woman; in the very nature of things it cannot be. Methinks these Nunneries would serve a better purpose were they schools from which to send women forth into the world to be good wives and mothers, rather than store-houses filled with sad samples of Nature's great purposes deliberately unfulfilled."

The merry schoolboy look had vanished. The Bishop's eyes were stern and searching; yet he looked not on the Prioress as he spoke.

Amazement was writ larger than ever, on her face; but she held herself well under control.

"Such views, my lord, if freely expressed and adopted, would change the entire monastic system."

"I know it," said the Bishop. "And I would not express them, saving to you and to one other, to whom I also talk freely. But the older I grow, the more clearly do I see that systems are man-made, and therefore often mistaken, injurious, pernicious. But Nature is Divine. Those who live in close touch with Nature, who rule their lives by Nature's rules, do not stray far from the Divine plan of the Creator. But when man takes upon himself to say 'Thou shalt,' or 'Thou shalt not,' quickly confusion enters. A false premise becomes the starting-point; and the goal, if it stop short of perdition, is, at best, folly and failure."

The Bishop paused.

The eyes of the woman before him were dark with sorrow, regret, and the dawning of a great fear. Presently she spoke.

"To say these things here, my lord, is to say them too late."

"It is never too late," replied Symon of Worcester. "'Too late' tolls the knell of the coward heart. If we find out a mistake while we yet walk the earth where we made it, it is not too late to amend it."

"Think you so, Reverend Father? Then what do you counsel me to do—with Seraphine?"

"Speak to her gently, and with great care and prudence. Say to her much of that which you have said to me, and a little of that which I have said to you, but expressed in such manner as will be suited to a foolish mind. You and I can hurl bricks at one another, my dear Prioress, and be the better for the exercise. But we must not fling at little Seraphine aught harder than a pillow of down. Empty heads, like empty eggshells, are soon broken. Tell her you have consulted me concerning her desire to return to the world; and that I, being lenient, and holding somewhat wider views on this subject than the majority of prelates, also being well acquainted with the mind of His Holiness the Pope concerning those who embrace the religious life for reasons other than a true vocation, have promised to arrange the matter of a dispensation. But add that there must be no possibility of any scandal connected with the Nunnery. Since the Lady Wulgeova, mother of Bishop Wulstan, of blessèd memory, took the veil here a century and a half ago, this house has ever been above reproach. You will tacitly allow her to slip away; and, once away, I will set matters right for her. But nothing must transpire which could stumble or scandalise the other members of the Community. The peculiar circumstances which the Knight made known to me—always, of course, without making any mention of the name of Seraphine—can hardly have occurred in any other case. It is not likely, for instance, that our worthy Sub-Prioress was torn by treachery from the arms of a despairing lover; and she would undoubtedly share your very limiting ideas of a lover's physical qualities and requirements; possibly not even allowing him a voice.

"Now I happen to know that the Knight daily spends the hour of Vespers in the Cathedral crypt, kneeling before the shrine of Saint Oswald beside a stretcher whereon lies one of his men, much bandaged about the head, swathed in linen, and covered with a cloak. The Knight has my leave to lay the sick man before the holy relics, daily, for five days. I asked of him what he expected would result from so doing. He made answer: 'A great recovery and restoration.'"

The Bishop paused, as if meditating upon the words. Then he slowly repeated them, taking evident pleasure in each syllable.

"A great recovery and restoration," said the Bishop, and smiled.

"Well? The blessèd relics can do much. They may avail to mend a broken head. Could they mend a broken heart? I know not. That were, of the two, the greater miracle."

The Bishop glanced at the Prioress.

Her face was averted.

"Well, my daughter, matters being as they are, you may inform Sister Mary Seraphine that, should she chance to lose her way among the hundred and forty-two columns, when passing through the crypt after Vespers, she will find a Knight, who will doubtless know what to do next. If he can contrive to take her safely from the Cathedral and out of the Precincts, she will have to ride with him to Warwick, where a priest will be in readiness to wed them. But it would be well that Sister Mary Seraphine should have some practice in mounting and riding, before she goes on so adventurous a journey. She may remember the crimson trappings of her palfrey, and yet have forgotten how to sit him. It is for us to make sure that the Knight's brave plans for the safe capture of his lady, do not fail for lack of any help which we may lawfully give."

The Bishop stretched out his hand and took up his biretta.

"When did the nuns last have a Play Day?" he asked.

"Not a month ago," replied the Prioress. "They made the hay in the river meadow, and carried it themselves. They thought it rare sport."

The Bishop put on his biretta.

"Give them a Play Day, dear Prioress, in honour of my visit. Tell them I asked that they should have it the day after to-morrow. I will then send you my white palfrey, suitably caparisoned. Brother Philip, who attends me when I ride, and who has the palfrey well controlled, shall lead him in. The nuns can then ride in turns, in the river meadow;

and our little foolish bird can try her wings, before she attempts the long flight from Worcester to Warwick."

The Bishop rose, crossed the cell, and knelt long, in prayer, before the crucifix.

When he turned toward the door, the Prioress said: "I pray you, give me your blessing, Reverend Father, before you go."

She knelt, and the Bishop extended his hand over her bowed head.

Expecting a Latin formula, she was almost startled when tender words, in the English tongue, fell softly from the Bishop's lips.

"The Lord bless thee, and keep thee; and grant unto thee grace and strength to choose and to do the harder part, when the harder part is His will for thee."

After which: "Benedictio Domini sit vobiscum," said the Bishop; and made the sign of the cross over the bowed head of the Prioress.

CHAPTER XX

HOLLY AND MISTLETOE

Symon, Bishop of Worcester, had bidden Sir Hugh d'Argent to sup with him at the Palace.

It was upon the second day after the Bishop's conversation with the Prioress in the Convent at Whytstone; the evening of the Nun's Play Day, granted in honour of his visit.

The Bishop and the Knight supped together, with much stately ceremony, in the great banqueting hall.

Knowing the Bishop's love of the beautiful, and his habit of being punctilious in matters of array and deportment, acquired no doubt during his lengthy sojourns in France and Italy, the Knight had donned his finest court suit—white satin, embroidered with silver; jewelled collar, belt, and shoes; a small-sword of exquisite workmanship at his side. A white cloak, also richly embroidered with silver, hung from his shoulders; white silk hose set off the shapely length of his limbs. The blood-red gleam of the magnificent rubies on his breast, sword-belt, and shoe-buckles, were the only points of colour in his attire.

The Bishop's keen eyes noted with quiet pleasure how greatly this somewhat fantastically beautiful dress enhanced the dark splendour of the Knight's noble countenance, displayed his superb carriage, and shewed off the supple grace of his limbs, which, in his ordinary garb, rather gave the idea of massive strength alone.

The Bishop himself wore crimson and gold; and, just as the dark beauty of the Knight was enhanced by the fair white and silver of his dress, so did these gorgeous Italian robes set off the frail whiteness of the Bishop's delicate face, the silvery softness of his abundant hair. And just as the collar of rubies gleamed like fiery eyes upon the Knight's white satin doublet, so from out the pallor of the Prelate's countenance the eyes shone forth, bright with the fires of eternal, youth, the gay joy of life, the twinkling humour of a shrewd yet kindly wit.

They supped at a round table of small size, in the very centre of the huge apartment. It formed a point of light and brightness from which all else merged into shadow, and yet deeper shadow, until the eye reached the dark panelling of the walls.

The light seemed to centre in the Knight—white and silver; the colour, in the figure of the Bishop—crimson and gold.

In and out of the shadows, swift and silent, on sandalled feet, moved the lay-brothers serving the feast; watchful of each detail; quickly supplying every need.

At length they loaded the table with fruit; put upon it fresh flagons of wine, and finally withdrew; each black-robed figure merging into the black shadows, and vanishing in silence.

The Bishop's Chaplain appeared in a distant doorway.

"Benedicite," said Symon of Worcester, looking up.

"Deus," replied the Chaplain, making a profound obeisance.

Then he stood erect—a grim, austere figure, hard features, hollow eyes, half-shrouded within his cowl.

He looked with sinister disapproval at the distant table, laden with fruit and flagons; at the Bishop and the Knight, now sitting nigh to one another; the Bishop in his chair of state facing the door, the Knight, on a high-backed seat at the Bishop's right hand, half-way round the table.

"Holly and Mistletoe," muttered the Chaplain, as he closed the great door.

"Yea, verily! Mistletoe and Holly," he repeated, as he strode to his cell. "The Reverend Father sups with the World, and indulges the Flesh. Methinks the Devil cannot be far off."

Nor was he.

He was very near.

He had looked over the Chaplain's shoulder as he made his false obeisance in the doorway.

But he liked not the pure white of the Knight's dress, and he feared the clear light in the Prelate's eyes. So, when the Chaplain closed the door, the Devil stayed on the outside, and now walked beside the Chaplain along the passage leading to his cell.

There is no surer way of securing the company of the Devil, than to make sure he is at that moment busy with another—particularly if that other chance to be the most saintly man you know, and merely displeasing to you, at the moment, because he hath not bidden you to sup with him. The Devil and the Chaplain made a night of it.

The Bishop's gentle "Benedicite" spread white wings and flew, like an affrighted dove, over the head of the bowing Chaplain, into the chill passage beyond.

But, just as the great door was closing, it darted in again, circled round the banqueting hall, and came back to rest in the safe nest of the kindly heart which had sent it forth.

No blessing, truly vitalised, ever ceases to live. If the blessed be unworthy, it returns on swift wing to the blesser.

CHAPTER XXI

SO MUCH FOR SERAPHINE!

A sense of peace fell upon the banqueting hall, with the closing of the door. All unrest and suspicion seemed to have departed. An atmosphere of confidence and serenity pervaded the great chamber. It was in the Bishop's smile, as he turned to the Knight.

"At length the time has come when we may talk freely; and truly, my son, we have much to say."

The Knight glanced round the spacious hall, and his look implied that he would prefer to talk in a smaller chamber.

"Nay, then," said the Bishop. "No situation can be better for a private conversation than the very centre of a very large room. Have you not heard it said that walls have ears? Well, in a small room, they may use them to some purpose. But here, we sit so far removed from the walls that, strain their ears as they may, they will hear nothing; even the very key-hole, opening wide its naughty eye, will see naught, neither will the adjacent ear hear anything. We may speak freely."

The Bishop, signing to the Knight to help himself to fruit, moved the wine toward him. At his own right hand stood a Venetian flagon and goblet of ruby glass, ornamented with vine leaves and clusters of grapes. The Bishop drank only from this flagon, pouring its contents himself into the goblet which he held to the light before he drank from it, enjoying the rich glow of colour, and the beauty of the engraving. His guests sometimes wondered what specially choice kind of wine the Bishop kept for his own, exclusive use. If they asked, he told them.

"The kind used at the marriage feast at Cana in Galilee, when the supply of an inferior quality had failed. This, my friends, is pure water, wholesome, refreshing, and not costly. I drink it from glass which gives to it the colour of the juice of the grape, partly in order that my guests may not feel chilled in their own enjoyment of more gay and luscious beverage; partly because I enjoy the emblem.

"The gifts of circumstance, life, and nature, vary, not so much in themselves, as in the human vessels which contain them. If the heart be a ruby goblet, the humblest form of pure love filling it, will assume the rich tint and fervour of romance. If the mind be, in itself, a thing of vivid tints and glowing colours, the dullest thought within it will take on a lustre, a sparkle, a glow of brilliancy. Thus, whensoever men or matters seem to me dull or wearisome, to myself I say: 'Symon! Thou art this day, thyself, a pewter pot.'"

Then the Bishop would fill up his goblet and hold it to the light.

"Aye, the best wine!" he would say. "'Thou hast kept the best wine until now.' The water of earth—drawn by faithful servants, acting in unquestioning obedience to the commands of the blessèd Mother of our Lord—transmuted by the word and power of the Divine Son; outpoured for others, in loving service; this is ever 'the best wine.'"

The Knight filled his goblet and took some fruit. Then, leaving both untouched, turned his chair sidewise, that he might the better face the Bishop, crossed his knees, leaned his right elbow on the table and his head upon his hand, pushing his fingers into his hair.

Thus, for a while, they sat in silence; the Knight's eyes searching the Bishop's face; the Bishop, intent upon the colour of his ruby goblet.

At length Hugh d'Argent spoke.

"I have been through deep waters, Reverend Father, since last I supped with you."

The Bishop put down the goblet.

"So I supposed, my son. Now tell me what you will, neither more nor less. I will then give you what counsel I can. On the one point concerning which you must not tell me more than I may rightly know, I will question you. Have you contrived to see the woman you loved, and lost, and are now seeking to regain? Tell me not how, nor when, nor where; but have you had speech with her? Have you made clear to her the treachery which sundered you? Have you pleaded with her to remember her early betrothal, to renounce these later vows, and to fly with you?"

The Knight looked straight into the Bishop's keen eyes.

At first he could not bring himself to answer.

This princely figure, with his crimson robes and golden cross, so visibly represented the power and authority of the Church.

His own intrusion into the Nunnery, his attempt to win away a holy nun, suddenly appeared to him, as the most appalling sacrilege.

With awe and consternation in his own, he met the Bishop's eyes.

79

At first they were merely clear and searching, and the Knight sat tongue-tied. But presently there flicked into them a look so human, so tender, so completely understanding, that straightway the tongue of the Knight was loosed.

"My lord, I have," he said. "All those things have I done. I have been in heaven, Reverend Father, and I have been in hell—"

"Sh, my son," murmured the Bishop. "Methinks you have been in a place which is neither heaven nor hell; though it may, on occasion, approximate somewhat nearly to both. How you got there, is a marvel to me; and how you escaped, without creating a scandal, an even greater wonder. Yet I think it wise, for the present, not to know too much. I merely required to be certain that you had actually found your lost betrothed, made her aware of your proximity, your discovery, and your desires. I gathered that you had succeeded in so doing; for, two days ago, the Prioress herself sent to beg a private interview with me, in order to ask whether, under certain circumstances, I could approve the return of a nun to the world, and obtain absolution from her vows."

The rubies on the Knight's breast suddenly glittered, as if a bound of his heart had caused them all to leap together. But, except for that quick sparkle, he sat immovable, and made no sign.

The Bishop had marked the gleam of the rubies.

He lifted his Venetian goblet to the light and observed it carefully, as he continued: "The Prioress—a most wise and noble lady, of whom I told you on the day when you first questioned me concerning the Nunnery—has been having trouble with a nun, by name Sister Mary Seraphine. This young and lovely lady has, just lately, heard the world loudly calling—on her own shewing, through the neighing of a palfrey bringing to mind past scenes of gaiety. But—the Prioress suspicioned the voice of an earthly lover; and I, knowing how reckless and resolute an earthly lover was attempting to invade the Nunnery, we both—the Prioress and I—drew our own conclusions, and proceeded to face the problem with which we found ourselves confronted, namely:—whether to allow or to thwart the flight of Seraphine."

The Knight, toying with walnuts, held at the moment four in the palm of his right hand. They broke with a four-fold crack, which sounded but as one mighty crunch. Then, all unconscious of what he did, the Knight opened his great hand and let fall upon the table, a little heap of crushed nuts, shells and white flesh inextricably mixed.

The Bishop glanced at the small heap. The veiled twinkle in his eyes seemed to say; "So much for Seraphine!"

"I know not any lady of that name," said the Knight.

"Not by that name, my son. The nuns are not known in the Convent by the names they bore before they left the world. I happen to know that the Prioress, before she professed, was Mora, Countess of Norelle. I know this because, years ago, I saw her at the Court, when she was a maid of honour to the Queen; very young and lovely; yet, even then remarkable for wisdom, piety, and a certain sweet dignity of deportment. Sometimes now, when she receives me in the severe habit of her Order, I find myself remembering the flow of beautiful hair, soft as spun silk, bound by a circlet of gold round the regal head; the velvet and ermine; the jewels at her breast. Yet do I chide myself for recalling things which these holy women have renounced, and doubtless would fain forget."

The Bishop struck a silver gong with his left hand.

At once a distant door opened in the dark panelling and two black-robed figures glided in.

"Kindle a fire on the hearth," commanded the Bishop; adding to his guest: "The evening air strikes chilly. Also I greatly love the smell of burning wood. It is pungent to the nostrils, and refreshing to the brain."

The monks hastened to kindle the wood and to fan it into a flame.

Presently, the fire blazing brightly, the Bishop rose, and signed to the monks to place the chairs near the great fireplace. This they did; and, making profound obeisance, withdrew.

Thus the Bishop and the Knight, alone once more, were seated in the firelight. As it illumined the white and silver doublet, and glowed in the rubies, the Bishop conceived the whimsical fancy that the Knight might well be some splendid archangel, come down to force the Convent gates and carry off a nun to heaven. And the Knight, watching the leaping flame flicker on the Bishop's crimson robes and silvery hair, saw the lenient smile upon the saintly face and took courage as he realised how kindly was the heart, filled with most human sympathy, which beat beneath the cross of gold upon the Prelate's breast.

Leaning forward, the Bishop lifted the faggot-fork and moved one of the burning logs so that a jet of blue smoke, instead of mounting the chimney, came out toward them on the hearth.

Symon of Worcester sat back and inhaled it with enjoyment.

"This is refreshing," he said. "This soothes and yet braces the mind. And now, my son, let us return to the question of your own private concerns. First, let me ask—Hugh, dear lad, as friend and counsellor I ask it—are you able now to tell me the name of the woman you desire to wed?"

"Nay, my dear lord," replied the Knight, "that I cannot do. I guard her name, as I would guard mine honour. If—as may our Lady be pleased to grant—she consent to fly with me, her name will still be mine to guard; yet then all men may know it, so they speak it with due respect and reverence. But if—as may our blessèd Lady forbid—she withhold herself from me, so that three days hence I ride away alone; then must I ride away leaving no shadow of reproach on her fair fame. Her name will be forever in my heart; but no word of mine shall have

81

left it, in the mind of any man, linked with broken vows, or a forsaken lover."

The Bishop looked long and earnestly at the Knight.

"That being so, my son," he said at length, "for want of any better name, I needs must call her by the name she bears in the Nunnery, and now speak with you of Sister Mary Seraphine."

Hugh d'Argent frowned.

"I care not to hear of this Seraphine," he said.

"Yet I fear me you must summon patience to hear of Seraphine for a few moments," said the Bishop, quietly; "seeing that I have here a letter from the Prioress herself, in which she sends you a message. . . . Ah! I marvel not that you are taken by surprise, my dear Knight; but keep your seat, and let not your hand fly so readily to your sword. To transfix the Reverend Mother's gracious epistle on your blade's keen point, would not tend to elucidate her meaning; nor could it alter the fact that she sends you important counsel concerning Sister Mary Seraphine."

The Bishop lighted a wax taper standing at his elbow, drew a letter from the folds of his sash, slowly unfolded and held it to the light.

The Knight sat silent, his face in shadow. The leaping flame of the fire played on his sword hilt and on the rubies across his breast.

As the parchment crackled between the Bishop's fingers, the Knight kept himself well in hand; but he prayed he might not have need to speak, nor to meet the Bishop's eyes. These—the saints be praised—were now intent upon the closely written page.

The light of the taper illumined the almost waxen whiteness of the gentle face, and gleamed upon the Bishop's ring. The Knight, fixing his eyes upon the stone, saw it the colour of red wine.

At last the Bishop began to speak with careful deliberation, his eyes upon the letter, yet telling, instead of reading; a method ofttimes maddening to an anxious listener, eager to snatch the parchment and master its contents for himself; yet who must perforce wait to receive them, with due patience, from another.

"The Prioress relates to me first of all a conversation she had, by my suggestion, with Sister Mary Serephine, in which she told that lady much of what passed between herself and me when she consulted me upon the apparent desire of this nun to escape from the Convent, renounce her vows, and return to her lover and the world—her lover who had come to save her."

The Bishop paused.

The Knight stirred uneasily in his seat. A net seemed to be closing around him. Almost he saw himself compelled to ride to Warwick in company with this most undesired and undesirable nun, Mary Seraphine.

The Bishop raised his eyes from the letter and looked pensively into the fire.

"A most piteous scene took place," he said, "on the day when Sister Seraphine first heard again the call of the outer world. Most moving it was, as told me by the Prioress. The distraught nun lay upon the floor of her cell in an abandonment of frantic weeping. She imitated the galloping of a horse with her hands and feet, a ride of some sort evidently being in her mind. At length she lifted a swollen countenance, crying that her lover had come to save her."

The Knight clenched his teeth, in despair. Almost, he and this fearsome nun had arrived at Warwick, and she was lifting a swollen countenance to him that he might embrace it.

Yet Mora well knew that he had not come for any Seraphine! Mora might deny herself to him; but she would not foist another upon him. Only, alas! this grave and Reverend Prioress of whom the Bishop spoke, hardly seemed one with the woman of his desire; she who, but three evenings before, had yielded her lips to his, clasping her arms around him; loving, even while she denied him.

The Bishop's eyes were again upon the letter.

"The Prioress," he said, "with her usual instinctive sense of the helpfulness of outward surroundings, and desiring, with a fine justice, to give Seraphine—and her lover—every possible advantage, arranged that the conversation should take place in the Nunnery garden, in a secluded spot where they could not be overheard, yet where the sunshine glinted, through overhanging branches, flecking, in golden patches, the soft turf; where birds carolled, and spread swift wings; where white clouds chased one another across the blue sky; in fact, my son," said the Bishop, suddenly looking up, "where all Nature sang aloud of liberty and nonrestraint."

The Knight's eyes, frowning from beneath a shading hand, were gloomy and full of sombre fury.

It mattered not to him in what surroundings this preposterous offer, that she should leave the Convent and fly with him to Warwick, had been made to Seraphine. Her swollen countenance would be equally unattractive, whether lifted in cell or cloister, or where white clouds chased one another across the blue sky!

The Knight felt as if he were being chased, and by something more to be feared than a white cloud. Grim Nemesis pursued him. This reverend prelate, whom he had deemed so wise, was well-nigh witless. Yet Mora knew the truth. Would her kind hands deal him so base a blow?

The Bishop saw the brooding rage in the Knight's eyes, and he lowered his own to the letter, in time to hide their twinkling.

Even the best and bravest of Knights, for having forced his way into a Nunnery, pressed a suit upon a nun, and escaped unscathed, deserved some punishment at the hands of the Church!

"Which was generous in the Reverend Mother," said the Bishop, "since she was inclined, upon the whole, to disapprove this offering of liberty to the restless nun. You can well understand that, the responsibility for the good conduct of that entire Community resting upon the Prioress, she is bound to regard with disfavour any innovation which might tend to provoke a scandal."

The Bishop did not look up, or he would have seen dull despair displacing the Knight's anger.

"However she appears faithfully to have laid before Sister Mary Seraphine, my view of the matter, giving her to understand that I am inclined to be lenient concerning vows made under misapprehension; also that, when there is not a true vocation, and a worldly spirit chafes against the cloistered life, I regard its presence within the Community as more likely to be harmful to the common weal, than the short-lived scandal which might arise if those in power should connive at an escape."

The Knight moved impatiently in his seat.

"Could we arrive, my lord," he said, "at the Lady Prioress's message, of which you spoke?"

"We are tending thither, my son," replied the Bishop, unruffled. "Curb your impatience. We of the Cloister are wont to move slowly, with measured tread—each step a careful following up of the step which went before—not with the leaps and bounds and capers of the laity. In due time we shall reach the message.

"Well, in this conversation the Prioress appears to have complied with my suggestions, excepting in the matter of one most important detail, concerning which she used her own discretion. I distinctly advised her to tell Seraphine that we were aware of your arrival, and that to my certain knowledge you were in the crypt each afternoon at the hour when the White Ladies pass to and from Vespers. In fact, my dear Knight, I even went so far as to suggest to the Reverend Mother to give Sister Mary Seraphine to understand that if she stepped aside, losing her way among the many pillars, you would probably know what to do next.

"But the Reverend Mother writes"—at last the Bishop began to read: "'I felt so sure from your description of the noble Knight who came to you in his trouble, that he cannot be the lover of this shallow-hearted little Seraphine, that I deemed it wise not to tell her of his arrival, nor to mention your idea, that the woman he seeks is to be found in this Nunnery.'"

The smothered sound which broke from the Knight was a mixture of triumph, relief, and most bitter laughter.

"Now that is like the Prioress," said the Bishop; "thus to use her own judgment, setting at naught my superior knowledge of the facts, and flouting my authority! A noble nature, Hugh, and most lovable; yet an imperious will, and a strength of character and purpose unusual in a woman. Had she remained in the world and married, her husband would have found it somewhat difficult wholly to mould her to his will.

Yet to possess such a woman would have been worth adventuring much. But I must not fret you, dear lad, by talking of the Prioress, when your mind is intent upon arriving at the decision of Seraphine.

"Well, I fear me, I have but sorry news for you. The Reverend Mother writes: 'Sister Mary Seraphine expressed herself as completely satisfied with the cloistered life. She declared that her desire to return to the world had been but a passing phase, of which she was completely purged by the timely discipline of Mother Sub-Prioress, and by the fact that she has been appointed, with Sister Mary Gabriel, to embroider the new altar-cloth for the Chapel. She talked more eagerly about a stitch she is learning from Mary Gabriel, than about any of those by-gone memories, which certainly had seemed most poignantly revived in her; and I had no small difficulty in turning her mind from the all-absorbing question as to how to obtain the right tint for the pomegranates. My lord, to a mind thus intent upon needle-work for the Altar of God, I could scarce have brought myself to mention the call of an earthly lover, even had I believed your Knight to be seeking Seraphine. Her heart is now wedded to the Cloister.'"

The Bishop looked up.

"Therefore, my son, we must conclude that your secret interview, whenever or wherever it took place, had no effect—will bear no lasting fruit." The Bishop could not resist this allusion to the pomegranates of Seraphine.

But Hugh d'Argent, face to face with the suspended portcullis of his fate, trampled all such gossamer beneath impatient feet.

He moistened his dry lips.

"The message," he said.

The Bishop lifted the letter.

"'But,'" he read, "'if you still believe your noble Knight to be the lover of Seraphine, then I pray you to tell him this from me. No nun worthy of a brave man's love, would consent to break her vows. A nun who could renounce her vows to go to him, would wrong herself and him, bringing no blessing to his home. Better an empty hearth, than a hearth where broods a curse. I ask you, my lord, to give this as a message to that noble Knight from me—the Prioress of this House—and to bid him go in peace, praying for a heart submissive to the will of God.'"

The Bishop's voice fell silent. He had maintained its quiet tones, yet perforce had had to rise to something of the dignity of this final pronouncement of the Prioress, and he spoke the last words with deep emotion.

Hugh d'Argent leaned forward, his elbows on his knees; then dropped his head upon his hands, and so stayed motionless.

The portcullis had fallen. Its iron spikes transfixed his very soul.

She was his, yet lost to him.

This final word of her authority, this speaking, through the

85

Bishop's mouth, yet with the dignity of her own high office, all seemed of set intent, to beat out the last ray of hope within him.

As he sat silent, with bowed head, wild thoughts chased through his brain. He was back with her in the subterranean way. He knelt at her feet in the yellow circle of the lantern's light. Her tender hands, her woman's hands, her firm yet gentle hands, fell on his head; the fingers moved, with soothing touch, in and out of his hair. Then—when his love and longing broke through his control—came her surrender.

Ah, when she was in his arms, why did he loose her? Or, when she had unlocked the door, and the dim, grey light, like a pearly dawn at sea, stole downward from the crypt, why, like a fool, did he mount the steps alone, and leave her standing there? Why did he not fling his cloak about her, and carry her up, whether she would or no? "Why?" cried the demon of despair in his soul. "Ah, why!"

But, even then, his own true heart made answer. He had loosed her because he loved her too well to hold her to him when she had seemed to wish to stand free. And he had gone alone, because never would he force a woman to come with him against her will. His very strength was safeguard to her weakness.

Presently Hugh heard the Bishop folding the Prioress's letter. He lifted his head and held out his hand.

The Bishop was slipping the letter into his sash.

He paused. Those eyes implored. That outstretched hand demanded.

"Nay, dear lad," said the Bishop. "I may not give it you, because it mentions the White Ladies by name, the Order, and poor little shallow, changeful Seraphine herself, But this much I will do: as you may not have it, none other shall." With which the Bishop, unfolding the Prioress's letter, flung it upon the burning logs.

Together they watched it curl and blacken; uncurl again, and slowly flake away. Long after the rest had fallen to ashes, this sentence remained clear: "Better an empty hearth; than a hearth where broods a curse." The flames played about it, but still it remained legible; white letters, upon a black ground; then, letters of fire upon grey ashes.

Of a sudden the Knight, seizing the faggot-fork, dashed out the words with a stroke.

"I would risk the curse," he cried, with passion. "By Pilate's water, I would risk the curse!"

"I know you would, my son," said the Bishop, "and, by our Lady's crown, I would have let you risk it, believing, as I do, that it would end in blessing. But—listen, Hugh. In asking what you asked, you scarce know what you did. You need not say 'yea,' nor 'nay,' but I incline to think with the Reverend Mother, that the woman you sought was not foolish little Seraphine, turned one way by the neighing of a palfrey, another by the embroidering of a pomegranate. There are women of finer mould in that Nunnery, any one of whom may be your lost betrothed. But of this we may be sure: whosoever she be, the Prioress knows her, and knew of whom she wrote when she sent you that message. She has the entire confidence of all in the Nunnery. I verily believe she knows them better than does their confessor—a saintly old man, but dim.

"Now, listen to me. I said you knew not what you asked. Hugh, my lad, if you had won your betrothed away, you would have had much to learn and much to unlearn. Believe me, I know women, as only a priest of many years' standing can know them. Women are either bad or good. The bad are bad below man's understanding, because their badness is not leavened by one grain of honour; a fact the worst of men will ever fail to grasp. The good are good above man's comprehension, because their perfect purity of heart causeth the spirit ever to triumph over the flesh; and their love-instinct is the instinct of self-sacrifice. Every true woman is a Madonna in the home, or fain would be, if her man would let her. To such a woman, each promise of a child is an Annunciation; our Lady's awe and wonder, whisper again in the temple of her inner being; for her love has deified the man she loves; and, it seems to her, a child of his and hers must be a holy babe, born into the world to help redeem it. And so it would be, could she but have her way. But too often the man fails to understand, and so spoils the perfect plan. And she to whom love means self-sacrifice, sacrifices all— even her noblest ideals—sooner than fail a call upon her love. Yet I say again, could the Madonna instinct have had full sway, the world would have been redeemed ere now to holiness, to happiness, to health.

"You looked high, my son, by your own shewing. You loved high. Your love was worthy, for you remained faithful, when you believed you had been betrayed. Let your consolation now be the knowledge that she also was faithful, and that it is a double faithfulness which keeps her from responding to the call of your love. Seek union with her on the spiritual plane, and some day—in the Realm where all noble things shall attain unto full perfection—you may yet give thanks that your love was not allowed to pass through the perilous pitfalls of an earthly union."

The Knight looked at the delicate face of the Bishop, with its wistful smile, its charm of extreme refinement.

Yes! Here spoke the Prelate, the Idealist, the Mystic.

But the Knight was a man and a lover.

His dark face flushed, and his eyes grew bright with inward fires such as the Bishop could hardly be expected to understand.

"I want not spiritual planes," he said, "nor realms of perfection. I want my own wife, in my own home; and, could I have won her there, I have not much doubt but that I could have lifted her over any perilous pitfalls that came in her way."

"True, my son," said the Bishop, at once gently acquiescent; for Symon of Worcester invariably yielded a point which had been misunderstood. For over-rating a mind with which he conversed, this was ever his self-imposed penance. "Your great strength would be fully equal to lifting ladies over pitfalls. Which recalls to my mind a scene in this day's events, which I would fain describe to you before we part."

CHAPTER XXII

WHAT BROTHER PHILIP HAD TO TELL

The Bishop sat back in his chair, smiling, as at a mental picture which gave him pleasure, coupled with some amusement.

Ignoring the Knight's sullen silence, he began his story in the cheerful voice which takes for granted a willing and an interested listener.

"When the Prioress and myself were discussing your hopes, my son, and I was urging, in your interests, liberty of flight for Sister Mary Seraphine, I informed the Reverend Mother that the carrying out of your plans, carefully laid in order to keep any scandal concerning the White Ladies from reaching the city, would involve for Seraphine a ride of many hours to Warwick, almost immediately upon safely reaching the Star hostel. This seemed as nothing to the lover who, by his own shewing, had ofttimes seen her 'ride like a bird, all day, on the moors.' But to us who know the effect of monastic life and how quickly such matters as these become lost arts through disuse, this romantic ride in the late afternoon and on into the summer night, loomed large as a possible obstacle to the successful flight of Seraphine.

"Therefore, in order that our little bird might try her wings, regain her seat and mastery of a horse, and rid herself of a first painful stiffness, I persuaded the Reverend Mother to grant the nuns a Play Day, in honour of my visit, promising to send them my white palfrey, suitably caparisoned, in safe charge of a good lay-brother, so that all nuns who pleased, might ride in the river meadow. You would not think it," said the Bishop, with a smile, "but the White Ladies dearly love such sport, when it is lawful. They have an agèd ass which they gleefully mount in turns, on Play Days, in the courtyard and in the meadow. Therefore riding is not altogether strange to them, although my palfrey, Iconoklastes, is somewhat of an advance upon their mild ass, Sheba."

The Knight's sad face had brightened at mention of the beasts.

"Wherefore 'Iconoklastes'?" he asked, with interest. It struck him as a curious name for a palfrey.

"Because," replied the Bishop, "soon after I had bought him he trampled to ruin, in a fit of misplaced merriment, some flower beds on which I had spent much precious time and care, and of which I was inordinately fond."

"Brute," said the Knight, puzzled, but unwilling to admit it. "Methinks I should have named him 'Devil,' for the doing of such diabolic mischief."

"Nay," said the Bishop, gently. "The Devil would have spared my flower beds. They were a snare unto me."

"And wherefore 'Sheba'?" queried the Knight.

"I named her so, when I gave her to the Prioress," said the Bishop, "in reply to a question put to me by the Reverend Mother. The ass was elderly and mild, even then, but a handsome creature, of good breed. The Prioress asked me whether she still had too much spirit to be easily managed by the lay-sisters. I answered that her name was 'Sheba.'"

The Bishop paused and rubbed his hands softly over each other, in gleeful enjoyment of the recollection.

But the Knight again looked blank.

"Did that content the Prioress?" he asked; but chiefly for love of mentioning her name.

"Perfectly," replied the Bishop. "She smiled and said: 'That is well.' And the name stuck to the ass, though the Reverend Mother and I alone understood its meaning."

"About the Play Day?" suggested the Knight, growing restive.

"Ah, yes! About the Play Day. The time chosen was after noon on this day, in order that the Prioress might first accomplish her talk with Seraphine, thus clearing the way for our experiment. Although written last evening, I had not received the Reverend Mother's decisive letter, when Iconoklastes set forth; and, I confess, I looked forward with keen interest, to questioning the lay-brother on his return. As I have told you, I had doubts concerning Seraphine; but I knew the Prioress would see to it that my meaning and intention reached the member of the Community actually concerned, were she Seraphine or another; and I should have light, both on the identity of the lady and on her probable course of action, when report reached me as to which of the nuns had taken the riding seriously. Therefore, with no little interest, I awaited the return of Iconoklastes, in charge of Brother Philip."

The Bishop lifted the faggot-fork and, bending over the hearth, began to build the logs, quickening the dying flame.

"Well?" cried the Knight, chafing like a charger on the curb. "Well, my lord? And then?"

The Bishop stood the faggot-fork in its corner.

"I paused, my son, that you might say: 'Wherefore "Philip"?'"

"The names of men interest me not," said the Knight, with impatience. "I care but to know the reason for the names of beasts."

"Quite right," said the Bishop. "Adam named the beasts; Eve named the men. Yet, I would like you to ask 'Wherefore "Philip,"' because the Prioress at once put that question, when she heard me call Brother Mark by his new name."

"Wherefore 'Philip'?" asked the Knight, with averted eyes.

"Because 'Philip' signifies 'a lover of horses.' I named the good brother so, when he developed a great affection for all the steeds in my stables.

"Well, at length Brother Philip returned, leading the palfrey. I had been riding upon the heights above the town, on my comely black mare, Shulamite."

Again the Bishop paused, and shot a merry challenge at Hugh d'Argent; but realising at once that the Knight could brook no more delay, he hastened on.

"Riding into the courtyard, just as Philip led in the palfrey, I bade him first to see to Icon's comfort; then come to my chamber and report. Before long the lay-brother appeared.

"Now Brother Philip is an excellent teller of stories. He does not need to mar them by additions, because his quickness of observation takes in every detail, and his excellent memory lets nothing slip. He has a faculty for recalling past scenes in pictures, and tells a story as if describing a thing just happening before his mental vision: the sole draw-back to so vivid a memory being, that if the picture grows too mirth provoking, Brother Philip is seized with spasms of the diaphragm, and further description becomes impossible. On this occasion, I saw at once that the good brother's inner vision teemed with pictures. I settled myself to listen.

"Aye, it had been a wonderful scene, and more merriment, so the lay-sisters afterwards told Brother Philip, than ever known before at any Play Day.

"Icon was led in state from the courtyard, down into the river meadow.

"At first the great delight was to crowd round him, pat him, stroke his mane, finger his trappings; cry out words of ecstatic praise and admiration, and attempt to feed him with all manner of unsuitable food.

"Icon, I gather, behaved much as most males behave on finding themselves the centre of a crowd of admiring women. He pawed the ground, and swished his tail; arched his neck, and looked from side to side; munched cakes he did not want, winking a large and roguish eye at Brother Philip; and finally, ignoring all the rest, fixed a languorous gaze upon the Prioress, she being the only lady present who stood apart, regarding the scene, but taking no share in the general adulation.

"At length the riding began; Brother Philip keeping firm hold on

Icon, while the entire party of nuns undertook to mount the nun who had elected to ride. Each time Brother Philip attempted a description of this part of the proceedings he was at once seized with such spasms in the region of his girdle, that speech became an impossibility; he could but hold himself helplessly, looking at me from out streaming eyes, until a fresh peep at his mental picture again bent him double.

"Much as I prefer a story complete, from start to finish, I was constrained to command Brother Philip to pass on to scenes which would allow him some possibility of articulate speech.

"The sternness of my tones gave to the good brother the necessary assistance. In a voice still weak and faltering, but gaining firmness as it proceeded, he described the riding.

"Most of the nuns rode but a few yards, held in place by so many willing hands that, from a distance, only the noble head of Icon could be seen above the moving crowd, surmounted by the terrified face of the riding nun; who, hastening to exclaim that her own delight must not cause her to keep others from participation, would promptly fall off into the waiting arms held out to catch her; at once becoming, when safely on her feet, the boldest encourager of the next aspirant to a seat upon the back of Icon.

"Sister Mary Seraphine proved a disappointment. She had been wont to boast so much of her own palfrey, her riding, and her hunting, that the other nuns had counted upon seeing her gallop gaily over the field.

"The humble and short-lived attempts were all made first. Then Sister Mary Seraphine, bidding the others stand aside, was swung by one tall sister, acting according to her instructions, neatly into the saddle.

"She gathered up the reins, as to the manner born," and bade Brother Philip loose the bridle. But the palfrey, finding himself no longer hemmed in by a heated, pressing crowd, gave, for very gladness of heart, a gay little gambol.

"Whereupon, Sister Mary Seraphine, almost unseated, shrieked to Brother

Philip to hold the bridle, rating him soundly for having let go.

"He then led Icon about the meadow, the nuns following in procession; Sister Seraphine all the while complaining; first of the saddle, which gripped her where it should not, leaving an empty space there where support was needed; then of the palfrey's paces; then of a twist in her garments—twice the procession stopped to adjust them; then of the ears of the horse which twitched for no reason, and presently pointed at nothing—a sure sign of frenzy; and next of his eye, which rolled round and was vicious.

"At this, Mother Sub-Prioress, long weary of promenading, yet determined not to be left behind while others followed on, exclaimed that if the eye of the creature were vicious, then must Sister Mary

91

Seraphine straightway dismount, and the brute be led back to the seat where the Prioress sat watching.

"To this Seraphine gladly agreed, and a greatly sobered procession returned to the top of the field.

"But gaiety was quickly restored by the old lay-sister, Mary Antony, who, armed with the Reverend Mother's permission, insisted on mounting.

"Willing hands, miscalculating the exceeding lightness of her aged body, lifted her higher than need be, above the back of the palfrey. Whereupon Mary Antony, parting her feet, came down straddling!

"Firm as a limpet, she sat thus upon Icon. No efforts of the nuns could induce her to shift her position. Commanding Brother Philip, seeing 'the Lord Bishop' was now safely mounted, to lead on and not keep him standing, old Antony rode off in triumph, blessing the nuns right and left, as she passed.

"Never were heard such shrieks of merriment! Even Mother Sub-Prioress sank upon a seat to laugh with less fatigue. Sister Seraphine's fretful complaints were forgotten.

"Twice round the field went old Antony, with fingers uplifted. Icon stepped carefully, arching his neck and walking as if he well knew that he bore on his back, ninety odd years of brave gaiety.

"Well, that made of the Play Day a success. But—the best of all was yet to come."

The Bishop took up the faggot-fork, and again tended the fire. He seemed to find it difficult to tell that which must next be told.

The Knight was breathing quickly. He sat immovable; yet the rubies on his breast glittered continuously, like so many eager, fiery eyes.

The Bishop went on, speaking rapidly, the faggot-fork still in his hand, his face turned to the fire.

"They had lifted Mary Antony down, and were crowding round Icon, patting and praising him, when a message came from the Reverend Mother, bidding Brother Philip to bring the palfrey into the courtyard; the nuns to remain in the field.

"They watched the beautiful creature pace through the archway and disappear, and none knew quite what would happen next. Philip heard them discussing it later.

"Some thought the Bishop had sent for his palfrey. Others, that the Reverend Mother had feared for the safety of the old lay-sister; or, lest her brave example should fire the rest to be too venturesome. Yet all eyes were turned toward the archway, vaguely expectant.

"And then—

"They heard the hoofs of Icon ring on the flagstones of the courtyard.

"They heard the calm voice of the Prioress. Could it be she who was coming?

92

"Out from the archway, into the sunshine, alone and fearless; the Prioress rode upon Icon. On her face was the light of a purposeful radiance. The palfrey stepped as if proud of the burden he carried.

"She smiled and would have cried out gaily to the groups as she passed. But, with one accord, the nuns dropped to their knees, with clasped hands, and faces uplifted, adoring. Always they loved her, revered her, and thought her beautiful. But this vision of the Prioress, whom none had ever seen mounted, riding forth into the sunshine on the snow-white palfrey, filled their hearts with praise and with wonder.

"Brother Philip leaned against the archway, watching. He knew his hand upon the bridle was no longer needed, from the moment when he saw the Reverend Mother gather up the reins in her left hand, lay her right gently on the neck of Icon, and, bending, speak low in his ear.

"She sat a horse—said Philip—as only they can sit, who have ridden from childhood.

"She walked him round the meadow once, then gently shook the reins, and he broke into a trot.

"The watching nuns, now on their feet again, shrieked aloud, with fright and glee.

"At the extreme end of the meadow, wheeling sharply, she let him out into a canter.

"The nuns at this were petrified into dumbness. One and all held their breath; while Mother Sub-Prioress—nobody quite knew why— turned upon Sister Mary Seraphine, and shook her.

"And the next moment the Prioress was among them, walking the palfrey slowly, settling her veil, which had streamed behind her as she cantered, bending to speak to one and another, as she passed.

"And the light of new life was in her eyes. Her cheeks glowed, she seemed a girl again.

"Reining in Iconoklastes, she paused beside Mother Sub-Prioress and said—"

The Bishop broke off, while he carefully stood the faggot-fork up in its corner.

"She paused and said: 'None need remain here longer than they will. But, being up and mounted, and our Lord Bishop in no haste for the return of his palfrey, it is my intention to ride for an hour.'"

Symon of Worcester turned and looked full at the Knight.

"And the Prioress rode for an hour," he said. "For a full hour, in the sunshine, on the soft turf of the river meadow, THE PRIORESS TRIED HER WINGS."

CHAPTER XXIII

THE MIDNIGHT ARRIVAL

Hugh d'Argent sat speechless, returning the Bishop's steady gaze. No fear was in his face; only a great surprise.

Presently into the eyes of both there crept a look which was half-smile, half-wistful sorrow, but wholly trustful; a look to which, as yet, the Bishop alone held the key.

"So you know, my lord," said Hugh d'Argent.

"Yes, my son; I know."

"Since this morning?"

"Nay, then! Since the first day you arrived with your story; asking such careful questions, carelessly. But be not wroth with yourself, Hugh. Faithful to the hilt, have you been. Only—no true lover was ever a diplomat! Matters which mean more than life, cannot be dissembled by true hearts from keen eyes."

"Then why all the talk concerning Seraphine?" demanded the Knight.

"Seraphine, my son, has served a useful purpose in various conversations. Never before, in the whole of her little shallow, selfish life has Seraphine been so disinterestedly helpful. That you sat here just now, thinking me witless beyond belief, just when I most desired not to appear to know too much, I owe to the swollen countenance of Seraphine."

"My lord," exclaimed the Knight, overcome with shame. "My lord! How knew you—"

"Peace, lad! Fash not thyself over it. Is it not a part of my sacred office to follow in the footsteps of my Master and to be a discerner of the thoughts and intents of the heart? Also, respecting, yea, approving your reasons for reticence, I would have let you depart not suspecting my knowledge of that which you wished to conceal, were it not that we must now face this fact together:—Since penning that message of apparent finality, the Prioress has tried her wings."

A rush of bewildered joy flooded the face of the Knight.

"Reverend Father!" he said, "think you that means hope for me?"

Symon of Worcester considered this question carefully, sitting in his favourite attitude, his lips compressed against his finger-tips.

At length; "I think it means just this," he said. "A conflict, in her, between the mental and the physical; between reason and instinct; thought and feeling. The calm, collected mind sent you that reasoned message of final refusal. The sentient body, vibrant with bounding life, instinctively prepares itself for the possibility of the ride with you to Warwick. This gives equal balance to the scale. But a third factor will be called in, finally to decide the matter. By that she will abide; and neither you nor I, neither earth nor hell, neither things past, things present, nor things to come, could avail to move her."

"And that third factor?" questioned the Knight.

"Is the Spiritual," replied the Bishop, solemnly, with uplifted face.

"With that, there came over the Knight a sudden sense of compunction. He began for the first time to see the matter as it must appear to the Bishop and the nun. His own obstinate and determined self-seeking shamed him.

"You have been very good to me, my lord," he said humbly. "You have been most kind and most generous, when indeed you had just cause to be angry."

The Bishop lowered his eyes from the rafters, and bent them in questioning gaze upon Hugh d'Argent.

"Angry, my son? And wherefore should I be angry?"

"That I should have sought, and should still be seeking, to tempt the Prioress to wrong-doing."

The Bishop's questioning gaze took on a brightness which almost became the light of sublime contempt.

"You—tempt her?" he said. "Tempt her to wrong-doing! The man lives not, who could succeed in that! She will not come to you unless she knows it to be right to come, and believes it to be wrong to stay. If I thought you were tempting her, think you I would stand aside and watch the conflict? Nay! But I stand aside and wait while she—of purer, clearer vision, and walking nearer Heaven than you or I—discerns the right, and, choosing it, rejects the wrong. Should she be satisfied that life with you is indeed God's will for her—and I tell you honestly, it will take a miracle to bring this about—she will come to you. But she will not come to you unless, in so doing, she is choosing what to her is the harder part."

"The harder part!" exclaimed the Knight. "You forget, my lord, she loves me."

"Do I forget?" replied the Bishop. "Have you found me given to forgetting? The very fact that she loves you, is the heaviest factor against you—just now. To such women there comes ever the instinctive feeling, that that which would be sweet must be wrong, and the hard path of renunciation the only right one. They climb not Zion's mount to reach the crown. They turn and wend their way through Gethsemane to Calvary, sure that thus alone can they at last inherit. And what can we say? Are they not following in the footsteps of the Son of God? I fear my nature turns another way. I incline to follow King David, or Solomon in all his glory, chanting glad Songs of Ascent, from the Palace on Mount Zion to the Temple on Mount Moriah. All things harmonious, in sound, form, or colour, seem to me good and, therefore, right. But long years in Italy have soaked me in the worship of the beautiful, inextricably

95

intermingled with the adoration of the Divine. I mistrust mine own judgment, and I fear me"—said the Prelate, whose gentle charity had won so many to religion—"I greatly fear me, I am far from being Christlike. But I recognise the spirit of self-crucifixion, when I see it. And the warning that I give you, is not because I forget, but because I remember."

As the last words fell in solemn utterance from the Bishop's lips, the silence without was broken by the loud clanging of the outer bell; followed by hurrying feet in the courtyard below, the flare of torches shining up upon the casements, and the unbarring of the gate.

"It must be close on midnight," said Hugh d'Argent; "a strange hour for an arrival."

The banqueting hall, on the upper floor of the Palace, had casements at the extreme end, facing the door, which gave upon the courtyard.

The Knight walked over to one of these casements standing open, kneeled upon the high window-seat, and looked down.

"A horseman has ridden in," he said, "and ridden fast. His steed is flecked with foam, and stands with spreading nostrils, panting. . . . The rider has passed within. . . . Your men, my lord, are leading away the steed." The Knight returned to his place. "Brave beast! Methinks they would do well to mix his warm mash with ale."

Symon of Worcester made no reply.

He sat erect, with folded hands, a slight flush upon his cheeks, listening for footsteps which must be drawing near.

They came.

The door, at the far end of the hall, opened.

The gaunt Chaplain stood in the archway, making obeisance.

"Well?" said the Bishop, dispensing with the usual formalities.

"My lord, your messenger has returned, and requests an audience without delay."

"Bid him enter," said the Bishop, gripping the arms of the chair, and leaning forward.

The Chaplain, half-turning, beckoned with uplifted hand; then stood aside, as rapid feet approached.

A young man, clad in a brown riding-suit, dusty and travel-stained, appeared in the doorway. Not pausing for any monkish salutations or genuflections, he strode some half-dozen paces up the hall; then swung off his hat, stopped short with his spurs together, and bowed in soldierly fashion toward the great fireplace.

Thrusting his hand into his breast, he drew out a packet, heavily sealed.

"I bring from Rome," he said—and his voice rang through the chamber—"for my Lord Bishop of Worcester, a letter from His Holiness the Pope."

The Knight sprang to his feet. The Bishop rose, a noble figure in

96

crimson and gold, and the dignity of his high office straightway enveloped him.

In complete silence, he stretched out his right hand for the letter.

The dusty traveller came forward quickly, knelt at the Bishop's feet, and placed the missive in his hands.

As the Bishop lifted the Pope's letter and, stooping his head, kissed the papal seal, the Knight kneeled on one knee, his hand upon his sword-hilt, his eyes bent on the ground.

So for a moment there was silence. The sovereignty of Rome, stretching a mighty arm across the seas, asserted its power in the English hall.

Then the Bishop placed the letter upon a small table at his right hand, seated himself, and signed to both men to rise.

"How has it fared with you, Roger?" he asked, kindly.

"Am I in time, Reverend Father?" exclaimed the youth, eagerly. "I acted on your orders. No expense was spared. I chartered the best vessel I could find, and had set sail within an hour of galloping into the port. We made a good passage, and being fortunate in securing relays of horses along the route, I was in Rome twenty-four hours sooner than we had reckoned. I rode in at sunset; and, your name and seal passing me on everywhere, your letter, my lord, was in the Holy Father's hands ere the glow had faded from the distant hills.

"I was right royally entertained by Cardinal Ferrari; and, truth to tell, a soft couch and silken quilts were welcome, after many nights of rough lodging, in the wayside inns of Normandy and Italy. Moreover, having galloped ahead of time, I felt free to take a long night's repose.

"But next morning, soon after the pigeons began to coo and circle, I was called and bid to hasten. Then, while I broke my fast with many strange and tasty dishes, seated in a marble court, with fountains playing and vines o'erhanging, the Cardinal returned, he having been summoned already to the bedchamber of the Pope, where the reply of His Holiness lay, ready sealed.

"Whereupon, my lord, I lost no time in setting forth, picking up on my return journey each mount there where I had left it, until I galloped into the port where our vessel waited.

"Then, alas, came delay, and glad indeed was I, that I had not been tempted to linger in Rome; for the winds were contrary; some days passed before we could set sail; and when at last I prevailed upon the mariners to venture, a great storm caught us in mid-channel, threatening to rend the sails to ribbons and, lifting us high, hurl us all to perdition. Helpless and desperate, for the sailors had lost all control, I vowed that if the storm might abate and we come safe to harbour I would—when I succeed to my father's lands in Gloucestershire—give to the worthy Abbot of an Abbey adjoining our estate, a meadow, concerning which he and his monks have long broken the tenth commandment and other commands as well, a trout stream running

97

through it, and the dearest delight of the Abbot being fat trout for supper; and of the monks, to lie on their bellies tickling the trout as they hide in the cool holes under the banks of the stream. But when my father finds the monks thus poaching, he comes up behind them, and up they get quickly—or try to! So, in mid-channel, remembering my sins, I remembered running to tell my father that if he came quickly he would find the good Brothers flat on their bellies, sleeves rolled back, heads hanging over the water, toes well tucked into the turf, deeply intent upon tickling. Then I would run by a short cut, hide in the hazels, and watch while my father stalked up through the meadow, caught and belaboured the poachers. My derisive young laughter seemed now to howl and shriek through the rigging. So I vowed that if the storm abated and we came safe to port, the monks should be given that meadow. Upon which the storm did abate, and to port we came— and what my father will say, I know not! Fearing vexation to you, my lord, from this untoward delay, on landing I rode as fast as mine own good horse could carry me. Am I in time?"

The Bishop smiled as he looked into the blue eyes and open countenance of young Roger de Berchelai, a youth wholly devoted to his service. Here was another who remembered in pictures, and Symon of Worcester loved the gallop, and rush, and breeze of the sea, which had swept through the chamber, in the eager young voice of his envoy.

"Yes, my son," said the Bishop. "You have returned, not merely in time, but with two days to spare. Was there ever fleeter messenger! Indeed my choice was well made and my trust well placed. Now you must sup and then take a much-needed rest, dear lad; and to-morrow tell me if you had need to spend more than I gave you."

Raising his voice, the Bishop called his Chaplain; whereupon that sinister figure at once appeared in the doorway.

The Bishop gave orders concerning the entertaining of the young Esquire of Berchelai; then added; "And let the chapel be lighted, Father Benedict. So soon as the aurora appears in the east, I shall celebrate mass, in thanksgiving for the blessing of a letter from the Holy Father, and for the safe return of my messenger. I shall not need your presence nor that of any of the brethren, save those whose watch it chances to be. . . . Benedicite."

"Deus," responded Father Benedict, bowing low.

Young Roger, gay and glad, knelt and kissed the Bishop's ring; then, rising, flung back a strand of fair hair which fell over his forehead, and said: "A bath, my lord, would be even more welcome than supper and bed. It shames me to have come in such travel-stained plight into your presence, and that of this noble knight," with a bow to Hugh d'Argent.

"Nay," said Hugh, smiling in friendly response. "Travel-stains gained in such fashion, are more to be desired than silks and fine linen.

98

I would I could go to rest this night knowing I had accomplished as much."

"Go and have thy bath, boy," said the Bishop. "This will give my monks time to tickle, catch, and cook, trout for thy supper! Ah, thou young rascal! But that field is Corban, remember. Sup well, rest well, and the blessing of the Lord be with thee."

The brown riding-suit vanished through the archway.

Father Benedict's lean hand pulled the door to.

The Bishop and the Knight were once more alone.

CHAPTER XXIV

THE POPE'S MANDATE

The Bishop and Hugh d'Argent were once more alone. It was characteristic of both that they sat for some minutes in unbroken silence.

Then the Bishop put out his hand, took up the packet from Rome, and looked at the Knight.

Hugh d'Argent rose, walked over to the casement, and leaned out into the still, summer night.

He could hear the Bishop breaking the seals of the Pope's letter.

Below in the courtyard, all was quiet. The great gates were barred. He wondered whether the steaming horse had been well rubbed down, clothed, and given a warm mash mixed with ale.

He could hear the Bishop unfolding the parchment, which crackled.

The moon, in her first quarter, rode high in the heavens. The towers of St. Mary's church looked black against the sky.

The Palace stood on the same side of the Cathedral as the main street of the city, in the direct route to the Foregate, the Tithing, and the White Ladies' Nunnery at Whytstone. How strange to remember, that beneath him lay that mile-long walk in darkness; that just under the Palace, so near the Cathedral, she and he, pacing together, had known the end of their strange pilgrimage to be at hand. Yet then—

He could hear the Bishop turning the parchment.

How freely the silvery moon sailed in this stormy sky, like a noble face looking calmly out, and ever out again, from amid perplexities and doubts.

In two nights' time, the moon would be well-nigh full. Would he be riding to Warwick alone, or would she be beside him?

As the Bishop had said, he had described her as riding all day, like a bird, on the moors. Yet now he loved best to picture her riding forth upon Icon into the river meadow, her veil streaming behind her; "on her face the light of a purposeful radiance."

Ah, would she come? Would she come, or would she stay? Would she stay, or would she come?

The moon was now hidden by a cloud; but he could see the edge of the cloud silvering.

If the moon sailed forth free, before he had counted to twelve, she would come.

He began to count, slowly.

At nine, the moon was still hidden; and the Knight's heart failed him.

But at ten, the Bishop called: "Hugh!" and turning from the casement the Knight answered to the call.

The Bishop held in his hands the Pope's letter, and also a legal-looking document, from which seals depended.

"This doth closely concern you, my son," said the Bishop, with some emotion, and placed the parchment in the Knight's hands.

Hugh d'Argent could have mastered its contents by the light of the wax taper burning beside the Bishop's chair. But some instinct he could not have explained, caused him to carry it over to the table in the centre of the hall, whereon four wax candles still burned. He stood to read the document, with his back to the Bishop, his head bent close to the flame of the candles.

Once, twice, thrice, the Knight read it, before his bewildered brain took in its full import. Yet it was clear and unmistakable—a dispensation, signed and sealed by the Pope, releasing Mora, Countess of Norelle, from all vows and promises taken and made when she entered the Nunnery of the White Ladies of Worcester, at Whytstone, in the parish of dairies, and later on when she became Prioress of that same Nunnery; and furthermore stating that this full absolution was granted because it had been brought to the knowledge of His Holiness that this noble lady had entered the cloistered life owing to a wicked and malicious plot designed to wrest her castle and estates from her, and also to part her from a valiant Knight, at that time fighting in the Holy Wars, to whom she was betrothed.

Furthermore the deed empowered Symon, Bishop of Worcester or any priest he might appoint, to unite in marriage the Knight Crusader, Hugh d'Argent, and Mora de Norelle, sometime Prioress of the White Ladies of Worcester.

The Knight walked back to the hearth and stood before the Bishop, the parchment in his hand.

"My Lord Bishop," he said, "do I dream?"

Symon of Worcester smiled. "Nay, my son. Surely no dream of thine was ever signed by His Holiness, nor bore suspended from it the great seal of the Vatican! The document you hold will be sufficient answer to all questions, and will ensure your wife's position at Court and her standing in the outer world—should she elect to re-enter it.

"But whether she shall do this, or no, is not a matter upon which the Church would give a decisive or even an authoritative pronouncement; and the Holy Father adds, in, his letter to me, further important instructions.

"Firstly: that it must be the Prioress's own wish and decision, apart from any undue pressure from without, to resign her office and to accept this dispensation, freeing her from her vows.

"Secondly; that she must leave the Nunnery and the neighbourhood, secretly; if it be possible, appearing in her new position, as your wife, without much question being raised as to whence she came.

"Thirdly: that when her absence becomes known in the Nunnery, I am authorized solemnly to announce that she has been moved on by me, secretly, with the knowledge and approval of the Holy Father, to a place where she was required for higher service."

The Bishop smiled as he pronounced the final words. There was triumph in his eye.

The Knight still looked as if he felt himself to be dreaming; yet on his face was a great gladness of expectation.

"And, my lord," he exclaimed joyously, "what news for her! Shall you send it, in the morn, or yourself take it to her?"

The Bishop's lips were pressed against his finger-tips.

"I know not," he answered, slowly; "I know not that I shall either take or send it."

"But, my lord, surely! It will settle all doubts, solve all questions, remove all difficulties—"

"Tut! Tut! Tut!" exclaimed the Bishop. "Good heavens, man! Dare I wed you to a woman you know so little? Not for one instant, into her consideration of the matter, will have entered any question as to what Church or State might say or do. For her the question stands upon simpler, truer, lines, not involved by rule or dogma: 'Is it right for me, or wrong for me? Is it the will of God that I should do this thing?'"

"But if you tell her, my lord, of the Holy Father's dispensation and permission; what will she then say?"

"What will she then say?" Symon of Worcester softly laughed, as at something which stirred an exceeding tender memory. "She will probably say: 'You amaze me, my lord! Indeed, my lord, you amaze me! His Holiness the Pope may rule at Rome; you, my Lord Bishop, rule in the cities of this diocese; but I rule in this Nunnery, and while I rule here, such a thing as this shall never be!'"

The Bishop gently passed his hands the one over the other, as was his habit when a recollection gave him keen mental pleasure.

"That is what the Prioress would probably say, my dear Knight, were I so foolish as to flaunt before her this most priceless parchment. And yet—I know not. It may be wise to send it, or to show it without much comment, simply in order that she may see the effect upon the mind of the Holy Father himself, of a full knowledge of the complete facts of the case."

"My lord," said the Knight, with much earnestness, "how came that full knowledge to His Holiness in Rome?"

"When first you came to me," replied the Bishop, "with this grievous tale of wrong and treachery, I knew that if you won your way with Mora, we must be armed with highest authority for the marriage and for her return to the world, or sorrow and much trial for her might follow, with, perhaps, danger for you. Therefore I resolved forthwith to lay the whole matter, without loss of time, before the Pope himself. I know the Holy Father well; his openness of mind, his charity and kindliness; his firm desire to do justly, and to love mercy. Moreover, his friendship for me is such, that he would not lightly refuse me a request. Also he would, of his kindness, incline to be guided by my judgment.

"Wherefore, no sooner were all the facts in my possession, those you told me, those I already knew, and those I did for myself deduce from both, than I sent for young Roger de Berchelai, whose wits and devotion I could safely trust, gave him all he would need for board and lodging, boats and steeds, that he might accomplish the journey in the shortest possible time, and despatched him to Rome with a written account of the whole matter, under my private seal, to His Holiness the Pope."

The Knight stood during this recital, his eyes fixed in searching question upon the Bishop's face.

Then: "My lord," he said, "such kindness on your part, passes all understanding. That you should have borne with me while I told my tale, was much. That you should tacitly have allowed me the chance to have speech with my betrothed, was more. But that, all this time, while I was giving you half-confidence, and she no confidence at all, you should have been working, spending, planning for us, risking much if the Holy Father had taken your largeness of heart and breadth of mind amiss! All this, you did, for Mora and for me! That you were, as you tell me, a frequent guest in my childhood's home, holding my parents in warm esteem, might account for the exceeding kindness of the welcome you did give me. But this generosity—this wondrous goodness—I stand amazed, confounded! That you should do so great a thing to make it possible that I should wed the Prioress— It passes understanding!"

When Hugh d'Argent ceased speaking, Symon of Worcester did not immediately make reply. He sat looking into the fire, fingering, with his left hand, the gold cross at his breast, and drumming, with the

102

fingers of his right, upon the carved lion's head which formed the arm of his chair.

It seemed as if the Bishop had, of a sudden, grown restive under the Knight's gratitude; or as if some train of thought had awakened within him, to which he did not choose to give expression, and which must be beaten back before he allowed himself to speak.

At length, folding his hands, he made answer to the Knight, still looking into the fire, a certain air of detachment wrapping him round, as with an invisible yet impenetrable shield.

"You overwhelm me, my dear Hugh, with your gratitude. It had not seemed to me that my action in this matter would demand either thanks or explanation. There are occasions when to do less than our best, would be to sin against all that which we hold most sacred. To my mind, the most useful definition of sin, in the sacred writings, is that of the apostle Saint James, most practical of all the inspired writers, when he said: 'To him that knoweth to do good, and doeth it not, to him it is sin.' I knew quite clearly the 'good' to be done in this case. Therefore no gratitude is due to me for failing to fall into the sin of omission.

"Also, my son, many who seem to deserve the gratitude of others, would be found not to deserve it, if the entire inward truth of motive could be fully revealed.

"With me it is well-nigh a passion that all good things should attain unto full completeness.

"It may be I was better able to give full understanding to your tale because, for love of a woman, I dwelt seven years in exile from this land, fearing lest my great love for her, which came to me all unsought, should—by becoming known to her—lead her young heart, as yet fresh and unawakened, to respond. There was never any question of breaking my vows; and I hold not with love-friendships between man and woman, there where marriage is not possible. They are, at best, selfish on the part of the man. They keep the woman from entering into her kingdom. The crown of womanhood is to bear children to the man she loves—to take her place in his home, as wife and mother. The man who cannot offer this, yet stands in the way of the man who can, is a poor and an unworthy lover."

The Bishop paused, unclasped his hands, withdrew his steadfast regard from the fire, and sat back in his chair. The stone in his ring gleamed blue, the colour of forget-me-nots beside a meadow brook.

Presently he looked at the silent Knight. There was a kindly smile, in his eyes, rather than upon his lips.

"It may be, my dear Hugh, that this heart discipline of mine—of which, by the way, I have never before spoken—has made me quick to understand the sufferings of other men. Also it may explain the great desire I always experience to see a truly noble woman come to the full completion of her womanhood.

"I returned to England not long after your betrothed had entered

103

the cloistered life in the Whytstone Nunnery. I was appointed to this See of Worcester, which appointment gave me the spiritual control of the White Ladies. My friendship with the Prioress has been a source of interest, pleasure, and true helpfulness to myself and I trust to her also. I think I told you while we supped that, many years ago, I had known her at the Court when I was confessor to the Queen, and preceptor to her ladies. But no mention has ever been made between the Prioress and myself of any previous acquaintance. I doubt whether she recognised, in the frail, white-haired, old prelate who arrived from Italy, the vigorous, bearded priest known to her, in her girlhood's days, as"—the Bishop paused and looked steadily at the Knight—"as Father Gervaise."

"Father Gervaise!" exclaimed Hugh d'Argent, lifting his hand to cross himself as he named the Dead, yet arrested in this instinctive movement by something in those keen blue eyes. "Father Gervaise, my lord, perished in a stormy sea. The ship foundered, and none who sailed in her were seen again."

The Knight spoke with conviction; yet, even as he spoke, the amazing truth rushed in upon him, and struck him dumb. Of a sudden he knew why the Bishop's eyes had instantly won his fearless confidence. A trusted friend of his childhood had looked out at him from their dear depths. Often he had searched his memory, since the Bishop had claimed knowledge of him in his boyhood, and had marvelled that no recollection of Symon as a guest in his parents' home came back to him.

Now—in this moment of revelation—how clearly he could see the figure of the famous priest, in brown habit, cloak, and hood, a cord at his waist, with tonsured head, full brown beard, and sandalled feet, pacing the great hall, standing in the armoury, or climbing the Cumberland hills to visit the chapel of the Holy Mount and the hermit who dwelt beside it.

As is the way with childhood's memories, the smallest, most trivial details leapt up vivid, crystal clear. The present was forgotten, the future disregarded, in the sudden intimate dearness of that long-ago past.

The Bishop allowed time for this realisation. Then he spoke.

"True, the ship foundered, Hugh; true, none who sailed in her were seen again. And, if I tell you that one swimmer, after long buffeting, was flung up on a rocky coast, lay for many weeks sick unto death in a fisherman's humble cot, rose at last the frail shadow of his former self, to find that his hair had turned white in that desperate night, to find that none knew his name nor his estate, that—leaving Father Gervaise and his failures at the bottom of the ocean—he could shave his beard, and make his way to Rome under any name he pleased; if I tell you all this, I trust you with a secret, Hugh, known to one other only, during all these years—His Holiness, the Pope."

104

"Father!" exclaimed the Knight, with deep emotion; "Father"—
Then, his voice broke. He dropped on one knee in front of the Bishop,
and clasped the bands stretched out to him.

What strange thing had happened? One, greatly loved and long
mourned, had risen from the dead; yet she who had best loved and
most mourned him, had herself passed to the Realm of Shadows, and
was not here to wonder and to rejoice.

"Father," said Hugh, when he could trust his voice, "in her last
words to me, my mother spoke of you. I went to her chamber to bid her
sleep well, and together we knelt before the crucifix. 'Let us repeat,'
whispered my mother, 'those holy words of comfort which Father
Gervaise ever bid his penitents to say, as they kneeled before the dying
Redeemer.' 'Mother,' said I, 'I know them not.' 'Thou wert so young, my
son,' she said, 'when Father Gervaise last was with us.' 'Tell me the
words,' I said; 'I should like well to have them from thy lips.' So, lifting
her eyes to the dead Christ, my mother said, with awe and reverence in
her voice and a deep gladness on her face: 'He—ever—liveth—to make
intercession for us.' And, in the dawn of the new day, her spirit passed."

The Bishop laid his hand upon the Knight's bowed head. "My
son," he said, "of all the women I have known, thy gentle mother bore
the most beautiful and saintly character. I would there were more such
as she, in our British homes."

"Father," said Hugh, brokenly, "knew you how much she had to
bear? My father's fierce feuds with all, shut her up at last to utter
loneliness. His anger against Holy Church and his contempt of Her
priests, cost my mother the comfort of your visits. His life-long quarrel
with Earl Eustace de Norelle caused that our families, though dwelling
within a three hours' ride, were allowed no intercourse. Never did I
enter Castle Norelle until I rode up from the South, with a message for
Mora from the King. And, to this day, Mora has never been within the
courtyard of my home! When we were betrothed, I dared not tell my
parents—though Earl Eustace and his Countess both were dead—lest
my father's wrath might reach Mora, when I had gone. News of his
death, chancing to me in a far-off land, brought me home. And truly, it
was home indeed, at last! Peace and content, where always there had
been turbulence and strain. Father, I tell you this because I know my
gentle mother feared you did not understand, and that you may have
thought her love for you had failed."

Symon of Worcester smiled.

"Dear lad," he said, "I understood."

"Ah why," cried Hugh, with sudden passion, "why should a
woman's whole life be spoiled, and other lives be darkened and made
sad, just by the angry, churlish, sullen whims of—"

"Hush, boy!" said the Bishop, quickly. "You speak of your father,
and you name the Dead. Something dies in the Living, each time they
speak evil of the Dead. I knew your father; and, though he loved me

not, yet, to be honest, I must say this of him: Sir Hugo was a good man and true; upright, and a man of honour. He carried his shield untarnished. If he was feared by his friends, he was also feared by his foes. Brave he was and fearless. One thing he lacked; and often, alas, they who lack just one thing, lack all.

"Hugo d'Argent knew not love for his fellow-men. To be a man, was to earn his frown; all things human called forth his disdain. To view the same landscape, breathe the same air, in fact walk the same earth as he, was to stand in his way, and raise his ire. Yet in his harsh, vexed manner he loved his wife, and loved his little son. Nor had he any self-conceit. He realised in himself his own worst foe. Lest we fall into this snare, it is well daily to pray: 'O Lover of Mankind, grant unto me truly to love my fellow-men; to honour them, until they prove worthless; to trust them, until they prove faithless; and ever to expect better of them, than I expect of myself; to think better of them, than I think of myself.' Let us go through life, my son, searching for good in others, not for evil; we may miss the good, if we search not for it; the evil, alas, will find us, quite soon enough, unsought."

Suddenly Hugh lifted his head.

"Father," he said, "the starling! Mind you the starling with the broken wing, which you and I found in the woods and carried home; and you did set his wing, and tamed him, and taught him to say 'Hugh'? Each time I brought him food, you said: 'Hugh! Hugh!' And soon the starling, seeing me coming, also said: 'Hugh! Hugh!' Do you remember, Father?"

"I do remember," said the Bishop. "I see thee now, coming across the courtyard, bread and meat in thy hands—a little lad, bareheaded in the sunshine, glowing with pleasure because the starling ran to meet thee, shouting 'Hugh!'"

"Then listen, dear Father. (Ah, how often have I wished to tell you this!) Soon after you were gone, that starling rudely taught me a hard lesson. Gaining strength, one day he left the courtyard, ran through the buttery, and wandered in the garden. I followed, whistling and watching. It greatly delighted the bird to find himself on turf. There had been rain. The grass was wet. Presently a rash worm, gliding from its hole, adventured forth. The starling ran to the worm, calling it 'Hugh.' 'Hugh! Hugh!' he cried, and tugged it from the earth. 'Hugh! Hugh!' and pecked it, where helpless it lay squirming. Then, shouting 'Hugh!' once more, gobbled it down. I stood with heavy heart, for I had thought that starling loved me with a true, personal love, when he ran at my approach shouting my name. Yet now I knew it was the food I carried, he called 'Hugh'; it was the food, not me, he loved. Glad was I when, his wing grown strong, he flew away. It cut me to the heart to hear the worms, the grubs, the snails, the caterpillars, all called 'Hugh'!"

The Bishop smiled, then sighed. "Poor little eager heart," he said, "learning so hard a lesson, all alone! Yet is it a lesson, lad, sooner or later learned in sadness by all generous hearts. . . . And now, leaving the past, with all its memories, let us return to the present, and face the uncertain future. Also, dear Knight, I must ask you to remember, even when we are alone, that your old friend, Father Gervaise, in his brown habit, lies at the bottom of the ocean; yet that your new friend, Symon of Worcester, holds you and your interests very near his heart."

The Bishop put out his hand.

Hugh seized and kissed it, knowing this was his farewell to Father Gervaise.

Then he rose to his feet.

The Bishop said nothing; but an indefinable change came over him. Again he extended his hand.

The Knight kneeled, and kissed the Bishop's ring.

"I thank you, my lord," he said, "for your great trust in me. I will not prove unworthy." With this he went back to his seat.

The Bishop, lifting the faggot-fork, carefully stirred and built up the logs.

"What were we saying, my dear Knight, when we strayed into a side issue? Ah, I remember! I was telling you of my appointment to the See of Worcester, and my belief that the Prioress failed to recognise in me, one she had known long years before."

The Bishop put by the faggot-fork and turned from the fire.

"I found the promise of that radiant girlhood more than fulfilled. She was changed; she shewed obvious signs of having passed through the furnace; but pure gold can stand the fire. The strength of purpose, the noble outlook upon life, the gracious tenderness for others, had matured and developed. Even the necessary restrictions of monastic life could not modify the grand lines—both mental, and physical—on which Nature had moulded her.

"I endeavoured to think no thoughts concerning her, other than should be thought of a holy lady who has taken vows of celibacy. Yet, seeing her so fitted to have made house home for a man, helping him upward, and to have been the mother of a fine race of sons and daughters, I felt it grievous that in leaving the world for a reason which in no sense could be considered a true vocation, she should have cut herself off from such powers and possibilities.

"So passed the years in the calm service of God and of the Church; yet always I seemed aware that a crisis would come, and that, when that crisis came, she would need me."

The Bishop paused and looked at the Knight.

Hugh's face was in shadow; but, as the Bishop looked at him, the rubies on his breast glittered in the firelight, as if some sudden thought had set him strongly quivering.

At sight of which, a flash of firm resolve, like the swift drawing of a sword, broke o'er the Bishop's calmness. It was quick and powerful; it

107

seemed to divide asunder soul and spirit, joints and marrow, and to discern the thoughts and intents of the heart. And before that two-edged blade could sheathe itself again, swiftly the Bishop spoke.

"Therefore, my dear Hugh, when you arrived with your tale of wrong and treachery, all unconsciously to yourself, every word you spoke of your betrothed revealed her to the man who had loved her while you were yet a youth, with your spurs to win, and all life before you.

"I saw in your arrival, and in the strange tale you told, a wondrous chance for her of that fuller development of life for which I knew her to be so perfectly fitted.

"It had seemed indeed the irony of fate that, while I had fled and dwelt in exile lest my presence should hold her back from marriage, the treachery of others should have driven her into a life of celibacy.

"Therefore while, with my tacit consent, you went to work in your own way, I sent my messenger to Rome bearing to the Holy Father a full account of all, petitioning a dispensation from vows taken owing to deception, and asking leave to unite in the holy sacrament of marriage these long-sundered lovers, undertaking that no scandal should arise therefrom, either in the Nunnery or in the City of Worcester.

"As you have seen, my messenger this night returned; and we now find ourselves armed with the full sanction of His Holiness, providing the Prioress, of her own free will, desires to renounce the high position she has won in her holy calling, and to come to you."

The quiet voice ceased speaking.

The Knight rose slowly to his feet. At first he stood silent. Then he spoke with a calm dignity which proved him worthy of the Bishop's trust.

"I greatly honour you, my lord," he said; "and were our ages and conditions other than they are, so that we might fight for the woman we love, I should be proud to cross swords with you."

The Bishop sat looking into the fire. A faint smile flickered at the corners of the sensitive mouth. The fights he had fought for the woman he loved had been of sterner quality than the mere crossing of knightly swords.

Hugh d'Argent spoke again.

"Profoundly do I thank you, Reverend Father, for all that you have done; and even more, for that which you did not do. It was six years after her first sojourn at the Court that I met Mora, loved her, and won her; and well I know that the sweet love she gave to me was a love from which no man had brushed the bloom."

Hugh paused.

Those kindly and very luminous eyes were still bent upon the fire. Was the Bishop finding it hard to face the fact that his life's secret had now, by his own act, passed into the keeping of another?

Hugh moved a pace nearer.

"And deeply do I love you, Reverend Father, for your wondrous goodness to her, and—for her sake—to me. And I pray heaven," added Hugh d'Argent simply, "that if she come to me, she may never know that she once won the love of so greatly better a man than he who won hers."

With which the Knight dropped upon one knee, and humbly kissed the hem of the Bishop's robe.

Symon of Worcester was greatly moved.

"My son," he said, "we are at one in desiring her happiness and highest good. For the rest, God, and her own pure heart, must guide her feet into the way of peace."

The Bishop rose, and went to the casement.

"The aurora breaks in the east. The dawn is near. Come with me, Hugh, to the chapel. We pray for His Holiness, giving thanks for his gracious letter and mandate; we praise for the safe return of my messenger. But we will also offer up devout petition that the Prioress may have clear light at this parting of the ways, and that our enterprise may be brought to a happy conclusion."

So, presently, in the dimly-lighted chapel, the Knight knelt alone; while, away at the high altar, remote, wrapt, absorbed in the supreme act of his priestly office, stood the Bishop, celebrating mass.

Yet one anxious prayer ascended from the hearts of both.

And, in the pale dawn of that new day, the woman for whom both the Knight and the Bishop prayed, kept vigil in her cell, before the shrine of the Madonna.

"Blessèd Virgin," she said; "thou who lovedst Saint Joseph, being betrothed to him, yet didst keep thyself an holy shrine consecrate to the Lord and His need of thee—oh, grant unto me strength to put from me this constant torment at the thought of his sufferings to whom once I gave my troth, and to reconsecrate myself wholly to the service of my Lord."

Thus these three knelt, as a new day dawned.

And the Knight prayed: "Give her to me!"

And the Bishop prayed: "Guide her feet into the way of peace."

And the Prioress, with hands crossed upon her breast and eyes uplifted, said: "Cause me to know the way wherein I should walk; for I lift up my soul unto Thee."

The silver streaks of the aurora paled before soaring shafts of gold, bright heralds of the rising sun.

Then from the Convent garden trilled softly the first notes, poignant but passing sweet, of the robin's song.

CHAPTER XXV

MARY ANTONY RECEIVES THE BISHOP

The morning after the return from Rome of the Bishop's messenger, the old lay-sister, Mary Antony, chanced to be crossing the Convent courtyard, when there came a loud knocking on the outer gates.

Mary Antony, hastening, thrust aside the buxom porteress, and herself opened the guichet, and looked out.

The Lord Bishop, mounted upon his white palfrey, waited without; Brother Philip in attendance.

What a bewildering surprise! What a fortunate thing, thought old Antony, that she should chance to be there to deal with such an emergency.

Never did the Bishop visit the Nunnery, without sending a messenger beforehand to know whether the Prioress could see him, stating the exact hour of his proposed arrival; so that, when the great doors were flung wide and the Bishop rode into the courtyard, the Prioress would be standing at the top of the steps to receive him; Mother Sub-Prioress in attendance in the background; the other holy ladies upon their knees within the entrance; Mary Antony, well out of sight, yet where peeping was possible, because she loved to see the Reverend Mother kneel and kiss the Bishop's ring, rising to her feet again without pause, making of the whole movement one graceful, deep obeisance. After which, Mary Antony, still peeping, greatly loved to see the Prioress mount the wide, stone staircase with the Bishop; each shewing a courtly deference to the other.

(One of Mary Antony's most exalted dreams of heaven, was of a place where she should sit upon a jasper seat and see the Reverend Mother and the great Lord Bishop mounting together interminable flights of golden stairs; while Mother Sub-Prioress and Sister Mary Rebecca looked through black bars, somewhere down below, whence they would have a good view of Mary Antony on her jasper seat, but no glimpse of the golden stairs or of the radiant figures which she watched ascending.)

So much for the usual visits of the Bishop, when everything was in readiness for his reception.

But now, all unexpected, the Bishop waited without the gate, and Mary
Antony had to deal with this emergency.

Crying to the porteress to open wide, she hastened to the steps. . . . It was impossible to summon the Reverend Mother in time. . . . The

Lord Bishop must not be kept waiting! . . . Even now the great doors were rolling back.

Mary Antony mounted the six steps; then turned in the doorway.

The Lord Bishop must be received. There was nobody else to do it. She would receive the Lord Bishop!

As she saw him riding in upon Icon, blessing the porteress as he passed, she remembered how she had ridden round the river meadow as the Bishop. Now she must play her part as the Prioress.

So it came to pass that, as he rode up to the door and dismounted, flinging his rein to Brother Philip, the Bishop found himself confronted by the queer little figure of the aged lay-sister, drawn up to its full height and obviously upheld by a sense of importance and dignity.

As the Bishop reached the entrance, she knelt and kissed his ring; then tried to rise quickly, failed, and clutching at his hand, exclaimed: "Devil take my old knee-joints!"

Never before had the Bishop been received with such a formula! Never had his ring been kissed by a lay-sister! But remembering the scene when old Antony rode round the field upon Icon, he understood that she now was playing the part of Prioress.

"Good-day, worthy Mother," he said, as he raised her. "The spirit is willing I know, but, in your case, the knee-joints are weak. But no wonder, for they have done you long service. Why, I get up slowly from kneeling, yet my knees are thirty years younger than yours. . . . Nay I will not mount to the Reverend Mother's chamber until you acquaint her of my arrival. Take me round to the garden, and there let me wait in the shade, while you seek her."

Greatly elated at the success of her effort, and emboldened by his charming condescension, Mary Antony led the Bishop through the rose-arch; and, casting a furtive glance at his face from behind the curtain of her veil, ventured to hope there was naught afoot which could bring trouble or care to the Reverend Mother.

Mary Antony was trotting beside the Bishop, down the long walk between the yew hedges, when she gave vent to this anxious question.

At once the Bishop slackened speed.

"Not so fast, Sister Antony," he said. "I pray you to remember mine age, and to moderate your pace. Why should you expect trouble or anxiety for the Reverend Mother?"

"Nay," said Mary Antony, "I expect naught; I saw naught; I heard naught! 'Twas all mine own mistake, counting with my peas. I told the Reverend Mother so, and set her mind at rest by carrying up six peas, saying that I had found six and not five in my wallet."

"Let us pause," said the Bishop, "and look at this lily. How lovely are its petals. How tall and white it shews against the hedge. Why did you need to set the Reverend Mother's mind at rest, Sister Antony, by carrying up six peas?"

"Because," said the old lay-sister, "when I had counted as they returned, the twenty holy ladies who had gone to Vespers, yet another passed making twenty-one. Upon which I ran and reported to the Reverend Mother, saying in my folly, that I feared the twenty-first was Sister Agatha, returned to walk amongst the Living, she being over fifty years numbered with the Dead. Yet many a time, just before dawn, have I heard her rapping on the cloister door; aye, many a time—tap! tap! tap! But what good would there be in opening to a poor lady you helped thrust into her shroud, nigh upon sixty years before? So 'Tap away!' says I; 'tap away, Sister Agatha! Try Saint Peter at the gates of Paradise. Old Antony knows better than to let you in.'"

"What said the Reverend Mother when you reported on a twenty-first White Lady?" asked the Bishop.

"Reverend Mother bid me begone, while she herself dealt with the wraith of Sister Agatha."

"And why did you not go?" asked the Bishop, quietly.

Completely taken aback, Mary Antony's ready tongue failed her. She stood stock still and stared at the Bishop. Her gums began to rattle and she clapped her knuckles against them, horror and dismay in her eyes.

The Bishop looked searchingly into the frightened old face, and there read all he wanted to know. Then he smiled; and, taking her gently by the arm, paced on between the yew hedges.

"Sister Antony," he said, and the low tones of his voice fell like quiet music upon old Antony's perturbed spirit; "you and I, dear Sister Antony, love the Reverend Mother so truly and so faithfully, that there is nothing we would not do, to save her a moment's pain. We know how noble and how good she is; and that she will always decide aright, and follow in the footsteps of our blessèd Lady and all the holy saints. But others there are, who do not love her as we love her, or know her as we know her; and they might judge her wrongly. Therefore we must tell to none, that which we know—how the Reverend Mother, alone, dealt with that visitor, who was not the wraith of Sister Agatha."

Mary Antony peeped up at the Bishop. A light of great joy was on her face. Her eyes had lost their look of terror, and began to twinkle cunningly.

"I know naught," she said. "I saw naught; I heard naught."

The Bishop smiled.

"How many peas were left in your wallet, Sister Antony?"

"Five," chuckled Mary Antony.

"Why did you shew six to the Reverend Mother?"

"To set her mind at rest," whispered the old lay-sister.

"To cause her to think that you had heard naught, seen naught, and knew naught?"

Mary Antony nodded, chuckling again.

112

"Faithful old heart!" said the Bishop. "What gave thee this thought?"

"Our blessèd Lady, in answer to her petition, sharpened the wits of old Antony."

The Bishop sighed. "May our blessèd Lady keep them sharp," he murmured, half aloud.

"Amen," said Mary Antony with fervour.

CHAPTER XXVI

LOVE NEVER FAILETH

The Bishop awaited the Prioress on that stone seat under the beech, from which the robin had carried off the pea.

He saw her coming through the sunlit cloisters.

As she moved down the steps, and came swiftly toward him, he was conscious at once of an indefinable change in her.

Had that ride upon Icon set her free from trammels in which she had been hitherto immeshed?

As she reached him, he took both her hands, so that she should not kneel.

"Already I have been received with obeisance, my daughter," he said; and told her of old Mary Antony's quaint little figure, standing to do the honours in the doorway.

The Prioress, at this, laughed gaily, and in her turn told the Bishop of the scene, on this very spot, when old Antony displayed her peas to the robin.

"What peas?" asked the Bishop; and so heard the whole story of the twenty-five peas and the daily counting, and of the identifying of certain of the peas with various members of the Community. "And a large, white pea, chosen for its fine aspect, was myself," said the Prioress; "and, leaving the Sub-Prioress and Sister Mary Rebecca, Master Robin swooped down and flew off with me! Hearing cries of distress, I hastened hither, to find Mary Antony denouncing the robin as 'Knight of the Bloody Vest,' and making loud lamentations over my abduction. Her imaginings become more real to her than realities."

"She hath a faithful heart," said the Bishop, "and a shrewd wit."

"Faithful? Aye," said the Prioress, "faithful and loving. Yet it is but lately I have realised, the love, beneath her carefulness and devotion." The Prioress bent her level brows, looking away to the overhanging branches of the Pieman's tree. "How quickly, in these places, we lose the very remembrance of the meaning of personal, human love. We grow so soon accustomed to allowing ourselves to dwell only upon the abstract or the divine."

"That is a loss," said the Bishop. He turned and began to pace slowly toward the cloister; "a grievous loss, my daughter. Sooner than that you should suffer that loss, beyond repair, I would let the daring Knight of the Bloody Vest carry you off on swift wing. Better a robin's nest, if, love be there, than a nunnery full of dead hearts."

He heard the quick catch of her breath, but gave her no chance to speak.

"'And now abideth faith, hope, love, these three,'" quoted the Bishop; "'but the greatest of these is love.'"

They were moving through the cloisters. The Prioress turned in the doorway, pausing that the Bishop might pass in before her.

"This, my lord," she said, with a fine sweep of her arm, "is the abode of Faith and Hope, and also of that divine Love, which excelleth both Hope and Faith."

"Nay," said the Bishop, "I pray you, listen. 'Love suffereth long, and is kind; love envieth not; love vaunteth not itself, is not puffed up; doth not behave itself unseemly; seeketh not her own; is not easily provoked, thinking no evil; rejoiceth not in iniquity, but rejoiceth in the truth; beareth all things, believeth all things, hopeth all things, endureth all things. Love never faileth.' Methinks," said the Bishop, in a tone of gentle meditation, as he entered the Prioress's cell, "the apostle was speaking of a most human love; yet he rated it higher than faith and hope."

"Are you still dwelling upon Sister Mary Seraphine, my lord?" inquired the Prioress, and in her voice he heard the sound of a gathering storm.

"Nay, my dear Prioress," said the Bishop, seating himself in the Spanish chair, and laying his biretta upon the table near by; "I speak not of self-love, nor does the apostle whose words I quote. I take it, he writes of human love, sanctified; upborne by faith and hope, yet greater than either; just as a bird is greater than its wings, yet cannot mount without them. We must have faith, we must have hope; then our poor earthly loves can rise from the lower level of self-seeking and self-pleasing and take their place among those things that are eternal."

The Prioress had placed her chair opposite the Bishop. She was very pale, and her lips trembled. She made so great an effort to speak with calmness, that her voice sounded stern and hard.

"Why this talk of earthly loves, my Lord Bishop, in a place where all earthly love has been renounced and forgotten?"

The Bishop, seeing those trembling lips, ignored the hard tones, and answered, very tenderly, with a simple directness which scorned all evasion:

"Because, my daughter, I am here to plead for Hugh."

114

CHAPTER XXVII

THE WOMAN AND HER CONSCIENCE

"For Hugh?" said the Prioress. And then again, in low tones of incredulous amazement, "For Hugh! What know you of Hugh, my lord?"

The Bishop looked steadfastly at the Prioress, and replied with exceeding gravity and earnestness:

"I know that in breaking your solemn troth to him, you are breaking a very noble heart; and that in leaving his home desolate, you are robbing him not only of his happiness but also of his faith. Men are apt to rate our holy religion, not by its theories, but by the way in which it causeth us to act in our dealings with them. If you condemn Hugh to sit beside his hearth, through the long years, a lonely, childless man, you take the Madonna from his home; if you take your love from him, I greatly fear lest you should also rob him of his belief in the love of God. I do not say that these things should be so; I say that we must face the fact that thus they are. And remember—between a man and woman of noble birth, each with a stainless escutcheon, each believing the other to be the soul of honour, a broken troth is no light matter."

"I did not break my troth," said the Prioress, "until I believed that Hugh had broken his. I had suffered sore anguish of heart and humiliation of spirit, over the news of his marriage with his cousin Alfrida, ere I resolved to renounce the world and enter the cloister."

"But Hugh did not wed his cousin, nor any other woman," said the Bishop. "He was true to you in every thought and act, even after he also had passed through sore anguish of heart by reason of your supposed marriage with another suitor."

"I learned the truth but a few days since," said the Prioress. "For seven long years I thought Hugh false to me. For seven long years I believed him the husband of another woman, and schooled myself to forget every memory of past tenderness."

"You were both deceived," said the Bishop. "You have both passed through deep waters. You each owe it to the other to make all possible reparation."

"For seven holy years," said the Prioress, firmly, "I have been the bride of Christ."

"Do you love Hugh?" asked the Bishop.

There was silence in the chamber.

The Prioress desired, most fervently, to take her stand as one dead to all earthly loves and desires. Yet each time she opened her lips to reply, a fresh picture appeared in the mirror of her mental vision, and closed them.

115

She saw herself, with hand outstretched, clasping Hugh's as they kneeled together before the shrine of the Madonna. She could feel the rush of pulsing life flow from his hand to the palm of hers, and so upward to her poor numbed heart, making it beat its wings like a caged bird.

She felt again the strength and comfort of the strong arm on which she leaned, as slowly through the darkness she and Hugh paced in silence, side by side.

She remembered each time when obedience had seemed strangely sweet, and she had loved the manly abruptness of his commands.

She saw Hugh, in the ring of yellow light cast by the lantern, kneeling at her feet. She felt his hair, thick and soft, between her fingers.

And then—she remembered that shuddering sob, and the instant breaking down of every barrier. He was hers, to comfort; she was his, to soothe his pain. Then—the exquisite moment of yielding; the relief of the clasp of his strong arms; the passing away of the suffering of long years, as she felt his lips on hers, and surrendered to the hunger of his kiss.

Then—one last picture—when loyal to her wish, felt rather than expressed, he had freed her, and passed, without further word or touch, up into that dim grey light like a pearly dawn at sea—passed, and been lost to view; she saw herself left in utter loneliness, the heavy door locked by her own turning of the key, he on one side, she on the other, for ever; she saw herself lying beneath the ground, in darkness and desolation, her face in the damp dust where his feet had stood.

"Do you love Hugh?" again demanded the Bishop.

And the Prioress lifted eyes full of suffering, reproach, and pain, but also full of courage and truth, to his face, and answered simply: "Alas, my lord, I do."

The silence thereafter following was tense with conflict. The Bishop turned his eyes to the figure of the Redeemer upon the cross, self-sacrifice personified, while the Prioress mastered her emotion.

Then: "'Love never faileth,'" said the Bishop gently.

But the Prioress had regained command over herself, and the gentle words were to her a challenge. She donned, forthwith, the breastplate of holy resolve, and drew her sword.

"My Lord Bishop, you have wrung from me a confession of my love; but in so doing, you have wrung from me a confession of sin. A nun may not yield to such love as Hugh d'Argent still desires to win from me. With long hours of prayer and vigil, have I sought to purge my soul from the stain of a weak yielding—even for 'a moment'—to the masterful insistence of this man, who forced himself, by the subterfuge of a sacrilegious masquerade, into the sacred precincts of our Nunnery.

116

I know not whom he bribed"—continued the Prioress, flashing an indignant glance of suspicion at the Bishop.

"'Love thinking no evil,'" murmured Symon of Worcester.

"But I do know, that somebody in high authority must have connived at his plotting, or he could not have found himself alone in the crypt at the hour of Vespers, in such wise as to assume our dress and, mingling with the returning procession, gain entrance to the cloisters. And somebody must still be aiding and abetting his plans, or he could not be, as he himself told me he would be, daily in the crypt alone, during the hour when we pass to and from the clerestory. It angers me, my lord, to think that one who should, in this, be on my side, taketh part against me."

"'Is not easily provoked,'" quoted the Bishop.

"In fact I am tempted, my lord," said the Prioress, rising to her feet, tall and indignant, "I am almost tempted, my Lord Bishop, to forget the reverence which I owe to your high office—"

"'Doth not behave itself unseemly,'" murmured Symon of Worcester, putting on his biretta.

The Prioress turned her back upon the Bishop, and walked over to the window. She was so angry that she felt the tears stinging beneath her eyelids; yet at the same time she experienced a most incongruous desire to kneel down beside that beautiful and dignified figure, rest her head against the Bishop's knees, and pour out the cruel tale of conflicts, uncertainties and strivings, temptations and hard-won victories, which, had lately made up the sum of her nights and days. He had been her trusted friend and counsellor during all these years. Yet now she knew him arrayed against her, and she feared him more than she feared Hugh. Hugh wrestled with her feelings; and, on the plane of the senses, she knew her will would triumph. But the Bishop wrestled with her mentality; and behind his calm gentleness was a strength of intellect which, if she yielded at all, would seize and hold her, as steel fingers in a velvet glove.

She returned to her seat, composed but determined.

"Reverend Father," she said, "I pray you to pardon my too swift indignation. To you I look to aid me in this time of difficulty. I grieve for the sorrow and disappointment to a brave and noble knight, a loyal lover, and a most faithful heart. But I cannot reward faith with un-faith. If I broke my sacred vows in order to give myself to him, I should not bring a blessing to his home. Better an empty hearth than a hearth where broods a curse. Besides, we never could live down the scandal caused. I should be anathema to all. The Pope himself would doubtless excommunicate us. It would mean endless sorrow for me, and danger for Hugh. On these grounds, alone, it cannot be."

Then the Bishop drew from his sash a folded sheet of vellum.

"My daughter," he said, "when Hugh came to me with his grievous tale of treachery and loss, he refused to give me the name of

117

the woman he sought, saying only that he believed she was to be found among the White Ladies of Worcester. When I asked her name he answered: 'Nay, I guard her name, as I would guard mine honour. If I fail to win her back; if she withhold herself from me, so that I ride away alone; then must I ride away leaving no shadow of reproach on her fair fame. Her name will be for ever in my heart,' said Hugh, 'but no word of mine shall have left it, in the mind of any man, linked with a broken troth or a forsaken lover.' I tell you this, my daughter, lest you should misjudge a very loyal knight.

"But no true lover was ever a diplomat. Hugh had not talked long with me, before you stood clearly revealed. A few careful questions settled the matter, beyond a doubt. Whereupon, my dear Prioress—"

The Bishop paused. It became suddenly difficult to proceed. The clear eyes of the Prioress were upon him.

"Whereupon, my lord?"

"Whereupon I realised—an early dream of mine seemed promised a possible fulfilment. I knew Hugh as a lad— It is a veritable passion with me that all things should attain unto their full perfection— In short, I sent a messenger to Rome, bearing a careful account of the whole matter, in a private letter from myself to His Holiness the Pope. Last evening, my messenger returned, bringing a letter from the Holy Father, with this enclosed."

The Bishop held out the folded document.

The Prioress rose, took it from him, and unfolded it.

As she read the opening lines, the amazement on her face quickly gathered into a frown.

"What!" she said. "The name and rank I resigned on entering this Order! Who dares to write or speak of me as 'Mora, Countess of Norelle'?"

"Merely His Holiness the Pope, and the Bishop of Worcester," said the Bishop meekly, in an undertone, not meaning the Prioress to hear; and, indeed, she ignored this answer, her words having been an angry ejaculation, rather than a question.

But there was worse to come.

"Dispensation!" exclaimed the Prioress.

"Absolution!" she cried, a little further on.

And at last, reading rapidly, in tones of uncontrollable anger and indignation: "'Empowers Symon, Lord Bishop of Worcester, or any priest he may appoint, to unite in the holy sacrament of marriage the Knight-Crusader, Hugh d'Argent, and Mora de Norelle, sometime Prioress of the White Ladies of Worcester.' Sometime Prioress? In very truth, they have dared so to write it! SOMETIME Prioress! It will be well they should understand she is Prioress NOW—not some time or any time, but NOW and HERE!"

She turned upon the Bishop.

"My lord, the Church seems to be bringing its powers to bear on

118

the side of the World, the Flesh, and the Devil, leaving a woman and her conscience to stand alone and battle unaided with the grim forces arrayed against her. But you shall see that she knows how to deal with any weapon of the adversary which happens to fall into her hands."

Upon which the Prioress rent the mandate from top to bottom, then across and again across; flung the pieces upon the floor, and set her foot upon them.

"Thus I answer," she cried, "your attempt, my lord, to induce the Pope to release me from vows which I hold to be eternally sacred and binding. And if you are bent upon divorcing a nun from her Heavenly Union, and making her to become the chattel of a man, you must seek her elsewhere than in the Convent of the White Ladies of Worcester, my Lord Bishop!"

So spoke the angry Prioress, making the quiet chamber to ring with her scorn and indignation.

The Bishop had made no attempt to prevent the tearing of the document. When she flung it upon the floor, placing her foot upon the fragments, he merely looked at them regretfully, and then back upon her face, back into those eyes which flamed on him in furious indignation. And in his own there was a look so sorrowful, so deeply wounded, and yet withal so tenderly understanding, that it quelled and calmed the anger of the Prioress.

Her eyes fell slowly, from the serene sadness of that quiet face, to the silver cross, studded with oriental amethysts, at his breast; to the sash girdling his purple cassock; to the hand resting on his knees; to the stone in his ring, from which the rich colour had faded, leaving it pale and clear, like a large teardrop on the Bishop's finger; to his shoes, with their strange Italian buckles; then along the floor to her own angry foot, treading upon the torn fragments of that precious document, procured, at such pains and cost, from His Holiness at Rome.

Then, suddenly, the Prioress faltered, weakened, fell upon her knees, with a despairing cry, clasped her hands upon the Bishop's knees, and laid her forehead upon them.

"Alas," she sobbed, "what have I done! In my pride and arrogance, I have spoken ill to you, my lord, who have ever shewn me most considerate kindness; and in a moment of ill-judged resentment, I have committed sacrilege against the Holy Father, rending the deed which bears his signature. Alas, woe is me! In striving to do right, I have done most grievous wrong; in seeking not to sin, lo, I have sinned beyond belief!"

The Prioress wept, her head upon her hands, clasped and resting upon the Bishop's knees.

Symon of Worcester laid his hand very gently upon that bowed head, and as he did so his eyes sought again the figure of the Christ upon the cross. The Prioress would have been startled indeed, had she lifted her head and seen those eyes—heretofore shrewd, searching,

119

kindly, or twinkling and gay,—now full of an unfathomable pain. But, sobbing with her face hidden, the Prioress was conscious only of her own sufferings.

Presently the Bishop began to speak.

"We did not mean to overrule your judgment, or to force your inclination, my daughter. If we appear to have done so, the blame is mine alone. This mandate is drawn up entirely along the lines of my suggestion, owing to my influence with His Holiness, and based upon particulars furnished by me. Now let me read to you the private letter from the Holy Father to myself, giving further important conditions."

The Bishop drew forth and unfolded the letter from Rome, and very slowly, that each syllable might carry weight, he read it aloud.

As the gracious and kindly words fell upon the Prioress's ear, commanding that no undue pressure should be brought to bear upon her, and insisting that it must be entirely by her own wish, if she resigned her office and availed herself of this dispensation from her vows, she felt humbled to the dust at thought of her own violence, and of the injustice of her angry words.

Her weeping became so heartbroken, that the Bishop again laid his left hand, with kindly comforting touch, upon her bowed head.

As he read the Pope's most particular injunctions as to the manner in which she must leave the Nunnery and take her place in the world once more, so as to prevent any public scandal, she fell silent from sheer astonishment, holding her breath to listen to the final clause empowering the Bishop to announce within the Convent, when her absence became known, that she had been moved on by him, secretly, with the knowledge and approval of the Pope, to a place where she was required for higher service.

"Higher service," said the Prioress, her face still hidden. "Higher service? Can it be that the Holy Father really speaks of the return to earthly love and marriage, the pleasures of the world, and the joys of home life, as 'higher service'?"

The grief, the utter disillusion, the dismayed question in her tone, moved the Bishop to compunction.

"Mine was the phrase, to begin with, my daughter," he admitted. "I used it to the Holy Father, and I confess that, in using it, I did mean to convey that which, as you well know. I have long believed, that wifehood and motherhood, if worthily performed, may rank higher in the Divine regard than vows of celibacy. But, in adopting the expression, the Holy Father, we may rest assured, had no thought of undervaluing the monastic life, or the high position within it to which you have attained. I should rather take it that he was merely accepting my assurance that the new vocation to which you were called would, in your particular case, be higher service."

The Prioress, lifting her head, looked long into the Bishop's face, without making reply.

Her eyes were drowned in tears; dark shadows lay beneath them. Yet the light of a high resolve, unconquerable within her, shone through this veil of sorrow, as when the sun, behind it, breaks through the mist, victorious, chasing by its clear beams the baffling fog.

Seeing that look, the Bishop knew, of a sudden, that he had failed; that the Knight had failed; that the all-powerful pronouncement from the Vatican had failed.

The woman and her conscience held the field.

Having conquered her own love, having mastered her own natural yearning for her lover, she would overcome with ease all other assailants.

In two days' time Hugh would ride away alone. Unless a miracle happened, Mora would not be with him.

The Bishop faced defeat as he looked into those clear eyes, fearless even in their sorrowful humility.

"Oh, child," he said, "you love Hugh! Can you let him ride forth alone, accompanied only by the grim spectres of unfaith and of despair? His hope, his faith, his love, all centre in you. Another Prioress can be found for this Nunnery. No other bride can be found for Hugh d'Argent. He will have his own betrothed, or none."

Still kneeling, the Prioress threw back her head, looking upward, with clasped hands.

"Reverend Father," she said, "I will not go to the man I love, trailing broken vows, like chains, behind me. There could be no harmony in life's music. Whene'er I moved, where'er I trod, I should hear the constant clanking of those chains. No man can set me free from vows made to God. But—"

The Prioress paused, looking past the Bishop at the gracious figure of the Madonna. She had remembered, of a sudden, how Hugh had knelt there, saying: "Blessèd Virgin . . . help this woman of mine to understand that if she break her troth to me, holding herself from me, now, when I am come to claim her, she sends me out to an empty life, to a hearth beside which no woman will sit, to a home forever desolate."

"But?" said the Bishop, leaning forward. "Yes, my daughter? But?"

"But if our blessèd Lady herself vouchsafed me a clear sign that my first duty is to Hugh, if she absolved me from my vows, making it evident that God's will for me is that, leaving the Cloister, I should wed Hugh and dwell with him in his home; then I would strive to bring myself to do this thing. But I can take release from none save from our Lord, to Whom those vows were made, or from our Lady, who knoweth the heart of a woman, and whose grace hath been with me all through the strivings and conflicts of the years that are past."

The Bishop sighed. "Alas," he said; "alas, poor Hugh!"

For that our Lady should vouchsafe a clear sign, would have to be a miracle; and, though he would not have admitted it to the Prioress, the Bishop believed, in his secret heart, that the age of miracles was past.

One so fixed in her determination, so persistent in her assertion, so loud in her asseveration, would scarce be likely to hear the inward whisperings of Divine suggestion.

Therefore, should our Lady intervene with clear guidance, that intervention must be miraculous. And the Bishop sighing, said: "Alas, poor Hugh!"

His eye fell upon the fragments of rent vellum on the floor. He held out his hand.

The Prioress gathered up the fragments, and placed them in the Bishop's outstretched hand.

"Alas, my lord," she said, "you were witness of my grievous sin in thus rending the gracious message of His Holiness. Will it please you to appoint me a penance, if such an act can indeed be expiated?"

"The sin, my daughter, as I will presently explain, is scarcely so great as you think it. But, such as it is, it arose from a lack of calmness and of that mental equipoise which sails unruffled through a sea of contradiction. The irritability which results in displays of sudden temper is so foreign to your nature that it points to your having passed through a time of very special strain, both mental and physical; probably overlong vigils and fastings, while you wrestled with this anxious problem upon which so much, in the future, depends.

"As you ask me for penance, I will give you two: one which will set right your ill-considered action; the other which will help to remedy the cause of that action.

"The first is, that you place these fragments together and, taking a fresh piece of vellum, make a careful copy of this writing which you destroyed.

"The second is that, in order to regain the usual equipoise of your mental attitude, you ride to-day, for an hour, in the river meadow. My white palfrey, Iconoklastes, shall be in the courtyard at noon. Yesterday, my daughter, you rode for pleasure. To-day you will ride for penance; and incidentally"—an irrepressible little smile crept round the corners of the Bishop's mouth, and twinkled in his eyes—"incidentally, my daughter, you will work off a certain stiffness from which you must be suffering, after the unwonted exercise. Ah me!" said the Bishop, "that is ever the Divine method. Punishments should be remedial, as well as deterrent. There is much stiffness of mind of which we must be rid before we can stoop to the portal of God's 'whosoever' and, passing through the narrow gate, enter the Kingdom of Heaven as little children."

The Bishop rose, and giving his hand to the Prioress raised her to her feet.

"My lord," she said, "as ever you are most kind to me. Yet I fear you have been too lenient for my own peace of mind. To have destroyed in anger the mandate of His Holiness—"

"Nay, my daughter," said the Bishop. "The mandate of His Holiness, inscribed upon parchment, from which hangs the great seal of the Vatican, is safely placed among my most precious documents. You have but destroyed the result of an hour's careful work. I rose betimes this morning to make this copy. I should not have allowed you to tear it, had not the writing been my own. But I took pains to reproduce exactly the peculiar style of lettering they use in Rome, and you will do the same in your copy."

Turning, the Bishop knelt for a few moments in prayer before the Madonna. He could not have explained why, but somehow the only hope for Hugh seemed to be connected with this spot.

Yet it was hardly reassuring that, when he lifted grave and anxious eyes, our Lady gently smiled, and the sweet Babe looked merry.

Rising, the Bishop turned, with unwonted sternness, to the Prioress.

"Remember," he said, "Hugh rides away to-morrow night; rides away, never to return."

Her steadfast eyes did not falter.

"He had better have ridden away five days ago, my lord. He had my answer, and I bade him go. By staying he has but prolonged his suspense and my pain."

"Yes," said the Bishop slowly, "he had better have ridden away; or, better still, have never come upon this fruitless quest."

He moved toward the door.

The Prioress reached it before him.

With her hand upon the latch: "Your blessing, Reverend Father," entreated the Prioress, rather breathlessly.

"Benedicite," said the Bishop, with uplifted fingers, but with eyes averted; and passed out.

CHAPTER XXVIII

THE WHITE STONE

Old Mary Antony was at the gate, when the Bishop rode out from the courtyard.

Thrusting the porteress aside, she pressed forward, standing with anxious face uplifted, as the Bishop approached.

He reined in Icon, and, bending from the saddle, murmured: "Take care of her, Sister Antony. I have left her in some distress."

"Hath she decided aright?" whispered the old lay-sister.

"She always decides aright," said the Bishop. "But she is so made that she will thrust happiness from her with both hands unless our Lady should herself offer it, by vision or revelation. I could wish thy gay little Knight of the Bloody Vest might indeed fly with her to his nest and teach her a few sweet lessons, in the green privacy of some leafy paradise. But I tell thee too much, worthy Mother. Keep a silent tongue in that shrewd old head of thine. Minister to her; and send word to me if I am needed. Benedicite."

An hour later, mounted upon his black mare, Shulamite, the Bishop rode to the high ground, on the north-east, above the city, from whence he could look down upon the river meadow.

As he had done on the previous day, he watched the Prioress riding upon Icon.

Once she put the horse to so sudden and swift a gallop that the Bishop, watching from afar, reined back Shulamite almost on to her haunches, in a sudden fear that Icon was about to leap into the stream.

For an hour the Prioress rode, with flying veil, white on the white steed; a fair marble group, quickened into motion.

Then, that penance being duly performed, she vanished through the archway.

Turning Shulamite, Symon of Worcester rode slowly down the hill, passed southward, and entered the city by Friar's Gate; and so to the Palace, where Hugh d'Argent waited.

The Bishop led him, through a postern, into the garden; and there on a wide lawn, out of earshot of any possible listeners, the Bishop and the Knight walked up and down in earnest conversation.

At length: "To-morrow, in the early morn," said the Knight, "I send her tire-woman on to Warwick, with all her effects, keeping back only the riding suit. Should she elect to come, we must be free to ride without drawing rein. Even so we shall reach Warwick only something before midnight."

"She tore it up and planted her foot upon it," remarked the Bishop.

"I will not give up hope," said the Knight.

"Nothing short of a miracle, my son, will change her mind, or move her from her fixed resolve."

"Then our Lady will work a miracle," declared the Knight bravely. "I prayed 'Send her to me!' and our blessèd Lady smiled."

"A sculptured smile, dear lad, is ever there. Had you prayed 'Hold her from me!' our Lady would equally have smiled."

"Nay," said the Knight; "I keep my trust in prayer."

They paused at the parapet overhanging the river.

"I was successful," said the Knight, "in dealing with Eustace, her

124

nephew. There will be no need to apply to the King. The ambition was his mother's. Now Eleanor is dead, he cares not for the Castle. Next month he weds an heiress, with large estates, and has no wish to lay claim to Mora's home. All is now once more as it was when she left it. Her own people are in charge. I plan to take her there when we leave Warwick, riding northward by easy stages."

The Bishop, stooping, picked up a smooth, white stone, and flung it into the river. It fell with a splash, and sank. The water closed upon it. It had vanished instantly from view.

Then the Bishop spoke. "Hugh, my dear lad, she thought it was the Pope's own deed and signature, yet she tore it across, and then again across; flung it upon the ground, and set her foot upon it. I deem it now as impossible that the Prioress should change her mind upon this matter, as that we should ever see again that stone which now lies deep on the river-bed."

It was a high dive from the parapet; and, to the Bishop, watching the spot where the Knight cleft the water, the moments seemed hours.

But when the Knight reappeared, the white stone was in his hand.

The Bishop went down to the water-gate.

"Bravely done, my son!" he called, as the Knight swam to the steps.

"You deserve to win."

But to himself he said: "Fighting men and quick-witted women will be ever with us, gaining their ends by strenuous endeavour. But the age of miracles is past."

Hugh d'Argent mounted the steps.

"I shall win," he said, and shook himself like a great shaggy dog.

The Bishop, over whom fell a shower, carefully wiped the glistening drops from his garments with a fine Italian handkerchief.

"Go in, boy," he said, "and get dry. Send thy man for another suit, unless it would please thee better that Father Benedict should lend thee a cassock! Give me the stone. It may well serve as a reminder of that famous sacred stone from which the Convent takes its name. Methinks we have, between us, contrived something of an omen, concluding in thy favour."

Presently the Bishop, alone in his library, stood the white stone upon the iron-bound chest within which he had placed the Pope's mandate.

"The age of miracles is past," he said again. "Iron no longer swims, neither do stones rise from the depths of a river, unless the Divine command be supplemented by the grip of strong human fingers.

"Stand there, thou little tombstone of our hopes. Mark the place where lies the Holy Father's mandate, ecclesiastically all-powerful, yet rendered null and void by the faithful conscience and the firm will of a woman. God send us more such women!"

125

The Bishop sounded a silver gong, and when his body-servant appeared, pointed to the handkerchief, damp and crumpled, upon the table.

"Dry this, Jasper," he said, "and bring me another somewhat larger. These dainty trifles cannot serve, when 'tears run down like a river.' Nay, look not distressed, my good fellow. I do but jest. Yonder wet Knight hath given me a shower-bath."

CHAPTER XXIX

THE VISION OF MARY ANTONY

On the afternoon following the Bishop's unexpected visit to the Nunnery, the Prioress elected to walk last in the procession to and from the Cathedral, placing Mother Sub-Prioress first. It was her custom occasionally to vary the order of procession. Sometimes she walked thirteenth, with twelve before, and twelve behind her.

She had at first inclined on this day, after her strenuous time with the Bishop, followed by the hour's ride upon Icon, not to go to Vespers.

Then her heart failed her, and she went. On these two afternoons—this and the morrow—Hugh would still be in the crypt. She should not so much as glance toward the pillar at the foot of the winding stairway leading to the clerestory; yet it would be sweet to feel him to be standing there as she passed; sweet to know that he heard the same sounds as fell upon her ear.

To-day, and again on the morrow, she might yield to this yearning for the comfort of his nearness; but never again, for Hugh would not return.

She had wondered whether she dared ask him, by the Bishop, on a given date once a year to attend High Mass in the Cathedral, so that she might know him to be under the same roof, worshipping, at the same moment, the same blessèd manifestation of the Divine Presence.

But almost at once she had dismissed the desire, realising that comfort such as this, could be comfort but to the heart of a woman, more likely torment to a man. Also that should his fancy incline him to seek companionship and consolation in the love of another, a yearly pilgrimage to Worcester for her sake, would stand in the way of his future happiness.

126

Walking last in that silent procession back to the Nunnery, the Prioress walked alone with her sadness. Her heart was heavy indeed.

She had angered her old friend, Symon of Worcester. After being infinitely patient, when he might well have had cause for wrath, he had suddenly taken a sterner tone, and departed in a certain aloofness, leaving her with the fear that she had lost him, also, beyond recall.

Thus she walked in loneliness and sorrow.

As she passed up the steps into the cloisters, she noted that Mary Antony was not in her accustomed place.

Slightly wondering, and half unconsciously explaining to herself that the old lay-sister had probably for some reason gone forward with the Sub-Prioress, the Prioress moved down the now empty passage and entered her own cell.

On the threshold she paused, astonished.

In front of the shrine of the Madonna, knelt Mary Antony in a kind of trance, hands clasped, eyes fixed, lips parted, the colour gone from her cheeks, yet a radiance upon her face, like the after-glow of a vision of exceeding glory.

She appeared to be wholly unconscious of the presence of the Prioress, who recovering from her first astonishment, closed the door, and coming forward laid her hand gently upon the old woman's shoulder.

Mary Antony's eyes remained fixed, but her lips moved incessantly. Bending over her, the Prioress could make out disjointed sentences.

"Gone! . . . But it was at our Lady's bidding. . . . Flown? Ah, gay little Knight of the Bloody Vest! Nay, it must have been the archangel Gabriel, or maybe Saint George, in shining armour. . . . How shall we live without the Reverend Mother? But the will of our blessèd Lady must be done."

"Antony!" said the Prioress. "Wake up, dear Antony! You are dreaming again. You are thinking of the robin and the pea. I have not gone from you; nor am I going. See! I am here."

She turned the old face about, and brought herself into Mary Antony's field of vision.

Slowly a light of recognition dawned in those fixed eyes; then came a cry, as of fear and of a great dismay; then a gasping sound, a clutching of the air. Mary Antony had fallen prone, before the shrine of the Madonna.

An hour later she lay upon her bed, whither they had carried her. She had recovered consciousness, and partaken of wine and bread.

The colour had returned to her cheeks, when the Prioress came in, dismissed the lay-sister in attendance, closed the door, and sat down beside the couch.

"Thou art better, dear Antony," said the Prioress. "They tell me

127

thy strength has returned, and this strange fainting is over. Thou must lie still yet awhile; but will it weary thee to speak?"

"Nay, Reverend Mother, I should dearly love to speak. My soul is full of wonder; yet to none saving to you, Reverend Mother, can I tell of that which I have seen."

"Tell me all, dear Antony," said the Prioress. "Sister Mary Rebecca says thy symptoms point to a Divine Vision."

Mary Antony chuckled. "For once Sister Mary Rebecca speaks the truth," she said. "Have patience with me, Reverend Mother, and I will tell you all."

The Prioress gently stroked the worn hands lying outside the coverlet.

Mary Antony looked very old in bed. Were it not for the bright twinkling eyes, she looked too old ever again to stand upon her feet. Yet how she still bustled upon those same old feet! How diligently she performed her own duties, and shewed to the other lay-sisters how they should have performed theirs!

Forty years ago, she had chosen her nook in the Convent burying-ground. She was even then, among the older members of the Community; yet most of those who saw her choose it, now lay in their own.

"She will outlive us all," said Mother Sub-Prioress one day, sourly; angered by some trick of Mary Antony's.

"She is like an ancient parrot," cried Sister Mary Rebecca, anxious to agree with Mother Sub-Prioress.

Which when Mary Antony heard, she chuckled, and snapped her fingers.

"Please God, I shall live long enough," she said, "to thrust Mother Sub-Prioress into a sackcloth shroud; also, to crack nuts upon the sepulchre of Sister Mary Rebecca."

But none of these remarks reached the Prioress. She loved the old lay-sister, knowing the aged body held a faithful and zealous heart, and a mind which, in its quaint simplicity, oft seemed to the Prioress like the mind of a little child—and of such is the Kingdom of Heaven.

"There is no need for patience, dear Antony," said the Prioress. "I can sit in stillness beside thee, until thy tale be fully told. Begin at the beginning."

The slanting rays of the late afternoon sun, piercing through the narrow window, fell in a golden band of light upon the folded hands, lighting up the aged face with an almost unearthly radiance.

"I was in the cloisters," began Mary Antony, "awaiting the return from Vespers of the holy Ladies.

"I go there betimes, because at that hour I am accustomed to hold converse with a little vain man in a red jerkin, who comes to see me, when he knows me to be alone. I tell him tales such as he never hears elsewhere. To-day I planned to tell him how the great Lord

Bishop, arriving unannounced, rode into the courtyard; and, seeing old Antony standing in the doorway, mistook her for the Reverend Mother. That was a great moment in the life of Mary Antony, and confers upon her added dignity.

"'So turn out thy toes, and make thy best bow, and behave thee as a little layman should behave in the presence of one who hath been mistaken for one holding so high an office in Holy Church.'

"Thus," explained Mary Antony, "had I planned to strike awe into the little red breast of that over-bold robin."

"And came the robin to the cloisters?" inquired the Prioress, presently, for Mary Antony lay upon her pillow laughing to herself, nodding and bowing, and making her fingers hop to and fro on the coverlet, as a bird might hop with toes out turned. Nor would she be recalled at once to the happenings of the afternoon.

"The great Lord Bishop did address me as 'worthy Mother,'" she remarked; "not 'Reverend Mother,' as we address our noble Prioress. And this has given me much food for thought. Is it better to be worthy and not reverend, or reverend and not worthy? Our large white sow, when she did contrive to have more little pigs in her litters, than ever our sows had before; and, after a long and fruitful life, furnished us with two excellent hams, a boar's head, and much bacon, was a worthy sow; but never was she reverend, not even when Mother Sub-Prioress pronounced the blessing over her face, much beautified by decoration— grand ivory tusks, and a lemon in her mouth! Never, in life, had she looked so fair; which is indeed, I believe, the case with many. Yet, for all her worthiness, she was not reverend. Also I have heard tell of a certain Prior, not many miles from here, who, borrowing money, never repays it; who oppresses the poor, driving them from the Priory gate; who maltreats the monks, and is kind unto none, saving unto himself. He—it seems—is reverend but not worthy. While thou, Master Redbreast, art certainly not reverend; the saints, and thine own conscience, alone know whether thou art worthy.

"This," explained Mary Antony, "was how I had planned to point a moral to that jaunty little worldling."

"They who are reverend must strive to be also worthy," said the Prioress; "while they who count themselves to be worthy, must think charitably of those to whom they owe reverence. Came the robin to thee in the cloisters, Antony?"

The old woman's manner changed. She fixed her eyes upon the Prioress, and spoke with an air of detachment and of mystery. The very simplicity of her language seemed at once to lift the strange tale she told, into sublimity.

"Aye, he came. But not for crumbs; not for cheese; not to gossip with old Antony.

"He stood upon the coping, looking at me with his bright eye.

"'Well, little vain man!' said I. But he moved not.

"'Well, Master Pieman,' I said, 'art come to spy on holy ladies?' But never a flutter, never a chirp, gave he.

"So grave and yet war-like was his aspect, that at length I said: 'Well, Knight of the Bloody Vest! Hast thou come to carry off again our noble Prioress?' Upon which, instantly, he lifted up his voice, and burst into song; then flew to the doorway, turning and chirping, as if asking me to follow.

"Greatly marvelling at this behaviour on the part of the little bird I love, I forthwith set out to follow him.

"Along the passage, on swift wing, he flew; in and out of the empty cells, as if in search of something.' Then, while I was yet some little way behind, he vanished into the Reverend Mother's cell, and came not forth again.

"Laughing to myself at such presumption, I followed, saying: 'Ha, thou Knight of the Bloody Vest! What doest thou there? The Reverend Mother is away. What seekest thou in her chamber, Knight of the Bloody Vest?'

"But, reaching the doorway, at that moment, I found myself struck dumb by what I saw.

"No robin was there, but a most splendid Knight, in shining armour, kneeled upon his knees before the shrine of our Lady. A blood-red cross was on his breast. His dark head was uplifted. On his noble face was a look of pleading and of prayer.

"Marvelling, but unafraid, I crept in, and kneeled behind that splendid Knight. The look of pleading upon his face, inclined me also to prayer. His lips moved, as I had seen at the first; but while I stood upon my feet, I could hear no words. As soon as I too kneeled, I heard the Knight saying: 'Give her to me! Give her to me!' And at last: 'Mother of God, send her to me! Take pity on a hungry heart, a lonely home, a desolate hearth, and send her to me!'"

Mary Antony paused, fixing her eyes upon the rosy strip of sky, seen through her narrow window. Absorbed in the recital of her vision, she appeared to have forgotten the presence of the Prioress. She paused; and there was silence in the cell, for the Prioress made no sound.

Presently the old voice went on, once more.

"When the splendid Knight said: 'Send her to me,' a most wondrous thing did happen.

"Our blessèd Lady, lifting her head, looked toward the door. Then raising her hand, she beckoned.

"No sooner did our Lady beckon, than I heard steps coming along the passage—that passage which I knew to be empty. The Knight heard them, also; for his heart began to beat so loudly that—kneeling behind—I could hear it.

"Our blessèd Lady smiled.

"Then—in through the doorway came the Reverend Mother,

130

walking with her head held high, and sunlight in her eyes, as I have ofttimes seen her walk in the garden in Springtime, when the birds are singing, and a scent of lilac is all around.

"She did not see old Mary Antony; but moving straight to where the Knight was kneeling, kneeled down beside him.

"Then the splendid Knight did hold out his hand. But the Reverend Mother's hands were clasped upon the cross at her breast, and she would not put her hand into the Knight's; but lifting her eyes to our Lady she said: 'Holy Mother of God, except thou thyself send me to him, I cannot go."

"And again the Knight said: 'Give her to me! Give her to me! Blessèd Virgin, give her to me!'

"And the tears ran down the face of old Antony, because both those noble hearts were wrung with anguish. Yet only the merry Babe, peeping over the two bowed heads, saw that old Antony was there.

"Then a wondrous thing did happen.

"Stooping from her marble throne our Lady leaned, and taking the Reverend Mother's hand in hers, placed it herself in the outstretched hand of the Knight.

"At once a sound like many chimes of silver bells filled the air, and a voice, so wonderful that I did fall upon my face to the floor, said:

"'TAKE HER; SHE HATH BEEN EVER THINE. I HAVE BUT KEPT HER FOR THEE.'"

"When I lifted my head once more, the Reverend Mother and the splendid Knight had risen. Heaven was in their eyes. Her hand was in his. His arm was around her.

"As I looked, they turned together, passed out through the doorway, and paced slowly down the passage.

"I heard their steps growing fainter and yet more faint, until they reached the cloisters. Then all was still."

"Then I heard other steps arriving. I still kneeled on, fearful to move; because those earthly steps were drowning the sound of the silver chimes which filled the air.

"Then—why, then I saw the Reverend Mother, returned—and returned alone.

"So I cried out, because she had left that splendid Knight. And, as I cried, the silver bells fell silent, all grew | dark around me, and I knew no more, until I woke up in mine own bed, tended by Sister Mary Rebecca, and Sister Teresa; with Abigail—noisy hussy!—helping to fetch and carry.

"But—when I close mine eyes—Ah, then! Yes, I hear again the sound of silver chimes. And some day I shall hear—shall hear again—that wondrous voice of—voice of tenderness, which said: 'Take her, she hath been ever—ever'—"

The old voice which had talked for so long a time, wavered, weakened, then of a sudden fell silent.

131

Mary Antony had dropped off to sleep.

Slowly the Prioress rose, feeling her way, as one blinded by too great a light.

She stood for some moments leaning against the doorpost, her hand upon the latch, watching the furrowed face upon the pillow, gently slumbering; still illumined by a halo of sunset light.

Then she opened the door, and passed out; closing it behind her.

As the Prioress closed the door, Mary Antony opened one eye.

Yea, verily! She was alone!

She raised herself upon the couch, listening intently.

Far away in the distance, she fancied she could hear the door of the Reverend Mother's chamber shut—yes!—and the turning of the key within the lock.

Then Mary Antony arose, tottered over to the crucifix, and, falling on her knees, lifted clasped hands to the dying Redeemer.

"O God," she said, "full well I know that to lie concerning holy things doth damn the soul forever. But the great Lord Bishop said she would thrust happiness from her with both hands, unless our Lady vouchsafed a vision. Gladly will I bear the endless torments of hell fires, that she may know fulness of joy and pleasures for evermore. But, oh, Son of Mary, by the sorrows of our Lady's heart, by the yearnings of her love, I ask that—once a year—I may come out—to sit just for one hour on my jasper seat, and see the Reverend Mother walk, between the great Lord Bishop and the splendid Knight, up the wide golden stair. And some day at last, O Saviour Christ, I ask it of Thy wounds, Thy dying love, Thy broken heart, may the sin of Mary Antony—her great sin, her sin of thus lying about holy things—be forgiven her, because—because—she loved"—

Old Mary Antony fell forward on the stones. This time, she had really swooned.

It took the combined efforts of Sister Teresa, Sister Mary Rebecca, and Mother Sub-Prioress, to bring her back once more to consciousness.

It added to their anxiety that they could not call the Reverend Mother, she having already sent word that she would not come to the evening meal, and must not be disturbed, as she purposed passing the night in prayer and vigil.

CHAPTER XXX

THE HARDER PART

Dawn broke—a silver rift in the purple sky—and presently stole, in pearly light, through the oriel window. Upon the Prioress's table, lay a beautifully executed copy of the Pope's mandate. Beside it, carefully pieced together, the torn fragments of the Bishop's copy.

Also, open upon the table, lay the Gregorian Sacramentary, and near to it strips of parchment upon which the Prioress had copied two of those ancient prayers, appending to each a careful translation.

These are the sixth century prayers which the Prioress had found comfort in copying and translating, during the long hours of her vigil.

O God, the Protector of all that trust in Thee, without Whom nothing is strong, nothing is holy; Increase and multiply upon us Thy mercy, that Thou being our ruler and guide, we may so pass through things temporal, that we finally lose not the things eternal; Grant this, O heavenly Father, for Jesus Christ's sake our Lord. Amen.

And on another strip of parchment:

O Lord, we beseech Thee mercifully to receive the prayers of Thy people who call upon Thee; and grant that they may both perceive and know what things they ought to do, and also may have grace and power faithfully to fulfil the same: through Jesus Christ our Lord. Amen.

Then, in that darkest hour before the dawn, she had opened the heavy clasps of an even older volume, and copied a short prayer from the Gelasian Sacramentary, under date A.D. 492.

Lighten our darkness, we beseech Thee O Lord, and my Thy great mercy defend us from all perils and dangers of this night; for the love of Thy only Son, our Saviour, Jesus Christ. Amen.

This appeared to have been copied last of all. The ink was still wet upon the parchment.

The candles had burned down to the sockets, and gone out. The Prioress's chair, pushed back from the table, was empty.

As the dawn crept in, it discovered her kneeling before the shrine of the Madonna, absorbed in prayer and meditation.

She had not yet taken her final decision as to the future; but her hesitation was now rather the slow, wondering, opening of the mind to accept an astounding fact, than any attempt to fight against it.

Not for one moment could she doubt that our Lady, in answer to Hugh's impassioned prayers, had chosen to make plain the Divine will, by means of this wonderful and most explicit vision to the aged lay-sister, Mary Antony.

When, having left Mary Antony, as she supposed, asleep, the Prioress had reached her own cell, her first adoring cry, as she prostrated herself before the shrine, had taken the form of the thanksgiving once offered by the Saviour: "I thank Thee, O Father, Lord of Heaven and earth, that Thou hast hid these things from the wise and prudent, and hast revealed them unto babes."

She and the Bishop had indeed been wise and prudent in their own estimation, as they discussed this difficult problem. Yet to them no clear light, no Divine vision, had been vouchsafed.

It was to this aged nun, the most simple—so thought the Prioress—the most humble, the most childlike in the community, that the revelation had been given.

The Prioress remembered the nosegay of weeds offered to our Lady; the games with peas; the childish pleasure in the society of the robin; all the many indications that second-childhood had gently come at the close of the long life of Mary Antony; just as the moon begins as a sickle turned one way and, after coming to the full, wanes at length to a sickle turned the other way; so, after ninety years of life's pilgrimage, Mary Antony was a little child again—and of such is the Kingdom of Heaven; and to such the Divine will is most easily revealed.

The Prioress was conscious that she and the Bishop—the wise and prudent—had so completely arrived at decisions, along the lines of their own points of view, that their minds were not ready to receive a Divine unveiling. But the simple, childlike mind of the old lay-sister, full only of humble faith and loving devotion, was ready; and to her the manifestation came.

No shade of doubt as to the genuineness of the vision entered the mind of the Prioress. She and the Bishop alone knew of the Knight's intrusion into the Nunnery, and of her interview with him in her cell.

Before going in search of the intruder, she had ordered Mary Antony to the kitchens; and disobedience to a command of the Reverend Mother, was a thing undreamed of in the Convent.

Afterwards, her anxiety lest any question should come up concerning the return of a twenty-first White Lady when but twenty had gone, was completely set at rest by that which had seemed to her old Antony's fortunate mistake in believing herself to have been mistaken.

In recounting the fictitious vision, with an almost uncanny cleverness, Mary Antony had described the Knight, not as he had appeared in the Prioress's cell, in tunic and hose, a simple dress of velvet and cloth, but in full panoply as a Knight-Crusader. The shining armour and the blood-red cross, fully in keeping with the vision, would have precluded the idea of an eye-witness of the actual scene, had such a thought unconsciously suggested itself to the Prioress.

As it was, it seemed beyond question that all the knowledge of Hugh shewn by the old lay-sister, of his person his attitude, his very words, could have come to her by Divine revelation alone. That being so, how could the Prioress presume to doubt the climax of the vision, when our blessèd Lady placed her hand in Hugh's, uttering the wondrous words: "Take her. She hath been ever thine. I have but kept her for thee."

Over and over the Prioress repeated these words; over and over she thanked our Lady for having vouchsafed so explicit a revelation. Yet was she distressed that her inmost spirit failed to respond, acclaiming the words as divine. She knew they must be divine, yet could not feel that they were so.

As dawn crept into the cell, she found herself repeating again and again "A sign, a sign! Thy will was hid from me; yet I accept its revelation through this babe. But I ask a sign which shall speak to mine own heart, also! A sign, a sign!"

She rose and opened wide the casement, not of the oriel window, but of one to the right of the group of the Virgin and child, and near by it.

She was worn out both in mind and body, yet could not bring herself to leave the shrine or to seek her couch.

She remembered the example of that reverend and holy man, Bishop Wulstan. She had lately been reading, in the Chronicles of Florence, the monk of Worcester, how "in his early life, when appointed to be chanter and treasurer of the Church, Wulstan embraced the opportunity of serving God with less restraint, giving himself up to a contemplative life, going into the church day and night to pray and read the Bible. So devoted was he to sacred vigils that not only would he keep himself awake during the night, but day and night also; and when the urgency of nature at last compelled him to sleep, he did not pamper his limbs by resting on a bed or coverings, but would lie down for a short time on one of the benches of the Church, resting his head on the book which he had used for praying or reading."

The Prioress chanced to have read this passage aloud, in the Refectory, two days before.

As she stood in the dawn light, overcome with sleep, yet unwilling to leave her vigil at the shrine, she remembered the example of this greatly revered Bishop of Worcester, "a man of great piety and dovelike simplicity, one beloved of God, and of the people whom he ruled in all things," dead just over a hundred years, yet ever living in the memory of all.

So, remembering his example, the Prioress went to her table, and shutting the clasps of her treasured Gregorian Sacramentary, placed it on the floor before the shrine of the Virgin.

Then, flinging her cloak upon the ground, and a silk covering over the book, she sank down, stretched her weary limbs upon the cloak and laid her head on the Sacramentary, trusting that some of the many sacred prayers therein contained would pass into her mind while she slept.

135

Yet still her spirit cried: "A sign, a sign! However slight, however small; a sign mine own heart can understand."

Whether she slept a few moments only or an hour, she could not tell. Yet she felt strangely rested, when she was awakened by the sound of a most heavenly song outpoured. It flooded her cell with liquid trills, as of little silver bells.

The Prioress opened her eyes, without stirring.

Sunlight streamed in through the open window; and lo, upon the marble hand of the Madonna, that very hand which, in the vision, had taken hers and placed it within Hugh's, stood Mary Antony's robin, that gay little Knight of the Bloody Vest, pouring forth so wonderful a song of praise, and love, and fulness of joy, that it seemed as if his little ruffling throat must burst with the rush of joyous melody.

The robin sang. Our Lady smiled. The Babe on her knees looked merry.

The Prioress lay watching, not daring to move; her head resting on the Sacramentary.

Then into her mind there came the suggestion of a test—a sign.

"If he fly around the chamber," she whispered, "my place is here. But if he fly straight out into the open, then doth our blessèd Lady bid me also to arise and go."

And, scarce had she so thought, when, with a last triumphant trill of joy, straight from our Lady's hand, like an arrow from the bow, the robin shot through the open casement, and out into the sunny, newly-awakened world beyond.

The Prioress rose, folded her cloak, placed the book back upon the table; then kneeled before the shrine, took off her cross of office, and laid it upon our Lady's hand, from whence the little bird had flown.

Then with bowed head, pale face, hands meekly crossed upon her breast, the Prioress knelt long in prayer.

The breeze of an early summer morn, blew in at the open window, and fanned her cheek.

In the garden without, the robin sang to his mate.

At length the Prioress rose, moving as one who walked in a strange dream, passed into the inner cell, and sought her couch.

The Bishop's prayer had been answered.

The Prioress had been given grace and strength to choose the harder part, believing the harder part to be, in very deed, God's will for her.

And, as she laid her head at last upon the pillow, a prayer from the Gregorian Sacramentary slipped into her mind, calming her to sleep, with its message of overruling power and eternal peace.

Almighty and everlasting God, Who dost govern all things in heaven and earth; Mercifully bear the supplications of Thy people, and grant us Thy peace, all the days of our life; through Jesus Christ our Lord. Amen.

CHAPTER XXXI

THE CALL OF THE CURLEW

For the last time, the Knight waited in the crypt.

The men-at-arms, having deposited their burden before the altar, leaned each against a pillar, stolid and unobservant, but ready to drop to their knees so soon as the chanting of Vespers should reach the crypt from the choir above.

The man upon the stretcher lay motionless, with bandaged head; yet there was an alert brightness in his eyes, and the turn of his head betokened one who listened. A cloak of dark blue, bordered with silver, covered him, as a pall.

Hugh d'Argent stood in the shadow of a pillar facing the narrow archway in the wall from which the winding stairs led up to the clerestory.

From this position he could also command a view of the steps leading up into the crypt from the underground way, and of the ground to be traversed by the White Ladies as they passed from the steps to the staircase in the wall.

Here the Knight kept his final vigil.

A strange buoyancy possessed him. He seemed to have left his despondence, like a heavy weight, at the bottom of the river. From the moment when, his breath almost exhausted, he had seen and grasped the Bishop's stone, bringing it in triumph to the surface, Hugh had felt sure he would win. Aye, even before Symon had flung the stone; when, in reply to the doubt cast by him on our Lady's smile, the Knight had said: "I keep my trust in prayer," a joyous confidence had then and there awakened within him. He had stretched out the right hand of his withered faith, and lo, it had proved strong and vital.

Yet as, in the heavy silence of the crypt, he heard the turning of the key in the lock, his heart stood still, and every emotion hung suspended, as the first veiled figure—shadowy and ghostlike—moved into view.

It was not she.

The Knight's pulses throbbed again. His heart pounded violently as, keeping their measured distances, nine, ten, eleven, white figures passed.

Then—twelfth: a tall nun, almost her height; yet not she.

Then—thirteenth: Oh, blessèd Virgin! Oh, saints of God! Mora! She, herself. Never could he fail to recognize her carriage, the regal poise of her head. However veiled, however shrouded, he could not be mistaken. It was Mora; and that she should be walking in this central

137

position meant that she might with comparative safety, step aside. Yet, even this—

But, at that moment, passing him, she turned her head, and for an instant her eyes met the eyes of the Knight looking out from the shadows.

Another moment and she had vanished up the winding stairway in the wall.

But that instant was enough. As her eyes met his, Hugh d'Argent knew that his betrothed was once more his own.

His heart ceased pounding; his pulses beat steadily.

The calm of a vast, glad certainty enfolded him; a joy beyond belief. Yet he knew now that he had been sure of it, ever since he came up from the depths of the Severn into the summer sunshine, grasping the white stone.

"I keep my trust in prayer. . . . Give her to me! Give her to me! Blessèd Virgin, give her to me! 'A sculptured smile'? Nay, my lord. I keep my trust in prayer!"

The solemn chanting of the monks, stole down from the distant choir. Vespers had begun.

The Knight strode to the altar, and knelt for some minutes, his hands clasped upon the crossed hilt of his sword.

Then he rose, and spoke in low tones to his men-at-arms.

"When a thrush calls, you will leave the crypt, and guard the entrance from without; allowing none, on any pretext, to pass within. When a blackbird whistles you will return, lift the stretcher, and pass with it, as heretofore, from the Cathedral to the hostel."

Next the Knight, returning to the altar, bent over the bandaged man upon the stretcher.

"Martin," he said, speaking very low, so that his trusted foster-brother alone could hear him. "All is well. Our pilgrimage is about to end, as we have hoped, in a great recovery and restoration. When the call of a curlew sounds, leap from the stretcher, leave the bandages beside it; go to the entrance, guarding it from within; but turn not thy head this way, until a blackbird whistles; upon which lose thyself among the pillars, letting no man see thee, until we have passed out. After which, make thy way out, as best thou canst, and join me at the hostel, entering by the garden and window, without letting thyself be seen in the courtyard."

The keen eyes below the bandage, smiled assent.

Stooping, the Knight lifted the cloak, fastened it to his left shoulder, and drew it around him, holding the greater part of it in many folds in his right hand. Then he moved back into the shadow of the pillar.

Above, the monks sang Nunc Dimittis.

By and by the voices fell silent.

Vespers were over.

Careful, shuffling feet were coming down the stairs within the wall.

One by one the white figures reappeared.

The Knight stood back, rigid, holding his breath.

As each nun stepped from the archway in the wall, on to the floor of the crypt, and moved toward the steps leading down to the subterranean way, she passed from the view of the nun following her, who was still one turn up the staircase. It was upon this the Knight had counted, when he laid his plains.

Six

Seven

Eight

Blessèd Saint Joseph! How slowly they walked!

Nine

Ten

Eleven

The Knight gripped the cloak and moved a step further back into the shadow.

Twelve

Were all the pillars rocking? Was the great new Cathedral coming down upon his head?

Thirteen

The Prioress was beside him in the shadow.

She had stepped aside.

The twelfth White Lady was moving on, her back toward them.

The fourteenth was shuffling down, but had not yet appeared.

Hugh slipped his left arm about the Prioress, holding her close to him; then flung the folds of the cloak completely around her, and over his left shoulder, pressing her head down upon his breast.

Thus they stood, motionless; her face hidden, his eyes bent upon the narrow archway in the wall.

The fourteenth White Lady appeared; evidently noted a wider gap than she expected between herself and the distant figure almost at the steps, and hastened forward.

The fifteenth also hastened.

The sixteenth chanced to have taken the stairs more quickly and, appearing almost immediately, noticed no gap.

Seventeen

Eighteen

Nineteen

Twenty

Not one had turned her head in the direction of the pillar. The procession was moving, with stately tread, along its accustomed way.

A delicious sense of security enveloped Hugh d'Argent.

The woman he loved was in his arms; she was his to shield, to guard, to hold for evermore.

139

Twenty-one

Twenty-two

She had come to him—come to him of her own free will. Holding her thus, he remembered those wondrous moments at the entrance to the crypt. How hard it had been to loose her and leave her. Yet how glad he now was that he had done so.

Twenty-three

Twenty-four

When all these white figures are gone, safely started on their mile-long walk, the door shut and locked behind them—then he will fold back the cloak, turn her sweet face up to his, and lay his lips on hers.

Twenty-five

Praise the holy saints! The last! But what an old ferret!

Yes; Mother Sub-Prioress gave the Knight a moment of alarm. She peered to right and left. Almost she saw the glint of the silver on the blue. Almost, yet not quite.

Sniffing, she passed on, walking as if her feet were angry, each with the other for being before it. She tweaked at her veil, as she turned and descended the steps.

Hugh glowed and thrilled from head to foot.

At last!

Almost—

The sound of a closing door.

Slowly a key turned, grated in the lock, and was withdrawn.

Then—silence.

But at sound of the turning key, the woman in his arms shivered, the slow, cold shudder of a soul in pain; and suddenly he knew that in coming to him she had chosen that which now seemed to her the harder part.

With the first revulsion of feeling occasioned by this knowledge, came a strong impulse to put her from him, to leap down the stairway, force open the heavy door, thrust her into the passage leading to her Nunnery, and shut the door upon her; then go out himself into the world to seek, in one wild search, every possible form of sin and revelry.

But this ungoverned impulse lasted but for the moment in which his passionate joy, recoiling upon himself, struck him a blinding, a bewildering blow.

In ten seconds he had recovered. His arms tightened more securely around her.

She had come to him. Whatever complex emotions might now be stirring within her, this fact was beyond question. Also, she had come of her own free will. The foot which had dared to stamp upon the torn fragments of the Pope's mandate, had, with an equal courage, stepped

140

aside from the way of convention and had brought her within the compass of his arms.

He could not put her from him. She was his to hold and keep. But she was his also to shield and guard; aye, to shield not from outward dangers only, but from anything in himself which might cause her pain or perplexity, thus making more difficult her noble act of self-surrender.

Words spoken by the Bishop, in the banqueting hall, came back to him with fuller significance.

A joy arose within him, deeper far than the rapture of passion; the joy of a faithful patience, of a strong man's mastery over the strongest thing in himself, of a lover's comprehension, by sure instinct, of that which no words, however clear and forcible, could have succeeded in making plain.

His love arose, a kingly thing, crowned by her trust in him.

As he folded back the cloak, he stood with eyes uplifted to the arched roof above his head. And the vision he saw, in the dim pearly light, was a vision of the Madonna in his home.

The shelter of the cloak removed, the Prioress looked around with startled eyes, full of an unspeakable shrinking; then upward to the face of her lover, and saw it transfigured by the light of holy purpose and of a great resolve.

But, even as she looked, he took his arm from about her, stepped a pace forward, leaving her in the shadow, and whistled thrice the Do-it-now call of the thrush.

Instantly the men-at-arms leapt to their feet, and making quickly for the entrance to the Cathedral from the crypt, stood to hold it from without, against all comers.

As their running feet rang on the steps, softly there sounded through the crypt the plaintive call of the curlew.

The man lying upon the stretcher rose, leaving his bandages behind; and, without glancing to right or left, passed quickly in and out amongst the forest of columns, and was lost to view. The entrance he had to guard from within, was out of sight of the altar. To all intents and purposes, the two who still stood motionless in the shadow, were now alone.

Then the Knight turned to the Prioress, took her right hand with his left, and led her forward to the altar.

There he loosed her hand as they knelt side by side; he clasping his upon the crossed hilt of his sword; she crossing hers upon her breast.

Presently the Prioress drew the marriage ring from the third finger of her left hand, and gave it to the Knight.

Divining her desire, he rose, laid the ring upon the altar, then knelt again.

141

Then rising, he took the ring, kissed it reverently, and slipped it upon the little finger of his own left hand.

The sad eyes of the Prioress, watching him, said to this neither "yea" nor "nay."

Rising she waited meekly to know his will for her. The Knight, the blue cloak over his arm, turned to the stretcher, picked up the bandages, then, spoke, very low, without looking at the Prioress.

"Lay thyself down thereon," he said. "I grieve to ask it of thee, Mora; but there is no other way of taking thee hence, unobserved."

The Prioress took two steps forward, and stood beside the stretcher.

It was many years since she had lain in any human presence. Standing, walking, sitting, kneeling, she had been seen by the nuns; but lying—never.

Though her cross of office and sacred ring were gone, her dignity and authority seemed still to belong to her while she stood, stately and tall, upon her feet.

She hesitated. The apologetic tone the Knight had used, seemed warrant for her hesitancy, and rendered compliance more difficult.

Each moment it became more impossible to place herself upon the stretcher.

"Lie down," said the Knight, sternly.

At the curt word of command, the Prioress shuddered again; but, without a word, she laid herself down upon the stretcher, closing her eyes, and crossing her hands upon her breast. So white she was, so still, so rigid; as Hugh d'Argent, the bandages in his hand, stood looking down upon her, she seemed the marble effigy of a recumbent Prioress, graven upon a tomb; save that, as the Knight looked upon that beautiful, proud face, two burning tears forced their way from beneath the closed lids and rolled helplessly down the pale cheeks.

She did not see the look of tender compunction, of adoring love, in Hugh's eyes.

Her shame, her utter humiliation, seemed complete.

Not when she took off her jewelled cross, and placed it upon our Lady's hand; not when she stepped aside and allowed herself to be hidden by the cloak; not even when she removed her ring and handed it to Hugh, did she cease to be Prioress of the White Ladies of Worcester; but when she laid herself down before the shrine of Saint Oswald, full length upon the stretcher, at her lover's feet.

Hugh stooped, and hid the bandages beside her. He could not bring himself to touch or to disguise that lovely head. Instead, he covered her completely with the cloak; saying, in deep tones of infinite tenderness:

"Our Lady be with thee. It will not be for long."

Then, shrill through the silent crypt, rang the dear call of the blackbird.

142

CHAPTER XXXII

A GREAT RECOVERY AND RESTORATION

Symon, Bishop of Worcester, attended by his Chaplain, chanced to be walking through the Precincts on his way from the Priory to the Palace, just as the men-at-arms bearing the stretcher came through the great door of the Cathedral.

Father Benedict, cowled, and robed completely in black, a head and shoulders taller than the Bishop, walked behind him, a somewhat sinister figure.

The Bishop stopped. "Precede me to the Palace, Father Benedict," he said. "I wish to have speech with yonder Knight who, I think, comes this way."

The Chaplain stood still, made deep obeisance, jerked his cowl more closely over his face, and strode away.

The Bishop waited, a radiant figure, in the afternoon sunshine. His silken cassock, his silvery hair, his blue eyes, so vivid and searching, not only made a spot on which light concentrated, but almost seemed themselves to give forth light.

The steady tramp of the men-at-arms drew nearer.

Hugh d'Argent walked beside the stretcher, head erect, eyes shining, his hand upon the hilt of his sword.

When the Bishop saw the face of the Knight, he moved to meet the little procession as it approached.

He held up his hand, and the men-at-arms halted.

"Good-day to you, Sir Hugh," said the Bishop. "Hath your pilgrimage to the shrine of the blessèd Saint Oswald worked the recovery you hoped?"

"Aye, my lord," replied the Knight, "a great recovery and restoration. We start for Warwick in an hour's time."

"Wonderful!" said the Bishop. "Our Lady and the holy Saint be praised! But you are wise to keep the patient well covered. However complete the restoration, great care is required at first, and over-exertion must be avoided."

"Your blessing for the patient, Reverend Father," said the Knight, uncovering.

The Bishop moved nearer. He laid his hand upon the form beneath the blue and silver cloak.

"Benedictio Domini sit vobiscum," he said. Then added, in a lower tone: "Be not afraid, neither be thou dismayed. . . . Go in peace."

The two men who loved the Prioress, looked steadily at one another.

The men-at-arms moved forward with their burden.

The Knight smiled as he walked on beside the stretcher.

The Bishop hastened to the Palace.

It was the Knight who had smiled, and there was glory in his eyes, and triumph in the squaring of his broad shoulders, the swing of his stride, and the proud poise of his head.

The Bishop was white to the lips. His hands trembled as he walked.

He feared—he feared sorely—this that they had accomplished.

It was one thing to theorize, to speculate, to advise, when the Prioress was safe in her Nunnery. It was quite another, to know that she was being carried through the streets of Worcester, helpless, upon a stretcher; that when that blue pall was lifted, she would find herself in a hostel, alone with her lover, surrounded by men, not a woman within call.

The heart of a nun was a thing well known to the Bishop, and he trembled at thought of this, which he had helped to bring about.

Also he marvelled greatly that the Prioress should have changed her mind; and he sought in vain to conjecture the cause of that change.

Arrived in the courtyard of the Palace, he called for Brother Philip.

"Saddle me Shulamite," he said. "Also mount Jasper on our fastest nag, with saddle-bags. We ride to Warwick; and must start within a quarter of an hour."

A portion of that time the Bishop spent writing in the library.

When he was mounted, he stooped from the saddle and spoke to Brother Philip.

"Philip," he said, "a very noble lady, betrothed to Sir Hugh d'Argent, has just arrived at the Star hostel, where for some days he has awaited her. She rides with the Knight forthwith to Warwick, where they will join me at the Castle. It is my wish to lend Iconoklastes to the lady. Therefore I desire thee to saddle the palfrey precisely as he was saddled when he went to the Convent of the White Ladies for their pleasuring and play. Lead him, without delay, to the hostel; deliver him over to the men-at-arms of Sir Hugh d'Argent, and see that they hand this letter at once to the Knight, that he may give it to his lady. Lose not a moment, my good Philip. Look to see me return to-morrow."

The Bishop gathered up the reins, and started out, at a brisk pace, for the Warwick road.

The letter he had intrusted to Brother Philip, sealed with his own signet, was addressed to Sir Hugh d'Argent. But within was written:

Will the Countess of Norelle be pleased to accept of the palfrey Iconoklastes as a marriage gift from her old friend Symon Wygorn.

144

CHAPTER XXXIII

MARY ANTONY HOLDS THE FORT

Mary Antony awaited in the cloisters the return of the White Ladies from Vespers.

The old lay-sister was not in the mood for gay chatter to the robin, nor even for quaint converse with herself.

She sat upon the stone seat, looking very frail, and wearing a wistful expression, quite unlike her usual alert demeanour.

As she sat, she slowly dropped the twenty-five peas from her right hand, to her left, and back again.

A wonderful thing had happened on that afternoon, just before the White Ladies set forth to the Cathedral.

All were assembling in the cloisters, when word arrived that the Reverend Mother wished to speak, in her cell, with Sister Mary Antony.

Hastening thither she found the Reverend Mother standing, very white and silent, very calm and steadfast, looking out from the oriel window.

At first she did not turn; and Mary Antony stood waiting, just within the doorway.

Then she turned, and said: "Ah, dear Antony!" in tones which thrilled the heart of the old lay-sister.

"Come hither, Antony," she said; and even as she said it, moved to meet her.

A few simple instructions she gave, concerning matters in the Refectory and kitchen. Then said: "Now I must go. The nuns wait."

Then of a sudden she put her arms about the old lay-sister.

"Good-bye, my Antony," she said. "Thy love and devotion have been very precious to me. The Presence of the Lord abide with thee in blessing, while we are gone."

And, stooping, she kissed her gently on the brow; then passed from the cell.

Mary Antony stood as one that dreamed.

It was so many years since any touch of tenderness had reached her.

And now—those gracious arms around her; those serene eyes looking upon her with love in their regard, and a something more, which her old heart failed to fathom; those lips, whose every word of command she and the whole Community hastened to obey, leaving a kiss upon her brow!

Long after the White Ladies had formed into procession and left the cloisters, Mary Antony stood as one that dreamed. Then, remembering her duties, she hurried to the cloisters, but found them

145

empty; down the steps to the crypt passage; the door was locked on the inside; the key gone.

The procession had started, and Mary Antony had failed to be at her post. The White Ladies had departed uncounted. Mary Antony had not been there to count them.

Never before had the Reverend Mother sent for her when she should have been on duty elsewhere.

Hastening to remedy her failure, Mary Antony drew the bag of peas from her wallet, opened it, and hurrying from cell to cell, took out a pea at each, as she verified its emptiness; until five-and-twenty peas lay in her hand.

So now she waited, her error repaired; yet ever with her—then, as she ran, and now, as she waited—she felt the benediction of the Reverend Mother's kiss, the sense of her encircling arms, the wonder of her gracious words.

"The Presence of the Lord abide with thee in blessing."

Yes, a heavenly calm was in the cloisters. The Devil had stayed away. Heaven seemed very near. Even that little vain man, the robin, appeared to be busy elsewhere. Mary Antony was quite alone.

"While we are gone." But they would not now be long. Mary Antony could tell by the shadows on the grass, and the slant of the sunshine through a certain arch, that the hour of return drew near.

She would kneel beside the topmost step, and see the Reverend Mother pass; she would look up at that serene face which had melted into tenderness; would see the firm line of those beautiful lips—

Suddenly Mary Antony knew that she would not be able to look. Not just yet could she bear to see the Reverend Mother's countenance, without that expression of wonderful tenderness. And even as she realised this, the key grated in the lock below.

Taking up her position at the top of the steps, the five-and-twenty peas in her right hand, Mary Antony quickly made up her mind. She could not lift her eyes to the Reverend Mother's face. She would count the passing feet.

The young lay-sister who carried the light, stumped up the steps, and set down the lantern with a clatter. She plumped on to her knees opposite to Mary Antony.

"Sister Mary Rebecca leads to-day," she chanted in a low voice, "and all the way hath stepped upon my heels."

But Mary Antony took no notice of this information, which, at any other time, would have delighted her.

Head bowed, eyes on the ground, she awaited the passing feet.

They came, moving slow and sedate.

They passed—stepping two by two, out of her range of vision; moving along the cloister, dying away in the distance.

All had passed.

Nay! Not all? Another comes! Surely, another comes?

146

Sister Abigail, lifting the lantern, rose up noisily.

"What wait you for, Sister Antony? The holy Ladies have by now entered their cells."

Mary Antony lifted startled eyes.

The golden bars of sunlight fell across an empty cloister.

A few white figures in the passage, seen in the distance through the open door, were vanishing, one by one, into their cells.

Mary Antony covered her dismay with indignation.

"Be off, thou impudent hussy! Hold thy noisy tongue and hang thy rattling lantern on a nail; or, better still, hold thy lantern, and hang thyself, holding it, upon the nail. If I am piously minded to pray here until sunset, that is no concern of thine. Be off, I say!"

Left alone, Mary Antony slowly opened her right hand, and peered into the palm.

One pea lay within it.

She went over to the seat and counted, with trembling fingers, the peas from her left hand.

Twenty-four! One holy Lady had therefore not returned. This must be reported at once to the Reverend Mother. In her excitement, Mary Antony forgot the emotion which had so recently possessed her.

Bustling down the steps, she drew the key from the door, paused one moment to peep into the dank darkness, listening for running footsteps or a voice that called; then closed the door, locked it, drew forth the key, and hurried to the Reverend Mother's cell.

The door stood ajar, just as she had left it.

She knocked, but entered without waiting to be bidden, crying: "Oh, Reverend Mother! Twenty-five holy Ladies went to Vespers, and but twenty-four have"—

Then her voice died away into silence.

The Reverend Mother's cell was empty.

Stock-still stood Mary Antony, while her world crumbled from beneath her old feet and her heaven rolled itself up like a scroll, from over her head, and departed.

The Reverend Mother's cell was empty.

It was the Reverend Mother who had not returned.

"Good-bye, my Antony. The Presence of the Lord abide with thee in blessing, while we are gone." Ah, gone! Never to return!

Once again the old lay-sister stood as one that dreamed; but this time instead of beatific joy, there was a forlorn pathos in the dreaming.

Presently a door opened, and a step sounded, far away in the passage beyond the Refectory stairs.

Instantly a look of cunning and determination replaced the helpless dismay on the old face. She quickly closed the cell door, hung up the crypt key in its accustomed place; then kneeling before the shrine of the Madonna: "Blessèd Virgin," she prayed, with clasped

147

hands uplifted; "be pleased to sharpen once again the wits of old Mary Antony."

Rising, she found the key of the Reverend Mother's cell, passed out, closing the door behind her; locked it, and slipped the key into her wallet.

The passage was empty. All the nuns were spending in prayer and meditation the time until the Refectory bell should ring.

Mary Antony appeared in the kitchen, only a few minutes later than usual.

"Prepare you the evening meal," she said to her subordinates. "I care not what the holy Ladies feed upon this even, nor how badly it be served. Reverend Mother again elects to spend the night in prayer and fasting. So Mother Sub-Prioress will spit out a curse upon the viands; or Sister Mary Rebecca will miaul over them like an old cat that sees a tom in every shadow, though all toms have long since fled at her approach. Serve at the usual hour; and let Abigail ring the Refectory bell. I am otherwise employed. And remember. Reverend Mother is on no account to be disturbed."

The porteress, at the gate, jumped well-nigh out of her skin when, turning, she found Mary Antony at her elbow.

"Beshrew me, Sister Antony!" she exclaimed. "Wherefore"—

"Whist!" said Mary Antony. "Speak not so loud. Now listen, Mary Mark. Saw you the great Lord Bishop yesterday, a-walking with Mary Antony? Ha, ha! Yea, verily! 'Worthy Mother,' his lordship called me. 'Worthy Mother,' with his hand upon his heart. And into the gardens he walked with Mary Antony. Wherefore, you ask? Wherefore should the great Lord Bishop walk in the Convent garden with an old lay-sister, who ceased to be a comely wench more than half a century ago? Because, Sister Mark, if you needs must know, the Lord Bishop is full of anxious fears for the Reverend Mother, and knoweth that Mary Antony, old though she be, is able to tend and watch over her. The Lord Bishop and the Worthy Mother both fear that the Reverend Mother fasts too often, and spends too many hours in vigil. The Reverend Father has therefore deputed the Worthy Mother to watch in this matter, and to let him know at once if the Reverend Mother imperils her health again, by too lengthy a fast or vigil. And, lo! this very day, the Reverend Mother purposes not coming to the evening meal, and intends spending the whole night in prayer and vigil, before our Lady's shrine. Therefore the Worthy Mother—I, myself—must start at once to fetch the great Lord Bishop; and you, Sister Mary Mark, must open the gate and let me be gone."

The porteress gazed, round-eyed and amazed.

"Nay, Sister Mary Antony, that can I not, without an order from the Reverend Mother herself. And even then, you could not walk so far as to the Lord Bishop's Palace. I doubt if you would even reach the Fore-gate."

"That I should, and shall!" cried Mary Antony. "And, if my old legs fail me, many a gallant will dismount and offer me his horse. Thus in fine style shall I ride into Worcester city. Didst thou not see me bestride the Lord Bishop's white palfrey on Play Day?"

Sister Mary Mark broke into laughter.

"Aye," she said, "my sides have but lately ceased aching. I pray you, Sister Antony, call not that sight again into my mind."

"Then open the door, Mary Mark, and let me go."

"Nay, that I dare not do."

"Then, if I fail to do as bidden by the great Lord Bishop, I shall tell his lordship that thou, and thine obstinacy, stood in the way of the fulfilment of my purpose."

The porteress wavered.

"Bring me leave from the Reverend Mother, Sister Antony."

"Nay, that can I not," said Mary Antony, "as any fool might see, when I go without the Reverend Mother's knowledge to report to the Lord Bishop by his private command. Even the Reverend Mother herself obeys the commands of the Lord Bishop."

Sister Mary Mark hesitated. She certainly had seen the Lord Bishop pass under the rose-arch, and enter the garden, in close converse with Sister Mary Antony. Yet her trust at the gate was given to her by the Reverend Mother.

"See here, Mary Mark," said Sister Antony. "I must send a message forthwith to Mother Sub-Prioress. You shall take it, leaving me in charge of the gate, as often I am left, by order of the Reverend Mother, when you are bidden elsewhere. If, on your return—and you need not to hurry—you find me gone, none can blame you. Yet when the Lord Bishop rides in at sunset, he will give you his blessing and, like enough, something besides."

Mary Mark's hesitation vanished.

"I will take your message, Sister Antony," she said meekly.

"Go, by way of the kitchens and the Refectory stairs, to the cell of Mother Sub-Prioress. Say that the Reverend Mother purposes passing the night in prayer and vigil, will not come to the evening meal, and desires Mother Sub-Prioress to take her place. Also that for no cause whatever is the Reverend Mother to be disturbed."

Sister Mary Mark, being thus given a legitimate reason for leaving her post and gaining the Bishop's favour without giving cause for displeasure to the Prioress, departed, by way of the kitchens, to carry Mary Antony's message.

No sooner was she out of sight, than Mary Antony seized the key, unlocked the great doors, pulled them apart, and left them standing ajar, the key in the lock; then hastened back across the courtyard, passed under the rose-arch, and creeping beneath the shelter of the yew hedge, reached the steps up to the cloisters; slipped unobserved through the cloister door, and up the empty passage; unlocked the

Reverend Mother's cell, entered it, and softly closed and locked the door behind her.

Then—in order to make it impossible to yield to any temptation to open the door—she withdrew the key, and flung it through the open window, far out into the shrubbery.

Thus did Mary Antony prepare to hold the fort, until the coming of the Bishop.

CHAPTER XXXIV

MORA DE NORELLE

Symon, Bishop of Worcester, chid himself for restlessness. Surely for once his mind had lost control of his limbs.

No sooner did he decide to walk the smooth lawns around the Castle, than he found himself mounting to the battlements; and now, though he had installed himself for greatly needed repose in a deep seat in the hall chamber, yet here he was, pacing the floor, or moving from one window to another.

By dint of hard riding he had reached Warwick while the sun, though already dipped beneath the horizon, still flecked the sky with rosy clouds, and spread a golden mantle over the west.

The lord of the Castle was away, in attendance on the King; but all was in readiness for the arrival of the Bishop, and great preparations had been made for the reception of Sir Hugh d'Argent. His people, having left Worcester early that morning, were about in the courtyard, as the Bishop rode in.

As he passed through the doorway, an elderly woman, buxom, comely, and of motherly aspect, whom he easily divined to be the tire-woman of whom the Knight had spoken, came forward to meet him.

"Good my lord," she said, her eagerness allowing of scant ceremony, "comes Sir Hugh d'Argent hither this night?"

"Aye," replied the Bishop, looking with kindly eyes upon Mora's old nurse. "Within two hours, he should be here."

"Comes he alone, my lord?" asked Mistress Deborah.

"Nay," replied the Bishop, "the Countess of Norelle, a very noble lady to whom the Knight is betrothed, rides hither with him."

"The saints be praised!" exclaimed the old woman, and turned away to hide her tears.

Whilst his body-servant prepared a bath and laid out his robes, the Bishop mounted to the ramparts and watched the gold fade in the west. He glanced at the river below, threading its way through the pasture land; at the billowy masses of trees; at the gay parterre, bright with summer flowers. Then he looked long in the direction of the city from which he had come.

During his strenuous ride, the slow tramp of the men-at-arms, had sounded continually in his ears; the outline of that helpless figure, lying at full length upon the stretcher, had been ever before his eyes.

He could not picture the arrival at the hostel, the removal of the covering, the uprising of the Prioress to face life anew, enfolded in the arms of her lover.

As in a weary dream, in which the mind can make no headway, but returns again and yet again to the point of distress, so, during the entire ride, the Bishop had followed that stretcher through the streets of Worcester city, until it seemed to him as if, before the pall was lifted, the long-limbed, graceful form beneath it would have stiffened in death.

"A corpse for a bride! A corpse for a bride!" the hoofs of the black mare Shulamite had seemed to beat out upon the road. "Alas, poor Knight! A corpse for a bride!"

The Bishop came down from the battlements.

When he left his chamber an hour later, he had donned those crimson robes which he wore on the evening when the Knight supped with him at the Palace.

As he paced up and down the lawns, the gold cross at his breast gleamed in the evening light.

A night-hawk, flying high overhead and looking downward as it flew, might have supposed that a great scarlet poppy had left its clump in the flower-beds, and was promenading on the turf.

A steward came out to ask when it would please the Lord Bishop to sup.

To the hovering hawk, a blackbird seemed to have hopped out, confronting and arresting the promenading poppy.

The Bishop said he would await the arrival of Sir Hugh; but he turned and followed the man into the Castle.

And now he sat in the great hall chamber.

Two hours had passed since his arrival.

Unless something unforeseen had occurred the Knight's cavalcade must be here before long. He had planned to start within the hour; and, though the Bishop had ridden fast, they could scarcely have taken more than an hour longer to do the distance.

But supposing the Prioress had faltered at the last, and had besought to be returned to the Nunnery? Would the chivalry of the Knight have stood such a test? And, having left in secret, how could she return openly? Would the way through the crypt be possible?

151

The Bishop began to wish that he had ridden to the Star hostel and awaited developments there, instead of hastening on before.

The hall chamber was in the centre of the Castle. Its casements looked out upon the gardens. Thus it came about that he did not hear a cavalcade ride into the courtyard. He did not hear the shouting of the men, the ring of hoofs on the paving stones, the champing of horses.

He sat in a great carved chair beside the fireplace in the hall chamber, forcing himself to stillness, yet tormented by anxiety; half minded to order a fresh horse and to ride back to Worcester.

Suddenly, without any warning, the door, leading from the ante-chamber at the further end of the hall, opened.

Framed in the doorway appeared a vision, which for a moment led Symon of Worcester to question whether he dreamed, so beautiful beyond belief was the woman in a green riding-dress, looking at him with starry eyes, her cheeks aglow, a veil of golden hair falling about her shoulders.

Oh, Mora, child of delight! Has the exquisite promise of thy girlhood indeed fulfilled itself thus? Have the years changed thee so little—-and yet so greatly?

"The captive exile hasteneth"; exile, long ago, for thy sake; seeking to be free, yet captive still, caught once and forever in the meshes of that golden hair.

Oh, Mora, child of delight! Must all this planning for thy full development and perfecting of joy, involve the poignant anguish of thus seeing thee again?

Symon of Worcester rose and stood, a noble figure in crimson and gold, at the top of the hall. But for the silver moonlight of his hair, he might have been a man in his prime—so erect was his carriage, so keen and bright were his eyes.

The tall woman in the doorway gave a little cry; then moved quickly forward.

"You?" she said. "You! The priest who is to wed us? You!"

He stood his ground, awaiting her approach.

"Yes, I," he said; "I."

Half-way across the hall, she paused.

"No," she said, as if to herself. "I dream. It is not Father Gervaise. It is the Bishop."

She drew nearer.

Earnestly he looked upon her, striving to see in her the Prioress of Whytstone—the friend of all these happy, peaceful, blessèd years.

But the Prioress had vanished.

Mora de Norelle stood before him, taller by half a head than he, flushed by long galloping in the night breeze; nerves strung to breaking point; eyes bright with the great unrest of a headlong leap into a new world. Yet the firm sweet lips were there, unchanged; and, even as he marked them, they quivered and parted.

152

"Reverend Father," she said, "I have chosen, even as you prayed I might do, the harder part." She flung aside the riding-whip she carried; and folding her hands, held them up before him. "For Christ's sake, my Lord Bishop, pray for me!"

He took those folded hands in his, gently parted them, and held them against the cross upon his heart.

"You have chosen rightly, my child," he said; "we will pray that grace and strength may be vouchsafed you, so that you may continue, without faltering, along the pathway of this fresh vocation."

She looked at him with searching gaze. The kind and gentle eyes of the Bishop met hers without wavering; also without any trace of the fire—the keen brightness—which had startled her as she stood in the doorway.

"Reverend Father," she said, and there was a strange note of bewildered question in her voice: "I pray you, tell me what you bid penitents to remember as they kneel in prayer before the crucifix?"

The Bishop looked full into those starry grey eyes bent upon him, and his own did not falter. His mild voice took on a shade of sternness as befitted the solemn subject of her question.

"I tell them, my daughter, to remember, the sacred Wounds that bled and the Heart that broke for them."

She drew her hands from beneath his, and stepped back a pace.

"The Heart that broke?" she said. "That broke? Do hearts break?" she cried. "Nay, rather, they turn to stone." She laughed wildly, then caught her breath. The Knight had entered the hall.

With free, glad step, and head uplifted, Hugh d'Argent came to them, where they stood.

"My Lord Bishop," he said, "you have been too good to us. I sent Mora on alone that she might find you here, not telling her who was the prelate who had so graciously offered to wed us, knowing how much it would mean to her that it should be you, Reverend Father."

"Gladly am I here for that purpose, my son," replied the Bishop, "having as you know, the leave and sanction of His Holiness for so doing. Shall we proceed at once to the chapel, or do you plan first to sup?"

"Nay, Father," said the Knight. "My betrothed has ridden far and needs food first, and then a good night's rest. If it will not too much delay your return to Worcester, I would pray you to wed us in the morning."

Knowing how determined Hugh had been, in laying his plans, to be wed at once on reaching Warwick, the Bishop looked up quickly, wishing to understand what had wrought this change.

He saw on the Knight's face that look of radiant peace which the Prioress had seen, when first the cloak was turned back in the crypt; and the Bishop, having passed that way himself, knew that to Hugh had come the revelation which comes but to the true, lover—the deepest of

153

all joys, that of putting himself on one side, and of thinking, first and only, of the welfare of the belovèd.

And seeing this, the Bishop let go his fears, and in his heart thanked God.

"It is well planned, Hugh," he said. "I am here until the morning."

At which the Knight turning, strode quickly to the door, and beckoned.

Then back he came, leading by the hand the buxom, motherly old dame, seen on arrival by the Bishop. Who, when the Lady Mora saw, she gave a cry, and ran to meet her.

"Debbie!" she cried, "Oh, Debbie! Let us go home!"

And with that the tension broke all on a sudden, and with her old nurse's arms around her, she sobbed on the faithful bosom which had been the refuge of her childhood's woes.

"There, my pretty!" said Deborah, as best she could for her own sobs. "There, there! We are at home, now we are together. Come and see the chamber in which we shall sleep, just as we slept long years ago, when you were a babe, my dear."

So, with her old nurse's arms about her, she, who had come in so proudly, went gently out in a soft mist of tears.

The Bishop turned away.

"Love never faileth," he murmured, half aloud.

Hugh turned with him, and laughed; but in his laughter there was no vexation, no bitterness, no unrest. It was the happy laugh of a heart aglow with a hope amounting to certainty.

"There were two of us the other night, my dear lord," he said; "but now old Debbie has appeared, methinks there are three!"

CHAPTER XXXV

IN THE ARBOUR OF GOLDEN ROSES

The next day dawned, clear and radiant; a perfect summer morning.

Mora awoke soon after five o'clock.

Notwithstanding the fatigue of the previous day, the strain and stress of heart, and the late hour at which she had at length fallen asleep, the mental habit of years overcame the physical need of further slumber.

154

Her first conscious thought was for the rope which worked over a pulley through a hole in the wall of her cell, enabling her from, within to ring the great bell in the passage, thus rousing the entire community. It had been her invariable habit to do this herself. She liked the nuns to feel that the call to begin a new day came to them from the hand of their Prioress. Realising the difficulty of early rising, especially after night vigils, it pleased her that her nuns should know that the fact of the bell resounding through the Convent proved that the Reverend Mother was already on her feet.

Yet now, looking toward the door, she could see no rope. And what meant those sumptuous tapestry hangings?

She leapt from her couch, and gazed around her.

Why fell her hair about her, as a golden cloud?—that beautiful hair, which in some Orders would have been shorn from her head; and, in this, must ever be closely braided, covered, and never seen. Still half-bewildered, she flung it back; gazing at the unfamiliar, yet well-remembered, garments laid ready for her use.

Sometimes she had had such dreams as this—dreams in which she was back in the world, wearing its garments, tasting its pleasures, looking again upon forbidden things.

Why should she not now be dreaming?

Then a sound fell upon her ear; a sound, long forgotten, yet so familiar that as she heard it, she felt herself a child at home again—the soft, contented snoring of old Debbie, fast asleep.

Sound is ever more convincing than sight. The blind live in a world of certainties. Not so, the deaf.

Mora needed not to turn and view the comely countenance of her old nurse sleeping upon a couch in a corner. At sound of that soft purring snore, she knew all she needed to know—knew she was no longer Prioress, knew she had renounced her vows; knew that even now the Convent was waking and wondering, as last night it must have marvelled and surmised, and to-morrow would question and condemn; knew that this was her wedding morn; that this robe of softest white, with jewelled girdle, and jewelled circlet to crown her hair, were old Debbie's choice for her of suitable attire in which to stand beside her bridegroom at the altar.

Passing into an alcove, she bathed and clothed herself, even putting on the jewelled band to clasp the shining softness of her hair. Debbie's will on these points had never been disputed, and truly it mattered little to Mora what she wore, since wimple and holy veil were forever laid aside.

She passed softly from the chamber, without awakening the old nurse, made her way down a winding stair, out through a postern door, and so into the gardens bathed in early morning sunshine.

Seeking to escape observation from the Castle walls or windows, she made her way through a rose-garden to where a high yew hedge

155

surrounded a bowling-green. At the further end of this secluded place stood a rustic summer-house, now a veritable bower of yellow roses.

Bending her head, Mora passed through an archway of yew, down three stone steps, and so on to the lawn.

Then, out from the arbour stepped the Bishop, in his violet cassock and biretta, his breviary in his hand.

If this first sight of Hugh's bride, in bridal array, on her wedding morning, surprised or stirred him, he gave no sign of unusual emotion.

As he came to meet her, his lips smiled kindly, and in his eyes was that half whimsical, half tender look, she knew so well. He might have been riding into the courtyard of the Nunnery, and she standing on the steps to receive him, so natural was his greeting, so wholly as usual did he appear.

"You are up betimes, my daughter, as I guessed you would be; also you have come hither, as I hoped you might do. Am I the first to wish you joy, on this glad day?"

"The first," she said. "Even my good Deborah slept through my rising. I woke at the accustomed hour, to ring the Convent bell, and found myself Prioress no longer, but bride—an earthly bride—expected to deck herself with jewels for an earthly bridal."

"'Even the ornament of a meek and quiet spirit, which is in the sight of God of great price,'" quoted, the Bishop, a retrospective twinkle in his eye.

"Alas, my lord, I fear that ornament was never mine."

"Yet you must wear it now, my daughter. I have heard it is an ornament greatly admired by husbands."

Standing in the sunlight, all unconscious of her wondrous beauty, she opened startled eyes on him; then dropped to her knees upon the turf. "Your blessing, Reverend Father," she said, and there was a wild sob in her voice. "Oh, I entreat your blessing, on this my bridal day!"

The Bishop laid his hands upon the bright coronet of her hair, and blessed her with the threefold Aaronic blessing; then raised her, and bade her walk with him across the turf.

Into the arbour he led her, beneath a cascade of fragrant yellow roses. There, upon a rustic table was spread a dainty repast—new milk, fruit freshly gathered, white rolls, and most golden pats of butter, the dew of the dairy yet upon them.

"Come, my daughter," said Symon of Worcester, gaily. "We of the Church, who know the value of these early hours, let us break our fast together."

"Is it magic, my lord?" she asked, suddenly conscious of unmistakable hunger.

"Nay," said the Bishop, "but I was out a full hour ago. And the dairy wench was up before me. So between us we contrived this simple repast."

156

So, while the bridegroom and old Deborah still slumbered and slept, the bride and the Bishop broke their fast together in a bower of roses; and his eyes were the eyes of a merry schoolboy out on a holiday; and the colour came back to her cheeks and she smiled and grew light-hearted, as always in their long friendship, when he came to her in this gay mood.

Yet, presently, when she had eaten well, and seemed strengthened and refreshed, the Bishop leaned back in his seat, saying with sudden gravity:

"And now, my daughter, will you tell me how it has come to pass that you have been led to feel it right to take this irrevocable step, renouncing your vows, and keeping your troth to Hugh? When last we spoke together you declared that naught would suffice but a clear sign, vouchsafed you from our Lady herself, making it plain that your highest duty was to Hugh, and that Heaven absolved you from your vows. Was such a sign vouchsafed?"

"Indeed it was, my lord, in wondrous fashion, our Lady choosing as the mouthpiece of her will, by means of a most explicit and unmistakable revelation, one so humble and so simple, that I could but exclaim: 'Thou hast hid these things from the wise and prudent, and hast revealed them unto babes.'"

"And who," asked the Bishop, his eyes upon a peach which he was peeling with extreme care; "who, my daughter, was the babe?"

"The old lay-sister, Mary Antony."

"Ah," murmured the Bishop, "an ancient babe. Yet truly, a most worthy babe. Almost, I should be inclined to say, a wise and prudent babe."

"Nay, my Lord Bishop," cried Mora, with a sharp decision of tone which made it please him to imagine that, should he look up from the peach, he would see the severe lines of the wimple and scapulary: "you and I were the wise and prudent, arguing for and against, according to our own theories and reason. But to this babe, our Lady vouchsafed a clear vision."

"Tell me of it," said the Bishop, splitting his peach and removing the stone which he carefully washed, and slipped into his sash. The Bishop always kept peach stones, and planted them.

She told him. She began at the beginning, and told him all, to the minutest detail; the full description of Hugh—the amazingly correct repetition, in the vision, of the way in which she and Hugh had actually knelt together before the shrine of the blessèd Virgin, of their very words and actions; and, finally, the sublime and gracious tenderness of our Lady's pronouncement, clearly heard at the close of the vision, by the old lay-sister: "Take her; she hath been ever thine. I have but kept her for thee."

"What say you to that, Reverend Father?" exclaimed Mora, concluding.

157

"I scarce know what to say," replied the Bishop. "For lack of anything better, I fall back upon my favourite motto, and I say: 'Love never faileth.'"

Now, generally, she delighted in the exceeding aptness of the Bishop's quotations; but this time it seemed to Mora that his favourite motto bore no sort of relevance.

She felt, with a chill of disappointment and a sense of vexation, that the Bishop's mind had been so intent upon the fruit, that he had not fully taken in the wonder of the vision.

"It has naught to do with love, my lord," she said, rather coldly; "unless you mean the divine lovingkindness of our blessèd Lady."

"Precisely," replied the Bishop, leaning back in his seat, and at length looking straight into Mora's earnest eyes. "The divine lovingkindness of our blessèd Lady never faileth."

"You agree, my lord, that the vision shed a clear light upon all my perplexities?"

"Absolutely clear," replied the Bishop. "The love which arranged the vision saw to that. Revelations, my daughter, are useless unless they are explicit. Had our Lady merely waved her marble hand, instead of stooping to take yours and place it in that of the Knight, you might have thought she was waving him away, and bidding you to remain. If her marble hand moved at all, it is well that it moved in so definite and practical a manner."

"It seems to me, Reverend Father," said Mora, leaning upon the table, her face framed in her hands, and looking with knitted brows at the Bishop; "it almost seems to me that you regard the entire vision with a measure of secret incredulity."

"Nay, my daughter, there you mistake. On the contrary I am fully convinced, by that which you tell me, that the ancient babe, Mary Antony, was undoubtedly permitted to see you and your knightly lover kneeling hand in hand before our Lady's shrine; also I praise our blessèd Lady that by vouchsafing this sight to Mary Antony, and by allowing her to hear words which you yourself know to have been in very deed actually spoken, your mind has been led to accept as the divine will for you, this return to the world and union with your lover, which will, I feel sure, be not only for your happiness and his, but also a fruitful source of good to many. Yet, I admit—"

The Bishop paused, and considered; as if anxious to say just so much, and neither more nor less. Continuing, he spoke slowly, weighing each word. "Yet, I frankly admit, I would sooner for mine own guidance listen for the Voice of God within, or learn His will from the written Word, than ask for miraculous signs, or act upon the visions of others.

"No doubt you read, in the Chronicle I lately lent you, how 'in the year of our Lord eleven hundred and thirty-seven—that time of many sorrows, of burning, pillaging, rapine and torture, when the city of York

158

was burned together with the principal monastery; the city of Rochester was consumed; also the Church of Bath, and the city of Leicester; when owing to the absence of King Stephen abroad and the mildness of his rule when at home, the barons greatly oppressed and ill-used the Church and the people—while many were standing at the Celebration of Mass at Windsor, they beheld the Crucifix, which was over the altar, moving and wringing its hands, now the right hand with the left, now the left with the right, after the manner of those who are in distress.'

"This wondrous sight convinced those who saw it that the crucified

Redeemer sympathised with the grievous sorrows of the land.

"But no carven crucifix, wringing its hands before a gazing crowd, could so deeply convince me of the sympathy of the Redeemer as to sit alone in mine own chamber and read from the book of Isaiah the Prophet: 'Surely He hath borne our griefs, and carried our sorrows.'"

Mora's brow cleared.

"I think I understand, my lord; and that you should so feel, helps me to confess to you a thing which I have scarce dared admit to myself. I found it difficult in mine own soul to attach due weight to our blessèd Lady's words as heard by Mary Antony. Mine own test—the robin's flight, straight from the hand of the Madonna to the world without— spoke with more sense of truth to my heart. I blame myself for this; but so it is. Yet it was the vision which decided me as to my clear path of duty."

"Doubtless," remarked the Bishop, "the medium of Mary Antony took from the solemnity of the pronouncement. There would be a twist of quaintness in even the holiest vision, as described by the old lay-sister."

"Nay, my lord," said Mora. "Truth to tell, it was not so. Once fairly started on the telling, she seemed lifted into a strange sublimity of utterance. I marvelled at it, and at the unearthly radiance of her face. At the end, I thought she slept; but later I heard from the Sub-Prioress that she was found swooning before the crucifix and they had much ado to bring her round.

"My lord, my heart fails me when I think to-day of my empty cell, and of the sore perplexity of my nuns. How soon will it be possible that you see them and put the matter right, by giving the Holy Father's message?"

"So soon as you are wed, my daughter, I ride back to Worcester. I shall endeavour to reach the Convent before the hour when they leave for Vespers."

"May I beg, my lord, that you speak a word of especial kindness to old Antony, whose heart will be sore at my departure? I had thought to bid her be silent concerning the vision; but as she declares the

159

shining Knight was Saint George or Saint Michael, the nuns, in their devout simplicity, will doubtless hold the vision to have been merely symbolic of my removal to 'higher service.'"

"I will seek old Antony," said the Bishop, "and speak with her alone."

"Father," said Mora, with deep emotion, "during all these years, you have been most good to me; kind beyond words; patient always. I fear I ofttimes tried you by being too firmly set on my own will and way. But, I pray you to believe, I ever valued your counsel and could scarce have lived without your friendship. Last night, on first entering the Castle, I fear I spoke wildly and acted strangely. I was sore overwrought. I came in, out of the night, not knowing whom I should find in the hall chamber; and—for a moment, my lord, for one wild, foolish moment—I took you not for yourself but for another."

"For whom did you take me, my daughter?" asked the Bishop.

"For one of whom you have oft reminded me, my lord, if I may say so without offence, seeing I speak of a priest who was the ideal of my girlhood's dreams. Knew you, many years ago, one Father Gervaise, held in high regard at the Court, confessor to the Queen and her ladies?"

The Bishop smiled, and his blue eyes looked into Mora's with an expression of quiet interest.

"Father Gervaise?" he said. "Preacher at the Court? Indeed, I knew him, my daughter; and more than knew him. Father Gervaise and I had the same grandparents."

"Ah," cried Mora, eagerly, "then that accounts for a resemblance which from the first has haunted me, making of our friendship, at once, so sweetly intimate a thing. The voice and the eyes alone were like— but, ah, so like! Father Gervaise wore a beard, which hid his mouth and chin; but his blue eyes had in them that kindly yet searching look, though not merry as yours oft are, my lord; and your voice has ever made me think of his.

"And once—just once—his eyes looked at me, across the Castle hall at Windsor, with a deep glow of fire in them; a look which made me feel called to an altar whereon, if I could but stand the test of fire, I should be forever purified, uplifted, blest as was never earthly maid before, save only our blessèd Lady. All that night I dreamed of it, and my whole soul was filled with it, yet never again did I see Father Gervaise. The next morning he left the Court, and soon after sailed for Spain; and on the passage thither the ship foundered in a great storm, and he, with all on board, perished. Heard you of that, my lord?"

"I heard it," said the Bishop.

"All believed it, and mourned him; for by all he was belovèd. But never could I feel that he was dead. Always for me it seemed that he still lived. And last night—when I entered—across the great hall

160

chamber, it seemed as if, once more, the eyes of Father Gervaise looked upon me, with that glowing fire in them, which called me to an altar."

The Bishop smiled again, and there was in his look a gentle merriment.

"You were over-strained, my daughter. When you drew near, you found—instead of a ghostly priest with eyes of fire, drowned many years ago, off the coast of Spain—your old friend, Symon of Worcester, who had stolen a march on you, by reason of the swift paces of his good mare, Shulamite."

Mora leaned forward, and laid her hand on his.

"Mock not, my friend," she said. "There was a time when Father Gervaise stood to me for all my heart held dearest. Yet I loved him, not as a girl loves a man, but rather as a nun loves her Lord. He stood to me for all that was noblest and best; and, above all, for all that was vital and alive in life and in religion; strong to act; able to endure. He confessed me once, and told me, when I kneeled before the crucifix, to say of Him Who hangs thereon: 'He ever liveth to make intercession for us.' Never have I forgotten it. And—sometimes—when I say the sacred words, and, saying them, my mind turns to Father Gervaise, an echo seems to whisper to my spirit: 'He, also, liveth.'"

Symon of Worcester rose.

"My daughter," he said, "the sun is high in the heavens. We must not linger here. Hugh will be seeking his bride, and Mistress Deborah be waxing anxious over the escape of her charge. The morning meal will be ready in the banqueting hall; after which we must to the chapel, for the marriage. Then, without delay, I ride to Worcester to make all right at the Nunnery. Let us go."

As Mora walked beside him across the sunny lawn, "Father," she said, "think you the heart of a nun can ever become again as the heart of other women?"

CHAPTER XXXVI

STRONG TO ACT; ABLE TO ENDURE

Back to Worcester rode the Bishop.

Gallop! Gallop! along the grassy rides, beside the hard highway.

Hasten good Shulamite, black and comely still, though flecked with foam.

Important work lies ahead. Every moment is precious.

If Mother Sub-Prioress should send to the Palace, mischief will be done, which it will not be easy to repair.

If news of the flight of the Prioress reaches the city of Worcester, a hundred tongues, spiteful, ignorant, curious, or merely idle, will at once start wagging.

Gallop, gallop, Shulamite!

How impossible to overtake a rumour, if it have an hour's start of you. As well attempt to catch up the water which first rushed through the sluice-gates, opened an hour before you reached the dam.

How impossible to remake a reputation once broken. Before the priceless Venetian goblet fell from the table on to the flagged floor, one hand put forth in time might have hindered its fall. But—failing that timely hand—when, a second later, it lies in a hundred pieces, the hands of the whole world are powerless to make it again as it was before it fell.

Faster, faster, Shulamite!

When the messenger of Mother Sub-Prioress reports the absence of the Bishop, he will most certainly be sent in haste to Father Benedict, who will experience a sinister joy at the prospect of following his long nose into the Prioress's empty cell, who will scent out scandal where there is but a fragrance of lilies, and tear to pieces Mora's reputation, with as little compunction as a wolf tears a lamb.

Gallop, gallop, Shulamite! If no hand be put forth to save it, between Mother Sub-Prioress and Father Benedict, this crystal bowl will be broken into a hundred pieces.

At length the Bishop drew rein, and walked his mare a mile. He had left Warwick ten miles behind him. He would soon be half-way to Worcester.

He had left Warwick behind him!

It seemed to the Bishop that, ever since he had first known Mora de Norelle, he had always been riding away and leaving behind.

For her sake he rode away, leaving behind the Court, his various offices, his growing influence and popularity.

For her sake he left his identity as Father Gervaise at the bottom of the ocean, taking up his life again, in Italy, under his other name.

For her sake, when he heard that she had entered the Convent of the White Ladies, he obtained the appointment to the see of Worcester, leaving the sunny land he loved, and the prospect of far higher preferment there.

And now for her sake he rode away from Warwick as fast as steed could carry him, leaving her the bride of another, in whose hand he had himself placed hers, pronouncing the Church's blessing upon their union.

Riding away—leaving behind; leaving behind—riding away. This was what his love had ever brought him.

Yet he felt rich to-day, finding himself in possession of the certain knowledge that he had been right in judging necessary, that first departure into exile long years ago.

For had not Mora told him—little dreaming to whom she spoke—that there was a time when he had stood to her for all her heart held dearest; yet that she had loved him, not as a girl loves a man, but rather as a nun loves her Lord.

But surely a man would need to be divine to be so loved, and to hold such love aright. And, even then, when that other man arrived who would fain woo her to love him as a girl loves a man, would her heart be free to respond to the call of nature? Nay. To all intents and purposes, her heart would be a cloistered thing; yet would she be neither bride of Christ nor bride of man. The fire in his eyes would indeed have called her to an altar, and the sacrifice laid thereon would be the full completion of her womanhood.

"I did well to pass into exile," said the Bishop, reviewing the past, as he rode. Yet deep in his heart was the comfort of those words she had said: that once he had stood to her for all her heart held dearest. Mora, the girl, had felt thus; Mora, the woman, remembered it; and the Bishop, as he thought of both, offered up a thanksgiving that neither he nor Father Gervaise had done aught which was unworthy of the ideal of her girlhood's dream.

Gathering up the reins, he urged Shulamite to a rapid trot. There must be no lingering by the way.

Hasten, Shulamite! Even now the sluice-gates may be opening. Even now the crystal bowl may be slipping from its pedestal, presently to lie in a hundred fragments on the ground.

Nay, trotting will scarce do. Gallop, gallop, brave black mare!

The city walls are just in sight.

Well done!

* * * * * *

Not far from the Convent gate, the Bishop chanced, by great good fortune, upon Brother Philip, trying in the meadows the paces of a young horse, but lately purchased.

The Bishop bade the lay-brother ride with him to the Nunnery and, so soon as he should have dismounted, lead Shulamite to the Palace stables, carefully feed and tend her; then bring him out a fresh mount.

As they rode forward: "Hath any message arrived at the Palace from the Convent, Philip?" inquired the Bishop.

"None, my lord."

"Or at the Priory?"

"Nay, my lord. But I did hear, at the Priory, a strange rumour"—

163

"Rumours are rarely worth regarding or repeating, Brother Philip."

"True, my lord. Yet having so lately aided her to ride upon Icon"—

"'Her'? With whom then is rumour making free? And what saith this Priory rumour concerning 'her'?"

"They say the old lay-sister, Mary Antony, hath fled the Convent."

"Mary Antony!" exclaimed the Bishop, and his voice held the most extraordinary combination of amazement, relief, and incredulity. "But, in heaven's name, good brother, wherefore should the old lay-sister leave the Convent?"

"They say she was making her way into the city in search of you, my lord; but she hath not reached the Palace."

"Any other rumour, Philip?"

"Nay, my lord, none; save that the Prioress is distraught with anxiety concerning the aged nun, and has commanded that the underground way to the Cathedral crypt be searched; though, indeed, the porteress confesses to having let Sister Mary Antony out at the gate."

"Rumour again," said the Bishop, "and not a word of truth in it, I warrant. Deny it, right and left, my good Philip; and say, on my authority, that the Reverend Mother hath most certainly not caused the crypt way to be searched. I would I could lay hands on the originator of these foolish tales."

The Bishop spoke with apparent vexation, but his heart had bounded in the upspring of a great relief. Was he after all in time to save with outstretched hand that most priceless crystal bowl?

The Bishop dismounted outside the Convent gate. He took Shulamite's nose into his hand, and spoke gently in her ear.

Then: "Lead her home, Philip," he said, "and surround her with tenderest care. Her brave heart hath done wonders this day. It is for us to see that her body doth not pay the penalty. Here! Take her rein, and go."

Mary Mark looked out through the wicket, in response to a knocking on the door. She gasped when she saw the Lord Bishop, on foot, without the gate.

Quickly she opened, wide, and wider; hiding her buxom form behind the door.

But the Bishop had no thought for Mary Mark, nor inclination to play hide-and-seek with a conscience-stricken porteress.

Avoiding the front entrance, he crossed the courtyard to the right, passed beneath the rose-arch, along the yew walk, and over the lawn, to the seat under the beech, where two days before he had awaited the coming of the Prioress.

Here he paused for a moment, looking toward the silent cloisters, and picturing her tall figure, her flowing veil and stately tread, advancing toward him over the sunny lawn.

Yet no. Even in these surroundings he could not see her now as Prioress. Even across the Convent lawn there moved to meet him the lovely woman with jewelled girdle, white robe, and coronet of golden hair—the bride of Hugh.

Perhaps this was the hardest moment to Symon of Worcester, in the whole of that hard day.

It was the one time when he thought of himself.

"I have lost her!" he said. "Holy Jesu—Thou Whose heart did break after three hours of darkness and of God-forsaken loneliness—have pity! The light of my life is gone from me, yet must I live."

Overwhelmed by this sudden realisation of loss, worn out in mind and exhausted in body, the Bishop sank upon the seat.

Mora was safe with Hugh. That much had been accomplished.

For the rest, things must take their own course. He could do no more—go no further.

Then he heard again her voice in the arbour of golden roses, saying, in those low sweet tones which thrilled his very soul: "He stood to me for all that was vital and alive, in life and in religion; strong to act; able to endure."

During five minutes the Bishop sat, eyes closed, hands firmly clasped.

So still he sat, that the little Knight of the Bloody Vest, watching, with bright eyes, from the tree overhead, almost made up his mind to drop to the other end of the seat. He was missing Sister Mary Antony, who had not appeared at all that morning. This meant neither crumbs nor cheese, and the "little vain man" was hungry.

But at the end of five minutes the Bishop rose, calm and purposeful; moved firmly up the lawn, mounted the steps, and passed into the cloisters.

CHAPTER XXXVII

WHAT MOTHER SUB-PRIORESS KNEW

Mother Sub-Prioress had applied her eye, for the fiftieth time, to the keyhole; but naught could she see in the Prioress's cell, save a portion of the great wooden cross against the opposite wall.

Sister Mary Rebecca, mounted upon a stool, attempted to spy

through the hole over the rope and pulley by means of which the Reverend Mother rang the Convent bell. But all Sister Mary Rebecca saw, after bumping her head upon a beam, and her nose on the wall, owing to the impossibility of getting it out of the way of her eye, was a portion of the top of the Reverend Mother's window.

She cried out, as a great discovery, that the curtains were drawn back; upon which, Mother Sub-Prioress, exclaiming, tartly, that that had been long ago observed from the garden below, pushed the stool in her anger, and sent Sister Mary Rebecca flying.

Jumping to save herself, she alighted heavily on the feet of Sister Teresa, striking Mary Seraphine full in the face with her elbow, and scattering, to right and left, the crowd around the door.

This cleared a view for Mother Sub-Prioress straight down the passage and through the big open door, to the cloisters; when, looking up—to scold Mary Rebecca for taking such a leap, to bid Sister Teresa cease writhing, and Mary Seraphine to shriek in her cell with the door shut, if shriek she must—Mother Sub-Prioress saw the Bishop, alone and unattended, walking toward them from the cloisters.

"Benedicite," said the Bishop, as he approached. "I am fortunate in chancing to find the whole community assembled."

The Bishop's uplifted fingers brought the nuns to their knees; but they rose at once to their feet again and crowded behind Mother Sub-Prioress as, taking a step forward, she hastened to explain the situation.

"My Lord Bishop, you find us in much distress. The Reverend Mother is locked into her cell, and we fear that, after a long night of vigil and fasting, she hath swooned. We cannot get an answer by much knocking, and we have no means of forcing the door, which is of most massive strength and thickness."

The Bishop looked searchingly into the ferrety face of Mother Sub-Prioress, but he saw naught there save genuine distress and perplexity.

He looked at the massive door, and at the excited crowd of nuns. He even gave himself time to note that the nose and lip of Seraphine were beginning to swell, and to experience a whimsical wish that the Knight could see her.

Then his calm, observant eye turned again to Mother Sub-Prioress.

"And why do you make so sure, Mother Sub-Prioress, that the Reverend Mother is indeed within her cell?"

"Because we know her to be," replied Mother Sub-Prioress, as tartly as she dared, when addressing the Lord Bishop. "Permit me, Reverend Father, to recount to you the happenings of the last twenty hours.

"Soon after her return from Vespers, yestereven, the Reverend Mother sent word by Mary Antony that she purposed again spending

166

the night in prayer and vigil, and would not be present at the evening meal; also that she must not, on any account whatever, be disturbed. Mary Antony took this message to the kitchens, bidding the younger lay-sisters to prepare the meal without her, saying she cared not how badly it was served, seeing the Reverend Mother would not be there to partake of it."

Mother Sub-Prioress paused to sniff, and to give the other nuns an opportunity for ejaculations concerning Sister Antony. But their awe of the Lord Bishop, and their genuine anxiety for the old lay-sister, kept them silent.

The Bishop stroked his chin, keeping the corners of his mouth firmly in place by means of his thumb and finger. Old Antony was delectably funny when she said these things herself; but she was delectably funnier, when her remarks were repeated by Mother Sub-Prioress.

"The old creature," continued Mother Sub-Prioress, eyeing the Bishop's meditative hand suspiciously, "then betook herself to the outer gates, told the porteress that she had your orders, Reverend Father, to report to you if the Reverend Mother again elected to pass a night in vigil and in fasting, because you and she—you and she forsooth!—were made anxious by the too constant fasting and the too prolonged vigils of the Reverend Mother. Mary Mark very properly refused to allow the old"—

"Lay-sister," interposed the Bishop, sternly.

Mother Sub-Prioress gasped; then made obeisance:—"the old lay-sister to leave the Convent. Whereupon Sister Antony sent Mary Mark to deliver the Reverend Mother's message to me, bribing her, with the promise of a gift from you, my lord, to leave her the key. When the porteress returned, Mary Antony was gone, having left the great doors ajar, and the key within the lock. She has not been seen since. Did she reach the Palace, and speak with you, my lord? Is she now in safety at the Palace?"

"Nay," said the Bishop gravely. "Sister Mary Antony hath not been seen at the Palace."

"Alack-a-day!" exclaimed Sister Abigail; "she will have fallen by the way, and perished! She was too old to face the world or attempt to reach the city."

"Peace, girl!" commanded the Sub-Prioress. "Thy comments and thy wailings mend not the matter, and do but incense the Lord Bishop."

Nothing could have appeared less incensed than the Bishop's benign countenance. But he had spoken sternly to Mother Sub-Prioress, therefore she endeavoured to put herself in the right by charging him, at the first opportunity, with unreasonable irritation.

The Bishop reassured Sister Abigail, with a smile; then, pointing toward the closed door: "Proceed with your recital, Mother Sub-

Prioress," he said. "You have as yet given me no proof confirming your belief that the Prioress is within the cell."

"When the absence of Mary Antony became known, my lord," continued Mother Sub-Prioress, "we felt it right to acquaint the Reverend Mother with the old lay-sister's flight. I, myself, knocked upon this door; but the only reply I received was the continuous low chanting of prayers, from within; not so much a clear chanting, as a murmur; and whenever, during the night, nuns listened at the door, or ventured again to tap, the sound of the Reverend Mother's voice, reciting psalms or prayers, reached them. As you may remember, my lord, the ground upon the other side of the building is on a lower level than the cloister lawn. The windows of the Reverend Mother's cell are therefore raised above the shrubbery and it is not possible to see into the chamber. But Sister Mary Rebecca, who went round after dark, noted that the Reverend Mother had lighted her tapers and drawn her curtains. This morning the light is extinguished, the curtains are drawn back, and the casement flung open. Moreover at the usual hour for rising, the Reverend Mother rang the bell, as is her custom, to waken the nuns—rang it from within her cell, by means of this rope and pulley."

"Ah," said the Bishop.

"Sister Abigail, up already, thereupon ran to the Reverend Mother's cell; and, the bell still swinging, tapped and asked if she might bring in milk and bread. Once more the only answer was the low chanting of prayers. Also, Sister Abigail declares, the voice was so weak and faltering, she scarce knew it for the Reverend Mother's. And since then, my lord, there has been silence within the cell, and a sore sense of fear within our hearts; for it is unlike the Reverend Mother to keep her door locked, when the entire community calls and knocks without."

The Bishop lifted his hand.

"In that speak you truly, Mother Sub-Prioress," said he. "Also I must tell you without further delay, that the Prioress is not within her cell."

"Not within her cell!" exclaimed Mother Sub-Prioress.

"Not within her cell!" shrieked a score of terrified voices, like seagulls calling to each other, before a gathering storm.

"The Prioress left the Convent yesterday afternoon," said the Bishop, "with my knowledge and approval; travelling at once, with a sufficient escort, to a place some distance from Worcester, where I also spent the night. I have come to bring you a message from His Holiness the Pope, sent to me direct from Rome. . . . The Holy Father bids me say that your Prioress has been moved on by me, with his full knowledge and approval, to a place where she is required for higher service. Perhaps I may also tell you," added the Bishop, looking with kindly sympathy upon all the blankly disconcerted faces, "that this morning I myself performed a solemn rite, for which I held the Pope's

168

especial mandate, setting apart your late Prioress for this higher service. She grieved that it was not possible to bid you farewell. She sends you loving greetings, her thanks for loyalty and obedience, and prays that the blessing of the Lord may ever be with you."

The Bishop ceased speaking.

At first there was an amazed silence.

Then the unexpected happened. Mother Sub-Prioress, without any warning, broke into passionate weeping.

Never before had Mother Sub-Prioress been known to weep. The sight petrified the Convent. Yet somehow all knew that she wept because, in the hard old nut which did duty for her heart, there was a kernel of deep love for their noble Prioress.

The other nuns wept, because Mother Sub-Prioress wept.

The sobbing became embarrassing in its completeness. Wheresoever the Bishop looked he was confronted by a weeping nun.

Suddenly Mother Sub-Prioress dried her eyes, holding herself once more in control. It had just occurred to her that the Bishop's word could not be taken against the evidence of all their senses! On that very morning, at five o'clock the Convent call to rise had been rung from within the Prioress's cell!

So Mother Sub-Prioress dried her eyes, punished her nose for sharing in the general breakdown, and looking with belligerent eye at the Bishop, said: "If the Reverend Mother be not within her cell, perhaps it will please you, my lord, to inform the Convent who is within it!"

"That point," said the Bishop, "can speedily be settled."

He took from his girdle the Prioress's master-key, handed over to him before he left Warwick.

Fitting it into the lock, he opened the door of the cell, and entered, followed by the Sub-Prioress and a crowd of palpitating, eager nuns.

A few paces from the door the Bishop paused, signing to Mother Sub-Prioress to come forward, but restraining, with uplifted hand, those who pressed in behind her.

The chamber was very still.

The chair of the Prioress was empty.

But, before the shrine of the Madonna, there lay, stretched upon the floor, the unconscious form of the old lay-sister, Mary Antony.

CHAPTER XXXVIII

THE BISHOP KEEPS VIGIL

Old Mary Antony lay dying.

The Bishop had not allowed her to be carried from the cell of the Prioress, to her own.

He had commanded that the Reverend Mother's couch be moved from the inner room and placed before the shrine of the Virgin. On this lay Mary Antony, while the Bishop himself kept watch beside her.

The evening light came in through the open casement, illumining the calm old face, from which the soothing hand of death was already smoothing the wrinkles.

Five hours had passed since they found her.

It had taken long to restore her to consciousness; and so soon as she awoke to her surroundings, and recognised Mother Sub-Prioress, and the many faces around her, she relapsed into silence, refusing to answer any questions, yet keeping her eyes anxiously fixed upon the door.

Seeing which, Sister Teresa slipped from the room and ran secretly to tell the Lord Bishop, who had paid but a brief visit to the Palace and was now pacing the lawn below the cloisters.

The Bishop came at once; when, seeing him enter, Mary Antony gave a cry, striving to raise herself from the pillows.

Moving to the bedside, the Bishop laid his hand upon the shaking hands, which had been clasped at sight of him.

An eager question was in the eyes lifted to his.

The Bishop bent over the couch.

"Yes," he said, and smiled.

The anxious look faded. The eyes closed. A triumphant smile illumined the dying face.

Turning, the Bishop asked a few whispered questions of the Sub-Prioress.

Mary Antony had taken a sip of wine, but seemed to find it impossible to partake of food. She had been so long without, that now nature refused it.

"Undoubtedly she is dying," said Mother Sub-Prioress, not unkindly, but in the matter-of-fact tone of one to whom the hard outline of a fact is unsoftened by the atmosphere of imagination or of sympathy.

"I know it," said the Bishop, in low tones. "Therefore am I come to confess our sister and to administer the final rites and consolations of the Church. I have with me all that is needed. You may now withdraw, and leave me to watch alone beside Sister Mary Antony."

"We sent for Father Peter," began Mother Sub-Prioress, "but she paid no heed to any of his questions, neither would she"—

The Bishop took one step toward Mother Sub-Prioress, with uplifted hand, pointing to the door.

Mother Sub-Prioress hastened out.

The Bishop followed her into the passage, where a waiting crowd of nuns created that atmosphere of excited tension, which seizes certain minds at the near approach of death.

"I bid you all to go to your cells," said the Bishop, "there to spend the next hour in earnest prayer for the passing soul of this aged nun who, during so long a time, has lived and worked in this Convent. Let every door be closed. I keep the final vigil alone. When I need help I shall ring the Convent bell."

Immovable in the passage stood the Bishop, until every figure had vanished; every door had closed.

Then he re-entered the Prioress's cell, and shut the door.

He placed the holy oil on the step, before the shrine of the Madonna, just where old Antony had knelt when she had prayed our blessèd Lady to be pleased to sharpen her old wits.

Then he drew forth a tiny flask of rare Italian workmanship, let fall a few drops from it into a spoonful of wine, and firmly poured the liquid between the old lay-sister's parted lips.

One anxious moment; then he heard her swallow.

At that, the Bishop drew the Prioress's chair to the side of the couch, and sat down to await events.

In a few moments the stertorous breathing ceased, the open mouth closed. Mary Antony sighed thrice, as a little child that has wept before sleeping sighs in its sleep.

Then she opened her eyes, and fixed them on the Bishop.

"Reverend Father"—she began, then chuckled, gleefully. Her voice had come back, and with it a great activity of brain, though the hands upon the coverlet seemed to belong to someone else, and she hoped they would not rise up and strike her. Her feet, she could not feel at all; but, seeing that she was most comfortably lying there where she best loved to be, why should she require feet? Feet are such tired things. One rests better without them.

"Speak low," said the Bishop, bending forward. "Speak low, dear Sister Antony; partly to spare thy strength; and partly because, though I have sent all the White Ladies to their cells, our good Mother Sub-Prioress, in her natural anxiety for thy welfare, may be outside the door, even now."

Mary Antony chuckled.

"If we could but thrust a nail through into her ear," she whispered. Then suddenly serious, she put the question which already her eyes had asked: "Did I succeed in keeping from them the flight of the Reverend Mother, until you arrived, Reverend Father?"

171

"Yes, faithful heart, wise beyond all expectation, you did."

Again Mary Antony chuckled.

"I locked them out," she said, with a knowing wink, "but I also took them in. Yea, verily, I took them in! Scores of times they called me 'Reverend Mother.' 'Open the door, I humbly pray you, Reverend Mother,' pleaded Mother Sub-Prioress at the keyhole. 'Dixi: Custodiam vias meas,' chanted Mary Antony, in a beauteous voice! . . . 'Open, open, Reverend Mother!' besought a multitude without. 'Quid multiplicati sunt gui tribulant me!' intoned Mary Antony, within. . . . 'Most dear and Reverend Mother,' crooned Sister Mary Rebecca, at midnight, 'I have something of deepest importance to say'—'Dixit insipiens,' was Mary Antony's appropriate response. Eh, and Sister Mary Rebecca, thinking none could observe her, had already been round, in the moonlight, and attempted to climb a tree. All the Reverend Mother's windows were closely curtained; but old Antony had her eye to a crack, and the sight of Sister Mary Rebecca climbing, made all the other trees to shake with laughter, but is not a sight to be described to the great Lord Bishop. . . . Nay, then!"—with a startled cry—"Why doth this knotted finger rise up and shake itself at me?"

The Bishop took the worn old hand, now stone cold, laid it back upon the quilt, and covered it with his own.

The drug he had administered had indeed revived the powers, but the over-excited brain was inclined to wander.

He recalled it with a name which he knew would act as a potent spell.

"Would you have news of the Prioress, Sister Antony?"

Instantly the eyes grew eager.

"Is she safe, Reverend Father? Is she well? Hath she taken happiness to her with both hands, not thrusting it away?"

"Happiness hath taken her by both hands," said the Bishop. "This morning I blest her union with a noble knight to whom she was betrothed before she came hither."

"I know," whispered old Antony ecstatically. "I heard it all, I and my meat chopper, hidden in there; I and my meat chopper—not willing to let the Reverend Mother face danger alone. And I did thrust the handle of the chopper between my gums, that I might not cry 'Bravely done!' when the noble Knight and his men-at-arms flung a rope over a strong bough, and hanged that clerkly fellow—somewhat lean and out at elbows. Oh, ah? It was bravely done! I heard it all! I saw it all!"

Then the joy faded; a look of shame and grief came into the old face.

"But having thus seen and heard has led me into grievous sin, Reverend Father. Alas, I have lied about holy things, sinning, I fear me, beyond forgiveness, though indeed I did it, meaning to do well. May I tell you all, Reverend Father, that you may judge whether in that which I did, I acted according to our blessèd Lady's will and intention, or

172

whether the deceitfulness of mine own heart has led me into mortal sin?"

The Bishop looked anxiously at the sun dipping slowly in the west. The effect of the drug he had given should last an hour, if care were taken of this spurious strength. He judged a quarter of that time to have already sped.

"Tell me from the beginning, without reserve, dear Antony," he said. "But speak low, for my ear only. Remember possible listeners outside the door."

So presently the whole tale was told, with many a quaint twist of old Antony's. And the Bishop's heart melted to tenderness as she whispered the story, and he realised the greatness of the devotion which had gone forward, without a thought of self, in the bold endeavour to bring happiness to the Prioress she loved, yet the anxious conscience, which now trembled at the thought of that which the fearless heart had done.

"I lied about holy things; I put words into our blessèd Lady's mouth; I said she moved her hand. But you did tell me, Reverend Father, that the Reverend Mother was so made that unless there was a vision or revelation from our Lady, she would thrust away her happiness with both hands. And there would not have been a vision if old Antony had not contrived one. Yet I fear me, for the sin of that contriving, I shall never find forgiveness; my soul must ever stay in torment."

Tears coursed down the wrinkled cheeks.

The Bishop kneeled beside the bed.

"Dear Antony," he said. "Listen to me. 'Perfect love casteth out fear, because fear hath torment.' You have loved with a perfect love. You need have no fear. Trust in the love of God, in the precious blood of the Redeemer, which cleanseth from all sin, in the understanding tenderness of our Lady, who knoweth a woman's heart. You meant to do right; and if, honestly intending to do well, you used the wrong means, Divine love, judging you by your intention, will pardon the mistake. 'If we confess our sins, He is faithful and just to forgive us our sins, and to cleanse us from all unrighteousness.' Think no more of yourself, in this. Dwell solely on our Lord. Silence your own fears, by repeating: 'He is faithful and just.'"

"Think you, Reverend Father," quavered the pathetic voice, "that They will sometimes let old Antony out of hell for an hour, to sit on her jasper seat and see the Reverend Mother walk up the golden stairs, with the splendid Knight on one side and the great Lord Bishop on the other?"

"Sister Mary Antony," said the Bishop, clearly and solemnly, "there is no place in hell for so faithful and so loving a heart. You shall go straight to your jasper seat; and because, with the Lord, one day is as a thousand years, and a thousand years as one day, your eyes will

173

scarce have time to grow used to the great glory, before you see the
Reverend Mother coming, walking between the two who have faithfully
loved her; and you, who have also loved her faithfully, will also mount
the golden stair, and together we all shall kneel before the throne of
God, and understand at last the full meaning of those words of wonder:
GOD IS LOVE."

A look of ineffable joy lit up the dying face.

"Straight to my jasper seat," she said, "to watch—to wait"—

Then came the sudden fading of the spurious strength. The
Bishop put out his hand and reached for the holy oil.

* * * * * *

The golden sunset light flooded the chamber with radiance.

The Bishop still watched beside the couch.

Having rallied sufficiently to make her last confession, short and
simple as a child's; having received absolution and the last sacred rites
of the Church, Mary Antony had slipped into a peaceful slumber.

The Bishop had to bend over and listen, to make sure that she
still breathed.

Suddenly she opened her eyes and looked full into his.

"Did you wed the Reverend Mother to the splendid Knight?" she
asked, and her voice was strong again and natural, with the little
chuckle of curiosity and humour in it, as of old.

"This morning," answered the Bishop, "I wedded them."

"Did he kiss her?" asked old Antony, with an indescribable
twinkle of gleeful enjoyment, though those twinkling eyes seemed the
only living thing in the old face.

"Nay," said the Bishop. "They who truly kiss, kiss not in public."

"Ah," whispered Mary Antony. "Yea, verily! I know that to be
true."

She lifted wandering fingers and, after much groping, touched
her forehead, with a happy smile.

Not knowing what else the action could mean, the Bishop leaned
forward and made the sign of the cross on her brow.

Mary Antony gave that peculiar little chuckle of enjoyment,
which had always marked her pleasure when the very learned made
mistakes. It gave her so great a sense of cleverness.

After this the light faded from the old eyes, and the Bishop had
begun to think they would not again open upon this world, when a
strange thing happened.

There was a flick of wings, and in, through the open window, flew
the robin.

First he perched on the marble hand of the Madonna. Then, with
a joyful chirp, dropped straight to the couch on which lay Mary Antony.

174

At sound of that chirp, Mary Antony opened her eyes, and saw her much loved little bird hopping gaily on the coverlet.

"Hey, thou little vain man!" she said. "Ah, naughty Master Pieman! Art come to look upon old Antony in her bed? The great Lord Bishop will have thee hanged."

The robin hopped nearer, and pecked gently at the hand which so oft had fed him, now lying helpless on the quilt.

A look of exquisite delight came into the old woman's eyes.

"Ah, my little Knight of the Bloody Vest," she whispered, "dost want thy cheese? Wait a minute, while old Antony searches in her wallet."

She sat up suddenly, as if to reach for something.

Then a startled look came into her face. She stretched out appealing hands to the Bishop.

Instantly he caught them in his.

"Fear not, dear Antony," he said. "All is well."

The robin, spreading his wings, flew out at the window. And the loving spirit of Mary Antony went with him.

The Bishop laid the worn-out body gently back upon the couch, closed the eyes, and folded the hands upon the breast.

Then he walked over to the window, and stood looking at the golden ramparts of that sunset city, glowing against the delicate azure of the evening sky.

Great loneliness of soul came to the Bishop, standing thus in the empty cell.

The Prioress had gone; the robin had gone; Mary Antony had gone; and the Bishop greatly wished that he might go, also.

Presently he turned to the Prioress's table. She had sent to the Palace the copy she had made, and the copy she had mended, of the Pope's mandate. But she had left upon the table the strips of parchment upon which she had inscribed, on the night of her vigil, copies and translations of ancient prayers from the Sacramentaries. The Bishop gathered these up, reading them as he stood. Two he slipped into his sash, but the third he took to the couch and placed beneath the folded hands.

"Take this with thee to thy jasper seat, dear faithful heart," he said; "for truly it was given unto thee to perceive and know what things thou oughtest to do, and also to have grace and power faithfully to fulfil the same."

The peaceful face, growing beautiful with that solemn look of eternal youth which death brings, even to the aged, seemed to smile, as the precious parchment passed into the keeping of those folded hands.

The Bishop knelt long in prayer and thanksgiving. At length, with uplifted face, he said: "And grant, O my God, that I too may be faithful, unto the very end."

Then he rose, and rang the Convent bell.

175

CHAPTER XXXIX

THE "SPLENDID KNIGHT"

On the steps of Warwick Castle stood the Knight and his bride.

Their eyes still lingered on the archway through which the noble figure of Symon, Bishop of Worcester, mounted upon his black mare, Shulamite, had just disappeared from view.

The marriage had taken place in the Castle chapel, half an hour before, with an astonishing amount of pomp and ceremony. Priests and acolytes had appeared from unexpected places. Madonna lilies, on graceful stem, gleamed white in the shadows of the sacred place. Solemn music rose and fell; the deep roll of the Gregorian chants, beginning with a low hum as of giant bees in a vast field of clover; swelling, in full-throated unison, a majestic volume of sound which rang against the rafters, waking echoes in the clerestory; then rumbling back into silence.

Standing beneath the sacred canopy, the bridal pair lifted their eyes to the high altar and saw, amid a cloud of incense, the Bishop, in gorgeous vestments, descending the steps and coming toward them.

To Mora, at the time, and afterwards in most thankful remembrance, the wonder of that which followed lay in the fact that where she had dreaded an inevitable sense of sacrilege in giving to another that which had been already consecrated to God, the Bishop so worded the service as to make her feel that she could still be spiritually the bride of Christ, even while fulfilling her troth to Hugh; also that, in accepting the call to this new Vocation, she was not falling from her old estate, but rather rising above it.

As the words were spoken which made her a wife, it seemed as if the Bishop gently wrapped her about with a fresh mantle of dignity— that dignity which had fallen from her in those moments of humiliation when, at Hugh's bidding she laid herself down upon the stretcher.

The Bishop voiced the Church with a pomp and power which could not be withstood; and when, in obedience to his command Hugh grasped her right hand with his right hand, and the Bishop laid his own on either side of their clasped hands, and pronounced them man and wife, it seemed indeed as if a Divine touch united them, as if a Divine voice ratified their vows and sanctified their union.

Mora had never before seen the man so completely merged in his high office.

And, when all was over, even as he mounted Shulamite and rode away, he rode out of the courtyard with the air of a Knight Templar riding forth-to do battle in a Holy War.

It seemed to Mora that she had bidden farewell to her old friend

176

of the kindly smile, the merry eye, and the ready jest, in the early hours of that morning, as together they left the arbour of the golden roses.

There remained therefore but one man to be considered: the "splendid Knight" of old Antony's vision; the lover who had pursued her into her Nunnery; wooed her in her own cell, unabashed by the dignity of her office; mastered her will; forced her numbed heart to awaken, disturbed by the thrill of an unwilling tenderness; moved her to passion by the poignant anguish of a parting, which she regarded as inevitably final; won the Bishop over, to his side, and, through him, the Pope; and finally, by the persistence of his pleadings, moved our blessèd Lady to vouchsafe a vision on his behalf.

This was the "splendid Knight" against whom the stars in their courses had most certainly not fought. Principalities and powers had all been for him; against him, just a woman and her conscience, and—he had won.

When, at their first interview in her cell, in reply to her demand: "Why are you not with your wife?" he had answered: "I am with my wife; the only wife I have ever wanted, the only woman I shall ever wed, is here"—she stood ready to strike with ivory and steel, at the first attempt upon her inviolable chastity, and could afford to smile, in pitying derision, at so empty a boast.

But now? If he said: "My wife is here," and chose to seize her with possessive grasp, she must meekly fold her hands upon her breast, and say: "Even so, my lord. I am yours. Deal with me as you will."

As the Bishop's purple cloak and the hind quarters of his noble black mare, disappeared from view, the crowd which hitherto had surrounded the bridal pair, also vanished, as if at the wave of a magic wand. Thus for the first time, since those tense moments in the Cathedral crypt, Mora found herself alone with Hugh.

She was not young enough to be embarrassed; but she was old enough to be afraid; afraid of him, and afraid of herself; afraid of his masterful nature and imperious will, which had always inclined to break rather than bend anything which stood in his way; and afraid of something in herself which leapt up in response to this fierce strength in him, yearning to be mastered, hungry to yield, wishful to obey; yet which, if yielded to, would lay her spirit in the dust, and turn the awakened tenderness in her heart to scorn of herself, and anger against him.

So she feared as she stood in the sunshine, watching the now empty archway through which her sole remaining link with Convent life had vanished; conscious, without looking round, that Debbie, who had been curtseying behind her, was there no longer; that Martin Goodfellow, who had held Shulamite's bridle while the Bishop mounted, had disappeared in one direction, the rest of the men in another; intensely conscious that she and Hugh were now alone; and fearing, she shivered again, as she had shivered in the crypt; then, of a

177

sudden, knew that she had done so, and, with a swift impulse of shame and contrition, turned and looked at Hugh.

He was indeed the "splendid Knight" of Mary Antony's vision! He had donned for his bridal the dress of white and silver, which he had last put on when he supped at the Palace with the Bishop. This set off, with striking effect, his dark head and the noble beauty of his countenance; and Mora, who chiefly remembered him as a handsome youth, graceful and gay, realised for the first time his splendour as a man, and the change wrought in him by all he had faced, endured, and overcome.

In the crypt, the day before, and during the hours which followed, she had scarce let herself look at him; and he, though always close beside her, had kept out of her immediate range of vision.

Since that infolding clasp in the crypt when he had flung the cloak about her, not once had he touched her, until the Church just now bade him, with authority, to take her right hand, with his.

Her mind flew back to the happenings of the previous day. With the lightning rapidity of retrospective thought, she passed again through each experience from the moment when the call of the blackbird sounded in the crypt. The helpless horror of being lifted by unseen hands; the slow, swinging progress, to the accompaniment of the measured tread of the men-at-arms; the stifling darkness, air and light shut out by the heavy cloak, and yet the clear consciousness of the moment when the stretcher passed from the Cathedral into the sunshine without; the sudden pause, as the Bishop met the stretcher, and then—as she lay helpless between them—Symon's question and Hugh's reply, with their subtlety of hidden meaning, which filled her with impotent anger, shewing as it did the completeness of the Bishop's connivance at Hugh's conspiracy. Then Hugh's request, and the Bishop's hand laid upon her, the Bishop's voice uplifted in blessing. Then once again the measured tramp, tramp, and the steady swing of the stretcher; but now the men's heels rang on cobbles, and voices seemed everywhere; cheery greetings, snatches of song, chance words concerning a bargain or a meeting, a light jest, a coarse oath; and, all the while, the steady, tramp, tramp, and the ring of Hugh's spurs.

She grew faint and it seemed to her she was about to die beneath the cloak, and that when at length Hugh removed it, it would prove a pall beneath which he would find a dead bride.

"Dead bride! Dead bride!" sounded the tramping footsteps. And all the way she was haunted by the belief, assailing her confused senses in the darkness, that the spirit of Father Gervaise had met the stretcher; that his was the voice which murmured low and tenderly; "Be not afraid, neither be thou dismayed. Go in peace."

With this had come a horror of the outer world, a wild desire for the safety and shelter of the Cloister, and an absolute physical dread of the moment when the covering cloak should be removed, and she would find herself alone with her lover; and, on rising from the stretcher, be seized by his arms.

Yet when, having been tilted up steps, she was conscious of the silence of passages and soon the even more complete quiet of a room; when the stretcher was set down, and the bearers' feet died away, Hugh's deep voice said gently: "Change thy garments quickly, my belovèd. There is no time to lose." But he laid no hand upon the cloak, and his footsteps, also, died away.

Then pushing back the heavy folds and sitting up, she had found herself alone in a bedchamber, everything she could need laid ready to her hand; while, upon the bed, lay her green riding-dress, discarded forever, eight years before!

Her mind refused to look back upon the half-hour that followed.

She saw herself next appearing in the doorway at the top of a flight of eight steps, leading down into the yard of the hostelry, where a cavalcade of men and horses waited; while Icon, the Bishop's beautiful white palfrey, was being led to and fro, and Hugh stood with an open letter in his hand.

As she hesitated in the doorway, gazing down upon the waiting, restive crowd, Hugh looked up and saw her. Into his eyes flashed a light of triumphant joy, of adoring love and admiration. She had avoided looking at her own reflection; but his face, as he came up the steps, mirrored her loveliness. It had cost her such anguish of soul to divest herself of her sacred habit and don these gay garments belonging to a life long left behind, that his evident delight in the change, moved her to an unreasonable resentment. Also that sudden blaze of love in his dark eyes, dazzled her heart, even as a burst of sunshine might dazzle one used to perpetual twilight.

She took the Bishop's letter, with averted eyes; read it; then moved swiftly down the steps to where Icon waited.

"Mount me," she said to Martin Goodfellow, as she passed him; and it was Martin who swung her into the saddle.

Then she trembled at what she had done, in yielding to this impulse which made her shrink from Hugh.

As the black mane of his horse drew level with Icon's head, and side by side they rode out from the courtyard, she feared a thunder-cloud on the Knight's brow, and a sullen silence, as the best she could expect. But calm and cheerful, his voice fell on her ear; and glancing at him furtively, she still saw on his face that light which dazzled her heart. Yet no word did he speak which all might not have heard, and not once did he lay his hand on hers. Each time they dismounted, she saw him sign to Martin Goodfellow, and it was Martin who helped her to alight.

All this, in rapid retrospect, passed through Mora's mind as she stood alone beside her splendid Knight, miserably conscious that she had shivered, and that he knew it; and fearful lest he divined the

179

shrinking of her soul away from him, away from love, away from all for which love stood. Alas, alas! Why did this man—this most human, ardent, loving man—hang all his hopes of happiness upon the heart of a nun? Would it be possible that he should understand, that eight years of cloistered life cannot be renounced in a day?

Mora looked at him again.

The stern profile might well be about to say: "Shudder again, and I will do to thee that which shall give thee cause to shudder indeed!"

Yet, at that moment he spoke, and his voice was infinitely gentle.

"Yonder rides a true friend," he said. "One who has learned love's deepest lesson."

"What is love's deepest lesson?" she asked.

He turned and looked at her, and the fire of his dark eyes was drowned in tenderness.

"That true love means self-sacrifice," he said. "Come, my belovèd. Let us walk in the gardens, where we can talk at ease of our plans for the days to come."

CHAPTER XL

THE HEART OF A NUN

Hugh and Mora passed together through the great hall, along the armoury, down the winding stair and so out into the gardens.

The Knight led the way across the lawn and through the rose garden, toward the yew hedge and the bowling-green.

Old Debbie, looking from her casement, thought them beautiful beyond words as she watched them cross the lawn—she in white and gold, he in white and silver; his dark head towering above her fair one, though she was uncommon tall. And, falling upon her knees, old Debbie prayed to the Angel Gabriel that she might live to hold in her arms, and rock to sleep upon her bosom, sweet babes, both fair and dark: "Fair little maids," she said, "and fine, dark boys," explaining to Gabriel that which she thought would be most fit.

Meanwhile Hugh and Mora, walking a yard apart—all unconscious of these family plans, being so anxiously made for them at an upper casement—bent their tall heads and passed under the arch in the yew hedge, crossed the bowling-green, and entered the arbour of the golden roses.

Hugh led the way; yet Mora gladly followed. The Bishop's presence seemed to abide here, in comfort and protection.

All signs of the early repast were gone from the rustic table.

Mora took her seat there where in the early morning she had sat; while Hugh, not knowing he did so, passed into the Bishop's place.

The sun shone through the golden roses, hanging in clusters over the entrance.

The sense of the Bishop's presence so strongly pervaded the place, that almost at once Mora felt constrained to speak of him.

"Hugh," she said, "very early this morning, long before you were awake, the Bishop and I broke our fast, in this arbour, together."

The Knight smiled.

"I knew that," he said. "In his own characteristic way the Bishop told it me. 'My son,' he said, 'you have reversed the sacred parable. In your case it was the bride-groom who, this morning, slumbered and slept.' 'True, my lord,' said I. 'But there were no foolish virgins about.' 'Nay, verily!' replied the Bishop. 'The two virgins awake at that hour were pre-eminently wise: the one, making as the sun rose most golden pats of butter and crusty rolls; the other, rising early to partake of them with appetite. Truly there were no foolish virgins about. There was but one foolish prelate.'"

She, who so lately had been Prioress of the White Ladies, flushed with indignation at the words.

"Wherefore said he so?" she inquired, severely. "He, who is always wiser than the wisest."

Hugh noted the heightened colour and the ready protest.

"Perhaps," he suggested, speaking slowly, as if choosing his words with care, "the Bishop's head, being so wise, revealed to him, in himself, a certain foolishness of heart."

Mora struck the table with her hand.

"Nay then, verily!" she cried. "Head and heart alike are wise; and—unlike other men—the Bishop's head rules his heart."

"And a most noble heart,", the Knight said, with calmness; neither wincing at the blow upon the table, nor at the "unlike other men," flung out in challenge.

Then, folding his arms upon the table, and looking searchingly into the face of his bride: "Tell me," he said, "during all these years, has this friendship with Symon of Worcester meant much to thee?"

Something in his tone arrested Mora. She answered, with an equal earnestness: "Yes, Hugh. It has done more for me than can well be told. It has kept living and growing in me much that would otherwise have been stunted or dead; an ever fresh flow of thought, where, but for him, would have been a stagnant pool. My sad heart might have grown bitter, my nature too austere, particularly when advancement to high office brought with it an inevitable loneliness, had it not been for the interest and charm of his visits and missives; his constant gifts and kindness. There is about him a light-hearted gaiety, a whimsical humour, a joy in life, which cannot fail to wake responsive gladness in any heart with which he comes in contact. And mingled with his shrewd wisdom, his wide knowledge of men and matters, there is ever a tender charity, which thinks no evil, always believing in good and hoping for the best; a love which never fails; a kindness which makes one ashamed of harbouring hard or revengeful thoughts."

Hugh made no reply. He sat with his eyes fixed upon the beautiful face before him, now glowing with enthusiasm. He waited for something more. And presently it came.

"Also," said Mora, slowly: "a very precious memory of my early days at Court, when as a young maiden I attended on the Queen, was kept alive by a remarkable likeness in the Bishop to one who was, as I learned this morning for the first time, actually near of kin to him. Do you remember, Hugh, long years ago, that I spoke to you of Father Gervaise?"

"I do remember," said the Knight.

She leaned her elbows on the table, framed her face in her hands, and looked straight into his eyes.

"Father Gervaise was more to me than I then told you, Hugh."

"What was he to thee, Mora?"

"He was the Ideal of my girlhood. For a time, I thought of him by day, I dreamed of him by night. No word of his have I ever forgotten. Many of his sayings and precepts have influenced, and still deeply influence, my whole life. In fact, Hugh, I loved Father Gervaise; not as a woman loves a man—ah, no! But, rather, as a nun loves her Lord."

"I see," said the Knight. "But you were not then a nun, Mora."

"No, I was not then a nun. But I have been a nun since then; and that is how I can best describe my love for the Queen's Confessor."

"Long after," said the Knight, "you were betrothed to me?"

"Yes, Hugh."

"How did you love me, Mora?"

Across the rustic table they looked full into each other's eyes. Tragedy, stalking around that rose-covered arbour, drew very near, and they knew it. Almost, his grim shadow came between them and the sunshine.

Then the Knight smiled; and with that smile rushed back the flood-tide of remembrance; remembrance of all which their young love had meant, of the sweet promise it had held.

His eyes still holding hers, she smiled also.

The golden roses clustering in the entrance swayed and nodded in the sunlight, as a gently rising breeze fanned them to and fro.

"Dear Knight," she said, softly, a wistful tenderness in her voice, "I suppose I loved you, as a girl loves the man who has won her."

"Mora," said Hugh, "I have something to tell thee."

"I listen," she said.

"My wife—so wholly, so completely, do I love thee, that I would not consciously keep anything from thee. So deeply do I love thee, that I would sooner any wrong or sin of mine were known to thee and by thee forgiven, than that thou shouldest think me one whit better than I am."

He paused.

Her eyes were tender and compassionate. Often she had listened, with a patient heart of charity, to the tedious, morbid, self-centred confessions of kneeling nuns, who watched with anxious eyes for the sign which would mean that they might clutch at the hem of her robe and press it to their lips in token that they were forgiven.

But she had had no experience of the sins of men. What had the "splendid Knight" upon his conscience, which must now be told her, in this sunny arbour, on the morning of their bridal day?

Her heart throbbed painfully. Alas, it was still the heart of a nun. It would not be controlled. Must she hear wild tales of wickedness and shame, of which she would but partly understand the meaning?

Oh, for the calm of the Cloister! Oh, for the sheltered purity of her quiet cell!

Yet his eyes, still meeting hers, were clear and fearless.

"I listen," she said.

"Mora, not long ago a wondrous tale was told me of a man's great love for thee—a man, nobler than I, in that he mastered all selfish desires; a love higher than mine, in that it put thy welfare, in all things, first. Hearing this tale, I failed both myself and thee, for I said: 'I pray heaven that, if she come to me, she may never know that she once won the love of so greatly better a man than I.' But, since I clasped thy hand in mine, and the Bishop, laying his on either side, gave thee to be my wife, I have known there would be no peace for me if I feared to trust thee with this knowledge, because that the man who loved thee was a better man than the man who, by God's mercy and our Lady's grace, has won thee."

As the Knight spoke thus, the grey eyes fixed on his face grew wide with wonder; soft, with a great compunction; yet, at the corners, shewed a little crinkle in which the Bishop would instantly have recognised the sign of approaching merriment.

Was this then a sample of the unknown sins of men? Nothing here, surely, to cause the least throb of apprehension, even to the heart of a nun! But what strange tale had reached the ears of this most dear and loyal Knight? She leaned a little nearer to him, speaking in a tone which was music to his heart.

"Dear Knight of mine," she said, "no tale of a man's love for me can have been a true one. Yet am I glad that, deeming it true, and feeling as it was your first impulse to feel, you now tell me quite frankly what you felt, thus putting from yourself all sense of wrong, while giving me the chance to say to you, that none more noble than this faithful Knight can have loved me; for, saving a few Court pages, mostly popinjays, and Humphry of Camforth, of whom the less said the better, no other man hath loved me."

More kindly she looked on him than she yet had looked. She leaned across the table.

By reaching out his arms he could have caught her lovely face between his hands.

Her eyes were merry. Her lips smiled.

Greatly tempted was the Knight to agree that, saving himself, and Humphry of Camforth, of whom the less said the better, none save Court popinjays had loved her. Yet in his heart he knew that ever between them would be this fact of his knowledge of the love of Father Gervaise for her, and of the noble renunciation inspired by that love. He had no intention of betraying the Bishop; but Mora's own explanation, making it quite clear that she would not be likely to suspect the identity of the Bishop with his supposed cousin, Father Gervaise, seemed to the Knight to remove the one possible reason for concealment. He was willing to risk present loss, rather than imperil future peace.

With an effort which made his voice almost stern: "The tale was a true one," he said.

She drew back, regarding him with grave eyes, her hands folded before her.

"Tell me the tale," she said, "and I will pronounce upon its truth."

"Years ago, Mora, when you were a young maiden at the Court, attending on the Queen, you were most deeply loved by one who knew he could never ask you in marriage. That being so, so noble was his nature and so unselfish his love, that he would not give himself the delight of seeing you, nor the enjoyment of your friendship, lest, being so strong a thing, his love—even though unexpressed—should reach and stir your heart to a response which, might hinder you from feeling free to give yourself, when a man who could offer all sought to win you. Therefore, Mora, he left the Court, he left the country. He went to foreign lands. He thought not of himself. He desired for you the full completion which comes by means of wedded love. He feared to hinder this. So he went."

Her face still expressed incredulous astonishment.

"His name?" she demanded, awaiting the answer with parted lips, and widely-open eyes.

"Father Gervaise," said the Knight.

He saw her slowly whiten, till scarce a vestige of colour remained.

For some minutes she spoke no word; both sat silent, Hugh ruefully facing his risks, and inclined to repent of his honesty.

At length: "And who told you this tale," she said; "this tale of the love of Father Gervaise for a young maid, half his age?"

184

"Symon of Worcester told it me, three nights ago."

"How came the Bishop to know so strange and so secret a thing? And knowing it, how came he to tell it to you?"

"He had it from Father Gervaise himself. He told it to me, because his remembrance of the sacrifice made so long ago in order that the full completion of wifehood and motherhood might be thine, had always inclined him to a wistful regret over thy choice of the monastic life, with its resultant celibacy; leading him, from the first, to espouse and further my cause. In wedding us to-day, methinks the Bishop felt he was at last securing the consummation of the noble renunciation made so long ago by Father Gervaise."

With a growing dread at his heart, Hugh watched the increasing pallor of her face, the hard line of the lips which, but a few moments before, had parted in such gentle sweetness.

"Alas!" he exclaimed, "I should not have told thee! With my clumsy desire to keep nothing from thee, I have spoilt an hour which else might have been so perfect."

"You did well to tell me, dear Knight of mine," she said, a ripple of tenderness passing across her stern face, as swiftly and gently as the breeze stirs a cornfield. "Nor is there anything in this world so perfect as the truth. If the truth opened an abyss which plunged me into hell, I would sooner know it, than attempt to enter Paradise across the flimsy fabric of a lie!"

Her voice, as she uttered these words, had in it the ring which was wont to petrify wrong-doers of the feebler kind among her nuns.

"Dear Knight, had the Bishop not forestalled me when he named his palfrey, truly I might have found a fine new name for you! But now, I pray you of your kindness, leave me alone with my fallen image for a little space, that I may gather up the fragments and give them decent burial."

With which her courage broke. She stretched her clasped hands across the table and laid her head upon her arms.

Despair seized the Knight as he stood helpless, looking down upon that proud head laid low.

He longed to lay his hand upon the golden softness of her hair.

But her shoulders shook with a hard, tearless sob, and the Knight fled from the arbour.

As he paced the lawn, on which the Bishop had promenaded the evening before, Hugh cursed his rashness in speaking; yet knew, in the heart of his heart, that he could not have done otherwise. Mora's words concerning truth, gave him a background of comfort. Even so had he ever himself felt. But would it prove that his honesty had indeed shattered his chances of happiness, and hers?

A new name? . . . What might it be? . . . What the mischief, had the Bishop named his palfrey? . . . Sheba? Nay, that was the ass!

Solomon? Nay, that was the mare! Yet—how came a mare to be named Solomon?

In his disturbed mental state it irritated him unreasonably that a mare should be called after a king with seven hundred wives! Then he remembered "black, but comely," and arrived at the right name, Shulamite. Of course! Not Solomon but Shulamite. He had read that love-poem of the unnamed Eastern shepherd, with the Rabbi in the mountain fastness. The Rabbi had pointed out that the word used in that description signified "sunburned." The lovely Shulamite maiden, exposed to the Eastern sun while tending her kids and keeping the vineyards, had tanned a ruddy brown, beside which the daughters of Jerusalem, enclosed in King Solomon's scented harem, looked pale as wilting lilies. Remembering the glossy coat of the black mare, Hugh wondered, with a momentary sense of merriment, whether the Bishop supposed the maiden of the "Song of Songs" to have been an Ethiopian.

Then he remembered "Iconoklastes." Yes, surely! The palfrey was Iconoklastes. Now wherefore gave the Bishop such a name to his white palfrey?

Striding blindly about the lawn, of a sudden the Knight stepped full on to a flower-bed. At once he seemed to hear the Bishop's gentle voice: "I named him Iconoklastes because he trampled to ruin some flower-beds on which I spent much time and care, and of which I was inordinately fond."

Ah! . . . That was it! The destroyer of fair bloom and blossom, of buds of promise; of the loveliness of a tended garden. . . . Was this then what he seemed to Mora? He, who had forced her to yield to the insistence of his love? . . . In her chaste Convent cell, she could have remained true to this Ideal love of her girlhood: and, now that she knew it to have been called forth by love, could have received, mentally, its full fruition. Also, in time she might have discovered the identity of the Bishop with Father Gervaise, and long years of perfect friendship might have proved a solace to their sundered hearts, had not he—the trampler upon flower-beds—rudely intervened.

And yet—Mora had been betrothed to him, her love had been his, long after Father Gervaise had left the land.

How could he win her back to be once more as she was when they parted on the castle battlements eight years before?

How could he free himself, and her, from these intangible, ecclesiastical entanglements?

He was reminded of his difficulties when he tried to walk disguised in the dress of the White Ladies, and found his stride impeded by those trailing garments. He remembered the relief of wrenching them off, and stepping clear.

Why not now take the short, quick road to mastery?

But instantly that love which seeketh not its own, the strange new sense so recently awakened in him, laid its calm touch upon his

186

throbbing heart. Until that moment in the crypt the day before, he had loved Mora for his own delight, sought her for his own joy. Now, he knew that he could take no happiness at the cost of one pang to her.

"She must be taught not to shudder," cried the masterfulness which was his by nature.

"She must be given no cause to shudder," amended this new, loyal tenderness, which now ruled his every thought of her.

Presently, returning to the arbour, he found her seated, her elbows on the table, her chin cupped in her hands.

She had been weeping; yet her smile of welcome, as he entered, held a quality he had scarce expected.

He spoke straight to the point. It seemed the only way to step clear of immeshing trammels.

"Mora, it cuts me to the heart that, in striving to be honest with you, I have all unwittingly trampled upon those flower-beds in which you long had tended fair blossoms of memory. Also I fear this knowledge of a nobler love, makes it hard for you to contemplate life linked to a love which seems to you less able for self-sacrifice."

She gazed at him, wide-eyed, in sheer amazement.

"Dear Knight," she said, "true, I am disillusioned, but not in aught that concerns you. You trampled on no flower-beds of mine. My shattered idol is the image of one whom I, with deepest reverence, loved, as a nun might love her Guardian Angel. To learn that he loved me as a man loves a woman, and that he had to flee before that love, lest it should harm me and himself, changes the hallowed memory of years. This morning, three names stood to me for all that is highest, noblest, best: Father Gervaise, Symon of Worcester, and Hugh d'Argent. Now, the Bishop and yourself alone are left. Fail me not, Hugh, or I shall be bereft indeed."

The Knight laughed, joyously. The relief at his heart demanded that much vent. "Then, if I failed thee, Mora, there would be but the Bishop?"

"There would be but the Bishop."

"I will not fail thee, my belovèd. And I fear I must have put the matter clumsily, concerning Father Gervaise. As the Bishop told it to me, there was naught that was not noble. It seemed to me it should be sweet to the heart of a woman to be so loved."

"Hush," she said, sternly. "You know not the heart of a nun."

He did not reason further. It was enough for him to know that the shattered image she had buried was not the ideal of his love and hers, or the hope of future happiness together.

"Time flies, dear Heart," he said. "May I speak to thee of immediate plans?"

"I listen," she answered.

Hugh stood in the entrance, among the yellow roses, leaning against the doorpost, his arms folded on his breast, his feet crossed.

187

At once she was reminded of the scene in her cell, when he had taken up that attitude while still garbed as a nun, and she had said: "I know you for a man," and, in her heart had added: "And a stronger man, surely, than Mary Seraphine's Cousin Wilfred!"

"We ride on to-day," said the Knight, "if you feel able for a few hours in the saddle, to the next stage in our journey. It is a hostel in the forest; a poor kind of place, I fear; but there is one good room where you can be made comfortable, with Mistress Deborah. I shall sleep on the hay, without, amongst my men. Some must keep guard all night. We ride through wild parts to reach our destination."

He paused. He could not hold on to the matter of fact tones in which he had started. When he spoke again, his voice was low and very tender.

"Mora, I am taking thee first to thine own home; to the place where, long years ago, we loved and parted. There, all is as it was. Thy people who loved thee and had fled, have been found and brought back. Seven days of journeying should bring us there. I have sent men on before, to arrange for each night's lodging, and make sure that all is right. Arrived at thine own castle, Mora, we shall be within three hours' ride of mine—that home to which I hope to bring thee. Until we enter there, my wife, although this morning most truly wed, we will count ourselves but betrothed. Once in thy home, it shall be left to thine own choice to come to mine when and how thou wilt. The step now taken— that of leaving the Cloister and coming to me—had perforce to be done quickly, if done at all. But, now it is safely accomplished, there is no further need for haste. The wings of my swift desire shall be dipt to suit thine inclination."

Hugh paused, looking upon her with a half-wistful smile. She made no answer; so presently he continued.

"I have planned that, each day, Mistress Deborah, with the baggage and a good escort, shall go by the most direct route, and the best road. Thus thou and I will be free to ride as we will, visiting places we have known of old and which it may please thee to see again. To-day we can ride out by Kenilworth, and so on our first stage northward. Martin will take Mistress Deborah on a pillion behind him. Should she weary of travelling so, she can have a seat in the cart with the baggage. But they tell me she travels bravely on horseback. We will send them on ahead of us, and on arrival all will be in readiness for thee. If this weather holds, we shall ride each day through a world of sunshine and beauty; and each day's close, my wife, will find us one day nearer home. Does this please thee? Have I thought of all?"

Rising, she came and stood beside him in the entrance to the arbour.

A golden rose, dipping from above, rested against her hair.

Her eyes were soft with tears.

"So perfectly have you thought and planned, dear faithful Knight,

188

that I think our blessèd Lady must have guided you. As we ride out into the sunshine, I shall grow used to the great world once more; and you will have patience and will teach me things I have perhaps forgot."

She hesitated; half put out her hands; but his not meeting them, folded them on her breast.

"Hugh, it seems hard that I should clip your splendid wings; but—oh, Hugh! Think you the heart of a nun can ever become again as the heart of other women?"

"Heaven forbid!" said the Knight, fervently, thinking of Eleanor and Alfrida.

And, as leaving the arbour they walked together over the lawn, she smiled, remembering, how that morning the Bishop had answered the same question in precisely the same words. Whatever Father Gervaise might have said, the Bishop and the Knight were agreed!

Yet she wished, somewhat wistfully, that this most dear and loyal Knight had taken her hands when she held them out.

She would have liked to feel the strong clasp of his upon them.

Possibly our Lady, who knoweth the heart of a woman, had guided the Knight in this matter also.

CHAPTER XLI

WHAT THE BISHOP REMEMBERED

Symon, Bishop of Worcester, sat in his library, in the cool of the day.

He was weary, with a weariness which surpassed all his previous experience of weariness, all his imaginings as to how weary, in body and spirit, a man could be, yet continue to breathe and think.

With some, extreme fatigue leads to restlessness of body. Not so with the Bishop. The more tired he was, the more perfectly still he sat; his knees crossed, his elbows on the arms of his chair, the fingers of both hands pressed lightly together, his head resting against the high back of the chair, his gaze fixed upon the view across the river.

As he looked with unseeing eyes upon the wide stretch of meadow, the distant woods and the soft outline of the Malvern hills, he was thinking how good it would be never again to leave this quiet room; never to move from this chair; never again to see a human being; never to have to smile when he was heart-sick, or to bow when he felt ungracious!

Those who knew the Bishop best, often spoke together of his wondrous vitality and energy, their favourite remark being: that he was never tired. They might with more truth have said that they had never known him to appear tired.

It had long been a rule in the Bishop's private code, that weariness, either of body or spirit, must not be shewn to others. The more tired he was, the more ready grew his smile, the more alert his movements, the more gracious his response to any call upon his sympathy or interest.

He never sighed in company, as did Father Peter when, having supped too well off jolly of salmon, roast venison, and raisin pie, he was fain to let indigestion pass muster for melancholy.

He never yawned in Council, either gracefully behind his hand, as did the lean Spanish Cardinal; or openly and unashamed, as did the round and rosy Abbot of Evesham, displaying to the fascinated gaze of the brethren in stalls opposite, a cavernous throat, a red and healthy tongue, and a particularly fine set of teeth.

Moreover the Bishop would as soon have thought of carrying a garment from the body of a plague-stricken patient into the midst of a family of healthy children, as of entering an assemblage with a jaded countenance or a languorous manner.

Therefore: "He is never weary," said his friends.

"He knoweth not the meaning of fatigue," agreed his acquaintances.

"There is no merit in labour which is not in anywise a burden, but, rather, a delight," pronounced those who envied his powers.

"He is possessed," sneered his enemies, "by a most energetic demon! Were that demon exorcised, the Bishop would collapse, exhausted."

"He is filled," said his admirers, "by the Spirit of God, and is thus so energized that he can work incessantly, without experiencing ordinary human weakness."

And none knew that it was a part of his religion to Symon of Worcester, to hide his weariness from others.

Yet once when, in her chamber, he sat talking with the Prioress, she had risen, of a sudden, saying: "You are tired, Father. Rest there in silence, while I work at my missal."

She had passed to the table; and the Bishop had sat resting, just as he was sitting now, save that his eyes could then dwell on her face, as she bent, absorbed, over the illumination.

After a while he had asked: "How knew you that I was tired, my dear Prioress?"

Without lifting her eyes, she had made answer: "Because, my Lord Bishop, you twice smiled when there was no occasion for smiling."

Another period of restful silence, while she worked, and he

watched her working. Then he had remarked: "My friends say I am never tired."

And she had answered: "They would speak more truly if they said that you are ever brave."

It had amazed the Bishop to find himself thus understood. Moreover he could scarce put on his biretta, so crowned was his head by the laurels of her praise. Also this had been the only time when he had wondered whether the Prioress really believed Father Gervaise to be at the bottom of the ocean. It is ever an astonishment to a man when the unerring intuition of a woman is brought to bear upon himself.

Now, in this hour of his overwhelming fatigue, he recalled that scene. Closing his eyes on the distant view, and opening them upon the enchanted vistas of memory, he speedily saw that calm face, with its chastened expression of fine self-control, bending above the page she was illuminating. He saw the severe lines of the wimple, the folds of the flowing veil, the delicate movement of the long fingers, and—yes!—resting upon her bosom the jewelled cross, sign of her high office.

Thus looking back, he vividly recalled the extraordinary restfulness of sitting there in silence, while she worked. No words were needed. Her very presence, and the fact that she knew him to be weary, rested him.

He looked again. But now the folds of the wimple and veil were gone. A golden circlet clasped the shining softness of her hair.

The Bishop opened tired eyes, and fixed them once again upon the landscape.

He supposed the long rides on two successive days had exhausted him physically; and the strain of securing and ensuring the safety and happiness of the woman who was dearer to him than life, had reacted now in a mental lassitude which seemed unable to rise up and face the prospect of the lonely years to come.

The thought of her as now with the Knight, did not cause him suffering. His one anxiety was lest anything unforeseen should arise, to prevent the full fruition of their happiness.

He had never loved her as a man loves the woman he would wed;—at least, if that side of his love had attempted to arise, it had instantly been throttled and flung back.

It seemed to him that, from the very beginning he had ever loved her as Saint Joseph must have loved the maiden intrusted to his keeping—his, yet not his; called, in the inspired dream, "Mary, thy wife"; but so called only that he might have the right to guard and care for her—she who was shrine of the Holiest, o'ershadowed by the power of the Highest; Mother of God, most blessèd Virgin forever.

It seemed to the Bishop that his joy in watching over Mora, since his appointment to the See of Worcester, had been such as Saint Joseph could well have understood; and now he had accomplished the supreme thing; and, in so doing, had left himself desolate.

On the afternoon of the previous day, so soon as the body of the old lay-sister had been removed from the Prioress's cell, the Bishop had gathered together all those things which Mora specially valued and which she had asked him to secure for her; mostly his gifts to her.

The Sacramentaries, from which she so often made copies and translations, now lay upon his table.

His tired eyes dwelt upon them. How often he had watched the firm white fingers opening those heavy clasps, and slowly turning the pages.

The books remained; yet her presence was gone.

His weary brain repeated, over and over, this obvious fact; then began a hypothetical reversal of it. Supposing the books had gone, and her presence had remained? . . . Presently a catalogue formed itself in his mind of all those things which might have gone, unmissed, unmourned, if her dear presence had remained. . . . Before long the Palace . . . the City . . . the Cathedral itself . . . all had swelled the list. . . . He was alone with Mora and the sunset; . . . and the battlements of glory were the radiant walls of heaven; . . . and soon he and she were walking up old Mary Antony's golden stair together. . . .

Hush! . . . "So He giveth His belovèd sleep."

* * * * * *

The Bishop had but just returned from laying to rest, in the burying-ground of the Convent, the worn-out body of the aged lay-sister.

When he had signified that he intended himself to perform the last rites, Mother Sub-Prioress had ventured upon amazed expostulation.

Such an honour had never, in the history of the Community, been accorded even to the Canonesses, much less to a lay-sister. Surely Father Peter—or the Prior? Had it been the Prioress herself, why then—

Few can remember the petrifying effect of a flash of sudden anger in the kindly eyes of Symon of Worcester. Mother Sub-Prioress will never forget it.

So, with as much pomp and circumstance as if she had been Prioress of the White Ladies, old Mary Antony's humble remains were laid in that plot in the Convent burying-ground which she had chosen for herself, half a century before.

Much sorrow was shewn, by the entire Community. The great loss they had sustained by the mysterious passing of the Prioress from their midst, weighed heavily upon them; and seemed, in some way which they could not fathom, to be connected with the death of the old lay-sister.

As the solemn procession slowly wended its way from the

Chapel, along the Cypress Walk, and so, across the orchard, to the burying-ground, the tears which ran down the chastened faces of the nuns, were as much a tribute of love to their late Prioress, as a sign of sorrow for the loss of Mary Antony. The little company of lay-sisters sobbed without restraint. Sister Abigail, so often called "noisy hussy" by old Antony, fully, on this final occasion, justified the name.

As the procession was re-forming to leave the grave, Sister Mary Seraphine felt that the moment had now arrived, old Antony being disposed of, when she might suitably become the centre of attention, and be carried, on the return journey. She therefore fell prone upon the ground, in a fainting fit.

The Bishop, his chaplain, the priests and acolytes, paused uncertain what to do.

Sister Teresa, and other nuns, would have hastened to raise her, but the command of Mother Sub-Prioress rang sharp and clear.

"Let her lie! If she choose to remain with the Dead, it is but small loss to the Living."

And with hands devoutly crossed upon her breast, ferret face peering to right and left from out the curtain of her veil, Mother Sub-Prioress moved forward at the head of the nuns.

The Bishop's procession, which had wavered, continued to lead the way; solemn chanting began; and, as the Bishop turned into the Cypress Walk he saw the flying figure of Mary Seraphine running among the trees in the orchard, trying to catch up, and to take her place again, unnoticed, among the rest.

The Bishop smiled, remembering his many talks with the Prioress concerning Seraphine, and the Knight's dismay when he feared they were foisting the wayward nun upon him.

Then he sighed as he realised that the control of the Convent had now passed into the able hands of Mother Sub-Prioress; and that, in these unusual circumstances, the task of selecting and appointing a new Prioress, fell to him.

Perhaps his conversations on this subject, first with the Prior, and later on with Mother Sub-Prioress, partly accounted for his extreme fatigue, now that he found himself at last alone in his library.

But the reward of those "whose strength is to sit still," had come to the Bishop.

Soon after he fixed his eyes upon the Gregorian and Gelasian Sacramentaries, his eyelids gently began to droop. Sleep was already upon him when he decided to let the Palace, the City, yea, even the Cathedral go, if he might but keep the Prioress. And as he walked with Mora up the golden stair, his mind was at rest; his weary body slept.

A very few minutes of sleep sufficed the Bishop.

He awoke as suddenly as he had fallen asleep; and, as he awoke, he seemed to hear himself say: "Nay, Hugh. None save the old lay-sister, Mary Antony."

193

He sat up, wondering what this sentence could mean; also when and where it had been spoken.

As he wondered, his eye fell upon the white stone which he had flung into the Severn, and which the Knight, diving from the parapet, had retrieved from the river bed. The stone seemed in some way connected with this chance sentence which had repeated itself in his brain.

The Bishop rose, walked over to his deed chest, took the white stone in his hand and stood motionless, his eyes fixed upon it, wrapped in thought. Then he passed out on to the lawn, and paced slowly to and fro between the archway leading from the courtyard, to the parapet overlooking the river.

Yes; it was here.

He had ridden in on Shulamite, from the heights above the town, whence he had watched the Prioress ride in the river meadow.

He had found Hugh d'Argent awaiting him, and together they had paced this lawn in earnest conversation.

Hugh had been anxious to hear every detail of his visit to the Convent and the scene in the Prioress's cell when he had shewn her the copy of the Pope's mandate, just received from Rome. In speaking of the possible developments which might take place in the course of the next few hours, Hugh had asked whether any in the Convent, beside Mora herself, knew of his presence in Worcester, or that he had managed to obtain entrance to the cloisters by the crypt passage, to make his way disguised to Mora's cell, and to have speech with her.

The Bishop had answered that none knew of this, save the old lay-sister Mary Antony, who was wholly devoted to the Prioress, made shrewd by ninety years of experience in outwitting her superiors, and could be completely trusted.

"How came she to know?" the Bishop seemed to remember that the Knight had asked. And he had made answer that he had as yet no definite information, but was inclined to suspect that when the Prioress had bidden the old woman begone, she had slipped into some place of concealment from whence she had seen and heard something of what passed in the cell.

To this the Knight had made no comment; and now, walking up and down the lawn, the white stone in his hand, the Bishop could not feel sure how far Hugh had taken in the exact purport of the words; yet well he knew that sentences which pass almost unnoticed when heard with a mind preoccupied, are apt to return later on, with full significance, should anything occur upon which they shed a light.

This then was the complication which had brought the Bishop out to pace the lawn, recalling each step in the conversation, there where it had taken place.

Sooner or later, Mora will tell her husband of Mary Antony's wondrous vision. If she reaches the conclusion, uninterrupted, all will

194

be well. The Knight will realise the importance of concealing the fact of the old lay-sister's knowledge—by non-miraculous means—of his presence in the cell, and his suit to the Prioress. But should she preface her recital by remarking that none in the Community had knowledge of his visit, the Knight will probably at once say: "Nay, there you are mistaken! I have it from the Bishop that the old lay-sister, Mary Antony, knew of it, having stayed hidden where she saw and heard much that passed; yet being very faithful, and more than common shrewd, could—so said the Bishop—be most completely trusted."

Whereupon irreparable harm would be done; for, at once, Mora would realise that she had been deceived; and her peace of mind and calm of conscience would be disturbed, if not completely overthrown.

One thing seemed clear to the Bishop.

Hugh must be warned. Probably no harm had as yet been done. The vision was so sacred a thing to Mora, that weeks might elapse before she spoke of it to her husband.

With as little delay as possible Hugh must be put upon his guard.

CHAPTER XLII

THE WARNING

Alert, determined, all trace of lassitude departed, the Bishop returned to the library, laid the stone upon the deed chest, sat down at a table and wrote a letter. He had made up his mind as to what must be said, and not once did he pause or hesitate over a word.

While still writing, he lifted his left hand and struck upon a silver gong.

When his servant entered, the Bishop spoke without raising his eyes from the table.

"Request Brother Philip to come here, without loss of time."

When the Bishop, having signed his letter, laid down the pen, and looked up, Brother Philip stood before him.

"Philip," said the Bishop, "select a trustworthy messenger from among the stable men, one possessed of wits as well as muscle; mount him on a good beast, supply him with whatsoever he may need for a possible six days' journey. Bring him to me so soon as he is ready to set forth. He must bear a letter, of much importance, to Sir Hugh d'Argent; and, seeing that I know only the Knight's route and stopping places, on his northward ride, but not his time of starting, which may have been yesterday or may not be until to-morrow, my messenger must ride first to Warwick, which if the Knight has left, he must then follow in his tracks until he overtake him."

"My lord," said Brother Philip, "the sun is setting and the daylight fades. The messenger cannot now reach Warwick until long after nightfall. Would it not be safer to have all in readiness, and let him start at dawn. He would then arrive early in the day, and could speedily overtake the most worshipful Knight who, riding with his lady, will do the journey by short stages."

"Nay," said the Bishop, "the matter allows of no delay. Mount him so well, that he shall outdistance all dangers. He must start within half an hour."

Brother Philip, bowing low, withdrew.

The Bishop bent again over the table, and read what he had written. Glancing quickly through the opening greetings, he considered carefully what followed.

_"This comes to you, my son, by messenger, riding in urgent haste, because the advice herein contained is of extreme importance.

"On no account let Mora know that which I told you here, four days since, as we paced the lawn; namely: that the old lay-sister, Mary Antony, was aware of your visit to the Convent, and had, from some place of concealment, seen and heard much of what passed in Mora's cell. How far you realised this, when I made mention of it, I know not. You made no comment. It mattered little, then; but has now become a thing of extreme importance.

"On that morning, finding the old lay-sister knew more than any supposed, and was wholly devoted to the Prioress, I had chanced to remark to her as I rode out of the courtyard that the Reverend Mother would thrust happiness from her with both hands unless our Lady herself offered it, by vision or revelation.

"Whereupon, my dear Knight, that faithful old heart using wits she had prayed our Lady to sharpen, contrived a vision of her own devising, so wondrously contrived, so excellently devised, that Mora—not dreaming of old Antony's secret knowledge—could not fail to believe it true. In fact, my son, you may praise heaven for an old woman's wits, for, as you will doubtless some day hear from Mora herself, they gave you your wife!

"But beware lest any chance words of yours lead Mora to suspect the genuineness of the vision. It would cost HER her peace of mind. It might cost YOU her presence.

"Meanwhile the agèd lay-sister died yesterday, after having mystified the entire Community by locking herself into the Prioress's cell, and remaining there, from the time she found it empty when the nuns returned from Vespers, until I arrived on the following afternoon. She thus prevented any questionings concerning Mora's flight, and averted possible scandal. But the twenty-four hours without food or

196

drink cost the old woman her life. A faithful heart indeed, and a most shrewd wit!

"Some day, if occasion permit, I will recount to you the full story of Mary Antony's strategy. It is well worth the hearing.

"I trust your happiness is complete; and hers, Hugh, hers!

"But we must take no risks; and never must we forget that, in dealing with Mora, we are dealing with the heart of a nun.

"Therefore, my son, be wary. Heaven grant this may reach you without delay, and in time to prevent mischief."_

When the messenger, fully equipped for his journey, was brought before the Bishop by Brother Philip, this letter lay ready, sealed, and addressed to Sir Hugh d'Argent, at Warwick Castle in the first place, but failing there, to each successive stopping place upon the northward road, including Castle Norelle, which, the Bishop had gathered, was to be reached on the seventh day after leaving Warwick.

So presently the messenger swung into the saddle, and rode out through the great gates. In a leathern wallet at his belt, was the letter, and a good sum of money for his needs on the journey; and in his somewhat stolid mind, the Bishop's very simple instructions—simple, yet given with so keen a look, transfixing the man, that it seemed to the honest fellow he had received them from the point of a blue steel blade.

He was to ride to Warwick, without drawing rein; to wake the porter at the gate, and the seneschal within, no matter at what hour he arrived. If the Knight were still at the Castle, the letter must be placed in his hands so soon as he left his chamber in the morning. But had he already gone from Warwick, the messenger, after food and rest for himself and his horse, was to ride on to the next stage and, if needful, to the next, until he overtook Sir Hugh and delivered into his own hands, with as much secrecy as possible, the letter.

The Bishop passed along the gallery, after the messenger had left the library, mounted to the banqueting hall and watched him ride away, from that casement, overlooking the courtyard, from which Hugh had looked down upon the arrival of Roger de Berchelai, bringing the letter from Rome.

A great relief filled the mind of the Bishop as he heard the clattering hoofs of the fastest nag in his stables, ring on the paving stones without, and die away in the distance.

A serious danger would be averted, if the Knight were warned in time.

The Bishop prayed that his letter might reach Hugh's hands before Mora was moved to speak to him of Mary Antony's vision.

He blamed himself bitterly for not having sooner recalled that conversation on the lawn. How easy it would have been, after hearing Mora's story in the arbour, to have given Hugh a word of caution before leaving Warwick.

Just after sunset, one of the Bishop's men, who had remained behind at Warwick, reached the Palace, bringing news that the Knight, his Lady, and their entire retinue, had ridden out from Warwick in the afternoon of the previous day.

The Bishop chafed at the delay this must involve, yet rejoiced at the prompt beginning of the homeward journey, having secretly feared lest Hugh should find some difficulty in persuading his bride to set forth with him.

After all, they were but two days ahead of the messenger who, by fast riding, might overtake them on the morrow. Mistress Deborah, even on a pillion, should prove a substantial impediment to rapid progress.

But, alas, before noon on the day following, Brother Philip appeared in haste, with an anxious countenance.

The messenger had returned, footsore and exhausted, bruised and wounded, with scarce a rag to his back.

In the forest, while still ten miles from Warwick, overtaken by the darkness, he had met a band of robbers, who had taken his horse and all he possessed, leaving him for dead, in a ditch by the wayside. Being but stunned and badly bruised, when he came to himself he thought it best to make his way back to Worcester and there report his misadventure.

The Bishop listened to this luckless tale in silence.

When it was finished he said, gently: "My good Philip, thou art proved right, and I, wrong. Had I been guided by thee, I should not have lost a good horse, nor—which is of greater importance at this juncture—twenty-four hours of most precious time."

Brother Philip made a profound obeisance, looking deeply ashamed of his own superior foresight and wisdom, and miserably wishful that the Reverend Father had been right, and he, wrong.

"However," continued the Bishop, after a moment of rapid thought, "I must forgo the melancholy luxury of meditating upon my folly, until after we have taken prompt measures, so far as may be, to put right the mischief it has wrought.

"This time, my good Philip, you shall be the bearer of my letter. Take with you, as escort, two of our men—more, if you think needful. Ride straight from here, by the most direct route to Castle Norelle, the home of the noble Countess, lately wedded to Sir Hugh. I will make you a plan of the road.

"If, when you reach the place, Sir Hugh and his bride have arrived, ask to have speech with the Knight alone, and put the letter into his own hands. But if they are yet on the way, ride to meet them, by a road I will clearly indicate. Only be careful to keep out of sight of all save the Knight or his body-servant, Martin Goodfellow.

"The letter delivered, and the answer in thy hands, return, to me as speedily as may be, without overpressing men or steeds. How soon canst thou set forth?"

198

"Within the hour, my lord," said Brother Philip, joyfully, cured of his shame by this call to immediate service; "with an escort of three, that we may ride by night as well as by day."

"Good," said the Bishop; and, as the lay-brother, bowing low, hastened from the chamber, Symon of Worcester drew toward him writing materials, and penned afresh his warning to the Knight; not at such length as in the former missive, but making very clear the need for silence concerning Mary Antony's previous knowledge of his visit to the Nunnery, lest Mora should come to doubt the genuineness of the vision which had brought her to her great decision, and which in very truth had been wholly contrived by the loving heart and nimble wits of Mary Antony.

So once again the Bishop stood at the casement in the banqueting hall; and, looking down into the courtyard, saw faithful Philip, with an escort fully armed, ride out at the Palace gates.

No time had been lost in repairing the mistake. Yet there was heavy foreboding at the Bishop's heart, as he paced slowly down the hall.

Greatly he feared lest this twenty-four hours' delay should mean mischief wrought, which could never be undone.

Passing into the chapel, he kneeled long before the shrine of Saint Joseph praying, with an intense fervour of petition, that his warning might reach the Knight before any word had passed his lips which could shake Mora's belief in that which was to her the sole justification for the important step she had taken.

The Bishop prayed and fasted; fasted, prayed, and kept vigil. And all the night through, in thought, he followed Brother Philip and his escort as they rode northward, through the forests, up the glens, and over the moors, making direct for Mora's home, to which she and Hugh were travelling by a more roundabout way.

CHAPTER XLIII

MORA MOUNTS TO THE BATTLEMENTS

The moonlight, shining in at the open casement, illumined, with its clear radiance, the chamber which had been, during the years of her maidenhood, Mora de Norelle's sleeping apartment.

It held many treasures of childhood. Every familiar thing within it, whispered of the love and care of those long passed into the realm of silence and of mystery; a noble father, slain in battle; a gentle mother, unable to survive him, the call to her of the spirit of her Warrior, being more compelling than the need of the beautiful young daughter, to whom both had been devoted.

The chamber seemed to Mora full of tender and poignant memories.

How many girlish dreams had been dreamed while her healthy young body rested upon that couch, after wild gallops over the moors, or a long day's climbing among the rocky hills, searching for rare ferns and flowers to transplant into her garden.

In this room she had mourned her father, with her strong young arms wrapped around her weeping mother.

In this room she had wept for her mother, with none to comfort her, saving the faithful nurse, Deborah.

To this room she had fled in wrath, after the scene with, her half-sister, Eleanor, who had tried to despoil her of her heritage—the noble Castle and lands left to her by her father, and confirmed to her, with succession to her father's title, by the King. These Eleanor desired for her son; but neither bribes nor cajolery, threats, nor cruel insinuations, had availed to induce Mora to give up her rightful possession—the home of her childhood.

Before the effects of this storm had passed, Hugh d'Argent had made his first appearance upon the scene, riding into the courtyard as a King's messenger, but also making himself known to the young Countess as a near neighbour, heir to a castle and lands, not far distant, among the Cumberland hills.

With both it had been love at first sight. His short and ardent courtship had, unbeknown to him, required not so much to win her heart, as to overcome her maidenly resistance, rendered stubborn by the consciousness that her heart had already ranged itself on the side of her lover.

When at last, vanquished by his eager determination, she had yielded and become betrothed to him, it had seemed to her that life could hold no sweeter joy.

But he, hard to content, ever headstrong and eager, already having taken the cross, and being now called at once to join the King in Palestine, begged for immediate marriage that he might take her with him to the Court of the new Queen, to which his cousin Alfrida had already been summoned; or, if he must leave her behind, at least leave her, not affianced maid, but wedded wife.

Here Eleanor and her husband had interposed; and, assuming the position of natural guardians, had refused to allow the marriage to take place. This necessitated the consent of the King, which could not be obtained, he being in the Holy Land; and Hugh had no wish to make application to the Queen-mother, then acting regent during the absence of the King; or to allow his betrothed to be brought again into association with the Court at Windsor.

Mora—secretly glad to keep yet a little longer the sweet bliss of betrothal, with its promise of unknown yet deeper joys to come—resisted Hugh's attempts to induce her to defy Eleanor, flout her wrongful claim to authority, and wed him without obtaining the Royal sanction. Steeped in the bliss of having taken one step into an unimagined state of happiness, she felt no necessity or inclination hurriedly to take another.

Yet when, upheld by the ecstasy of those final moments together, she had let him go, as she watched him ride away, a strange foreboding of coming ill had seized her, and a restless yearning, which she could not understand, yet which she knew would never be stilled until she could clasp his head again to her breast, feel his crisp hair in her fingers, and know him safe, and her own.

This chamber then had witnessed long hours of prayer and vigil, as she knelt at the shrine in the nook between the casements, beseeching our Lady and Saint Joseph for the safe return of her lover.

Then came the news of Hugh's supposed perfidy; and from this chamber she had gone forth to hide her broken heart in the sacred refuge of the Cloister; to offer to God and the service of Holy Church, the life which had been robbed of all natural joys by the faithlessness of a man.

And this had happened eight years ago, as men count time. But as nuns count it? And lovers? A lifetime? A night?

It had seemed indeed a lifetime to the Prioress of the White Ladies, during the first days of her return to the world. But to the woman who now kneeled at the casement, drinking in the balmy sweetness of the summer night, looking with soft yearning eyes at the well-remembered landscape flooded in silvery moonlight, it seemed—a night.

A night—since she stood on the battlements, her lover's arms about her.

A night—since she said: "Thou wilt come back to me, Hugh. . . . My love will ever be around thee as a silver shield."

A night—since, as the last words he should hear from her lips, she had said: "Maid or wife, God knows I am all thine own. Thine, and none other's, forever."

Of all the memories connected with this chamber, the clearest to-night was of the hungry ache at her heart, when Hugh had gone. It had seemed to her then that never could that ache be stilled, until she could once again clasp his head to her breast. She knew now that it never had been stilled. Dulled, ignored, denied; called by other names; but stilled—never.

On this night it was as sweetly poignant as on that other night

201

eight years ago, when she had slowly descended to this very room, from the moonlit battlements.

Yet to-night she was maid and wife. Moreover Hugh was here, under this very roof. Yet had he bidden her a grave good-night, without so much as touching her hand. Yet his dark eyes had said: "I love thee."

Kneeling at the casement, Mora reviewed the days since they rode forth from Warwick.

It had been a wondrous experience for her—she, who had been Prioress of the White Ladies—thus to ride out into the radiant, sunny world.

Hugh was ever beside her, watchful, tender, shielding her from any possible pain or danger, yet claiming nothing, asking nothing, for himself.

One night, not being assured of the safety of the place where they lodged, she found afterwards that he had lain all night across the threshold of the chamber within which she and Debbie slept.

Another night she saw him pacing softly up and down beneath her window.

Yet when each morning came, and they began a new day together, he greeted her gaily, with clear eye and unclouded brow; not as one chilled or disappointed, or vexed to be kept from his due.

And oh, the wonder of each new day! The glory of those rides over the mossy softness of the woodland paths, where the sunlight fell, in dancing patches, through the thick, moving foliage, and shy deer peeped from the bracken, with soft eyes and gentle movements; out on to the wild liberty of the moors, where Icon, snuffing the fresher air, would stretch his neck and gallop for pure joy at having left cobbled streets and paved courtyards far behind him. And ever they rode northward, and home drew nearer. Looking back upon those long hours spent alone together, Mora realised how simply and easily she had grown used to being with Hugh, and how entirely this was due to his unselfishness and tact. He talked with her constantly; yet never of his own feelings regarding her.

He told her of his adventures in Eastern lands; of the happenings in England during the past eight years, so far as he had been able to learn them; of his home and property; of hers, and of the welcome which awaited her from her people.

He never spoke of the Convent, nor of the eventful days through which he and she had so recently passed.

So successfully did he dominate her mind in this, that almost it seemed to her she too was returning home after a long absence in a foreign land.

Her mind awoke to unrestrained enjoyment of each hour, and to the keen anticipation of the traveller homeward bound.

Each day spent in Hugh's company seemed to wipe out one, or more, of the intervening years, so that when, toward evening, on the seventh day, the grey turrets of her old home came in sight, it might have been but yesterday they had parted, on those same battlements, and she had watched him ride away, until the firwood from which they were now emerging, had hidden him from view.

Kneeling at her casement, her mind seemed lost in a whirlpool of emotion, as she reviewed the hour of their arrival. The road up to the big gates—every tree and hillock, every stock and stone, loved and familiar, recalling childish joys and sorrows, adventure and enterprise. Then the passing in through the gates, the familiar faces, the glad greetings; Zachary—white-haired, but still rosy and stalwart—at the foot of the steps; and, in the doorway, just where loneliness might have gripped her, old Debbie, looking as if she had never been away, waiting with open arms. So this was the moment foreseen by Hugh when he had planned an early start, that morning, for Mistress Deborah, and a more roundabout ride for her.

She turned, with an impulsive gesture, holding out to him her left hand, that he might cross the threshold with her. But the Knight was stooping to examine the right forehoof of her palfrey, she having fancied Icon had trod tenderly upon it during the last half-mile; so she passed in alone.

Afterwards she overheard old Debbie say, in her most scolding tones: "She did stretch out her hand to you, Sir Hugh, and you saw it not!" But the Knight's deep voice made courteous answer: "There is no look or gesture of hers, however slight, good Mistress Deborah, which doth escape me." And at this her heart thrilled far more than if he had met her hand, responsive; knowing that thus he did faithfully keep his pledge to her, and that he could so keep it, only by never relaxing his stern hold upon himself.

Yet almost she began to wish him less stern and less faithful, so much did she long to feel for one instant the strong clasp of his arms about her. By his rigid adherence to his promise, she felt herself punished for having shuddered. Why had she shuddered? . . . Would she shudder now? This wonderful first evening had quickly passed, in going from chamber to chamber, walking in the gardens, and supping with Hugh in the dining-hall, waited on by Mark and Beaumont, with Zachary to supervise, pour the wine, and stand behind her chair.

Then a final walk on the terrace; a grave good-night upon the stairs; and, at last, this time of quiet thought, in her own chamber.

She could not realise that she was wedded to Hugh; but her heart awoke to the fact that truly she was betrothed to him. And she was happy—deeply happy.

Leaving the casement, she kneeled before the shrine of the Virgin—there where she had put up so many impassioned prayers for the safe return of her lover.

"Blessèd Virgin," she said, "I thank thee for sending me home."

Years seemed to roll from her. She felt herself a child again. She longed for her mother's understanding tenderness. Failing that, she turned to the sweet Mother of God.

The image before which she knelt, shewed our Lady standing, tall and fair and gracious, the Infant Saviour, seated upon her left hand, her right hand holding Him leaning against her, His baby arms outstretched. Neither the Babe nor His Mother smiled. Each looked grave and somewhat sad.

"Home," whispered Mora. "Blessèd Virgin I thank thee for sending me home."

"Nay," answered a voice within her. "I sent thee not home. I gave thee to him to whom thou didst belong. He hath brought thee home. What said the vision? 'Take her. She is thine own. I have but kept her for thee.'"

Yet Hugh knew naught of this gracious message—knew naught of the vision which had given her to him. Until to-night she had felt it impossible to tell him of it. Now she longed that he should share with her the wonder.

She sought her couch, but sleep would not come. The moonlight was too bright; the room too sweetly familiar. Moreover it seemed but yesterday that she had parted from Hugh, in such an ecstasy of love and sorrow, up on the battlements.

A great desire seized her to mount to those battlements, and to stand again just where she had stood when she bade him farewell.

She rose.

Among the garments put ready for her use, chanced to be the robe of sapphire velvet which she had worn on that night.

She put it on; with jewels at her breast and girdle. Then, with the mantle of ermine falling from her shoulders, and her beautiful hair covering her as a veil, she left her chamber, passed softly along the passage, found the winding stair, and mounted to the ramparts.

As she stepped out from the turret stairway, she exclaimed at the sublime beauty of the scene before her; the sleeping world at midnight, bathed in the silvery light of the moon; the shadows of the firs, lying like black bars across the road to the Castle gate.

"There I watched him ride away," she said, with a sweep of her arm toward the road, "watched, until the dark woods swallowed him. And here"—with a sweep toward the turret—"here, we parted."

She turned; then caught her breath.

Leaning against the wall with folded arms, stood Hugh.

CHAPTER XLIV

"I LOVE THEE"

Mora stood, for some moments, speechless; and Hugh did not stir. They faced one another, in the weird, white light.

At last: "Did you make me come?" she whispered.

"Nay, my belovèd," he answered at once; "unless constant thought of thee, could bring thee to me. I pictured thee peacefully sleeping."

"I could not sleep," she said. "It seemed to me our Lady was not pleased, because, dear Knight, I have failed, in all these days, to tell you of her wondrous and especial grace which sent me to you."

"I have wondered," said the Knight; "but I knew there would come a time when I should hear what caused thy mind to change. That it was a thing of much import, I felt sure. The Bishop counselled me to give up hope. But I had besought our Lady to send thee to me, and I could not lose my trust in prayer."

"It was indeed our blessèd Lady who sent me," said Mora, very softly. "Hugh, dare I stay and tell you the whole story, here and now? What if we are discovered, alone upon the ramparts, at this hour of the night?"

Hugh could not forbear a smile.

"Dear Heart," he said, "we shall not be discovered. And, if we were, methinks we have the right to be together, on the ramparts, or off them, at any hour of the day or night."

A low wooden seat ran along beneath the parapet.

Mora sat down and motioned the Knight to a place beside her.

"Sit here, Hugh. Then we can talk low."

"I listen better standing," said the Knight; but he came near, put one foot on the seat, leaned his elbow on his knee, his chin in his hand, and stood looking down upon her.

"Hugh," she said, "I withstood your pleadings; I withstood the Bishop's arguments; I withstood the yearnings of my own poor heart. I tore up the Pope's mandate, and set my foot upon it. I said that nothing could induce me to break my vows, unless our Lady herself gave me a clear sign that my highest duty was to you, thus absolving me from my vows, and making it evident that God's will for me was that I should leave the Cloister, and keep my early troth to you."

"And gave our Lady such a sign?" asked the Knight, his dark eyes fixed on Mora's face.

She lifted it, white and lovely; radiant in the moonlight.

"Better than a sign," she said. "Our Lady vouchsafed a wondrous vision, in which her own voice was heard, giving command and consent."

The Knight, crossing himself, dropped upon his knees, lifting his eyes heavenward in fervent praise and adoration. He raised to his lips a gold medallion, which he wore around his neck, containing a picture of the Virgin, and kissed it devoutly; then overcome by emotion, he covered his face with his hands and knelt with bowed head, reciting in a low voice, the Salve Regina.

Mora watched him, with deep gladness of heart. This fervent joy and devout thanksgiving differed so greatly from the half-incredulous, whimsically amused, mental attitude with which Symon of Worcester had received her recital of the miracle. Hugh's reverent adoration filled her with happiness.

Presently he rose and stood beside her again, expectant, eager.

"Tell me more; nay, tell me all," he said.

"The vision," began Mora, "was given to the old lay-sister, Mary Antony."

"Mary Antony?" queried Hugh, with knitted brow. "'The old lay-sister, Mary Antony'? Why do I know that name? I seem to remember that the Bishop spoke of her, as we walked together in the Palace garden, the day following the arrival of the messenger from Rome. Methinks the Bishop said that she alone knew of my intrusion into the Nunnery; but that she, being faithful, could be trusted."

"Nay, Hugh," answered Mora, "you mistake. It was I who told you so, even before I knew you were the intruder, while yet addressing you as Sister Seraphine's 'Cousin Wilfred.' I said that you had been thwarted in your purpose by the faithfulness of the old lay-sister, Mary Antony, who never fails to count the White Ladies, as they go, and as they return, and who had reported to me that one more had returned than went. Afterward I was greatly perplexed as to what explanation I should make to Mary Antony; when, to my relief, she came and confessed that hers was the mistake, she having counted wrongly. Glad indeed was I to let it rest at that; so neither she, nor any in the Convent, knew aught of your entrance there or your visit to my cell. The Bishop, you, and I, alone know of it."

"Then I mistake," said the Knight. "But I felt certain I had heard the name, and that the owner thereof had some knowledge of my movements. Now, I pray thee, dear Heart, tell me all."

So sitting there on the ramparts of her old home, the stillness of the fragrant summer night all around, Mora told from the beginning the wondrous history of the trance of Mary Antony, and the blessèd vision then vouchsafed to her.

The Knight listened with glowing eyes. Once he interrupted to exclaim: "Oh, true! Most true! More true than thou canst know. Left alone in thy cell, I kneeled to our Lady, saying those very words: 'Mother of God, send her to me! Take pity on a hungry heart, a lonely

206

home, a desolate hearth, and send her to me.' I was alone. Only our Lady whom I besought, heard those words pass my lips."

Again Hugh kneeled, kissed the medallion, and lifted to heaven eyes luminous with awe and worship.

Continuing, Mora told him all, even to each detail of her long night vigil and her prayer for a sign which should be given direct to herself, so soon granted by the arrival and flight of the robin. But this failed to impress Hugh, wholly absorbed in the vision, and unable to see where any element of hesitation or of uncertainty could come in. Hearing it from Mora, he was spared the quaint turn which was bound to be given to any recital, however sacred, heard direct from old Mary Antony.

The Knight was a Crusader. Many a fight he had fought for that cause representing the highest of Christian ideals. Also, he had been a pilgrim, and had visited innumerable holy shrines. For years, his soul had been steeped in religion, in that Land where true religion had its birth, and all within him, which was strongest and most manly, had responded with a simplicity of faith, yet with a depth of ardent devotion, which made his religion the most vital part of himself. This it was which had given him a noble fortitude in bearing his sorrow. This it was which now gave him a noble exultation in accepting his great happiness. It filled him with rapture, that his wife should have been given to him in direct response to his own earnest petition.

When at length Mora stood up, stretching her arms above her head and straightening her supple limbs:

"My belovèd," he said, "if the vision had not been given, wouldst thou not have come to me? Should I have had to ride away from Worcester alone?"

Standing beside him, she answered, tenderly:

"Dear Hugh, my most faithful and loyal Knight, being here—and oh so glad to be here—how can I say it? Yet I must answer truly. But for the vision, I should not have come. I could not have broken my vows. No blessing would have followed had I come to you, trailing broken vows, like chains behind me. But our Lady herself set me free and bid me go. Therefore I came to you; and therefore am I here."

"Tell me again the words our Lady said, when she put thy hand in mine."

"Our Lady said: 'Take her. She hath been ever thine. I have but kept her for thee.'"

Then she paled, her heart began to beat fast, and the colour came and went in her cheeks; for he had come very near, and she could hear the sharp catch of his breath.

"Mora, my belovèd," he said, "every fibre of my being cries out for thee. Yet I want thy happiness before my own; and, above and beyond all else, I want the Madonna in my home. Even at our Lady's

207

bidding I cannot take thee. Not until thine own sweet lips shall say: 'Take me! I have been ever thine.'"

She lifted her eyes to his. In the moonlight, her face seemed almost unearthly, in its pure loveliness; and, as on that night so long ago, he saw her eyes, brighter than any jewels, shining with love and tears.

"Dear man of mine," she whispered, "to-night we are betrothed. But to-morrow I will ride home with thee. To-morrow shall be indeed our bridal day. I will say all—I will say anything—I will say everything thou wilt! Nay, see! The dawn is breaking in the east. Call it 'to-day'—TO-DAY, dear Knight! But now let me flee away, to fathom my strange happiness alone. Then, to sleep in mine own chamber, and to awake refreshed, and ready to go with thee, Hugh, when and where and how thou wilt."

The Knight folded his arms across his breast.

"Go," he said, softly, "and our Lady be with thee. Our spirits to-night have had their fill of holy happiness. I ask no higher joy than to watch the breaking of the day which gives thee to me, knowing thee to be safely sleeping in thy chamber below."

"I love thee!" she whispered; and fled.

Hugh d'Argent watched the dawn break—a silver rift in the purple sky.

His heart was filled with indescribable peace and gladness.

It meant far more to him that his bride should have come to him in obedience to a divine vision, than if his love had mastered her will, and she had yielded despite her own conscience.

Also he knew that at last his patient self-restraint had won its reward. The heart of a nun feared him no longer. The woman he loved was as wholly his as she had ever been.

As the sun began to gild the horizon, flecking the sky with little rosy clouds, Hugh turned into the turret archway, went down the steps, and sought his chamber. No sooner was he stretched upon his couch, than, for very joy, he fell asleep.

But—beyond the dark fir woods, and over the hills on the horizon, four horsemen, having ridden out from a wayside inn before the dawn, watched, as they rode, the widening of that silver rift in the sky, and the golden tint, heralding the welcome appearance of the sun.

So soundly slept Hugh d'Argent that, three hours later, be did not wake when a loud knocking on the outer gates roused the porter; nor, though his casement opened on to the courtyard, did he hear the noisy clatter of hoofs, as Brother Philip, with his escort of three mounted men, rode in.

Not until a knocking came on his own door did the Knight awake and, leaping from his bed, see—as in a strange, wild dream—Brother Philip, dusty and haggard, standing on the threshold, the Bishop's letter in his hand.

CHAPTER XLV

THE SONG OF THE THRUSH

The morning sun already poured into her room, when Mora opened her eyes, waking suddenly with that complete wide-awakeness which follows upon profound and dreamless slumber.

Even as she woke, her heart said: "Our bridal day! The day I give myself to Hugh! The day he leads me home."

She stretched herself at full length upon the couch, her hands crossed upon her breast, and let the delicious joy of her love sweep over her, from the soles of her feet to the crown of her head.

The world without lay bathed in sunshine; her heart within was flooded by the radiance of this new and perfect realisation of her love for Hugh.

She lay quite still while it enveloped her.

Ten days ago, our Lady had given her to Hugh.

Eight days ago, the Bishop, voicing the Church, had done the same.

But to-day she—she herself—was going to give herself to her lover.

This was the true bridal! For this he had waited. And the reward of his chivalrous patience was to be, that to-day, of her own free will she would say; "Hugh, my husband, take me home."

She smiled to remember how, riding forth from the city gates of Warwick, she had planned within herself that, once safely established in her own castle, she would abide there days, weeks, perhaps even, months!

She stretched her arms wide, then flung them above her head.

"Take me home," she whispered. "Hugh, my husband, take me home."

A thrush in the coppice below, whistled in liquid notes: *"Do it now! Do it now! Do it now!"*

Laughing joyously, Mora leapt from her bed and looked out upon a sunny summer's day, humming with busy life, fragrant with scent of flowers, thrilling with songs of birds.

"What a bridal morn!" she cried. "All nature says 'Awake! Arise!' Yet I have slept so late. I must quickly prepare myself to find and to greet my lover."

"Do it now!" sang the thrush.

Half an hour later, fresh and fragrant as the morn, Mora left her chamber and made her way to the great staircase.

Hearing shouting in the courtyard, and the trampling of horses' feet, she paused at a casement, and looked down.

To her surprise she saw the well-remembered figure of Brother Philip, mounted; with him three other horsemen wearing the Bishop's livery, and Martin Goodfellow leading Hugh's favourite steed, ready saddled.

Much perplexed, she passed down the staircase, and out on to the terrace where she had bidden them to prepare the morning meal.

From the terrace she looked into the banqueting hall, and her perplexity grew; for there Hugh d'Argent, booted and spurred, ready for a journey, strode up and down.

For two turns she watched him, noting his knitted brows, and the heavy forward thrust of his chin.

Then, lifting his eyes as he swung round for the third time, he saw her, outside in the sunlight; such a vision of loveliness as might well make a man's heart leap.

He paused in his rapid walk, and stood as if rooted to the spot, making no move toward her.

For a moment, Mora hesitated.

"*Do it now!*" sang the thrush.

CHAPTER XLVI

"HOW SHALL I LET THEE GO?"

Mora passed swiftly into the banqueting hall.

"Hugh," she said, and came to him. "Hugh, my husband, this is our bridal day. Will you take me to our home?"

His eyes, as they met hers, were full of a dumb misery.

Then a fierce light of passion, a look of wild recklessness, flashed into them. He raised his arms, to catch her to him; then let them fall again, glancing to right and left, as if seeking some way of escape.

But, seeing the amazement on her face, he mastered, by a mighty effort, his emotion, and spoke with calmness and careful deliberation.

"Alas, Mora," he said, "it is a hard fate indeed for me on this day, of all days, to be compelled to leave thee. But in the early morn there came a letter which obliges me, without delay, to ride south, in order to settle a matter of extreme importance. I trust not to be gone longer than nine days. You, being safely established in your own home, amongst your own people, I can leave without anxious fears. Moreover, Martin Goodfellow will remain here representing me, and will in all things do your bidding."

"From whom is this letter, Hugh, which takes you from me, on such a day?"

"It is from a man well known to me, dwelling in a city four days' journey from here."

"Why not say at once: 'It is from the Bishop, written from his Palace in the city of Worcester'?"

Hugh frowned.

"How knew you that?" he asked, almost roughly.

"My dear Knight, hearing much champing of horses in my courtyard, I looked down from a casement and saw a lay-brother well known to me, and three other horsemen wearing the Bishop's livery. What can Symon of Worcester have written which takes you from me on this day, of all days?"

"That I cannot tell thee," he made answer. "But he writes, without much detail, of a matter about which I must know fullest details, without loss of time. I have no choice but to ride and see the Bishop, face to face. It is not a question which can be settled by writing nor could it wait the passing to and fro of messengers. Believe me, Mora, it is urgent. Naught but exceeding urgency could force me from thee on this day."

"Has it to do with my flight from the Convent?" she asked.

He bowed his head.

"Will you tell me the matter on your return, Hugh?"

"I know not," he answered, with face averted. "I cannot say." Then with sudden violence: "Oh, my God, Mora, ask me no more! See the Bishop, I must! Speak with him, I must! In nine days at the very most, I will be back with thee. Duty takes me, my belovèd, or I would not go."

Her mind responded instinctively to the word "duty," "Go then, dear Knight," she said. "Settle this business with Symon of Worcester. I have no desire to know its purport. If it concerns my flight from the Convent, surely the Pope's mandate is all-sufficient. But, be it what it may, in the hands of my faithful Knight and of my trusted friend, the Bishop, I may safely leave it. I do but ask that, the work accomplished, you come with all speed back to me."

With a swift movement he dropped on one knee at her feet.

"Send me away with a blessing," he said. "Bless me before I go."

She laid her hands on the bowed head.

"Alas!" she cried, "how shall I let thee go?"

Then, pushing her fingers deeper into his hair and bending over him, with infinite tenderness: "How shall thy wife bless thee?" she whispered.

He caught his breath, as the fragrance of the newly gathered roses at her bosom reached and enveloped him.

"Bless me," he said, hoarsely, "as the Prioress of the White Ladies used to bless her nuns, and the Poor at the Convent gate."

211

"Dear Heart," she said, and smiled. "That seems so long ago!" Then, as with bent head he still waited, she steadied her voice, lifting her hands from off him; then laid them back upon his head, with reverent and solemn touch. "The Lord bless thee," she said, "and keep thee; and may our blessèd Lady, who hath restored me to thee, bring thee safely back to me again."

At that, Hugh raised his head and looked up into her face, and the misery in his eyes stirred her tenderness as it had never been stirred by the vivid love-light or the soft depths of passion she had heretofore seen in them.

Her lips parted; her breath came quickly. She would have caught him to her bosom; she would have kissed away this unknown sorrow; she would have smothered the pain, in the sweetness of her embrace.

But bending swiftly he lifted the hem of her robe and touched it with his lips; then, rising, turned and left her without a word; without a backward look.

He left her standing there, alone in the banqueting hall. And as she stood listening, with beating heart, to the sound of his voice raised in command; to the quick movements of his horse's hoofs on the paving stones, as he swung into the saddle; to the opening of the gates and the riding forth of the little cavalcade, a change seemed to have come over her. She ceased to feel herself a happy, yielding bride, a traveller in distant lands, after long journeyings, once more at home.

She seemed to be again Prioress of the White Ladies. The calm fingers of the Cloister fastened once more upon her pulsing heart. The dignity of office developed her.

And wherefore?

Was it because, when her lips had bent above him in surrendering tenderness, her husband had chosen to give her the sign of reverent homage accorded to a prioress, rather than the embrace which would have sealed her surrender?

Or was it because he had asked her to bless him as she had been wont to bless the Poor at the Convent gate?

Or was it the unconscious action of his mind upon hers, he being suddenly called to face some difficulty which had arisen, concerning their marriage, or the Bishop's share in her departure from the Nunnery?

The clang of the closing gates sounded in her ears as a knell.

She shivered; then remembered how she had shivered at sound of the turning of the key in the lock of the crypt-way door. How great the change wrought by eight days of love and liberty. She had shuddered then at being irrevocably shut out from the Cloister. She shuddered now because the arrival of a messenger from the Bishop, and something indefinable in Hugh's manner, had caused her to look back.

212

She stood quite still. None came to seek her. She seemed to have turned to stone.

It was not the first time this looking back had had a petrifying effect upon a woman. She remembered Lot's wife, going forward led by the gentle pressure of an angel's hand, yet looking back the moment that pressure was removed.

She had gone forward, led by the sweet angel of our Lady's gracious message. Why should she look back? Rather would she act upon the sacred precept: "Forgetting those things which are behind, and reaching forth unto those things which are before"—this, said the apostle Saint Paul, was the one thing to do. Undoubtedly now it was the one and only thing for her to do; leaving all else which might have to be done, to her husband and to the Bishop.

"This one thing I do," she said aloud; "this one thing I do." And moving forward, in the strength of that resolve, she passed out into the sunshine.

"Do it now!" sang the thrush, in the rowan-tree.

CHAPTER XLVII

THE BISHOP IS TAKEN UNAWARES

Symon of Worcester, seated before a table in the library, pondered a letter which had reached him the evening before, brought by a messenger from the Vatican.

It was a call to return to the land he loved best; the land of sunshine and flowers, of soft speech and courteous ways; the land of heavenly beauty and seraphic sounds; and, moreover, to return as a Cardinal of Holy Church.

His acceptance or refusal must be penned before night. The messenger expected to start upon his return journey early on the morrow.

Should he go? Or should he stay?

Was all now well for Mora? Or did she yet need him?

Surely never had Cardinal's hat hung poised for such a reason! How little would the Holy Father dream that a question affecting the happiness or unhappiness of a woman could be a cause of hesitancy.

Presently, with a quick movement, the Bishop lifted his head. The library was far removed from the courtyard; but surely he heard the clatter of horses' hoofs upon the raving stones.

He had hardly hoped for Brother Philip's return until after sunset; yet—with fast riding—

If the Knight's answer were in all respects satisfactory—If Mora's happiness was assured—why, then—

He sounded the silver gong.

His servant entered.

"What horsemen have just now ridden into the courtyard, Jasper?"

"My lord, Brother Philip has this moment returned, and with him—"

"Bid Brother Philip to come hither, instantly."

"May it please you, my lord—"

"Naught will please me," said the Bishop, "but that my commands be obeyed without parley or delay."

Jasper's obeisance took him through the door.

The Bishop bent over the letter from Rome, shading his face with his hand.

He could scarcely contain his anxiety; but he did not wish to give Brother Philip occasion to observe his tremulous eagerness to receive the Knight's reply.

He heard the door open and close, and a firm tread upon the floor. It struck him, even then, that the lay-brother had not been wont to enter his presence with so martial a stride, and he wondered at the ring of spurs. But his mind was too intently set upon Hugh d'Argent's letter, to do more than unconsciously notice these things.

"Thou art quickly returned, my good Philip," he said, without looking round. "Thou has done better than my swiftest expectations. Didst thou give my letter thyself into the hands of Sir Hugh d'Argent, and hast thou brought me back an answer from that most noble Knight?"

Wherefore did Brother Philip make no reply?

Wherefore did his breath come sharp and short—not like a stout lay-brother who has hurried; but, rather, like a desperate man who has clenched his teeth to keep control of his tongue?

The Bishop wheeled in his chair, and found himself looking full into the face of Hugh d'Argent—Hugh, haggard, dusty, travel-stained, with eyes, long strangers to sleep, regarding him with a sombre intensity.

"You!" exclaimed the Bishop, surprised out of his usual gentle calm. "You? Here!"

"Yes, I," said the Knight, "I! Does it surprise you, my Lord Bishop, that I should be here? Would it not rather surprise you, in view of that which you saw fit to communicate to me by letter, that I should fail to be here—and here as fast as horse could bring me?"

"Naught surprises me," said the Bishop, testily. "I have lived so long in the world, and had to do with so many crazy fools, that human

214

vagaries no longer have power to surprise me. And, by our Lady, Sir Knight, I care not where you are, so that you have left safe and well, her peace of mind undisturbed, the woman whom I—acting as mouthpiece of the Pope and Holy Church—gave, not two weeks ago, into your care and keeping."

The Knight's frown was thunderous.

"It might be well, my Lord Bishop, to leave our blessèd Lady's name out of this conversation. It hath too much been put to shameful and treacherous use. Mora is safe and well. How far her peace of mind can be left undisturbed, I am here to discover. I require, before aught else, the entire truth."

But the Bishop had had time to recover his equanimity. He rose with his most charming smile, both hands out-stretched in gracious welcome.

"Nay, my dear Knight, before aught else you require a bath! Truly it offends my love of the beautiful to see you in this dusty plight." He struck upon the gong. "Also you require a good meal, served with a flagon of my famous Italian wine. You did well to come here in person, my son. If naught hath been said to Mora, no harm is done; and together we can doubly safeguard the matter. I rejoice that you have come. But the strain of rapid travelling, when anxiety drives, is great. . . . Jasper, prepare a bath for Sir Hugh d'Argent in mine own bath-chamber; cast into it some of that fragrant and refreshing powder sent to me by the good brethren of Santa Maria Novella. While the noble Knight bathes, lay out in the ante-chamber the complete suit of garments he was wearing on the day when the sudden fancy seized him to have a swim in our river. I conclude they have been duly dried and pressed and laid by with sweet herbs? . . . Good. That is well. Now, my dear Hugh, allow Jasper to attend you. He will give his whole mind to your comfort. Send word to Brother Philip, Jasper, that I will speak with him here."

The Bishop accompanied the Knight to the door of the library; watched him stride along the gallery, silent and sullen, in the wake of the hastening Jasper; then turned and walked slowly back to the table, smiling, and gently rubbing his hands together as he walked.

He had gained time, and he had successfully regained his sense of supremacy. Taken wholly by surprise, he had not felt able to cope with this gaunt, dusty, desperately determined Knight. But the Knight would leave more than mere travel stains behind, in the scented waters of the bath! He would reappear clothed and in his right mind. A good meal and a flagon of Italian wine would further improve that mind, mellowing it and rendering it pliable and easy to convince; though truly it passed comprehension why the Knight should need convincing, or of what! Even more incomprehensible was it, that a man wedded to Mora, not two weeks since, should of his own free will elect to leave her.

The Bishop turned.

Brother Philip stood in the doorway, bowing low.

"Come in, my good Philip," said the Bishop; "come in, and shut the door. . . . I must have thy report with fullest detail; but, time being short, I would ask thee to begin from the moment when the battlements of Castle Norelle came into view."

CHAPTER XLVIII

A STRANGE CHANCE

On the fourth day of her husband's absence, Mora climbed to the battlements to watch the glories of a most gorgeous sunset.

Also she loved to find herself again there where she and Hugh had spent that wonderful hour in the moonlight, when she had told him of the vision, and afterwards had given him the promise that on the morrow he should take her to his home.

She paused in the low archway at the top of the winding stair, remembering how she had turned a moment there, to whisper: "I love thee." Ah, how often she had said it since: "Dear man of mine, I love thee! Come back to me safe; come back to me soon; I love thee!"

That he should have had to leave her just as her love was ready to respond to his, had caused that love to grow immeasurably in depth and intensity.

Also she now realised, more fully, his fine self-control, his chivalrous consideration for her, his noble unselfishness. From the first, he had been so perfect to her; and now her one desire was that, if her love could give it, he should have his reward.

Ah, when would he come! When would he come!

She could not keep from shading her eyes and looking along the road to the point where it left the fir wood, though this was but the fourth day since Hugh's departure—the day on which, by fast riding and long hours, he might arrive at Worcester—and the ninth was the very earliest she dared hope for his return.

How slowly, slowly, passed the days. Yet they were full of a quiet joy and peace.

From the moment when she had stepped out into the sunshine, resolved to go steadily forward without looking back, she had thrown herself with zest and pleasure into investigating and arranging her house and estate.

Also, on the second day an idea had come to her with her first waking thoughts, which she had promptly put into execution.

Taking Martin Goodfellow with her she had ridden over to Hugh's home; had found it, as she expected, greatly needing a woman's hand and mind, and had set to work at once on those changes and arrangements most needed, so that all should be in readiness when Hugh, returning, would take her home.

Under her direction the chamber which should be hers was put into perfect order; her own things were transported thither, and all was made so completely ready, that at any moment she and Hugh could start, without need of baggage or attendants, and ride together home.

This chamber had two doors, the one leading down a flight of steps on to a terrace, the other opening directly into the great hall, the central chamber of the house.

Mora loved to stand in this doorway, looking into the noble apartment, with its huge fireplace, massive carved chairs on either side of the hearth, weapons on the walls, trophies of feats of arms, all those things which made it home to Hugh, and to remember that of this place he had said in his petition to our Lady: "Take pity on a lonely home, a desolate hearth . . . and send her to me."

No longer should it be lonely or desolate. Aye, and no longer should his faithful heart be hungry.

On this day she had been over for the third time, riding by the road, because she and Martin both carried packages of garments and other things upon their saddles; but returning by a shorter way through the woods, silent and mossy, most heavenly cool and green.

This journey had served to complete her happy preparations. So now, should Hugh arrive, even at sunset, and be wishful to ride on without delay, she could order the saddling of Icon, and say: "I am ready, dear Knight; let us go."

She stood on the Castle wall, gazing at the blood-red banners of the sunset, flaming from the battlements of a veritable city of gold; then, shading her eyes, turned to look once again along the road.

And, at that moment, out from the dark fir wood there rode a horseman, alone.

For one moment only did her heart leap in the wild belief that Hugh had returned. The next instant she knew this could not be he; even before her eyes made out a stranger.

She watched him leave the road, and turn up the winding path which led to the Castle gate; saw the porter go to the grating in answer to a loud knocking without; saw him fetch old Zachary, who in his turn sent for Martin Goodfellow; upon which the gates were opened wide, and the stranger rode into the courtyard.

Whereupon Mora thought it time that she should descend from the battlements and find out who this unexpected visitor might be.

At the head of the great staircase, she met Martin.

217

"Lady," he said, "there waits a man below who urgently desires speech with Sir Hugh. Learning from us that the Knight hath ridden south, and is like to be away some days longer, he begs to have word with you, alone; yet refuses to state his business or to give his name. Master Zachary greatly hopeth that it may be your pleasure that we bid the fellow forthwith depart, telling him—if he so will—to ride back in six days' time, when the worshipful Knight, whom he desires to see, will have returned."

Mora knitted her brows. It did not please her that Zachary and Martin Goodfellow should arrange together what she should do.

"Describe him, Martin," she said. "What manner of man is he?"

"Swarthy," said Martin, "and soldierly; somewhat of a dare-devil, but on his best behaviour. Zachary and I would suggest—"

"I will see him," said Mora, beginning to descend the stairs. "I will see him in the banqueting hall, and alone. You, Martin, can wait without, entering on the instant if I call. Tell Zachary to bid them prepare a meal of bread and meat, with a flagon of wine, or a pot of good ale, which I may offer to this traveller, should he need refreshment."

She was standing in the banqueting hall, on the very spot where Hugh had kneeled at their parting, when the swarthy fellow, soldierly, yet somewhat of a dare-devil, entered.

Most certainly he was on his best behaviour. He doffed his cap at first sight of her, advanced a few paces, then stood still, bowing low; came forward a few more paces, then bowed again.

She spoke.

"You wished to see my husband, Friend, and speak with him? He is away and hardly can return before five days, at soonest. Is your business with Sir Hugh such as I can pass on to him for you, by word of mouth?"

She hoped those bold, dark eyes did not perceive how she glowed to speak for the first time, to another, of Hugh as her husband.

He answered, and his words were blunt; his manner, frank and soldierly.

"Most noble Lady, failing the Knight, whom I have ridden far to find, my business may most readily be told to you.

"Years ago, on a Syrian battle-field it was my good fortune, in the thick of the fray, to find myself side by side with Sir Hugh d'Argent. The Infidels struck me down; and, sorely wounded, I should have been at their mercy, had not the noble Knight, seeing me fall, wheeled his horse and, riding back, hewn his way through to me, scattering mine assailants right and left. Then, helping me to mount behind him, galloped with me back to camp. Whereupon I swore, by the holy Cross at Lucca, that if ever the chance came my way to do a service to Sir Hugh of the Silver Shield, I would travel to the world's end to do it.

"Ten nights ago, I chanced to be riding through a wood

218

somewhere betwixt Worcester and Warwick. A band of lawless fellows coming by, I and my steed drew off the path, taking cover in a thicket. But a solitary horseman, riding from Worcester, failed to avoid them. Within sight of my hiding-place he was set upon, made to dismount, stripped and bidden to return on foot to the place from whence he came. I could do naught to help him. We were two, to a round dozen. The robbers took the money from his wallet. Within it they found also a letter, which they flung away as worthless. I marked where it fell, close to my hiding-place.

"When the affray was over, their victim having fled and the lawless band ridden off, I came forth, picked up the letter and slipped it into mine own wallet. So soon as the sun rose I drew forth the letter, when, to my amaze, I found it addressed to my brave rescuer, the Knight of the Silver Shield and Azure Pennant. It appeared to be of importance as, failing Warwick Castle, six halting places, all on the northward road, were named on the outside; also it was marked to be delivered with most urgent haste.

"It seemed to me that now had come my chance, to do this brave Knight service. Therefore have I ridden from place to place, following; and, after some delay, I find myself at length at Castle Norelle, only to hear that he to whom I purposed to hand the letter has ridden south by another road. Thus is my endeavour to serve him rendered fruitless."

"Nay, Friend," said Mora, much moved by this recital. "Not fruitless. Give me the letter you have thus rescued and faithfully attempted, to deliver. My husband returns in five days. I will then hand him the letter and tell him your tale. Most grateful will he be for your good service, and moved by your loyal remembrance."

The swarthy fellow drew from his wallet a letter, heavily sealed, and inscribed at great length. He placed it in Mora's hands.

Her clear eyes dwelt upon his countenance with searching interest. It was wonderful to her to see before her a man whose life Hugh had saved, so far away, on an Eastern battle-field.

"In my husband's name, I thank you, Friend," she said. "And now my people will put before you food and wine. You must have rest and refreshment before you again set forth."

"I thank you, no," replied the stranger. "I must ride on, without delay. I bid you farewell, Lady; and I do but wish the service, which a strange chance has enabled me to render to the Knight, had been of greater importance and had held more of risk or danger."

He bowed low, and departed. A few moments later he was riding out at the gates, and making for the northward road.

Had Brother Philip chanced to be at hand, he could not have failed to note that the swarthy stranger was mounted upon the fastest nag in the Bishop's stable.

For a life of lawlessness, rapine, and robbery, does not debar a

219

man from keeping an oath sworn, out of honest gratitude, in cleaner, better days.

Left alone, Mora passed on to the terrace and, in the clearer light, examined this soiled and much inscribed missive.

To her amazement she recognised the well-known script of Symon, Bishop of Worcester. How many a letter had reached her hands addressed in these neat characters.

Yet Hugh had left her, and gone upon this ride of many days to Worcester in order to see the Bishop, because he had received a letter telling him, without sufficient detail, a matter of importance. Probably the letter she now held in her hands should have reached him first. Doubtless had he received it, he need not have gone.

Pondering this matter, and almost unconscious that she did so, Mora broke the seals. Then paused, even as she began to unfold the parchment, questioning whether to read it or to let it await Hugh's return.

But not long did she hesitate. It was upon a matter which closely concerned her. That much Hugh had admitted. It might be imperative to take immediate action concerning this first letter, which by so strange a mishap had arrived after the other. Unless she mastered its contents, she could not act.

Ascending the turret stairway, Mora stepped again on to the battlements.

The golden ramparts in the west had faded; but a blood-red banner still floated above the horizon. The sky overhead was clear.

Sitting upon the seat on which she had sat while telling Hugh of old Mary Antony's most blessèd and wondrous vision, Mora unfolded and read the Bishop's letter.

CHAPTER XLIX

TWICE DECEIVED

The blood-red banner had drooped, dipped, and vanished.

The sky overhead had deepened to purple, and opened starry eyes upon the world beneath. Each time the silent woman, alone upon the battlements, lifted a sorrowful face to the heavens, yet another bright eye seemed to spring wide and gaze down upon her.

At length the whole expanse of the sky was studded with stars; the planets hung luminous; the moon, already waning, rose large and golden from behind the firs, growing smaller and more silvery as she mounted higher.

Mora covered her face with her hands. The summer night was too full of scented sweetness. The stars sang together. The moon rode triumphant in the heavens. In this her hour of darkness she must shut out the brilliant sky. She let her face sink into her hands, and bowed her head upon her knees.

Blow after blow had fallen upon her from the Bishop's letter.

First that the Bishop himself was plotting to deceive her, and seemed to take Hugh's connivance for granted.

Then that she had been hoodwinked by old Mary Antony, on the evening of Hugh's intrusion into the Nunnery; that this hoodwinking was known to the Bishop, and appeared but to cause him satisfaction, tempered by a faint amusement.

Then the overwhelming news that Mary Antony's vision had been an imposition, devised and contrived by the almost uncannily shrewd wits of the old woman; and that the Bishop advised the Knight to praise heaven for those wits, and to beware lest any chance word of his should lead her—Mora—to doubt the genuineness of the vision, and to realise that she had been hocussed, hoodwinked, outwitted! In fact the Bishop and her husband were to become, and to continue indefinitely, parties to old Antony's deception.

She now understood the full significance of the half-humorous, half-sceptical attitude adopted by the Bishop, when she recounted to him the history of the vision. No wonder he had called Mary Antony a "most wise and prudent babe."

But even as her anger rose, not only against the Bishop, but against the old woman she had loved and trusted and who had so deceived her, she came upon the news of the death of the aged lay-sister and the account of her devoted fidelity, even to the end.

Mary Antony living, was often a pathetic figure; Mary Antony dead, disarmed anger.

And, after all, the old lay-sister and her spurious vision faded into insignificance in view of the one supreme question: What course would Hugh take? Would he keep silence and thus tacitly become a party to the deception; or would he, at all costs, tell her the truth?

It was evidence of the change her love had wrought in her, that this one point was so paramount, that until it was settled, she could not bring herself to contemplate other issues.

She remembered, with hopeful comfort, his scrupulous honesty in the matter of Father Gervaise. Yet wherefore had he gone to consult with the Bishop unless he intended to fall in with the Bishop's suggestions?

Not until she at last sought her chamber and knelt before the shrine of the Madonna, did she realise that her justification in leaving the Convent was gone, if there had been no vision.

"Blessèd Virgin," she pleaded, with clasped hands uplifted; "I, who have been twice deceived—tricked into entering the Cloister, and tricked into leaving it—I beseech thee, by the sword which pierced through thine own soul also, grant me now a vision which shall be, in very deed, a VISION OF TRUTH."

CHAPTER L

THE SILVER SHIELD

The Bishop sat at the round table in the centre of the banqueting hall, sipping water from his purple goblet while the Knight dined.

They were not alone. Lay-brethren, with sandalled feet, moved noiselessly to and fro; and Brother Philip stood immovable behind the Reverend Father's chair.

The Bishop discoursed pleasantly of many things, watching Hugh the while, and blessing the efficacy of the bath. It had, undoubtedly, cleansed away much beside travel-stains.

The thunder-cloud had lifted from the Knight's brow; his eyes, though tired, were no longer sombre; his manner was more than usually courteous and deferential, as if to atone for the defiant brusquerie of his first appearance.

He listened in absolute silence to the Bishop's gentle flow of conversation; but this was a trait the Bishop had observed in him before; and, after all, a lapse into silence could be easily understood when a man had travelled far, on meagre fare, and found himself seated at a well-spread board.

Yet the Knight ate but sparingly of the good cheer, so lavishly provided; and the famous Italian wine, he scarce touched at all.

The meal over, the Bishop dismissed Brother Philip and the attendant monks, and, rising, went to his chair near the hearth, motioning the Knight to the one opposite.

Thus they found themselves seated again as they had sat on the night of the arrival of the Pope's messenger; save that now no fire burned upon the hearth; no candles were lighted on the table. Instead, the summer sunshine poured in through open casements.

"Well, my dear Hugh," said the Bishop, "suppose you now tell me the reason which brings you hither. It must surely be a matter of grave importance which could cause so devoted a lover and husband to leave

222

his bride, and go a five days' journey from her, within two weeks of the bridal day."

"I have come, my lord," said the Knight, speaking slowly and with evident effort, "to learn from your lips the entire truth concerning that vision which caused the Prioress of the White Ladies to hold herself free to renounce her vows, leave her Nunnery, and give herself in marriage where she had been betrothed before entering the Cloister."

"Tut!" said the Bishop. "The White Ladies have no Prioress. Mother Sub-Prioress doth exercise the functions of that office until such time as the Prior and myself shall make a fresh appointment. We are not here to talk of prioresses, my son, but of that most noble and gracious lady who, by the blessing of God and our Lady's especial favour, is now your wife. See to it that you continue to deserve your great good fortune."

The Knight made no protest at the mention of our Lady; but his left hand moved to the medallion hanging by a gold chain from his neck, covered it and clasped it firmly.

The Bishop paused; but finding that the Knight had relapsed into silence, continued:

"So you wish the entire history of the inspired devotion of the old lay-sister, Mary Antony—may God rest her soul." Both men crossed themselves devoutly, as the Bishop named the Dead. "Shall I give it you now, my son, or will you wait until the morrow, when a good night's rest shall fit you better to enjoy the recital?"

"My lord," said Hugh, "ere this sun sets, I hope to be many miles on my homeward way."

"In that case," said the Bishop, "I must tell you this moving story, without further delay."

So, beginning with her custom of counting the White Ladies by means of the dried peas, the Bishop gave the Knight the whole history of Mary Antony's share in the happenings in the Nunnery on the day of his intrusion, and those which followed; laying especial stress on her devotion to Mora, and her constant prayers to our Lady to sharpen her old wits.

The Bishop had undoubtedly intended to introduce into the recital somewhat more of mysticism and sublimity than the actual facts warranted. But once launched thereon, his sense of humour could not be denied its full enjoyment in this first telling of the entire tale. Full justice he did to the pathos, but he also shook with mirth over the ludicrous. As he quoted Mary Antony, the old lay-sister's odd manner and movements could be seen; her mumbling lips, and cunning wink. And here was Mother Sub-Prioress, ferret-faced and peering; and here Sister Mary Rebecca, long-nosed, flat-footed, eager to scent out and denounce wrong doing. And at last the Bishop told of his talk with Mora in the arbour of golden roses; and lo, there was Mora, devout, adoring, wholly believing. "Thou hast hid these things from the wise and prudent and hast revealed them unto babes"; and here, the Bishop himself, half amused, half incredulous: "An ancient babe! Truly, a most wise and prudent babe." Then the scene outside the Prioress's cell when the Bishop unlocked the door; the full confession and the touching death of old Mary Antony.

To it all the Knight listened silently, shading his face with his right hand.

"Therefore, my son," concluded Symon of Worcester, "when on a sudden I remembered our conversation on the lawn, and that I had told you of my belief that the old lay-sister knew of your visit to the Convent and had seen you in Mora's cell, I hastened to send you a warning, lest you should, unwittingly, mention this fact to Mora, and raise a doubt in her mind concerning the genuineness of the vision, thus destroying her peace, and threatening her happiness and your own. Hath she already told you of the vision?"

Still shielding his face the Knight spoke, very low:

"The evening before the messenger arrived, bringing your letter, my lord, Mora told me of the vision."

"Said you aught concerning my words to you?"

"So soon as she mentioned the name of Mary Antony, I said that I seemed to recall that you, my lord, had told me she alone knew of my visit to the Convent. But Mora at once said nay, that it was she herself who had told me so, even while I stood undiscovered in her cell; but that afterward the lay-sister had confessed herself mistaken. This seemed to me to explain the matter, therefore I said no more; nor did I, for a moment, doubt the truth and wonder of the vision."

"For that, the saints be praised," said the Bishop. "Then no harm is done. You and I, alone, know the entire story; and you and I, who would safeguard Mora's happiness with our lives, must see to it that she never has cause for misgivings."

Hugh d'Argent lifted his head, and looked full at the Bishop.

"My lord," he said, "had there been no vision, no message from our Lady, no placing by her of Mora's hand in mine, think you she would have left the Nunnery and come to me?"

"Nay, dear lad, that I know she would not. On that very morning, as I told you, she set her foot upon the Pope's mandate, and would accept no absolving from her vows. Naught would suffice, said she, but a direct vision and revelation from our Lady herself."

"But," said the Knight, slowly, "was there a vision, my lord? Was there a revelation? Was there a spoken message or a given sign?"

The Bishop met the earnest eyes, full of a deep searching. He stirred uneasily; then smiled, waving a deprecatory hand.

"Between ourselves, my dear Hugh—though even so, it is not well to be too explicit—between ourselves of course nothing—well—miraculous happened, beyond the fact that our Lady most certainly

224

sharpened the wits of old Antony. Therefore is it, that you undoubtedly owe your wife to those same wits, and may praise our Lady for sharpening them."

Then it was that the Knight rose to his feet.

"And I refuse," he said, "to owe my wife to sacrilege, fraud, and falsehood."

The Bishop leaned forward, gripping with both hands the arms of his chair. His face was absolutely colourless; but his eyes, like blue steel, seemed to transfix the Knight, who could not withdraw his regard from those keen points of light.

The Bishop's whisper, when at length he spoke, was more alarming than if he had shouted.

"Fool!" he said. "Ungrateful, unspeakable fool! What mean you by such words?"

"Call me fool if you will, my Lord Bishop," said the Knight, "so long as I give not mine own conscience cause to call me knave."

"What mean you by such words?" persisted the Bishop. "I mean, my lord, that if the truth opened out an abyss which plunged me into hell, I would sooner know it than attempt to enter Paradise across the flimsy fabric of a lie."

Now during many days, Symon of Worcester had worked incessantly, suffered much, accomplished much, surrendered much, lost much. Perhaps it is hardly to be wondered at, that, at this juncture, he lost his temper.

"By Saint Peter's keys!" he cried, "I care not, Sir Knight, whether you drop to hell or climb to Paradise. But it is my business to see to it that you do not disturb the peace of mind of the woman you have wed. Therefore I warn you, that if you ride from here set upon so doing, you will not reach your destination alive."

The Knight smiled. The film of weariness lifted as if by magic from his eyes, and they shone bright and serene.

"I cannot draw my sword upon threats, my Lord Bishop; but let those threats take human shape, and by Saint George, I shall find pleasure in rendering a good account of them. With this same sword I once did hew my way through a score of Saracens. Think you a dozen Worcester cut-throats could keep me from reaching my wife?"

Something in the tone with which the Knight spoke these final words calmed the Bishop; something in the glance of his eye quelled the angry Prelate. In the former he recognised a depth of love such as he had not hitherto believed possible to Hugh d'Argent; in the latter, calm courage, nay, a serene joy at the prospect of danger, against which his threats and fury could but break themselves, even as stormy waves against the granite rocks of the Cornish coast.

The Bishop possessed that somewhat rare though valuable faculty, the ability to recognise instantly, and instantly to accept, the inevitable. Also when he had made a false move, he knew it, and was preparing to counteract it almost before his opponent had perceived the mistake.

So rarely was the Bishop angry, that his anger now affected him physically, with a sickening sense of faintness. With closed eyes, he leaned his head against the back of the chair. His face, always white and delicate, now appeared as if carved in ivory. His lips fell apart, but no breath issued from them. Except for a slight twitching of the eyelids, the Bishop's countenance was lifeless.

Startled and greatly alarmed, Hugh looked around for some means whereby he might summon help, but could see none.

Hastening to the table, he poured wine into the Venetian goblet, brought it back, and moistened the Bishop's lips. Then kneeling on one knee loosed the cold fingers from their grip.

Presently the Bishop opened his eyes—no longer points of blue steel, but soft and dreamy like a mist of bluebells on distant hills. He looked, with unseeing gaze, into the anxious face on a level with his own; then turned his eyes slowly upon the ruby goblet which the Knight had lifted from the floor and was trying to hold to his lips.

Waving it away, the Bishop slipped the finger and thumb of his left hand into his sash, and drew out a small gold box of exquisite workmanship, set with emeralds.

At this he gazed for some time, as if uncertain what to do with it; then touched a spring and as the lid flew open, sat up and took from the box a tiny white tablet. This he dropped into the wine.

The Knight, watching with anxious eyes, saw it rapidly dissolve as it sank to the bottom.

But all consciousness of the tablet, the wine, or the kneeling Knight, appeared to have instantly faded from the Bishop's mind. He lay back gazing dreamily at a banner which, for no apparent reason, stirred and wafted to and fro, as it hung from an oaken beam, high up among the rafters.

"Wherefore doth it waft?" murmured the Bishop, thereby adding greatly to the Knight's alarm. "Wherefore?—Wherefore?—Wherefore doth it waft?"

"Drink this, Reverend Father," urged the Knight. "I implore you, my dear lord, raise yourself and drink."

"Methinks there must be a draught," mused the Bishop.

"Yea, truly," said the Knight, "of your famous Italian wine. Father, I pray you drink."

"Among the rafters," said the Bishop. But he sat up, took the goblet from the Knight's hand, and slowly sipped its contents.

Almost at once, a faint tinge of colour shewed in his cheeks and on his lips; his eyes grew bright. He smiled at the Knight, as he placed the empty goblet on the table beside him.

"Ah, my dear Hugh," he said, extending his hand; "it is good to

226

find you here. Let us continue our conversation, if you are sufficiently rested and refreshed. I have much to say to you."

In the reaction of a great relief, Hugh d'Argent seized the extended hand and fervently kissed the Bishop's ring.

It was the reverent homage of a loyal heart. Symon of Worcester, as with a Benedicite he graciously acknowledged it, suffered a slight twinge of conscience; almost as unusual an experience as the ebullition of temper. He took up the conversation exactly at that point to which it best suited him to return, namely, there where he had made the first false step.

"Therefore, my dear Hugh, I have now given you in detail the true history of the vision, making it clear that we owe it, alas! to earthly devotion, rather than to Divine interposition—though indeed the one may well be the means used by the other. It remains for us to consider, and to decide upon, the best line to take with Mora in order to safeguard most surely her peace of mind, and permanently to secure her happiness."

"I have considered, Reverend Father," said the Knight, simply; "and I have decided."

"What have you decided to do, my son?" questioned Symon of Worcester, in his smoothest tones.

"To make known to Mora, so soon as I return, the entire truth."

The Bishop cast his eyes upward, to see whether the banner still waved.

It did.

Undoubtedly there must be a current of air among the rafters.

"And what effect do you suppose such a communication will have, my son, upon the mind of your wife?"

"I am not called to face suppositions, Reverend Father; I am simply confronted by facts."

"Precisely, my son, precisely," replied the Bishop, pressing his finger-tips together, and raising them to his lips. "Yet even while dealing with causes, it is well sometimes to consider effects, lest they take us wholly unawares. Do you realise that, as your wife felt justified in leaving the Nunnery and wedding you, solely by reason of our Lady's miraculously accorded permission, when she learns that that permission was not miraculous, she will cease to feel justified?"

"I greatly fear it," said the Knight.

"Do you yourself now consider that she was not justified?"

"Nay!" answered the Knight, with sudden vehemence. "Always, since I learned how we had been tricked by her sister, I have held her to be rightfully mine. Heaven knew, when she made her vows, that I was faithful, and she therefore still my betrothed. Heaven allowed me to discover the truth, and to find her—alive, and still unwed. To my thinking, no Divine pronouncement was required; and when the Holy Father's mandate arrived bringing the Church's sanction, why then

227

indeed naught seemed to stand between us. But Mora thought otherwise."

A tiny gleam came into the Bishop's eyes; an exceedingly refined edition of the look of cunning which used to peep out of old Mary Antony's.

"Have you ever heard tell, my son, that two negatives make an affirmative? Think you not that, in something the same way, two deceptions may make a truth. Mora was deceived into entering the Convent, and deceived into leaving it; but from out that double deception arises the great truth that she has, in the sight of Heaven, been all along yours. The first deception negatives the second, and the positive fact alone remains that Mora is wedded to you, is yours to guard and shield from sorrow; and those whom God hath joined together, let no man put asunder."

Hugh d'Argent passed his hand across his brow.

"I trust the matter may appear thus to Mora," he said.

The banner still wafted, gently. The Bishop gave himself time to ponder whence that draught could come.

Then: "It will not so appear," he said. "My good Hugh, when your wife learns from you that she was tricked by Mary Antony, she will go back in mind to where she was before the spurious vision, and will feel herself to be still Prioress of the White Ladies."

"I have so felt her, since the knowledge reached me," agreed the Knight.

The efficacy of the soothing drug taken by the Bishop was strained to its utmost.

"And what then do you propose to do, my son, with this wedded Prioress? Do you expect her to remain with you in your home, content to fulfil her wifely duties?"

"I fear," said the Knight sadly, "that she will leave me."

"And I am certain she will leave you," said the Bishop.

"It was largely this fear for the future which brought me at once to you, my lord. If Mora desires, as you say, to consider herself as she was, before she was tricked into leaving the Convent, will you arrange that she shall return, unquestioned, to her place as Prioress of the White Ladies of Worcester?"

"Impossible!" said the Bishop, shortly. "It is too late. We can have no Madonna groups in Nunneries, saving those carven in marble or stone."

To which there followed a silence, lasting many minutes.

Then the Knight said, with effort, speaking very low: "It is not too late."

Instantly the keen eyes were searching his face. A line of crimson leapt to the Bishop's cheek, as if a whip-lash had been drawn across it.

Presently: "Fool!" he whispered, but the word savoured more of pitying tenderness than of scorn. Alas! was there ever so knightly a fool,

228

or so foolish a knight! "What was the trouble, boy? Didst find that after all she loved thee not?"

"Nay," said Hugh, quickly, "I thank God, and our Lady, that my wife loves me as I never dreamed that such as I could be loved by one so perfect in all ways as she. But—at first—all was so new and strange to her. It was wonder enough to be out in the world once more, free to come and go; to ride abroad, looking on men and things. I put her welfare first. . . . Nay, it was easy, loving her as I loved, also greatly desiring the highest and the best. Father, I wanted what you spoke of as the Madonna in the Home. Therefore—'twas I who made the plan—we agreed that, the wedding having of necessity been so hurried, the courtship should follow, and we would count ourselves but betrothed, even after reaching Castle Norelle, for just so many days or weeks as she should please; until such time as she herself should tell me she was wishful that I should take her home. But—each day of the ride northward had been more perfect than that which went before; each hour of each day, sweeter than the preceding. Thus it came to pass that on the very evening of our arrival at Mora's home, after parting for the night at the door of her chamber, we met again on the battlements, where years before we had said farewell; and there, seated in the moonlight, she told me the wonder of our Lady's grace in the vision; and, afterwards, in words of perfect tenderness, the even greater wonder of her love, and that she was ready on the morrow to ride home with me. So we parted in a rapture so deep and pure, that sleep came, for very joy of it. But early in the morning I was wakened by a rapping at my door, and there stood Brother Philip, holding your letter, Reverend Father."

"Alas!" said the Bishop. "Would that I had known she would have whereby to explain away thy memory of that which I had said."

Yet the Bishop spoke perfunctorily; he spoke as one who, even while speaking, muses upon other matters. For, within his secret soul, he was fighting the hardest temptation yet faced by him, in the whole history of his love for Mora.

By rapid transition of mind, he was back on the seat in the garden of the White Ladies' Nunnery, left there by Mary Antony while she went to fetch the Reverend Mother. He was looking up the sunny lawn toward the cloisters, from out the shade of the great beech tree. Presently he saw the Prioress coming, tall and stately, her cross of office gleaming upon her breast, her sweet eyes alight with welcome. And at once they were talking as they always talked together—he and she—each word alive with its very fullest meaning; each thought springing to meet the thought which matched it.

Next he saw himself again on that same seat, looking up the lawn to the sunlit cloisters; realising that never again would the Prioress come to greet him; facing for the first time the utter loneliness, the irreparable loss to himself, of that which he had accomplished for Hugh and Mora.

The Bishop's immeasurable loss had been Hugh's infinite gain. And now that Hugh seemed bent upon risking his happiness, the positions were reversed. Would not his loss, if he persisted, be the Bishop's gain?

How easy to meet her on the road, a few miles from Worcester; to proceed, with much pomp and splendour, to the White Ladies' Nunnery; to bid them throw wide the great gates; to ride in and, then and there, reinstate Mora as Prioress, announcing that the higher service upon which the Holy Father had sent her had been duly accomplished. Picture the joy in the bereaved Community! But, above and beyond all, picture what it would mean to have her there again; to see her, speak with her, sit with her, when he would. No more loneliness of soul, no more desolation of spirit; and Mora's conscience at rest; her mind content.

But at that, being that it concerned the woman he loved, the true soul of him spoke up, while his imaginative reason fell silent.

Never again could the woman who had told Hugh d'Argent, in words of perfect tenderness, the wonder of her love, and that she was ready on the morrow to ride home with him, be content in the calm of the Cloister.

If Hugh persisted in this folly of frankness and disturbed her peace, she might leave him.

If the Bishop made the way easy, she might return to the Nunnery.

But all the true life of her would be left behind with her lover.

She would bring to the Cloister a lacerated conscience, and a broken heart.

Surely the two men who loved her, if they thrust away all thought of self, and thought only of her, could save her this anguish.

At once the Bishop resolved to do his part.

"My dear Hugh," he said, "you did well to come to me in order to consult over these plans before taking the irrevocable step which should set them in motion. I, alone, could reinstate your wife as Prioress of the White Ladies; moreover my continued presence here would be essential, to secure her comfort in that reinstatement. And I shall not be here. I am shortly leaving Worcester, leaving this land and returning to my beauteous Italy. The Holy Father has been pleased to tell me privately of high preferment shortly to be offered me. I have to-day decided to accept it. I return to Italy a Cardinal of Holy Church."

Hugh rose to his feet and bowed. An immense scorn blazed in his eyes.

"My Lord High Cardinal, I congratulate you! That a cardinal's hat should tempt you from your cathedral, from this noble English city, from your people who love you, from the land of your birth, may perhaps be understood. But that, for the sake of Church preferment, however high, you should willingly depart, leaving Mora in sorrow, Mora in difficulty, Mora needing your help—"

The Knight paused, amazed. The Bishop, who seldom laughed aloud, was laughing. Yet no! The Bishop, who never wept, seemed near to weeping.

The scales fell from Hugh's eyes, even before the Bishop spoke. He realised a love as great as his own.

"Ah, foolish lad!" said Symon of Worcester; "bent upon thine own ways, and easy to deceive. When I spoke of going, I said it for her sake, hoping the prospect of my absence might hold you from your purpose. But now truly am I convinced that you are bent upon risking your own happiness, and imperilling hers. Therefore will I devise some means of detaining the Holy Father's messenger, so that my answer need not be given until two weeks are past. You will reach Mora, at longest, five days from this. As soon as she decides what she will do, send word to me by a fast messenger. Should she elect to return to the Nunnery, state when and where, upon the road, I am to meet her. Her habit as Prioress, and her cross of office, I have here. The former you returned to me, from the hostel; the latter I found in her cell. You must take them with you. If she returns, she must return fully robed. If, on the other hand, she should decide to remain with you; if—as may God grant—she is content, and requires no help from me, send me this news by messenger. I can then betake myself to that fair land to which I first went for her sake; left for her sake, and to which I shall most gladly return, if her need of me is over. The time I state allows a four days' margin for vacillation."

"My lord," said the Knight, humbly, "forgive the wrong I did you. Forgive that I took in earnest that which you meant in jest; or rather, I do truly think, that which you hoped would turn me from my purpose. Alas, I would indeed that I might rightly be turned therefrom."

"Hugh," said the Bishop, eagerly, "you deemed her justified in coming to you, apart from any vision."

"True," replied the Knight, "but I cannot feel justified in taking her, and all she would give me, knowing she gives it, with a free heart, because of her faith in the vision. Moments of purest joy would be clouded by my secret shame. Being aware of the deception, I too should be deceiving her; I, whom she loves and trusts."

"To withhold a truth is not to lie," asserted the Bishop.

"My lord," replied Hugh d'Argent, rising to his feet and standing erect, his hand upon his sword, "I cannot reason of these things; I cannot define the difference between withholding a truth and stating a lie. But when mine Honour sounds a challenge, I hear; and I ride out to do battle—against myself, if need be; or, if it must so be, against another. On Eastern battle-fields, in Holy War, I won a name known throughout all the camp, known also to the enemy: 'The Knight of the

231

Silver Shield.' Our name is Argent, and we ever have the right to carry a pure silver shield. But I won the name because my shield was always bright; because not once in battle did it fall in the dust; because it never was allowed to tarnish. So bright it was, that as I rode, bearing it before me, reflecting the rays of the sun, it dazzled and blinded the enemy. My lord, I cannot tarnish my silver shield by conniving at falsehood, or keeping silence when mine Honour bids me speak."

Looking at the gallant figure before him, the Bishop's soul responded to the noble words, and he longed to praise them and applaud. But he thought of Mora's peace of mind, Mora's awakened heart and dawning happiness. For her sake he must make a final stand.

"My dear Hugh," he said, "all this talk, of a silver shield and of the challenge of honour, is well enough for the warrior on the battle-field. But the lover has to learn the harder lesson; he has to give up Self, even the Self which holds honour dear. When you polished your silver shield, keeping it so bright, what saw you reflected therein? Why, your own proud face. Even so, now, you fear the faintest tarnish on your sense of honour, but you will keep that silver shield bright at Mora's expense, riding on proudly alone in your glory, reflecting the sun, dazzling all beholders, while your wife who loved and trusted you, Mora, who told you the sweet wonder of her love in words of deepest tenderness, lies desolate in the dark, with a shattered life, and a broken heart. Hugh, I would have you think of the treasure of her golden heart, rather than of the brightness of your own selfish, silver shield."

"Selfish!" cried the Knight. "Selfish! Is it selfish to hold honour dear? Is it selfish to be ashamed to deceive the woman one loves? Have I, who have so striven in all things to put her welfare first, been selfish towards my wife in this hour of crisis?"

He sat down, heavily; leaned his elbows on his knees, and dropped his head into his hands.

This attitude of utter dejection filled the Bishop with thankfulness. Was he, in the very moment when he had given up all hope of winning, about to prove the victor?

"Perilously selfish, my dear Hugh," he said. "But, thank Heaven, no harm has yet been done. Listen to me and I will shew you how you may keep your honour safely untarnished, yet withhold from Mora all knowledge which might cause her disquietude of mind, thus securing her happiness and your own."

CHAPTER LI

TWO NOBLE HEARTS GO DIFFERENT WAYS

On that same afternoon, an hour before sunset, the two men who loved Mora faced one another, for a final farewell.

The Bishop had said all he had to say. Without interruption, his words had flowed steadily on; eloquent, logical, conciliatory, persuasive.

At first he had talked to the top of the Knight's head, to the clenched hands, to the arms outstretched across the table.

He had wondered what thoughts were at work beneath the crisp thickness of that dark hair. He had wished the rigid attitude of tense despair might somewhat relax. He had used the most telling inflexions of his persuasive voice in order to bring this about, but without success. He had wished the Knight would break silence, even to rage or to disagree. To that end he had cast as a bait an intentional slip in a statement of facts; and, later on, a palpable false deduction in a weighty argument. But the Knight had not risen to either.

After a while Hugh had lifted his head, and leaned back in his chair; fixing his eyes, in his turn, upon the banner hanging from the rafters.

It had ceased to wave gently to and fro. Probably Father Benedict had closed the trap-door, concealed behind an upright beam, through which he was wont to peer down into the banqueting hall below, in order to satisfy himself that all was well and that the Reverend Father needed naught.

Let it be here recorded that this exceeding vigilance, on the part of Father Benedict, met with but scant reward. For, having deduced a draught, and its reason, from the slight stirring of the banner during his conversation with the Knight, the Bishop gave certain secret instructions to Brother Philip, with the result that the next time the Chaplain peered down upon a private conference he found, at its close, the door by which he had gained access to the roof chamber barred on the outside, and, forcing it, he was in no better case, the ladder which connected it with another disused chamber below having been removed. Thereafter Father Benedict watched the Bishop, and his guest, partake of three meals, before he could bring himself to make known his predicament, and beg to be released. And, even then, the Bishop was amazingly slow in locating the place from which issued the agitated voice imploring assistance. Several brethren were summoned to help; so that quite a little crowd stood gazing up at the pallid countenance of Father Benedict, framed in the trap-door as, lying upon his very empty stomach, he called down replies to the Bishop's

233

questions; vainly striving to give a plausible reason for the peculiar situation in which he was discovered.

But, to return to the interview which brought about this later development.

The Knight had lifted his head, yet had still remained silent and impassive.

Where at length the Bishop had paused, awaiting comment of some kind, Hugh d'Argent, removing his eyes from the rafters, had asked:

"When, my lord, do you propose to meet the Prioress, should my wife, upon learning the truth, elect to return to the Nunnery?"

Thus had the Bishop been forced to realise that the flow of his eloquence, the ripple of his humour, the strong current of his arguments, the gentle lapping of his tenderness, the breakers of his threats, and the thunderous billows of his denunciations, had alike expended themselves against the rock of the Knight's unshakable resolve, and left it standing.

Whereupon, in silence, the Bishop had risen, and had led the way to the library.

Here they now faced one another in final farewell.

Each knew that his loss would be the other's gain; his gain, the other's irreparable loss.

Yet, at that moment, each thought only of Mora's peace of soul. They did but differ in their conception of the way in which that peace might best be preserved and maintained.

"I must take her cross of office, my Lord Bishop," said the Knight, with decision.

The Bishop went to a chest, standing in one corner of the room, opened it, and bent over it, his back to Hugh d'Argent; then, slipping his hand into his bosom drew therefrom a cross of gold gleaming with emeralds. Shutting down the massive lid of the chest, he returned, and placed the cross in the outstretched hand of the Knight.

"I entrust it to you, my dear Hugh, only on one condition: that it shall without fail return to me in two weeks' time. Should you decide to tell your wife the true history of the vision, I must see this cross of office upon her breast when I meet her riding back to Worcester, once more Prioress of the White Ladies. If, on the other hand, wiser counsel prevails, and you decide not to tell her, you must, by swift messenger, at once return it to me in a sealed packet."

"I shall tell her," said the Knight. "If she elects to leave me, you will see the cross upon her breast, my lord. If she elects to stay, you shall receive it by swift messenger."

"She will leave you," said the Bishop. "If you tell her, she will leave you."

"She loves me," said the Knight; and he said it with a tender

234

reverence, and such a look upon his face, as a man wears when he speaks of his faith in God.

"Hugh," said the Bishop, sadly; "Hugh, my dear lad, you have but little experience of the heart of a nun. The more she loves, the more determined will she be to leave you, if you yourself give her reason to think her love unjustified. The very thing which is now a cause of bliss will instantly become a cause for fear. She will flee from joy, as all pure hearts flee from sin; because, owing to your folly, her joy will seem to her to be sinful. My son!"—the Bishop stretched out his hands; a passion of appeal was in his voice—"God and Holy Church have given you your wife. If you tell her this thing, you will lose her."

"I must take with me the dress she left behind," said the Knight, "so that, should she decide to go, she may ride back fully robed."

The Bishop went again to the chest, raised the heavy lid, and lifted out the white garments rolled together. At sight of them both men fell silent, as in presence of the dead; and the Knight felt his heart grow cold with apprehension, as he received them from the Bishop's hand.

They passed together through the doorway leading to the river terrace, and so down the lawn, under the arch, and into the courtyard.

There Brother Philip waited, mounted, while another lay-brother held the Knight's horse.

As they came in sight of the horses: "Philip will see you a few miles on your way," said the Bishop.

"I thank you, Father," replied the Knight, "but it is not needful. The good Brother has had many long days in the saddle."

"It is most needful," said the Bishop. "Let Philip ride beside you until you have passed through the Monk's Wood, and are well on to the open ground beyond. There, if you will, you may bid him turn back."

"Is this to ensure the safety of the Worcester cut-throats, my lord?"

The Bishop smiled.

"Possibly," he said. "Saracens may be hewn in pieces, with impunity. But we cannot allow our Worcester lads rashly to ride to such a fate. Also, my dear Hugh, you carry things of so great value that we must not risk a scuffle. These are troublous times, and dangers lurk around the city. Three miles from here you may dismiss Brother Philip, and ride forward alone."

Arrived at the horses, the Knight put away safely, that which he carried, into his saddle-bag. Then he dropped on one knee, baring his head for the Bishop's blessing.

Symon of Worcester gave it. Then, bending, added in low tones: "And may God and the blessèd Saints aid thee to a right judgment in all things."

"Amen," said Hugh d'Argent, and kissed the Bishop's ring.

Then he mounted; and, without one backward look, rode out through the Palace gates, closely followed by Brother Philip.

235

CHAPTER LII

THE ANGEL-CHILD

Symon of Worcester turned, walked slowly across the courtyard, made his way to the parapet above the river, and stood long, with bent head, watching the rapid flow of the Severn.

His eyes rested upon the very place where the Knight had cleft the water in his impulsive dive after the white stone, made, by the Bishop's own words, to stand to him for his chances of winning the Prioress.

Yet should that sudden leap be described as "impulsive"? The Bishop, ever a stickler for accuracy in descriptive words, considered this.

Nay, not so much "impulsive" as "prompt." Even as the warrior who, having tested his trusty sword, knowing its readiness in the scabbard and the strength of his own right arm, draws, on the instant, when surprised by the enemy. Prompt, not impulsive. A swift action, based upon an assured certainty of power, and a steadfast determination, of long standing, to win at all costs.

The Bishop's hand rested upon the parapet. The stone in his ring held neither blue nor purple lights. Its colour had paled and faded. It shone—as the Prioress had once seen it shine—like a large tear-drop on the Bishop's finger.

Deep dejection was in the Bishop's attitude. With the riding away of the Knight, something strong and vital seemed to have passed out of his life.

A sense of failure oppressed him. He had not succeeded in bending Hugh d'Argent to his will, neither had he risen to a frank appreciation of the loyal chivalry which would not enjoy happiness at the expense of honour.

While his mind refused to accept the Knight's code, his soul yearned to rise up and acclaim it.

Yet, working to the last for Mora's peace of mind, he had maintained his tone of scornful disapproval.

He would never again have the chance to cry "Hail!" to the Silver Shield. The deft fingers of his sophistry had striven to loosen the Knight's shining armour. How far they had succeeded, the Bishop could not tell. But, as he watched the swiftly moving river, he found himself wishing that his task had been to strengthen, rather than to weaken; to gird up and brace, rather than subtly to unbuckle and disarm. Yet by so doing, would he not have been ensuring his own happiness, bringing back the joy of life to his own heart, at the expense of the two whom he had given to be each other's in the Name of the Divine Trinity?

If Hugh persisted in his folly, he would lose his bride, yet would the Bishop meet and reinstate the Prioress with a clear conscience, having striven to the very last to dissuade the Knight.

If, on the other hand, Hugh, growing wiser as he rode northward, decided to keep silence, why then the sunny land he loved, and the Cardinal's office, for Symon, Bishop of Worcester.

But meanwhile, two weeks of uncertainty; and the Bishop could not abide uncertainty.

He turned from the river and began to pace the lawn slowly from end to end, his head bent, his hands clasped behind him.

Each time he reached the wall between the garden and the courtyard, he found himself confronted by two rose trees, a red and a white, climbing so near together that their branches intertwined, crimson blooms resting their rich petals against the fragrant fairness of their white neighbours.

Presently these roses became symbolic to the Bishop—the white, of the fair presence of the Prioress; the red, of the high honour awaiting him in Rome.

He was seized by the whimsical idea that, were he to close his eyes, beseech the blessèd Saint Joseph to guide his hand, take three steps forward, and pluck the first blossom his fingers touched, he might put an end to this tiresome uncertainty.

But he smiled at the childishness of the fancy. It savoured of the old lay-sister, Mary Antony, playing with her peas and confiding in her robin. Moreover the Bishop never did anything with his eyes shut. He would have slept with them open, had not Nature decreed otherwise.

Once again he paced the full length of the lawn, his hands clasped behind his back, his eyes looking beyond the river to the distant hills.

"Will she come, or shall I go? Shall I depart, or will she return?"

As he turned at the parapet, a voice seemed to whisper with insistence: "A white rose for her pure presence in the Cloister. A red rose for Rome."

And, as he reached the wall again, the bright eyes of a little maiden peeped at him through the archway.

He stood quite still and looked at her.

Never had he seen so lovely an elf. A sunbeam had made its home in each lock of her tumbled hair. Her little brown face had the soft bloom of a ripe nectarine; her eyes, the timid glance of a startled fawn.

The Bishop smiled.

The bright eyes lost their look of fear, and sparkled responsive.

The Bishop beckoned.

The little maid stole through the archway; then, gaining courage flew over the turf, and stood between the Bishop and the roses.

237

"How camest thou here, my little one?" questioned Symon of Worcester, in his softest tones.

"The big gate stood open, sir, and I ran in."

"And what is thy name, my little maid?"

"Verity," whispered the child, shyly, blushing to speak her own name.

"Ah," murmured the Bishop. "Hath Truth indeed come in at my open gate?"

Then, smiling into the little face lifted so confidingly to his: "Dost thou want something, Angel-child, that I can give thee?"

One little bare, brown foot rubbed itself nervously over the other. Five little brown, bare toes wriggled themselves into the grass.

"Be not afraid," said the Bishop. "Ask what thou wilt and I will give it thee, unto the half of my kingdom. Yea, even the head of Father Benedict, in a charger."

"A rose," said the child, eagerly ignoring the proffered head of Father Benedict and half the Bishop's kingdom. "A rose from that lovely tree! Their pretty faces looked at me over the wall."

The Bishop's lips still smiled; but his eyes, of a sudden, grew grave.

"*Blessèd Saint Joseph*!" he murmured beneath his breath, and crossed himself.

Then, bending over the little maid, he laid his hand upon the tumbled curls.

"Truly, my little Verity," he said, "thou shalt gather thyself a rose, and thou shall gather one for me. I leave thee free to make thy choice. See! I clasp my hands behind me—thus. Then I shall turn and walk slowly up the lawn. So soon as my back is turned, pluck thou two roses. Fly with those little brown feet after me, and place one of the roses—whichever thou wilt—in my hands. Then run home thyself, with the other. Farewell, little Angel-child. May the blessing of Bethlehem's purple hills be ever thine."

The Bishop turned and paced slowly up the lawn, head bent, hands clasped behind him.

The small bare feet made no sound on the turf. But before the Bishop was half-way across the lawn, the stem of a rose was thrust between his fingers. As they closed over it, a gay ripple of laughter sounded behind him, fading fleetly into the distance.

The Angel-child had made her choice, and had flown with her own rose, leaving the Bishop's destiny in his clasped hands.

Without pausing or looking round, he paced onward, gazing for a while at the sparkling water; then beyond it, to the distant woods through which the Knight was riding.

Presently he turned, still with his hands behind him, passed to the garden-door, left standing wide, and entered the library.

But not until he kneeled before the shrine of Saint Joseph did he

238

move forward his right hand, and bring into view the rose placed therein by Verity.

It was many years since the Bishop had wept. He had not thought ever to weep again. Yet, at sight of the rose, plucked for him by the Angel-child, something gave way within him, and he fell to weeping helplessly.

Saint Joseph, bearded and stalwart, seemed to look down with compassion upon the bowed head with its abundant silvery hair.

Even thus, it may be, had he himself wept when, after his time of hard mental torture, the Angel of the Lord appeared unto him, saying: "Fear not."

After a while the Bishop left the shrine, went over to the deed chest, and laid the rose beside the white stone.

"There, my dear Hugh," he murmured; "thy stone, and my rose. Truly they look well together. Each represents the triumph of firm resolve. Yet mine will shortly fade and pass away; while thine, dear lad, will abide forever."

The Bishop seated himself at his table, and sounded the silver gong.

A lay-brother appeared.

"Benedicite," said the Bishop. "Request Fra Andrea Filippo at once to come hither. I must have speech with him, without delay."

CHAPTER LIII

ON THE HOLY MOUNT

On the ninth day since Hugh's departure, the day when fast riding might make his return possible before nightfall, Mora rose early.

At the hour when she had been wont to ring the Convent bell, she was walking swiftly over the moors and climbing the heather-clad hills.

She had remembered a little chapel, high up in the mountains, where dwelt a holy Hermit, held in high repute for his saintliness of life, his wisdom in the giving of spiritual counsel, and his skill in ministering to the sick.

It had come to Mora, as she prayed and pondered during the night, that if she could make full confession to this holy man, he might be able to throw some clear beam of light upon the dark tangle of her perplexity.

This hope was strongly with her as she walked.

239

"Lighten my darkness! Lead me in a plain path!" was the cry of her bewildered soul.

It seemed to her that she had two issues to consider. First: the question as to whether Hugh, guided by the Bishop, would keep silence; thus making himself a party to her deception. Secondly: the position in which she was placed by the fact that she had left the Convent, owing to that deception. But, for the moment the first issue was so infinitely the greater, that she found herself thrusting the second into the background, allowing herself to be conscious of it merely as a question to be faced later on, when the all-important point of Hugh's attitude in the matter should be settled.

She walked forward swiftly, one idea alone possessing her: that she hastened toward possible help.

She did not slacken speed until the chapel came into view, its grey walls glistening in the morning light, a clump of feathery rowan trees beside it; at its back a mighty rock, flung down in bygone centuries from the mountain which towered behind it. From a deep cleft in this rock sprang a young oak, dipping its fresh green to the roof of the chapel; all around it, in every crack and cranny, parsley fern, hare-bells on delicate, swaying stalks, foxgloves tall and straight, and glorious bunches of purpling heather.

Nearby was the humble dwelling of the Hermit. The door stood ajar.

Softly approaching, Mora lifted her hand, and knocked.

No voice replied.

The sound of her knock did but make evident the presence of a vast solitude.

Pushing open the door, she ventured to look within.

The Hermit's cell was empty. The remains of a frugal meal lay upon the rough wooden table. Also an open breviary, much thumbed and worn. At the further end of the table, a little pile of medicinal herbs heaped as if shaken hastily from the wallet which lay beside them. Probably the holy man, even while at an early hour he broke his fast, had been called to some sick bedside.

Mora turned from the doorway and, shading her eyes, scanned the landscape.

At first she could see only sheep, slowly moving from tuft to tuft as they nibbled the short grass; or goats, jumping from rock to rock, and suddenly disappearing in the high bracken.

But soon, on a distant ridge, she perceived two figures and presently made out the brown robe and hood of the Hermit, and a little, barefoot peasant boy, running to keep up with his rapid stride. They vanished over the crest of the hill, and Mora—alone in this wild solitude—realised that many hours might elapse ere the Hermit returned.

This check to the fulfilment of her purpose, instead of disappointing her, flooded her heart with a sudden sense of relief.

The interior of the Hermit's cell had recalled, so vividly, the austerities of the cloistered life.

The Hermit's point of view would probably have been so completely from within.

It would have been impossible that he should comprehend the wonder—the growing wonder—of these days, since she and Hugh rode away from Warwick, culminating in that exquisite hour on the battlements when she had told him of the vision, whispered her full surrender, and yet he—faithful and patient even then—had touched her only with his glowing eyes.

How could a holy Hermit, dwelling alone among great silent hills, realise the tremendous force of a strong mutual love, the glow, the gladness, the deep, sweet unrest, the call of soul to soul, the throb of hearts, filling the purple night with the soft beat of angels' wings?

How could a holy Hermit understand the shock to Hugh, how fathom the maddening torment of suspense, the abyss of hope deferred, into which the Bishop's letter must have plunged him, coming so soon after he had said: "I ask no higher joy, than to watch the breaking of the day which gives thee to my home"? But the breaking of the day had brought the stern necessity which took him from her.

Yet why? How much was in that second letter? Was it less detailed than the first? Had Hugh ridden south to learn the entire truth? Or had he ridden south to arrange with the Bishop for her complete and permanent deception?

Standing on this mountain plateau—the morning breeze blowing about her, the sun mounting triumphant in the heavens "as a bridegroom coming out of his chamber," and all around the scent of heather, the hum of bees, the joyful trill of the soaring lark; her own body bounding with life after the swift climb—it seemed to Mora impossible that Hugh should withstand the temptation to hold to his happiness, at all costs. And how could a saintly Hermit judge him as mercifully as she—the woman who loved him—knew that he should be judged?

She felt thankful for the good man's absence, yet baffled in her need for help.

Looking back toward the humble dwelling, she perceived a rough device of carved lettering on a beam over the doorway. She made out Latin words, and going nearer she, who for years had worked so continuously at copying and translating, read them without difficulty.

"WITH HIM, IN THE HOLY MOUNT," was inscribed across the doorway of the Hermit's dwelling.

Mora repeated the words, and again repeated them; and, as she did so there stole over her the sense of an Unseen Presence in this solitude.

241

"With Him, in the Holy Mount."

She turned to the chapel. Over that doorway also were carven letters. Moving closer, she looked up and read them.

"AND WHEN THEY HAD LIFTED UP THEIR EYES, THEY SAW NO MAN, SAVE JESUS ONLY."

Mora opened the door and entered the tiny chapel. At first, coming in from the outer brightness it seemed dark; but she had left the door standing wide, and light poured in behind her.

Then she lifted up her eyes and saw; and seeing, understood the meaning of the legend above the entrance.

In that little chapel was one Figure, and one Figure only. No pictured saints were there. No image of our Lady. No crucifix hung on the wall.

But, in a niche above the altar, stood a wondrous figure of the Christ; not dying, not dead; not glorified and ascending; but the Christ as very man, walking the earth in human form, yet calmly, unmistakably, triumphantly Divine. The marble form was carved by the same hand as the Madonna which the Bishop had brought from Rome, and placed in Mora's cell at the Convent. It had been his gift to his old friend the Hermit. At first sight of it, Mora remembered hearing it described by the Bishop himself. Then the beauty of the sculpture took hold upon her, and she forgot all else.

It lived! The face wore a look of searching tenderness; on the lips, a smile of loving comprehension; in the out-stretched hands, an attitude of infinite compassion.

Mora fell upon her knees. Instinctively she recalled the earnest injunction of Father Gervaise to his penitents that, when kneeling before the crucifix, they should repeat: "He ever liveth to make intercession for us." And, strangely enough, there came back with this the remembrance of the wild voice of Mary Seraphine, shrieking, when told to contemplate the dying Redeemer: "I want life—not death!"

Here was Life indeed! Here was the Saviour of the world, in mortal guise, the Word made manifest.

Mora lifted her eyes and read the words, illumined in letters of gold around the arch of the niche, gleaming in the sunlight above the patient head of the Man Divine.

"IN ALL POINTS TEMPTED LIKE AS WE ARE, YET WITHOUT SIN."

And higher still, above the arch:

"A GREAT HIGH PRIEST. . . . PASSED INTO THE HEAVENS."

In the silence and stillness of that utter solitude, she who had so lately been Prioress of the White Ladies kneeled and worshipped.

The Unseen Presence drew nearer.

She closed her eyes to the sculptured form.

The touch of her Lord was upon her heart.

She had prayed in her cell that His piercèd feet nailed to the wood might become as dear to her as the Baby feet on the Virgin Mother's knees. In her anguish of cloistered sorrow, that prayer had been granted.

But out in the world of living men and things, she needed more. She needed Feet that walked and moved, passed in and out of house and home; paused by the hearth; went to the wedding feast; moved to the fresh closed grave; Feet that had sampled the dust of life's highway; Feet that had trod rough places, yet never tripped nor stumbled.

"Tempted in all points." . . . Then here was One Who could understand Hugh's hard temptation; Who could pity, if Hugh fell. Here was One Who would comprehend the breaking of her poor human heart if, loving Hugh as she now loved, she yet must leave him.

"A great High Priest." . . . What need of any other priest, while "with Him in the Holy Mount"? Passed into the heavens, yet ever living to make intercession for us.

Deep peace stole into her heart, as she knelt in absorbed communion in this sacred place, where, for the first time, in her religious life, she had found herself with "Jesus only."

"Ah, blessèd Lord!" she cried at length, "Thou Who knowest the heart of a man, and canst divine the heart of a woman, grant unto me this day a true vision; a vision which shall make clear to me, without any possibility of doubt, what is Thy will for me."

CHAPTER LIV

THE UNSEEN PRESENCE

The world was a new and a wonderful world as, leaving the chapel, Mora turned her steps homeward. She had been wont to regard temptation itself as sinful, but now this sacred fact "in all points tempted like as we are" seemed to sanctify the state of being tempted, providing she could add the three triumphant words: "Yet without sin."

As she walked, with springy step, down the grassy paths among the heather, the Unseen Presence moved beside her.

It seemed strange that she should have found in the world this sweet secret of the Perpetual Presence, which had evaded her in the Nunnery. Often when her duties had taken her elsewhere in the Convent, or during the walk through the underground way on the return from the Cathedral, or even when walking for refreshment in the Convent garden, she would yearn for the holy stillness of the chapel, or to be back in her cell that she might kneel at the shrine of the Virgin and there realise the adorable purity of our blessèd Lady's heart; or, prostrating herself before the crucifix, gaze upon those piercèd feet, then slowly lift her eyes to the other sacred wounds, and force her mind to realise and her cold heart to receive the mighty fact that the Divine Redeemer thus hung and suffered for her sins.

Transports of realisation had come to her in her cell, or when she kept vigil in the Convent chapel, or when from the height of the Cathedral clerestory she gazed down upon the High Altar, the lighted candles, the swinging censers, and heard the chanting of the monks, and the tinkle of the silver bell. But these transports had resulted from her own determination to realise and to respond. The mental effort over, they faded, and her heart had seemed colder than before, her spirit more dead, her mind more prone to apathy. The greater the effort to force herself to apprehend, the more complete had been the reaction of non-realisation.

But now, in this deep wonder of new experience, there was no effort. She had but waited with every inlet of her being open to receive. And now the power was a Real Presence within, revealing an equally Real Presence without. The Risen Christ moved beside her as she walked. Her eyes were no longer holden that she should not know Him, for the promised Presence of the Paracletos filled her, unveiling her spiritual vision, whispering within her glowing heart; "It is the Lord!"

"Which Voice we heard," wrote Saint Peter, "when we were with Him in the Holy Mount." She, too, had first heard it there; but, as she descended, it was with her still. The songs of the birds, the rush of the stream, the breeze in the pines, the bee on the wing, all Nature seemed to say: "It is the Lord!"

Sorrow, suffering, disillusion might await her on the plain; but, with the Presence beside her, and the Voice within, she felt strong to face them, and to overcome.

Noon found her in her garden, calm and serene; yet wondering, with quickening pulses, whether at nightfall or even at sunset, Hugh would ride in; and what she must say if, giving some other reason for his journey to Worcester, he deceived her as others had deceived; failed her as others had failed.

And wondering thus, she rose and moved with slow step to the terrace.

For a while she stood pondering this hard question, her eyes lifted to the distant hills.

Then something impelled her to turn and glance into the banqueting hall, and there—on the spot where he had knelt that she might bless him at parting—stood Hugh, his arms folded, his eyes fixed upon her, waiting till she should see him.

CHAPTER LV

THE HEART OF A WOMAN

For a space, through the casement, they looked into one another's eyes; she, standing in the full glory of the summer sunshine, a radiant vision of glowing womanhood; he, in the shade of the banqueting-hall, gaunt and travel-stained, yet in his eyes the light of that love which never faileth. But, even as she looked, those dark eyes wavered, shifted, turned away, as if he could not bear any longer to gaze upon her in the sunlight.

An immense pity filled Mora's heart. She knew he was going to fail her; yet the pathos of that failure lay in the fact that it was the very force of his love which rendered the temptation so insuperable.

Swiftly she passed into the banqueting hall, went to him where he stood, put up her arms about his neck, and lifted her lips to his.

"I thank God, my belovèd," she said, "that He hath brought thee in safety back to me."

Hugh's arms, flung around her, strained her to him. But he kept his head erect. The muscles of his neck were like iron bands under her fingers. She could see the cleft in his chin, the firm curve of his lips. His eyes were turned from her.

She longed to say: "Hugh, the Bishop's first letter, lost on its way, hath reached my hands. Already I know the true story of the vision."

Yet instead she clung to his neck, crying: "Kiss me, Hugh! Kiss me!"

She could not rob her man of his chance to be faithful. Also, if he were going to fail her, it were better he should fail and she know it, than that she should forever have the torment of questioning: "Had I not spoken, would he have kept silence?"

Yet, while he was still hers, his honour untarnished, she longed for the touch of his lips.

"Kiss me," she whispered again, not knowing how ten-fold more hard she thus made it for him.

But loosing his arms from around her, he took her face between his hands, looking long into her eyes, with such a yearning of hunger, grief, and regret, that her heart stood still. Then, just as, rendered dizzy by his nearness, she closed her eyes, she felt his lips upon her own.

For a moment she was conscious of nothing save that she was his.

Then her mind flew back to the last time they had stood, thus. Again the underground smell of damp earth seemed all about them; again her heart was torn by love and pity; again she seemed to see Hugh, passing up from the darkness into that pearly light which came stealing down from the crypt—and she realised that this second kiss held also the anguish of parting, rather than the rapture of reunion.

Before she could question the meaning of this, Hugh released her, gently loosed her hands from about his neck, and led her to a seat.

Then he thrust his hand into his breast, and when he drew it forth she saw that he held something in his palm, which gleamed as the light fell upon it.

Standing before her, his eyes bent upon that which lay in his hand, Hugh spoke.

"Mora, I have to tell thee a strange tale, which will, I greatly fear, cause thee much sorrow and perplexity. But first I would give thee this, sent to thee by the Bishop with his most loving greetings; who also bids me say that if, after my tale is told, thy choice should be to return to Worcester, he himself will meet thee, and welcome thee, conduct thee to the Nunnery and there reinstate thee Prioress of the White Ladies, with due pomp and highest honour. I tell thee this at once to spare thee all I can of shock and anguish in the hearing of that which must follow."

Kneeling before her, Hugh laid her jewelled cross of office on her lap.

"My wife," he said simply, speaking very low, with bent head, "before I tell thee more I would have thee know thyself free to go back to the point where first thy course was guided by the vision of the old lay-sister, Mary Antony. Therefore I bring thee thy cross of office as Prioress of the White Ladies."

She laughed aloud, in the great gladness of her relief; in the rapture of her pride in him.

"How can thy wife be Prioress of the White Ladies?" she cried, and caught his head to her breast, there where the jewelled cross used to lie, raining tears and kisses on his hair.

For a moment he yielded, speaking, with his face pressed against her, words of love beyond her imagining.

Then he regained control.

"Oh, hush, my belovèd!" he said. "Hold me not! Let me go, or our Lady knoweth I shall even now fail in the task which lies before me."

"Our Lord, Who knoweth the heart of a man," she said, "hath made my man so strong that he will not fail."

But she let him go; and rising, the Knight stood before her.

"The letter brought to me by Brother Philip," he began, "told me something of that which I am about to tell thee. But I could not speak of it to thee until I knew it in fullest detail, and had consulted with the Bishop concerning its possible effect upon thy future. Hence my instant departure to Worcester. That which I now shall tell thee, I had, in each particular, from the Bishop in most secret conversations. He and I, alone, know of this matter."

Then with his arms folded upon his breast, his eye fixed upon the sunny garden, beyond the window, deep sorrow, compunction, and, at times, awe in his voice, Hugh d'Argent recited the entire history of the pretended vision; beginning with the hiding of herself of old Antony in the inner cell, her anxiety concerning the Reverend Mother, confided to the Bishop; his chance remark, resulting in the old woman's cunningly devised plan to cheat the Prioress into accepting happiness.

And, as he told it, the horror of the sacrilege fell as a dark shadow between them, eclipsing even the radiance of their love. Upon which being no longer blinded, Mora clearly perceived the other issue which she was called upon to face: If our Lady's sanction miraculously given to the step she had taken in leaving the Nunnery had after all not been given, what justification had she for remaining in the world?

Presently Hugh reached the scene of the full confession and death of the old lay-sister. He told it with reverent simplicity. None of the Bishop's flashes of humour had found any place in the Knight's recital.

But now his voice, of a sudden, fell silent. The tale was told.

Mora had sat throughout leaning forward, her right elbow on her knee, her chin resting in the palm of her right hand; her left toying with the jewelled cross upon her lap.

Now she looked up.

"Hugh, you have made no mention of the Bishop's opinion as regards the effect of this upon myself. Did he advise that I be told the entire truth?"

The Knight hesitated.

"Nay," he admitted at length, seeing that she must have an answer. "The Bishop had, as you indeed know, from the first considered our previous betrothal and your sister's perfidy, sufficient justification for your release from all vows made through that deception. Armed with the Pope's mandate, the Bishop saw no need for a divine manifestation, nor did he, from the first, believe in the vision of this old lay-sister. Yet, knowing you set great store by it, he feared for your peace of mind, should you learn the truth."

"Did he command you not to tell me, Hugh?"

"For love of you, Mora, out of tender regard for your happiness, the Bishop counselled me not to tell you."

"He would have had you to become a party, with himself, and old Mary Antony, in my permanent deception?"

Hugh was a loyal friend.

"He would have had me to become a party, with himself, in securing your permanent peace, Mora," he said, sternly.

She loved his sternness. So much did she adore him for having triumphed where she had made sure that he would fail, so much did she despise herself for having judged him so poorly, rated him so low, that she could have knelt upon the floor and clasped his feet! Yet must she strive for wisdom and calmness.

247

"Then how came you to tell me, Hugh, that which might well imperil not only my peace but your own happiness?"

"Mora," said the Knight, "if I have done wrong, may our blessèd Lady pardon me, and comfort you. But I could not take my happiness knowing that it came to me by reason of a deception practised upon you. Our love must have its roots in perfect truthfulness and trust. Also you and I had together accepted the vision as divine. I had kneeled in your sight and praised our blessèd Lady for this especial grace vouchsafed on my behalf. But now, knowing it to have been a sacrilegious fraud, every time you spoke with joy of the special grace, every time you blessed our Lady for her loving-kindness, I, by my silence, giving mute assent, should have committed sacrilege afresh. Aye, and in that wondrous moment which you promised should soon come, when you would have said: 'Take me! I have been ever thine. Our Lady hath kept me for thee!' mine honour would have been smirched forever had I, keeping silence, taken advantage of thy belief in words which that old nun had herself invented, and put into the mouth of the blessèd Virgin. The Bishop held me selfish because I put mine honour before my need of thee. He said I saw naught but mine own proud face, in the bright mirror of my silver shield. But"—the Knight held his right hand aloft, and spoke in solemn tones—"methinks I see there the face of God, or the nearest I know to His face; and, behind Him, I see thy face, mine own belovèd. I needs must put this, which I owe to honour and to our mutual trust, before mine own content, and utter need of thee. I should be shamed, did I do otherwise, to call thee wife of mine, to think of thee as mistress of my home, and of my heart the Queen."

Mora's hand had sought the Bishop's letter; but now she let it lie concealed. She could not dim the noble triumph of that moment, by any revelation of her previous knowledge. Had Hugh failed, she must have produced the first letter. Hugh having proved faithful, it might well wait.

A long silence fell between them. Mora, fingering the cross, looked on it with unseeing eyes. To Hugh it seemed that this token of her high office was becoming to her a thing of first importance.

"The dress is also here," he said.

"What dress?" she questioned, starting.

He pointed to where he had laid it: her white habit, scapulary, wimple, veil and girdle; the dress of a Prioress of the Order of the White Ladies.

She turned her startled eyes upon it. Then quickly looked away.

"Did you yourself think a vision needed, in order that I might be justified in leaving the Convent, Hugh?"

"Nay, then," he cried, "always from the first I held thee mine in the sight of Heaven."

"Are you of opinion that, the vision being proved no vision, I should go back?"

248

"No!" said the Knight; and the word fell like a blow from a battle-axe.

"Does the Bishop expect that I shall return?"

"Yes," replied the Knight, groaning within himself that she should have chanced to change the form of her question.

"He would so expect," mused Mora. "He would be sure I should return. He remembers my headstrong temper, and my imperious will. He remembers how I tore the Pope's mandate, placing my foot upon it. He knows I said how that naught would suffice me but a divine vision. Also he knoweth well the heart of a nun; and when I asked him if the heart of a nun could ever become as the heart of other women, he did most piously ejaculate: 'Heaven forbid?'"

Little crinkles of merriment showed faintly at the corners of her eyes. The Bishop would have seen them, and smiled responsive. But the sad Knight saw them not.

"Mora," he said, "I leave thee free. I hold thee to no vows made through falsehood and fraud. I rate thy peace of mind before mine own content; thy true well-being, before mine own desires. Leaving thee free, dear Heart, I must leave thee free to choose. Loving thee as I love thee, I cannot stay here, yet leave thee free. My anguish of suspense would hamper thee. Therefore I purpose now to ride to my own home. Martin will ride with me. But tomorrow he will return, to ask if there is a message; and the next day, and the next. The Bishop allowed four days for hesitation. If thy decision should be to return to the Nunnery, his command is that thou ride the last stage of the journey fully robed, wearing thy cross of office. He himself will meet thee five miles this side of Worcester, and riding in, with much pomp and ceremony, will announce to the Community that, the higher service to which His Holiness sent thee, being accomplished—"

"Accomplished, Hugh?"

The Knight smiled, wearily. "I quote the Bishop, Mora. He will explain that he now reinstates thee as Prioress of the Order. The entire Community will, he says, rejoice; and he himself will be ever at hand to make sure that all is right for thee."

"These plans are well and carefully laid, Hugh."

"They who love thee have seen to that, Mora."

"Who will ride with me from here to Worcester?"

"Martin Goodfellow, and a little band of thine own people. A swifter messenger will go before to warn the Bishop of thy coming."

"And what of thee?" she asked.

"Of me?" repeated the Knight, as if at first the words conveyed to him no meaning. "Oh, I shall go forth, seeking a worthy cause for which to fight; praying God I may soon be counted worthy to fall in battle."

She pressed her clasped hands there where his face had rested.

"And if I find I cannot go back, Hugh? If I decide to stay?"

He swung round and looked at her.

"Mora, is there hope? The Bishop said there was none."

"Hugh," she made answer slowly, speaking with much earnestness, "shall I not be given a true vision to guide me in this perplexity?"

"Our Lady grant it," he said. "If you decide to stay, one word will bring me back. If not, Mora—this is our final parting."

He took a step toward her.

She covered her face with her hands.

In a moment his arms would be round her. She could not live through a third of those farewell kisses. She had not yet faced out the second question. But—vision or no vision—if he touched her now, she would yield.

"Go!" she whispered. "Ah, for pity's sake, go! The heart of a nun might endure even this. But I ask thy mercy for the heart of a woman!"

She heard the sob in his throat, as he knelt and lifted the hem of her robe to his lips.

Then his step across the floor.

Then the ring of horses' hoofs upon the paving stones.

She was trembling from head to foot, yet she rose and went to the window overlooking the courtyard.

Mark was shutting the gates. Beaumont held a neglected stirrup cup, and laughed as he drained it himself. Zachary, stout and pompous, was mounting the steps.

Hugh, her husband—Hugh, faithful beyond belief—Hugh, her dear Knight of the Silver Shield—had ridden off alone, to the home to which he so greatly longed to take her; alone, with his hopeless love, his hungry heart, and his untarnished honour.

Turning from the window she gathered up the habit of her Order and, clasping her cross of office, mounted to her bedchamber, there to face out in solitude the hard question of the second issue.

CHAPTER LVI

THE TRUE VISION

To her bedchamber went Mora—she who had been Prioress of the White Ladies—bearing in her arms the full robes of her Order, and in her hand the jewelled cross of her high office. She went, expecting to spend hours in doubt and prayer and question before the shrine of the Virgin. But, as she pushed open the door and entered the sunlit chamber, on the very threshold she was met by a flash of inward illumination. Surely every question had already been answered; the second issue had been decided, while the first was yet wholly uncertain.

She had said she must have a divine vision. Had she not this very day been granted a two-fold vision, both human and divine; the Divine, stooping in unspeakable tenderness and comprehension to the human; the Human, upborne on the mighty pinions of pure love and stainless honour in a self-sacrifice which lifted it to the Divine?

In the lonely chapel on the mountain, she had seen her Lord. Not as the Babe, heralded by angels, worshipped by Eastern shepherds, adored by Gentile kings, throned on His Mother's knee, wise-eyed and God-like, stretching omnipotent baby hands toward this mysterious homage which was His due; accepting, with baby omniscience, the gold, the frankincense, the myrrh, which typified His mission; nor as the Divine Redeemer nailed helpless to the cross of shame; dead, that the world might live. These had been the visions of her cloistered years.

But in the chapel on the mountain she had seen Him as the human Jesus, tempted in all points like as we are, His only visible halo the "yet without sin," which set upon His brow in youth and manhood the divine seal of perfect purity, and in His eyes the clear shining of uninterrupted intercourse with Heaven.

As she had left the chapel, turning from the sculptured figure which had helped her to this realisation, she had become wondrously aware of the Unseen Presence of the Christ, close beside her. "As seeing Him Who is invisible" she had come down from the mount, conscious that He went on before. She seemed to be following those blessèd footsteps over the heather of her native hills, even as the disciples of old followed them through the cornfields of Judea, and over the grassy slopes of Galilee. Yet conscious also that He moved beside her, with hand outstretched in case her spirit tripped; and that, should a hidden foe fling shafts from an ambush in the rear, even there that Unseen Presence would be behind her as a shield. "Lo I am with you always, even unto the end of the world."

Strong in this most human vision of the Divine, she had come down from the Holy Mount, prepared to face the dumb demon she dreaded, the silent acquiescence in deception, which threatened to tear her happiness, bruise her spirit, and cast into the fire and into the waters to destroy them, those treasures which her heart had lately learned to hold so dear.

Prepared for this, she came; and lo, Heaven granted her the second vision. She saw deep into the heart of a true man's faithfulness; an example of chivalry, of profound reverence for holy things, which shamed her doubts of him; a self-sacrifice which lifted the great human love, to which she, in her cloistered sanctity, had pictured herself as stooping, far above her, to the ideal of the divine. Was not this indeed a Vision of Truth?

251

Crossing the room, Mora laid the robes she carried upon the couch. While mounting the stairs she had planned, in the secret of her own chamber, to clothe herself in them once again, to hang her jewelled cross about her neck, and thus—once more Prioress of the White Ladies—to kneel at our Lady's shrine, and implore guidance in this final decision. But now, she laid them gently down upon the bed.

She could not stand fast in this new liberty, with the heavy folds of that white habit entangling her feet in a yoke of bondage.

The heart, filled with a love so full of glowing tenderness for her Knight of the Silver Shield proved worthy, could not beat beneath a scapulary. Nor could her cross of office lie where his dear head had rested.

She stood before the shrine. The Madonna looked gravely upon her. The holy Babe gazed with omniscient eyes, holding forth tiny hands of omnipotence.

Even so had they looked in her hour of joy, when she had kneeled in a transport of thanksgiving.

Even so had they looked in her hour of anguish, when she had poured out her despair at having been twice deceived.

Yet help had not come, until she had lifted her eyes unto the hills.

She turned from the shrine, went swiftly to the open casement, and stood looking over the green tree tops, to the heavenly blue beyond, flecked by swift moving clouds.

She, who had now learned to "look . . . at the things that are not seen," could not find help through gazing on carven images.

Thoughts of our Lady seemed more living and vital while she kept her eyes upon the fleecy whiteness of those tiny clouds, or watched a flight of mountain birds, silver-winged in the sunshine.

What was the one command recorded as having been given, by the blessed Mother of our Lord, to men? "Whatsoever He saith unto you, do it." And what was His last injunction to His Church on earth? "Go ye into all the world and preach glad tidings to every creature. . . . And lo, I am with you always."

Mora could not but know that she had come forth into her world bringing the glad tidings of love requited, of comfort, and of home.

By virtue of this promise the feet of the risen Christ would move beside her "all the days."

It seemed to her, that if she went back now into her Convent cell, she would nail those blessèd feet to the wood again. In slaying this new life within herself, she would lose forever the sense of living companionship, retaining only the religion of the Crucifix. Enough, perhaps, for the cloistered life. But this life more abundant, demanded that grace should yet more abound.

A great apostolic injunction sounded, like a clarion call, from the stored chancel of her memory. "As ye have therefore received Christ Jesus the Lord, so walk ye in Him."

252

She flung wide her arms. A sense of all-pervading liberty, a complete freedom from all bondage of spirit, soul, or body, leapt up responsive to the call.

"I will!" she said. "Without any further fear or faltering, I will!"

She passed to the couch, folded the robes she had worn so long, and laid them away in an empty chest.

This done, she took her cross of office, and went down to the terrace. Her one thought was to reach Hugh with as little delay as possible. She could not leave that noble heart in suspense, a moment longer than she need.

The sun was still high in the heavens. By the short way through the woods, she could reach the castle long before sunset.

She owed Hugh much. Yet there was another to whom she also owed a debt; how much she owed to him, this day's new light had shewn her. She would go forward to her joy with a freer heart if she gave herself time to discharge, by acknowledgment and thanks, the great debt she owed to her old and faithful friend, Symon, Bishop of Worcester.

She sent for her steward.

"Zachary," she said, "Sir Hugh has ridden on before. I follow by the short way through the forest, and shall not return to-night. Bid them saddle my white palfrey, Icon. I shall be ready to start within an hour. But first I must despatch to Worcester, a packet of importance. Bid two of the men, who rode with us from Worcester, prepare to mount and return thither. If they start in an hour's time, they can be well on their way, and make a safe lodging, before nightfall."

She passed into the library, laid the cross before her on the table, and began her letter to the Bishop.

Straight from her hand to his, that letter went; straight from her heart to his, that letter spoke; and Symon's comfort in it, lies largely in the knowledge that she was alone when she wrote it, alone when she sealed it, and that none in this world, saving they two, will ever know exactly what the woman, whom he had loved so purely and served so faithfully, said to him in this letter.

Bare facts, however, may be given.

She told him, as briefly as might be, of that morning's great experience; of Hugh's return, and noble self-effacement; of the clear light she had received, and the decision to which she had come; and of how she was now going forward, with a free heart, to her great happiness.

And then, in glowing words, she told him all she owed to his faithful, patient friendship, to the teaching of long years, the trend of which had always been life, light, liberty; a wider outlook, a fearless judgment, a clear knowledge of God, based on inspired writings; and, above all, belief in those words, often on his lips, always in his heart: "Love never faileth."

"Truly, my dear lord," she wrote, "your love—" Nay, it may not be quoted!

She told him how his teaching, following along the same lines as that of Father Gervaise years before, had prepared her mind for this revelation of the ever-living Saviour.

"Now the mystery is unveiled to me also," she wrote, "I realise that you knew it all along; and that, had I but been more teachable, Reverend Father, you could have taught me more. Oh, I pray you, take heart of grace, and teach these great truths to others."

She blessed him for his faithfulness in striving to make her see her duty to Hugh, and her life's true vocation.

She blessed him for her great happiness, yet thanked him for his care in sending her cross of office, thus making all easy in order that, had her conscience so required, she could have safely returned. She herewith sent him the cross, and begged that he would keep it, remembering when he chanced to look upon it—

She also begged him to forgive her the many times when she had tried his patience, and been herself impatient of his wise counsel and control.

And, finally, she signed herself — — —

Mora held the cross to her lips, then placed it within the letter, folded the packet, sealed it with her own seal, addressed it with full directions, and called for the messenger.

Thus, fully four days before he had looked to have it, the answer for which he waited, reached the Bishop's hand. As he opened it, and perceived the gleam of gold and emeralds, he glanced across to the deed chest, where lay the Knight's white stone.

The rose beside it had not yet faded. It might have been plucked and placed in the water that morning, so fair it bloomed—a red, red rose. Ah, Verity! Little Angel Child!

* * * * * *

It was said in sunny Florence in the years that followed, and, later on, it was remarked in Rome, that if the Lord High Cardinal—kindest of men—was tried almost beyond bearing, if even his calm patience seemed in danger of ruffling, or if he was weary, or sad, or disheartened, he had a way of slipping his hand into the bosom of his scarlet robe, as if he gently fingered something that lay against his heart.

Whereupon at once his brow grew serene again, his blue eyes kindly and bright, his lips smiled that patient smile which never failed; and, as he drew forth his hand, the stone within his ring, though pale before, glowed deep red, as juice of purple grapes in a goblet.

CHAPTER LVII

"I CHOOSE TO RIDE ALONE"

Mora escaped from the restraining arms of old Debbie, and appeared at the top of the steps leading down to the courtyard.

Framed in the doorway, in her green riding dress, she stood for a moment, surveying the scene before her.

The two men bound for Worcester, bearing her packet to the Bishop, had just ridden out at the great gates. Through the gates, still standing open, she could see them guiding their horses down the hill and taking the southward road.

The porter was attempting to close the gates, but a stable lad hindered him, pointing to Icon, whom a groom was leading, ready saddled, to and fro, before the door; Icon, with proudly arched neck and swishing tail, as conscious of his snowy beauty as when, in the river meadow at Worcester, he found himself the centre of an admiring crowd of nuns.

At sight of his flowing mane, powerful forequarters, and high stepping action, Mora was irresistibly reminded of the scene in the courtyard at the Nunnery, when the Bishop rode in on his favourite white palfrey, she standing at the top of the steps to receive him. Never again would she stand so, to receive the Bishop; never again would Icon proudly carry him. The Bishop had given her to Hugh and Icon to her. A faint sense of compunction stirred within her. Perhaps at that moment she came near to realising something of what both gifts had cost the Bishop.

Bending her head, she looked across the courtyard and under the gateway. The messengers were riding fast. Even as she looked, they disappeared into the pine wood.

Her letter to Symon was well on its way. She remembered with comfort and gladness certain things she had written in that letter.

Then—as the pine wood swallowed the messengers—with a joyous bound of reaction her whole mind turned to Hugh.

Three steps below her, a page waited, holding a dagger which she had been wont to wear, when riding in the forests. She had sent it out to be sharpened. She took it from him, tested its point, slipped it into the sheath at her belt, smiled upon the boy, descended the remaining steps, and laid her hand upon Icon's mane.

Then it was that Mistress Deborah's agitated signals from within the doorway, took effect upon old Zachary.

Coming forward, he bared his white head, and adventured a humble expostulation.

"My lady," he said, "it is not safe nor well that you should ride

255

alone. A few moments' delay will suffice Beaumont to saddle a horse and be ready to attend you."

She mounted before she made answer.

She kept her imperious temper well in hand, striving to remember that to old Debbie and Zachary she seemed but the child they had loved and watched over from infancy, of a sudden grown older. They had not known the Prioress of the White Ladies.

Bending from the saddle, her hand on Icon's mane:

"I go to my husband, Zachary," she said, "and I choose to ride alone."

Then gathering up the reins, she turned Icon toward the gates and so rode across the courtyard, looking, neither back to where Mistress Deborah alternately wrung her hands and shook her fist at Zachary; nor to right or left, where Mark and Beaumont, standing with doffed caps waited till she should have passed, to yield to the full enjoyment of Mistress Deborah's gestures, and of Master Zachary's discomfiture.

She rode forth looking straight before her, over the pointed ears of Icon. She was riding to Hugh, and, they who stood by must not see the love-light in her eyes.

Grave and serene, her head held high, she paced the white palfrey through the gates. And if the porter marked a wondrous shining in her eyes—well, the sun began to slant its rays, and she rode straight toward the west.

Zachary mounted the steps and hastened across the hall, followed by Deborah.

Mark thereupon enacted Mistress Deborah, and Beaumont, Master Zachary; while the page sat down on the steps to laugh.

The porter clanged to the gates.

The day's work was done.

CHAPTER LVIII

THE WARRIOR HEART

As Mora turned off the highway, and pressed Icon deep into the glades, she cried over and over aloud, for there was none to hear: "I go to my husband, and I choose to ride alone."

How wondrous it seemed, this going to him; a second giving, a deeper surrender, a fuller yielding.

When she went to him in the crypt, her body had recoiled, her spirit had shrunk, shamed, humbled, and unwilling. Her mind alone, governed by her will, had driven her along the path of her resolve, holding her upon the stretcher, until too late to cry out or to return.

Now—how different! Free as air, alone, uncoerced, even unexpected, she left her own home, and her own people, to ride, unattended, straight to the arms of the man who had won her.

A wild joy seized and shook her.

The soft, mysterious glades, beneath vast, leafy domes, seemed enchanted ground. The hoofs of Icon thudded softly on the moss. The stillness seemed alive with whispering life. Rabbits sat still to peep, then whisked and ran. Great birds rose suddenly, on whirring wings. Tiny birds, fearless, stayed on their twigs and sang.

There was scurrying among ferns and rocks, telling of bright, watchful eyes; of life, safeguarding itself, unseen. Yet all these varied sounds, Nature disturbed in the shady haunts which were her rightful home, did but emphasize the vast stillness, the utter solitude, the complete remoteness from human dwelling-place.

Shining through parted boughs and slowly moving leaves, the sunlight fell, in golden bars or shifting yellow patches, on the glade.

The joy which thrilled his rider, seemed to communicate itself to Icon. He galloped over the moss on the broad rides, and would scarce be restrained when passing between great rocks, or turning sharply into an unseen way.

Mora rode as in a dream. "I ride to my husband," she cried to the forest, "and I choose to ride alone!" And once she sang, in an irrepressible burst of praise: "Jesu dulsis memoria!" Then, when she fell silent: "Dulsis! Dulsis!" carolled unseen choristers in leafy clerestories overhead. And each time Icon heard her voice, he laid back his ears and cantered faster.

Not far from her journey's end, the way lay through a deep gorge in the very heart of the pine wood.

Here the sun's rays could scarce penetrate; the path became rough and slippery; a hidden stream oozed up between loose stones.

Icon picked his way, with care; yet even so, he slipped, recovered, and slipped again.

With a sudden rush, some wild animal, huge and heavy, went crashing through the undergrowth.

Stealthy footsteps seemed to keep pace with Icon's, high up among the tree trunks.

Yet this valley of the shadow held no terrors for the woman whose heart was now so blissfully at rest.

Having left behind forever the dark vale of doubt and indecision, she mounted triumphant on the wings of trust and certainty.

"I ride to my husband," she whispered, as if the words were a charm which might bring the sense of his strong arms about her, "and I choose to ride alone."

With a gentle caress on the arch of his snowy neck, and with soft words in the anxiously pointing ears, she encouraged the palfrey to go forward.

At length they rounded a great grey rock jutting out into the path, and the upward slope of a mossy glade came into view.

With a whinny of pleasure, Icon laid back his ears and broke into a swift canter.

Up the glade they flew; out into the sunshine; clear into the open.

Here was the moor! Here the highroad, at last! And there in the distance, the grey walls of Hugh's castle; the portals of home.

* * * * * *

It was the Knight's trusted foster-brother, Martin Goodfellow, amazed, yet smiling a glad welcome, who held Icon's bridle as Mora dismounted in the courtyard.

She fondled the palfrey's nose, laying her cheek against his neck. For the moment it became imperative that she should hide her happy eyes even from this faithful fellow, in whom she had learned to place entire confidence.

"Icon, brave and beautiful!" she whispered. "Thou hast carried me here where I longed to be. Thy feet were well-nigh as swift as my desire."

Then she turned, speaking quickly and low.

"Martin, where is my husband? Where shall I find Sir Hugh?"

"My lady," said Martin, "I saw him last in the armoury."

"The armoury?" she questioned.

"A chamber opening out of the great hall, facing toward the west, with steps leading down into the garden."

"Even as my chamber?"

"The armoury door faces the door of your chamber, Countess. The width of the hall lies between."

"Can I reach my chamber without entering the hall, or passing the armoury windows? I would rid me of my travel-stains, before I make my presence known to Sir Hugh."

"Pass round to the right, and through the buttery; then you reach the garden and the steps up to your chamber from the side beyond the armoury."

"Good. Tell no one of my presence, Martin. I have here the key of my chamber. Has Sir Hugh asked for it?"

"Nay, my lady; nor guessed how often we rode hither. We reached the castle scarce two hours ago. The Knight bathed, and changed his dusty garments; then dined alone. After which he went into the armoury."

"When did you see him last, Martin?"

"Two minutes ago, lady. I come this moment from the hall."

"What was he doing, Martin?"

Martin Goodfellow hesitated. He knew something of love, and as much as an honest man may know, of women. He shrewdly suspicioned what she would expect the Knight to be doing. He was sorely tempted to give a fancy picture of Sir Hugh d'Argent, in his lovelorn loneliness.

He looked into the clear eyes bent upon him; glanced at the firm hand, arrested for a moment in its caress of Icon's neck; then decided that, though the truth might probably be unexpected, a lie would most certainly be unwise.

"Truth to tell," said Martin Goodfellow, "Sir Hugh was testing his armour, and sharpening his battle-axe."

As Mora passed into the dim coolness of the buttery, she was conscious of a very definite sense of surprise. She had pictured Hugh in his lonely home, nursing his hungry heart, beside his desolate hearth. She had seen herself coming softly behind him, laying a tender hand upon those bowed shoulders; then, as he lifted eyes in which dull despair would quickly give place to wondering joy, saying: "Hugh, I am come home."

But now, as she passed through the buttery, Mora had to realise that yet again she had failed to understand the man she loved.

It was not in him, to sit and brood over lost happiness. If she failed him finally, he was ready in this, as in all else, to play the man, going straight on, unhindered by vain regret.

Once again her pride in him, in that he was finer than her own conceptions, quickened her love, even while it humbled her, in her own estimation, to a place at his feet.

A glory of joy was on her face as, making her way through to the terrace, now bathed in sunset light, she passed up to the chamber she had prepared during Hugh's absence.

All was as she had left it.

Fastening the door by which she had entered from the garden, she noiselessly opened that which gave on to the great hall.

The hall was dark and deserted, but the door into the armoury stood ajar.

A shaft of golden sunshine streamed through the half-open door.

She heard the clang of armour. She could not see Hugh, but even as she stood in her own doorway, looking across the hall, she heard his voice, singing, as he worked, snatches of the latest song of Blondel, the King's Minstrel.

With beating heart, Mora turned and closed her door, making it fast within.

CHAPTER LIX

THE MADONNA IN THE HOME

Hugh d'Argent had polished his armour, put a keen edge on his battle-axe, and rubbed the rust from his swords.

The torment of suspense, the sickening pain of hope deferred, could be better borne, while he turned his mind on future battles, and his muscles to vigorous action.

Of the way in which the cup of perfect bliss had been snatched from his very lips, he could not trust himself to think.

His was the instinct of the fighter, to bend his whole mind upon the present, preparing for the future; not wasting energy in useless reconsideration of an accomplished past.

He had acted as he had felt bound in honour to act. Gain or loss to himself had not been the point at issue. Even as, in the hot fights with the Saracens, slaying or being slain might incidentally result from the action of the moment, but the possession of the Holy Sepulchre was the true object for which each warrior who had taken the cross, drew his sword or swung his battle-axe.

Was honour, held unsullied, to prove in this case, the tomb of his life's happiness? Three days of suspense, during which Mora considered, and he and the Bishop waited. On the third day, would Love arise victorious, purified by suffering, clad in raiment of dazzling whiteness? Would there be Easter in his heart, and deep peace in his home? Or would his belovèd wind herself once more in cerements, would the seal of the Vatican be set upon the stone of monastic rules and regulations, making it fast, secure, inviolable? Would he, turning sadly from the Zion of hopes fulfilled, be walking in dull despair to the Emmaus of an empty home, of a day far spent, holding no promise of a brighter dawn?

But, even as his mind dwelt on the symbolism of that sacred scene, the Knight remembered that the two who walked in sadness did not long walk alone. One, stepping silently, came up with them; knowing all, yet asking tenderest question; the Master, Whom they mourned, Himself drew near and went with them.

It seemed to Hugh d'Argent that if so real a Presence as that, could draw near to him and to Mora at this sad parting of the ways, if their religion did but hold a thing so vital, then might they have a true vision of Life, which should make clear the reason for the long years of suffering, and point the way to the glory which should follow. Then, being blessèd, not merely by the Church and the Bishop but by the Christ Himself—He Who at Cana granted the best wine when the earthly vintage failed the wedding feast—they might leave behind forever the empty tomb of hopes frustrated, and return together, with exceeding joy, to the Jerusalem of joys fulfilled.

Hugh laid down his sword, rose, stretched himself, and stood looking full into the golden sunset.

He could not account for it, but somehow the darkness had lifted. The sense of loneliness was gone. An Unseen Presence seemed with him. The thought of prayer throbbed through his helpless spirit, like the uplifting beat of strong white wings.

"O God," he said, "Thou seemest to me as a stranger, when I meet Thee on mine own life's way. I know Thee as Babe divine; I know Thee, crucified; I know Thee risen, and ascending in such clouds of glory as hide Thee from mine earthbound sight. But, if Thou hast drawn near along the rocky footpath of each day's common happenings, then have mine eyes indeed been holden, and I knew Thee not."

Hugh stood motionless, his eyes on the glory of the sunset battlements. And into his mind there came, as clearly as if that moment uttered, the words of Father Gervaise: "He ever liveth to make intercession for us."

The Knight raised his right arm. "Oh, if Thou livest," he said, "and living, knowest; and knowing, carest; grant me a sign of Thy nearness—a Vision of Life and of Love, which shall make clear this mist of uncertainty."

Turning back to his work, so great a load seemed lifted from his heart, that he found himself singing as he put a keener edge on his weapons.

Presently he went over to the corner where stood the silver shield. Hitherto he had kept his eyes turned from it. It called up thoughts which he had striven to beat back. Now, he set to work and polished it until its surface shone clear as a mirror.

And as he worked, he thought within himself: "What said the Bishop? That I saw reflected in my silver shield naught save mine own proud face? But I told my wife that I see there the face of God, or the nearest I know to His face; and, behind Him, her face—the face of my beloved; for, had I not put reverence and honour first, my very love for her would have been tarnished."

Hugh stood the silver shield at such an angle as that it reflected the sunset, yet as he kneeled upon one knee before it he could not see his own reflection.

The sun, round and blood red, almost dipping below the horizon, shone out in crimson glory from the deepest heart of the silver.

Hugh remembered two verses of a Hebrew poem which the Rabbi used to recite at sunset. "The Lord God is a Sun and Shield: The Lord will give Grace and Glory; No good thing will He withhold from them that walk uprightly. O Lord of Hosts, blessèd is the man that trusteth in Thee."

His eyes upon the shield, his hands clasped around his knee, Hugh said, softly: "The face of God, my belovèd, or the nearest I know to His face: and behind Him, thy face"—

And then his voice fell of a sudden silent; his heart beat in his throat, his fingers gripped his knee; for something moved softly in the shining surface, and there looked out at him from his own silver shield, the face of the woman he loved.

How long he kneeled and gazed without stirring, Hugh could not tell. At that moment life paused suspended, and he ceased to be conscious of time. But, at length, pressing nearer, his own dark head appeared in the shield, and above him, bending toward him, Mora, shimmering in softest white, as on her wedding morn, her hands outstretched, her eyes full of a tender yearning, gazing into his.

"The Vision for which I prayed!" cried the Knight. "O, my God! Is this the sign of Thy nearness? Is this a promise that my wife will come to me?"

He hid his face in his hands.

A gentle touch fell lightly on his hair.

"Not a promise, Hugh," came a tender whisper close behind him. "A sign of God's nearness; a proof of mine. Hugh, my own dear Knight, lift up your head and look. Your wife has come home."

Leaping to his feet, he turned; still dazzled, incredulous.

No shadowy reflection this. His wife stood before him, fair as on her wedding morning, a jewelled circlet clasping the golden glory of her hair. But his eyes saw only the look in hers.

Yet he kept his distance.

"Mora?" he whispered. "Home? To stay? Hath a true vision then been granted thee?"

"Oh, Hugh," she answered, "I have seen deep into the heart of a true man. I have seen myself unworthy, in the light of thy great loyalty. I have seen all others fail, but my Knight of the Silver Shield stand faithful. I have been shewn this by so strange a chance, that I humbly take it to be the Finger of God pointing out the pathway of His will. My pride is in the dust. My self-will lies slain. But my love for thee has become as great a thing as the heart of a woman may know. Thy faithfulness shames my poor doubts of thee. The richness of thy giving, beggars my yearning to bestow. Yet now at last thy wife can come to thee without a doubt, without a tremor, all hesitancy gone, all she is, and all she has, quite simply, thine. Oh, Hugh, thine own—to do with as thou wilt. All these years—kept for thee. Take me—Ah! . . . . Oh, Hugh, thy strength! Is this love, or is there some deeper, more rapturous word? Oh, dear man of mine, how strong must have been the flood-gates, if this was the pent-up force behind them!"

He carried her to the hearth in the great hall, and placed her in the chair in which his mother used to sit.

Then, his arms still around her, he kneeled before her, lifting his face in which the dark eyes glowed with a deeper light than passion's transient fires.

"The Madonna!" he said. "The Madonna in my home."

He stooped and lifted the hem of her robe to his lips.

"Not as Prioress," he said, "but as my adored wife."

Again he stooped and pressed it to his lips.

"Not as Reverend Mother to a score of nuns," he said, "but as—"

She caught his head between her hands, hiding his glowing eyes against her breast.

Presently: "And did thy people come with thee, my sweetheart? And how could a three hours' ride be accomplished in this bridal array? Oh, Heaven help me, Mora! Thou art so beautiful!"

"Hush," she said, "thou dear, foolish man! Heaven hath helped thee through worse straits than that! Nay, I rode alone, and in my riding dress of green. Arrived here, I changed, in mine own chamber, to these marriage garments."

"In thine own chamber?" He looked at her, with bewildered eyes.

"Here—here, in thine own chamber, Mora?"

The mother in her thrilled with tenderness, as she bent and looked into those bewildered eyes. For once, she felt older than he, and wiser. The sense of inexperience fell from her. For very joy she laughed as she made answer.

"Dear Heart," she said, "I could scarce come home unless I had a chamber to which to come! Martin shewed me which had been thy mother's, and daily in thine absence he and I rode over, and others with us, bringing all things needful, thus making it ready, against thy return."

"Ready?" he said. "Against my return?"

She laid her lips upon his hair.

"I hope it will please thee, my lord," she said. "Come and see."

She made for to rise, but with masterful hands he held her down. His great strength must have some outlet, lest it should overmaster the gentleness of his love. Also, perhaps, the primitive instincts of wild warrior forefathers arose, of a sudden, within him.

"I must carry thee," he said. "Not a step thither shalt thou walk. Thine own feet brought thee to the crypt; others bore thee thence. Thy palfrey carried thee home; thy palfrey bore thee here. But to our chamber, my wife, I carry thee, alone."

She would sooner have gone on her own feet; but her joy this day, was to give him all he wished, and as he wished it.

As he bent above her, she slipped her arms around his neck. "Then carry me, dear Heart," she said, "but do not let me fall."

He laughed; and as he swung her out of the seat, and strode across the great hall to where the western glow still gleamed from the doorway of his mother's chamber, she knew of a sudden, why he had wished to carry her. His great strength gave him such easy mastery; helped her to feel so wholly his.

On the threshold of the chamber he paused.

Bending his face to hers, he touched her lips with exceeding gentleness. Then spoke in her ear, deep and low. "Say again what thou didst say ten nights ago when we parted in the dawning, on the battlements."

"I love thee," she whispered, and closed her eyes.

Then Hugh passed within.

CHAPTER LX

THE CONVENT BELL

The slanting rays of the setting sun lay, in golden bands, upon the flags of the Convent cloister.

Complete silence reigned.

The White Ladies had returned from Vespers. Each, in the solitude of her own cell, was spending, in prayer and meditation, the hour until the Refectory bell should ring.

The great door into the cloisters stood wide.

Mother Sub-Prioress appeared in the far distance, moving down the passage. As she passed between the long line of closed doors, she turned her face quickly from side to side, pausing occasionally to listen, ear laid against the panelling.

Presently she stepped from the cool shadow into the sunny brightness of the cloister.

She did not blink, as old Mary Antony used to blink. Her small eyes peered from out her veil as sharply in sunshine as in shadow.

Yet was there something curiously furtive about Mother Sub-Prioress, when she entered the cloister. Listening at the doors in the cell passage, she had been merely official, acting with a precise celerity which bespoke long practice. Now she hesitated; looked around as if to make sure she was not observed, and obviously held, with her left hand, something concealed.

Moving along the cloister, she seated herself upon the stone slab in the archway overlooking the lawn and the pieman's tree; then drew forth from beneath her scapulary, the worn leathern wallet which had belonged to the old lay-sister, Mary Antony.

At the same moment there came a gentle flick of wings, and the robin alighted on the stone coping, not three feet from the elbow of Mother Sub-Prioress.

Very bright-eyed, and tall on his legs, was Mary Antony's little vain man. With his head on one side, he looked inquiringly at Mother Sub-Prioress; and Mother Sub-Prioress, from out the curtain of her veil, frowned back at him.

There was a solemn quality in the complete silence. No naughty tales of bakers' boys or piemen. No gay chirps of expectation. Receiving cheese from Mother Sub-Prioress, bestowed for conscience' sake, partook of the nature of a sacred ceremony. Yet the robin had come for his cheese, and the Sub-Prioress had come to give it to him.

Presently she slowly opened the wallet, took therefrom some choice morsels, and strewed them on the coping.

"Here, bird," she said, grimly; "I cannot let thee miss thy cheese because the foolish old creature who taught thee to look for it, comes this way no more. Take it and begone!"

This was the daily formula.

The "jaunty little layman," undismayed—though the look was austere, and the voice, forbidding—hopped gaily nearer, pecking eagerly. No gaping mouths now waited his return. His nestlings were grown and flown. At last he could afford to feast himself.

Mother Sub-Prioress turned her back upon the coping and stared at the archway opposite. She had no wish to see the bird's enjoyment.

Then a strange thing happened.

Having pecked up all he wanted, the robin turned his bright eye upon the motionless figure, seated so near him, wrapped in the aloofness of an impenetrable silence.

Excepting in her dying moments, Mary Antony's much loved little bird had never adventured nearer to her than to hop along the coping, pecking at her fingers when, to test his boldness, she reached out and with them covered the cheese.

Yet now, with a gentle flick of wings, lo, he alighted on the knee of Mother Sub-Prioress! Then, while she scarce dared breathe, for wonder and amaze, hopped to her arm and pecked gently at her veil.

Whereupon something broke in the cold heart of Mother Sub-Prioress. Tears ran slowly down the thin face. She would not stir nor lift her hand to wipe them away, and they fell in heavy drops upon her folded fingers.

At length she spoke, in a broken whisper.

"Oh, thou little winged thing," she said, "who so easily could'st fly from me! Dost thou use those wings of liberty to draw yet nearer? In this place of high walls and narrow cells, they who have not full freedom, use to the full what freedom they possess, to turn, at my approach and fly from me. Not one if she could choose, would choose to come to me. . . . Is there any honour so great as that of being feared by all? Is there any loneliness so great as by all to be hated? That honour, little bird, is mine; also that loneliness. Who then hath sent thee thus to essay to take both from me?"

Heavy tears continued to fall upon the clasped hands; the worn face was distorted by mental suffering. The frozen soul of Mother Sub-Prioress having melted, the iron of self-knowledge was entering into it, causing the dull ache of a pain unspeakable. Yet she dared not sob, lest the heaving of her bosom should frighten away the little bird perched so lightly on her arm.

This evidence of the trust in her of a little living thing, was the one rope to which Mother Sub-Prioress clung in those first moments, during which the black waters of remorse and despair passed over her head—a rope made of frail enough strands, God knows: bright eyes alert, small clinging feet, a pair of folded wings. Yet do the frailest threads of love and trust, make a safer rope to which to cling when shipwreck threatens the heart, than the iron chains of obligation and duty.

Presently a sordid doubt seized upon Mother Sub-Prioress. Had the robin finished the cheese, and come to her thus, merely to ask for more?

Very slowly she ventured to turn her head, until the stone coping at her elbow came into her range of vision.

Then a glow of pride and happiness warmed her heart. Three—four—five fragments remained! Not for greed or favour had this little wild thing of his own free will drawn near.

For what, then? . . .

Mother Sub-Prioress whispered the answer; and as she whispered it, her tears fell afresh; but now they were tears without bitterness; a healing fount seemed to well up within her softening heart.

For love? Yea, verily! For love of her, those small brown wings had brought him near, those bright eyes were unafraid.

"For love of me," she whispered. "For love of me."

When at length he chirped and flew, she still sat motionless, listening as he sang his evening song high up in the pieman's tree.

Then she rose and swept the untouched fragments back into the wallet. There was triumph in the action.

"For love!" she said. "Not of that which I brought and gave, but of that which he thought me to be."

Slowly she left the cloister, moving, with bent head, until she reached the open door of the empty chamber which had been the Reverend Mother's.

Before long this chamber would be hers. At noon she had received word from the Bishop that it was his intention to appoint her to be Prioress, for the years which yet remained of the Reverend Mother's term of office.

She had experienced a sinister pleasure in being thus promoted

266

to this high office by the Bishop, owing to the certainty that had the usual election by ballot taken place, her name would not have been inscribed by a single member of the Community.

Yet now, in this strangely softened mood, she began wistfully to desire that there might be looks of pleasure and satisfaction on at least a few faces, when the announcement should be made on the morrow.

Mother Sub-Prioress passed into the cell, and closed the door.

She was drawn, by the glow of the sunset, to the oriel window. But on her way thither she found herself unexpectedly arrested before the marble group of the Virgin and Child.

Mother Sub-Prioress never could see a naked babe without experiencing a feeling of irritation against those who had failed to provide it with suitable clothing. Possibly this was why she had hurriedly looked the other way if her eye chanced to fall upon the beautiful sculpture in the Prioress's cell.

Now, for the first time, she really saw it.

She stood and gazed; then knelt, and tried to understand.

The tenderness reached her heart and shook it. The encircling arms, the loving breast, the watchful mother-eyes; the exquisite human love, called forth by the necessity, the dependence, the helplessness of a little child.

And were there not souls equally helpless, and hearts just as dependent upon sympathy and tenderness?

The Prioress had understood this, and had ruled by love.

But Mother Sub-Prioress had ever preferred the briers and the burning.

She recalled a conversation she had had a day or two before with the Prior and the Chaplain, when they came to consult with her concerning the future of the Community, and her possible appointment. In speaking of the late Prioress, the Prior had said: "She ever seemed as one apart, who walked among the stars; yet full, to overflowing, of the milk of human kindness and the gracious balm of sympathy." He had then asked Mother Sub-Prioress if she felt able to follow in her steps. To which Mother Sub-Prioress, vexed at the question, had answered, tartly: Nay; that she knew no Milky Way! Whereupon Father Benedict, a sudden gleam of approval on his sinister face, had interposed, addressing the Prior: "Nay, verily! Our excellent Sub-Prioress knows no Milky Way! She is the brier, which hath sharply taught the tender flesh of each. She is the bed of nettles from which the most weary moves on to rest elsewhere. She is the fearsome burning, from which the frightened brands do snatch themselves!"

These words, spoken in approbation, had been meant to please; and at first she had been flattered. Then the look upon the kind face of the Prior, had given her the sense of being shut up with Father

Benedict in a fearsome Purgatory of their own making—nay rather, in a hell, where pity, mercy, and loving-kindness were unknown.

Perhaps this was the hour when the change of mind in Mother Sub-Prioress really had its beginning, for Father Benedict's terrible yet true description of her methods and her rule, now came forcefully back to her.

Putting out a trembling hand, she touched the little foot of the Babe.

"Give me tenderness," she said, and an agony of supplication was in her voice; also a rain of tears softened the hard lines of her face.

Our blessèd Lady smiled, and the sweet Babe looked merry.

Mother Sub-Prioress passed to the window. The sun, round and blood red, as at that very moment reflected in Hugh d'Argent's shield, was just about to dip below the horizon. When next it rose, the day would have dawned which would see her Prioress of the White Ladies of Worcester.

She turned to the place where the Prioress's chair of state stood empty. During the walk to and from the Cathedral, she had planned to come alone to this chamber, and seat herself in the chair which would so soon be hers. But now a new humbleness restrained her.

Falling upon her knees before the empty chair, she lifted clasped hands heavenward.

"O God," she said, "I am not worthy to take Her place. My heart is hard and cold; my tongue is ofttimes cruel; my spirit is censorious. But I have learned a lesson from the bird and a lesson from the Babe; and that which I know not teach Thou me. Create in me a new heart, O God, and renew a right spirit within me. Grant unto me to follow in Her gracious steps, and to rule, as She ruled, by that love which never faileth."

Then, stooping to the ground, she kissed the place where the feet of the Prioress had been wont to rest.

The sun had set behind the distant hills, when Mother Sub-Prioress rose from her knees.

An unspeakable peace filled her soul. She had prayed, by name, for each member of the Community; and as she prayed, a gift of love for each had been granted to her.

Ah, would they make discovery, before the morrow, that instead of the brier had come up the myrtle tree?

With this hope filling her heart, Mother Sub-Prioress hastened along the passage, and rang the Convent bell.

* * * * * *

And at that moment, Mora stood within her chamber, looking over terrace, valley, and forest to where the sun had vanished below the horizon, leaving behind a deep orange glow, paling above to clear blue where, like a lamp just lit, hung luminous the evening star.

Hugh's arms were still wrapped about her. As they stood together at the casement, she leaned upon his heart. His strength enveloped her. His love infused a wondrous sense of well-being, and of home.

Yet of a sudden she lifted her head, as if to listen.

"What is it," questioned Hugh, his lips against her hair.

"Hush!" she whispered. "I seem to hear the Convent bell."

His arms tightened their hold of her.

"Nay, my belovèd," he said. "There is no place for echoes of the Cloister, in the harmony of home."

She turned and looked at him.

Her eyes were soft with love, yet luminous with an inward light, that moment kindled.

"Dear Heart," she said—hastening to reassure him, for an anxious question was in his look—"I have come home to thee with a completeness of glad giving and surrender, such as I did not dream could be, and scarce yet understand. But Hugh, my husband, to one who has known the calm and peace of the Cloister there will always be an inner sanctuary in which will sound the call to prayer and vigil. I am not less thine own—nay, rather I shall ever be free to be more wholly thine because, as we first stood together in our chamber, I heard the Convent bell."

One look she gave, to make sure he understood; then swiftly hid her face against his breast.

Hugh spoke his answer very low, his lips close to her ear.

But his eyes—with that light in them, which her happy heart scarce yet dared see again—were lifted to the evening star.